Demons in the Sanctuary

Miriam E. Bellamy

Order this book online at www.trafford.com/08-1088
or email orders@trafford.com

Most Trafford titles are also available at major online book retailers.

Cover Design by Miriam E. Bellamy.

Note for Librarians: A cataloguing record for this book is available from Library and Archives Canada at www.collectionscanada.ca/amicus/index-e.html

Printed in Victoria, BC, Canada.

ISBN: 978-1-4251-8582-4

www.trafford.com

North America & international
toll-free: 1 888 232 4444 (USA & Canada)
phone: 250 383 6864 • fax: 250 383 6804 • email: info@trafford.com

The United Kingdom & Europe
phone: +44 (0)1865 487 395 • local rate: 0845 230 9601
facsimile: +44 (0)1865 481 507 • email: info.uk@trafford.com

10 9 8 7 6 5 4 3 2

1

THE NIGHT SKY WAS clear, a full moon shedding it's brilliance over the worn asphalt highway. A twinkling myriad of stars provided a lustrous panorama across the dark heavens. Two men walked rapidly down the road past a few scattered houses and farm properties on the outskirts of the tiny community of Badin. They were handsome and rugged, tall in stature, one being fair with piercing blue eyes and tousled blond hair of shoulder-length, while the other was dark-skinned with brown eyes and short, curly black hair.

They walked in silence, each swinging a large staff, which seemed unnecessary as an aid to their long, sure stride. A warm breeze fanned their cheeks while the steady chirping of insects and drone of mosquitoes trying to fulfill their bloodlust, filled the air.

A train rumbled by in the distance, the blaring whistle receding quickly into a velvety blanket of darkness. Although the hour was late, a few cars still sped by, their occupants anxious to get home to families, to relax and dream of their tomorrows.

The men moved steadily onward leaving the lights of the town far behind. Turning from the highway, they started down a deserted country road. A large greenhouse loomed on their left, quiet and desolate until the morning, which would bring a straggle of customers looking for stray blooms to replace the dead ones in their drought-ridden gardens and flower boxes.

"We are almost there." It was the fair haired man who spoke. "Remember Valin, we are here only to observe and report," he said quietly.

"Yes, Caelen, I know." The dark-skinned man spoke softly, barely above a whisper. "We must be careful not to be seen."

The road ended abruptly after they passed by a small factory, forcing them to turn onto a narrow gravel road. On their immediate right they caught sight of their destination. A church, with it's great cross stretching toward heaven, etched in relief against the silvery cast of a moonlit sky.

Splashes of illumination from strategically placed floodlights showed a double row of stark stone pillars, each pair connected by wide granite banners proclaiming some of the names of Christ; Redeemer, Savior, King of Kings and Lord of Lords. Immaculately manicured shrubbery and blooms graced picturesque flower beds under the pillar canopy. An imposing fountain bubbled serenely in its midst. Special lighting enhanced gigantic creamy pillars which crowned the broad sweep of steps leading to a wide piazza. They were just a shade lighter than the milky stucco exterior of the building.

A garish billboard at the front corner of the lot announced the church name in bold red letters as, *The Good Shepherd Church*. It was crowned with the national flag and proclaimed *Rev. Rafe Rutherford* as senior pastor. This was followed by the service times in smaller black lettering.

Soundlessly, the two men angled across the end of the unpaved parking lot, careful now to stay within the shadows of shrubbery and trees at the edge of the property. Reaching an unobtrusive spot, they stopped, and for a time just stood quietly watching the building.

Time passed slowly, the shadows lengthening as the moon hastened its path across the sky. No movement was apparent from their vantage point either around the church property or inside the structure. The long row of windows on the side of the building facing the men was dark and silent.

Finally, with a simple quick gesture of his hand, Caelen melted soundlessly into the darkness. Straining his ears to listen, the remaining solitary figure stared into the night, waiting, his eyes sweeping the darkness, his body rigid with intent. The night air felt cloyingly heavy and rife with danger. Large winged insects buzzed annoyingly about his head. Still, Valin stood motionless, leaning on his staff, his gaze piercing the darkness between him and the church.

He could taste the wrongness in the air even before his sharp eyes picked out the strange thick black cloud swirling around the entryway. It seeped through the walls of the building; a numbing mist that bespoke horror and disease. Valin straightened and leaned forward. A furtive movement within the dense, churning blackness caught his attention.

Slowly disengaging itself in a single fluid motion from the roiling black haze, a gigantic shadowy apparition, red eyes gleaming luridly in the glow of the floodlights, shambled down the steps. Its grotesque body was twisted and gnarled; its countenance nightmarish and evil. A flash of yellowed fangs, dripping with saliva, glistened with almost palpable brutality. Thick powerful arms hung from a set of massive shoulders. From its back, gigantic black serrated wings billowed and snapped with every stray gust of wind. A second pair of long undulating appendages with cruel looking claws swayed menacingly in front of the beast. These appeared to be attached at the waist of the thick hairy torso.

Behind the huge monster, a host of ebony-winged creatures followed, small and large, tumbling out of the walls and through the locked doors and windows. They clustered about the great beast, with faces distorted by hatred and demonic glee, their bodies bent and deformed. Some had the appearance of vultures swooping through the air; others resembled wolf-like creatures with wide, dripping maws. A number of creatures slithered along the ground like serpents, with scaly skins and jaundiced eyes.

One hapless being, capering about, leaped too vigorously into the air and unable to control his flight careened into the demon-master. Snarling with fury, the brute turned, smashing the startled little imp with a murderous blow from his massive clenched fist. It tumbled, head over heels, into the mass of demons milling about behind him. The tiny creature screamed in terror as it pitched about, pummelled by beating wings and grasping claws. Mocking shrieks of mirth filled the air as the horde of demons kicked, bit and clawed cruelly at the unfortunate beast, showing no mercy, until it lay on the gravel in a contorted heap, exhausted and whimpering pitifully.

The demon-master did not slow his pace. Striding forward purposefully, he moved towards a large old stone house on the far side of the property. Raging at his heels, the vast horde of savage underlings trotted, flew and slithered along, all radiating a fathomless blood-hunger. Struggling to regain its feet, the damaged imp alternately limped and fluttered behind the demon forces.

Valin, watching in silence from the shadow of the trees, saw the entire throng disappear, fading through the outside walls of the home as if they did not exist. Caelen loomed unexpectedly in front of him, materializing out of the darkness.

"It is much worse than I thought," he whispered. "We must make all speed to bring our report to Michael."

The two men hastily retraced their steps, but this time they cut directly across the farmer's field at the side of the road and did not stop until they had reached the main highway. Satisfied that at last they were a safe distance from the church property, they raised their staffs in unison toward the moonlit sky. A flicker of pure white light cut through the night shadows. Two wooden cudgels shimmered; a momentary distortion and then they were transformed into gigantic blazing swords.

Simultaneously, a glimmering aura crept down over the two figures which now appeared to be expanding, changing into giant beings of towering height. Huge, iridescent wings appeared on their backs, swelling to vast proportions. Enormous glowing shields materialized in their hands while countenance and clothing began to shine, radiating the same white, pure light which emanated from the uplifted swords. A heart-beat later they vanished, leaving only brilliant streaks like shooting stars across the heavens.

In a field close by, a loping shadow, immense and fierce, stopped short - startled. Gazing about with flat, yellow eyes and body hair bristling like porcupine quills, it snarled as it caught sight of the streaking bright lights now disappearing over the horizon. With a cruel, calculating look, the foul spirit turned and resumed its gallop towards the road that led to the church.

Mira Grant pushed back several strands of dark brown, shoulder-length hair that had fallen over her face and tried to contain the sobs that had become a wrenching pain in her chest. Getting up from her knees and wiping the traces of tears from her face, she looked disconsolately at her reflection in the mirror of her dressing table seeing red-rimmed, swollen eyes and a splotchy complexion.

"God, I need your help!" She threw the statement into the air with some vehemence as she reached for a tissue.

"I need wisdom, Lord! My husband is so angry and upset with the pastor that he won't sit through a service under him any more. I'm tired of going to service after service all by myself. I want to see him enjoying church again and growing in faith instead of losing ground day by day. I want to see him living a consistent, happy, Christian life; the way he used to."

Mira grabbed a brush and jerked it through her tangled locks. Sighing deeply, she wandered into the bathroom to splash some cool water on her perspiring face and neck as she pondered the problem.

It seemed that every time Dan appeared at the church, the pastor would ask him to fix something; either in the building itself or over at the parsonage. In the past, he had always responded promptly and cheerfully to every request, never expecting anything more than a "*thank you*". An easy-going man with a generous heart, her husband delighted in using his talents as electrician and handyman to help out with projects and repairs.

But things had changed over the past couple of years. Mira had tried to ignore Dan's claims that he had caught the minister in several lies completely souring him on the man. She had hoped it would all blow over. Recently however, his grumblings had increased and now he complained bitterly about the pastor's shabby treatment of volunteers. As his resentment and anger grew, her husband rapidly reached the point of feeling used whenever asked to do anything around the church. Mira had anxiously watched his attendance drop off as he found various flimsy excuses to absence himself from each service.

"I'm worried about his health too, Lord." A lump filled her throat. Dan had not been well lately. It seemed as if he was always in pain. She had finally persuaded him to let her make a doctor's appointment.

Why does Pastor Rafe never ask Dan how he's doing? she wondered. *If he would only show a little personal interest in him, it might make a big dif-*

ference in his attitude towards the man. It seems as if he's only interested in what Dan can do for him.

As she went about her household chores, a kaleidoscope of memories crowded her thoughts. Only three years had passed since Mira had lost her accounting job at a company where she had worked for fifteen years. At the time, she had worried over the loss of employment and the financial implications, but God had taken care of them and every need had been met. Now she could honestly be thankful that door had been closed, removing her permanently from a situation that could have destroyed her.

She was happy with their choice of a smaller home. Dan had found a darling little bungalow that they could easily afford in a city only a half hour's drive away. It had a wonderful tiny garden full of flowers that Mira fell in love with. The day they moved in, she felt as if the old life had been left behind forever, replaced by a sense of peace and tranquility that had always evaded her in the old house.

Looking back now, it was clear to Mira that she had allowed her job to consume her. Because her life was tragically out of balance, the daily stress of her work environment had eventually hurtled her into a horrible pit of depression which culminated in several hospitalizations. For five years she had struggled in wretched, miserable despondency, trying to overcome feelings of helplessness and hopelessness. Life simply hadn't been worth living! Along with self abnegation and feelings of worthlessness came an abject fear that she would never make it as a Christian; never experience heaven or eternal life as it was promised in the bible.

At the time, it had seemed to Mira that everyone around her was experiencing God's love and forgiveness, except her. Lost in her own pit of despair, she couldn't even comprehend the love of her Heavenly Father much less experience it. Where was the God who loved her so much that He sent his only Son to die for her sins?

Intellectually, she had always known there was a God. She had even made a commitment as a child, giving her heart to the Lord Jesus Christ at a church altar one Sunday when an invitation had been given. But the cares of life, accompanied by unrepentant sin, had choked out the assurance of her salvation years ago. Her conscience had then smote her heavily with her unworthiness; her unfitness to be part of the kingdom of heaven.

Reminiscences catapulted her ahead to the wonderful deliverance she had experienced on the day she finally gave the mess of her life over to God. She had thrown herself on His mercy in deep sorrow and remorse, knowing that there was nothing she could offer beyond her repentance for the things she had done. That was when God's peace and love had entered her heart, bringing with it immediate contentment and joy that overwhelmed her starved soul.

God really loved her! Not because of anything she had done or left undone, but rather because His only begotten Son, Jesus Christ had already paid the price for her sin. She caught a glimpse of who the Father really was and with that came the total assurance that her sins were all covered forever by the precious blood He had shed on her behalf when He was nailed to a cross to suffer and die for the sins of the world.

The mood-enhancing, prescription drugs Mira had been using were now a thing of the past. She didn't need them any longer. Christ had given her life back to her and she was determined in her heart to serve Him for as long as she lived. With the assurance of her salvation came an overwhelming joy which she resolved never to let go of again!

When she and Dan had moved to Campbelton, it had brought them closer to Krysta and Jason, their daughter and son-in-law, who lived in the same city. Married for only a few years, the young couple seemed to be doing well in their life together.

Mira smiled. It was as if those two had always known they were meant for one another. Since high school, they had shared their hopes and dreams, laying careful plans for their future together.

Of late, she had noticed a great transformation in her daughter. Krysta had shared with her parents a powerful, life-changing experience that had occurred after watching a movie on a Christian television station about the rapture of the church. That night, after she retired to her bedroom, there had been a real *God-moment* in her life. She had heard His audible voice in her bedroom telling her that she must believe on Him.

Since that moment, Krysta's priorities had altered dramatically. She now devoured her bible with eagerness, growing in grace by leaps and bounds. The tears that Mira had shed over her seeming indifference to God had been changed to overwhelming joy and happiness. She almost had to pinch herself to see if she was really awake and not dreaming about this quick and powerful work that had somehow been wrought in her daughter.

Krysta had always had a gift of music but after her encounter with God, it was enhanced greatly as the Holy Spirit gave her songs and a powerful anointing to touch hearts. Jason was also showing an interest in God and a desire to learn about Him, although he was a little jealous of his wife's experience, wanting a supernatural sign from God for himself. As a couple, they were finally letting God into their busy lives and were coming to church on a regular basis.

Mira recalled the years – almost fourteen now – that she had attended the Good Shepherd Church. It had been the one constant in her life. She was grateful that she hadn't been forced to give it up when they moved.

The church was uniquely situated on a country road outside the small bedroom community of Badin, which lay on the outskirts of the larger twin cities of Kittimer and Waterville. Mira's new home in Campbelton was almost the same distance, about a half hour drive, from their place of worship as their old house had been in the city of Greydon.

Mira felt fortunate that she was able to use her God-given talent as a soloist in the church. For many years, she had been a part of the worship team there and she loved it. For the last three years, she served as president of the Women's Ministries. How humbled she had been when she was chosen by the pastor and his wife for this great honor! She had thrown herself into the ministry with a passion, drawing closer to the women of the congregation as they shared their hearts and struggles with her.

Just a year ago, Mira had increased her involvement in the church even more when requested to let her name stand for the board of directors. Elated to be especially chosen by the pastor and elected on the first ballot, she was asked to serve as Secretary-Treasurer. Dan had been very supportive, even proud of her.

Her first year on the board had gone well with some minor hitches. There were a few things she couldn't help but notice. In particular, it bothered her the way the pastor sometimes treated people. It didn't seem quite right for a man of God, but knowing where she had come from spiritually, Mira determined to overlook what she felt was certainly just a minor personality flaw. Perfectionism was something she could relate to, as she struggled with it herself. Her beloved pastor was only human after all! He just liked things done well, she reasoned.

It sometimes occurred to her that she may have made an idol of him, placing him upon a high pedestal even before she had started coming to the church. She had grown up listening to his television ministry. Her dearly loved parents, now long departed, had thought he was wonderful! He called himself a prophet, so she reasoned that he must be on a higher level than everyone else.

It disturbed her that some members of the church had disappeared from the ranks with little or no explanation. Even more distressing was the truth that they were usually those that had served faithfully in some leadership capacity for a period of time. Associate ministers didn't seem to last long nor did the heads of the various ministries.

From time to time, she had questioned Pastor Rafe about many of these disappearances. He had seemed forthright in his explanations and even rather willing to recount the reasons for their leaving, telling her of numerous wicked deeds that had been perpetrated against him. Some, he told her, had been out to steal his pulpit and others had either a controlling spirit or selfish agenda that would ultimately damage his good name or that of the church. Mira readily believed his accounts of these situations, feeling fervently that his sufferings had indeed been horrendous.

In one of their conversations, Pastor Rafe shared his personal devastation over being abandoned by his ministerial organization some twenty years earlier for what he considered a relatively minor infraction. He told her how a close male friend had completely betrayed his confidence by exposing an indiscretion. The details were rather vague, but Mira's tender heart was incensed over how badly he had been treated, especially after seeing the tear on his cheek and hearing the tremble in his voice as he talked about it. Vehemently, he had protested his innocence, telling her that he had never even had the fun of the sexual escapade he was accused of, but had stepped away from the man's advance after a brief hesitation. That was his only guilt, he had stated in tremulous tones.

There were other abuses he only hinted at. Things he had endured over the years. A prior board of directors in the church had risen up against him, locking him out of the church. Again the details were hazy, but he had made it abundantly clear that God had always been on his side and he had ultimately triumphed in the midst of every adverse circumstance. Since those revelations, he had never mentioned anything of the kind again.

Mira sighed. Clouds were forming on the horizon for this board that she was now a part of and she didn't know what to do about it. Things had begun to sour between the pastor and the directors in the spring, shortly after the new constitution was voted in. With only a year's board experience under her belt, Mira had been honored and excited to play a small part in the drafting of the new by-laws for the church and it had been a thrill to see it accepted unanimously by the membership.

Before taking the document to the congregation, the approval of the pastor had been no easy matter to obtain. Some of the changes incorporated into the new by-laws seemed to bother him immensely, particularly anything that touched his control over the assembly in any way. The inclusion of a section on the discipline of the pastor was a particularly sticky one. They had gone over the document so many times that she very familiar with its content. Finally, after some minor changes, Pastor Rafe had reluctantly given the long-sought-after approval and it appeared a new era had begun.

Mira had been excited to be a part of it all. Change was coming! She could feel it! A great change had even been prophesied to the congregation during the annual summer camp meeting the prior year. The speaker, who was billed as a prophet-evangelist, had told them that in eight months, by the end of April in fact, the Good Shepherd Church would experience dramatic change.

Along with many others, Mira had prayed about the prophesy, looking eagerly for its fulfillment as the designated month approached. She remembered the whole thing vividly. The man had stopped in the middle of his sermon and given the prophetic word. Turning in the middle of his pronouncement, and looking directly at Pastor Rafe, he had twice boldly proclaimed, "You might not like the change." He had also said that he didn't know if it would be good or bad, but he was certain that the church would never be the same again.

When the time of fulfillment drew near, as people questioned and speculated, Pastor Rutherford invited the prophet-evangelist to return for special services to speak further about the Word he had given. He himself showed little interest in the matter leaving his associate in charge while he flew off to another part of the country to attend a long anticipated conference.

The prophet had told the people that the Word of the Lord must have been fulfilled in the spirit realm rather than the temporal one. Indeed that seemed to be the only explanation for it. After his departure, when nothing momentous happened, interest flagged and memories faded, leaving only a few to still wonder whether his prophesy had been true or false.

Mira shivered in remembrance of the peculiar feeling she had experienced when the Word was first given. There had been a strong witness in her spirit that the man was speaking truth and yet she had to admit that the only noteworthy things that had happened in April were the new constitution coming into effect and a newly elected board of directors. Of course there were a couple of other matters that were causing the board some headaches now, she thought ruefully.

Pastor Rutherford had certainly wasted no time in pressuring the new board to give his grandson, Jonas, the position of youth pastor in the church. The very night of their election he had asked to meet with them regarding the issue. Mira had tried to raise an objection at the time but the others hadn't supported her. Somehow she had found the nerve to speak up and say that she thought nepotism unwise because if there were any future problems in the youth ministry or with Jonas, in particular, no one would want to address them with the pastor, due to the relationship that existed between them.

Pastor Rafe's color had heightened slightly but he had stated, pleasantly enough, that he was always harder on his own kids than on anyone else. He suggested they try Jonas out for a period of time and pay him a generous travel honorarium. No one else had offered any objection and so the new board, anxious to start off on the right foot with their pastor, had acquiesced easily, giving him his way. They agreed to a three month trial period without interviewing or even seeing the young man but trusting their dearly loved pastor's wisdom in the matter.

The first inkling they had that caused them to feel they may have erred in their decision was when young Jonas showed up with his fiancée in tow the following Sunday to be introduced as the new youth pastor. The older members of the church were upset with his body piercings but, more importantly, numerous complaints were made regarding the way he and his girlfriend laughed and talked with one another throughout the service. The lack of respect and scornful attitude noted during the worship, in particular, was as unpalatable to the board as it was to the congregants.

Mira didn't know if that qualified as any great change in the church but it certainly had raised some problems. Oh yes, there was also the start of the tiling project in the large banquet hall. What a fiasco that had turned into! There had been one problem after another. She would be glad to have it done and behind them!

Mira heard a key in the lock and the front door opened and swung shut with a bang.

"Hi Hon. I'm home." Dan kicked off his shoes and strode into kitchen. He was a tall man, strong and well-built with a thick shock of white hair.

Leaning over Mira, he kissed the top of her head. "How was your day, Dear?"

"Good." Mira smiled up at him fondly. "Nothing special happened."

Dan busied himself making a pot of coffee. When it was ready, he poured himself a cup and settled down at the kitchen table to read the newspaper. Glancing at Mira's face, he put the paper aside and taking a long sip, quietly studied her for a few moments.

"What's the matter?" He finally asked.

"Nothing really," she said hesitantly. "I've just been praying."

"Oh!" He waited for her to talk about it and when she didn't reply, he tried again. "Well? ... What were you praying about? Is anything wrong?"

"It's just some board stuff, Hon," Mira shifted uncomfortably in her chair.

Dan's face turned red. He grabbed the newspaper and then slammed it down again almost immediately. "It's that lying pastor again, isn't it?" he demanded. "What scheme has he cooked up now? It's no great surprise to me that you're having trouble with him. I already know he's a liar! I've been trying to tell you for months but you won't listen to me."

"There are some issues that we're trying to deal with," she admitted casually. Mira didn't want to get into it with him. Things were already bad enough between her husband and the pastor. In truth though, Dan was already somewhat involved in the tiling project. Fraught with problems from the start, the job had quickly gone awry and his help with the supervision of the latest worker had proved invaluable.

Mira was keenly aware that many of the same issues that dogged them now, Dan had already experienced when he had supervised the renovation of the church kitchen a couple of years ago. That job had been major headache for him with Pastor Rafe nullifying decisions made by the kitchen committee, changing and adding things on a constant basis, all the while insisting that the price with the contractor must remain fixed.

She remembered how frustrated Dan had been, even enraged on several occasions, accusing Pastor Rafe of being untruthful and dishonest in his dealings. He had lost respect for the man and things had never been the same between them since. Now the board was facing many of the same issues again with the latest project.

"Huh!" Dan snorted. "I already know what's going on! It's just like last time! He'll go ahead and make his little private deals on the side and none of you will even attempt to stop him! He won't be able to keep his hands out of it and if he gets caught doing anything wrong, he'll lie his head off!"

"I don't think he means it, Hon, I truly don't. He just forgets what he says sometimes or he gets confused or mixed up – or maybe we get mixed up, I don't know." Tears started in Mira's eyes.

"A liar is a liar! Don't make excuses for him! He knows exactly what the truth is," Dan said disgustedly. "He's just incapable of telling it! He'll just skate around it and blame any problems or fault on everyone else."

"But he's a man of God and the bible says – "*Touch not mine anointed and do my prophets no harm*". We need to pray for him – not speak against him," Mira quavered.

"Well, doesn't the bible have something to say about all liars going to hell?" Dan asked angrily. "I'm telling you, that man is going straight to hell! He's a liar and that's all there is to it! He couldn't tell the truth if his life depended on it!"

"Oh Hon, you shouldn't say such terrible things!" Mira expostulated. It frightened her that he would speak so against a man of the cloth. "He is our pastor after all."

"Huh," Dan grunted. "He might be your pastor but he isn't mine any more. I've had it with him! I can't sit under him and listen to him talk about himself all the time. When was the last time you heard him preach anything out of the bible? You just tell me!"

"Oh Honey, it isn't that bad!" Mira exclaimed.

"You just pay attention and you'll see I'm right," Dan snorted. "But you won't listen to me. Someone else will have to tell you before you'll listen."

"He's still my pastor and I love him!" she cried defensively.

Dan pushed back his chair. "Well he's not my pastor! Not any more!" he roared. "You'll see! Just give him time and you'll see that I'm right about the man! You need to stand up to him and tell the truth!" He stormed noisily out of the room.

Mira bowed her head, breathing a prayer for both her husband's attitude and also for her pastor and the board of directors. She felt that clouds were indeed looming on the horizon and threatening an ugly storm unless God's hand moved quickly and her prayers were answered.

2

Together, the two angels entered a vast room, the walls of which seemed to pulsate and glow with dazzling, unearthly light. The atmosphere exuded righteousness, purity and holiness. Row upon row of angelic beings with flaming swords and shields stood before a huge dais upon which was seated a wondrous immortal creature, whose beauty and majesty transcended that of everyone present. His fierce visage shone with the likeness of purest gold. Rife with authority, his compelling presence dominated the room. Caelen and Valin knew they were beholding the great and mighty Archangel, Michael.

Without delay, they were approached by a tall, magisterial angel who beckoned them to follow him down a broad aisle to a spot at one side of the platform. Standing respectfully at attention, they patiently awaited recognition.

A deep discussion was taking place between Michael and several warrior angels. Eventually, their dialogue concluded and receiving new orders, these quickly withdrew receiving a blessing in the name of the Lord of Heaven's Armies. The great Archangel then turned his attention to the waiting pair and signalled their approach.

"What news do you bring me of the Good Shepherd Church?"

"It is not good," Caelen answered grimly, coming straight to the point. "There is a great gathering of demonic forces in that place the like of which is staggering. They have established such a stronghold that we fear the church could be lost entirely to the enemy. It also appears that they have legal ground to be there, which complicates matters considerably. The guardian at the manse tells me that he has little or no influence over the shepherd. He has no legal right."

"What does the angel of the church have to say?"

"That would be Jarah," asserted Caelen. "He agrees that the church's covering has been seriously damaged. There was a time when this shepherd knew and followed the ways of God, but sins of pride and greed gained a foothold in his life many years ago. Left unchecked, they have blossomed and grown and are now so deeply rooted that his ear is no longer attuned to hear the voice of the Spirit."

"What is known of his past behaviours?" asked Michael.

"He was at a crossroads when he came to this church," Caelen answered. "A great transgression had been exposed in his life at his last pastorate, which should have brought deep repentance and humility. Had that taken place, there could have been a lasting change affected in his life. He was offered aid and counselling by spiritual advisors, but his heart was too full of pride and arrogance. Fearful for his image, he refused to accept their help. He chose instead to deny his behaviour with lies and excuses, rather than humbling himself and showing true remorse. His former church suffered greatly because of his actions."

"Nevertheless, God is long-suffering and merciful. Because of His great love, it is not His will to lose any that are called to fulfill His purpose."

"True," Caelen replied, "but there is more that I must tell you. Because he refused to be held accountable in this matter, other sins have crept into the life of this shepherd, until they now have a stranglehold on him. He lives a secret life, dabbling in abominations. His conscience has been seared. Jarah reports that he is becoming more unstable as time passes, driven to control everyone and everything in his life."

"Then his very soul hangs in the balance," Michael declared. "What about the other spiritual leaders in the church? How do they fare?"

"Those that serve under him are in a miserable state, suffering esteem and confidence issues due to long-term intimidation and manipulation. Some have fallen by the wayside, broken, wounded and desolate.

Because the church is independent, it has no other governing body to appeal to outside of its own board. However, there is hope. Several, who have come into positions of authority only recently, have not yet succumbed to the spirit that controls the shepherd, so they have promise. They have not served long enough to understand the depth of depravity in his life or to become disillusioned."

Michael spoke firmly. "A further attempt must be made to reach him or he could be lost forever. His soul is very precious in the eyes of the Lord of Hosts. We must also bring help and strength to the rest of the leadership. The whole body of believers there must be in turmoil and suffering greatly."

"We will certainly do our utmost to destroy the enemy and take back the ground that has been lost," Caelen replied quietly, "but we will need help. A host of powerful and wise warriors are required to aid us or we will not be able to get near the place."

He quickly related what intelligence he had acquired in his probe of both the church and the parsonage, regarding the current size of the opposing army, as well as the type of demons they would be dealing with. Valin, in turn, added what he had witnessed outside of the church the night of their surveillance.

Michael nodded. "I have knowledge of the activities of the Prince of that region which has been a growing concern to us. His secretive gathering of forces has been reported by others and therefore does not take us by surprise. Recent intelligence would suggest that corruption is widespread with conditions worsening dramatically in the last few years. Our position needs reinforcements now or we risk losing much of the territory. We have had our share of skirmishes and ugly battles in the past, some of which have been victorious, but our enemy is also powerful and very patient. By any means possible, he will gain a foothold and build upon it with subtle cunning and deception. You must prepare for war, Caelen!"

"I believe the Evil One has some great plan in the works for this place," he continued. "Many churches in the region have been infiltrated but this particular assembly seems to interest him greatly. It is unfortunate that he has been permitted access because it now appears he wishes to establish a permanent base there. Over time, a formidable army has been entrenched. His wicked plans must be thwarted or many precious souls will be lost! I have received Word that we must make our stand now or risk a total rout! I will assign a full detachment of warriors to accompany you. Fight wisely and well, Caelen. Search out those among the believers that will pray. Encourage them and protect them. You must not fail! This battle must be fought with strategy and cunning, as well as power and might. Whether we win or lose the territory, there are precious souls hanging in the balance. Remember, there will always be a remnant of God's chosen ones. These must be saved at any cost!"

"We will not fail!" Caelen assented fiercely. "

The Archangel signalled a powerful looking commander standing at attention in the forefront of the multitude. "Captain Darshan, I have chosen your division for this fight." The mighty warrior nodded, accepting the assignment with a crisp salute.

Michael returned the gesture. "God speed you on your way!"

Caelen and Valin raised their swords which flamed brightly and shouted, "The name of Jesus, the Lord of Hosts, the King of Kings, be glorified forever!"

As they turned to leave, a large detachment of angels, at the command of Captain Darshan, instantly separated themselves from the vast crowd. At the warning blast of a multitude of trumpets, with uplifted swords and voices raised in a great battle cry, they descended towards the earth. The sound of their wings filled the air with an echoing roar like a mighty rush of wind. A great cheer ascended, reverberating through the heavens, as the vast assembled host expressed their approval and support for those going into battle with the enemy of the Lord God Almighty.

~

A multitude of evil yellow eyes flickered like dancing flames throughout the darkened banquet hall of the Good Shepherd Church. Amid bolts of greenish fire, the demons revelled in savage ecstasy, howling their blood lust and fury. Reeking of attar, a monstrous apparition with hideous facial deformities flared in the blackness, cackling with venomous hunger like a fragment of insanity. Frogs, the color of bile, issued from its mouth. Red-rimmed eyes peered malevolently at the assembled throng of foul spirits.

"Jezebel!" shrieked the demonic horde wildly. The air sizzled like frying flesh. It appeared molten and dangerous as noxious gas.

Unfurling its great ebony wings and raising huge black fists, the demon-master cursed and spewed forth a blast of profanity. A pair of cruel claws curled and uncurled, snapping viciously at the end of horrifying, undulating appendages.

The air thickened. It seemed to ripple and dance. Abruptly, red fire erupted from the wall behind the monstrous creature. The demon-master whirled about, surprise evident in its savage features. Slithering through its thick hairy legs, a massive serpent's head suddenly appeared, undulating slowly into full view of the roiling mass of evil spirits. Thick leathery scales coiled and uncoiled as it expanded to its full height.

"Hail, mighty Python!" cried the throng shifting their allegiance to one of greater rank and higher authority.

The demon-master, Jezebel, slouched to one side, twisting his crooked mouth in savage hatred. He knew better than to challenge the power and authority of the Python spirit who was unquestionably in charge. For one that craved domination and control over everything and everyone, it was a bitter pill to swallow. His hatred for the stronger spirit was as corrosive as vitriol. He waited in seething fury, maddened by the obsequious worship from the horde of lesser demons, lavished upon another. Red flared in his eyes but he managed to choke out a feral grin of approval.

The mass of creatures began to seethe as a powerful wolf-like being pushed and shoved its way to the forefront. "Master," growled the beast, addressing the enormous serpent. "I have news to report." The spiny poisonous quills on his back quivered in anticipation of the reward he would receive for this timely warning.

Red rimmed eyes glared evilly, while a long, forked tongue darted wickedly forth like a black tentacle, twisting and coiling eagerly." Who are you?" it hissed.

"Rejection, your Greatness." The cunning creature bared his teeth in a cruel semblance of a grin. His merciless barbs had paved the way for mistrust, anger, fear, rebellion and bitterness to accomplish their dirty work in the minds of many a child of God. "I witnessed two brilliant flashes of light streaking across the sky last night just a few hundred yards from this place," he rasped sharply.

"What do I care, you sssnivelling fool!" Tension crackled in the air. The demon host whispered hoarsely to one another, waiting to see the malevolent crushing force of Python turned against the lesser demon.

"The lights were two powerful angels," snarled the wolf, his lolling tongue slavering with acid drops of drool.

A red mist steamed in lazy tendrils from the serpent's nostrils. He regarded the beast with smoldering hatred. "Two angelsss!" His aching gaze transfixed the smaller creature holding him helpless in its inexorable grip. "What are two angelsss to such as me?" The maw of the demon serpent opened with a roar, displaying a fearsome set of elongated, curved, razor-sharp fangs.

Fear and uncertainty penetrated the ferocious visage of the underling. He slowly backed away from his superior, his grizzled tail slinking between his powerful hind legs. With lightening quick reflexes, the snake lunged. Sinking its dripping fangs into the back of the demon spawn, it shook him violently. The wolf howled in fear and panic until he was unceremoniously flung into the swirling mass of demons scrambling to get out of his way.

"Our plansss and ssstrategiesss are sssure. They will not fail! We are too ssstrong for the angels to ssstop us now." He spat on the floor. A fiery red vapor rose from the spittle. "Thisss territory isss mine!!" he lisped and no one dared to oppose his statement. His superior intelligence was evident as, with uncanny simplicity, he outlined the next phase of his plans.

The demon-master stood mute with silent fury and burning jealousy. It seemed as if the powerful Python spirit would never leave. The time finally came however, when its strategy was unveiled and it slithered away, as abruptly as it had come, leaving the underling once again in charge of the troops.

"Discouragement," barked Jezebel. A horrible creature with a multitude of long undulating limbs adorned with suction cups separated itself from the horde of demons. "You must concentrate on the board members. They are the legal entity of the assembly and their authority must be undermined and made ineffective."

The ruthless demon nodded his agreement. "I have already begun," he responded with a chuckle. "I don't expect much opposition. They are a poor lot."

"No?" The question dripped with sarcasm. "The lack of opposition has made you too cocky. Never underestimate the power of the enemy. Unlike others, I will not ignore the news brought by Rejection." The wolf preened self-consciously.

"The angels will undoubtedly come," sneered Jezebel, "and they will make every effort to oppose us, but we will triumph because we will not be caught unprepared." He called out a number of names in quick succession. "Deception, Fear, Jealousy, Bitterness, Rejection, Accusation, Witchcraft." Each of these commanders stepped forward with a begrudging salute. Legions of demons served under their dreaded rule, but they lusted after the power and authority of the Jezebel spirit.

The demon-master spat out his orders rapidly. "You must continue to infiltrate this body of believers. I commend you for their weakened state but we cannot be slack. We must use every trick and lie in our formidable arsenal to increase our hold over this house. All of your forces must be brought to bear, not only on the assembly, but the board and council members in particular. I want extra guardians placed around the perimeter of the church and manse. Antichrist and Lust! I have a special assignment for you."

~

A burly angel, with a shock of auburn hair and a fiery red beard, met Caelen and Valin in an open meadow several miles from the church. He greeted them with a crisp salute recognizing Captain Darshan with a pleased grin. "Hail Captain! We are grateful for the reinforcements," he said waving his hand toward the full contingent of warriors standing in readiness.

An answering smile lit up the handsome rugged features of the Captain. "Jarah! It will be good to fight alongside you again." Huddling together, they discussed war strategies and made a series of well considered plans to defend the body of Christ against the attack of the enemy forces.

"You must be careful in any attempt to breach the church sanctuary," Jarah advised the commanders. "The demons pretty much ignore me. They have such a stranglehold on the pastor and the people here that they do not think me much of a threat."

"You have others here though, do you not?" asked a surprised Darshan.

"A few," responded Jarah, "but they try to be as inconspicuous as possible now. The ears of the people are dull. They do not hear us any more. The shepherd does not pray nor does he feed the people enough of the Word of God to make a difference. He relies on story-telling so their strength has eroded and only a few still pursue an active prayer life. They have been our only source of entrance into the church for some time now. Any approach must be handled with care or you will wear out these warriors very quickly with little or no gain."

The angels conferred together for a time before they separated. When Jarah returned again to the church, he took with him the two commanders, Caelen and Valin. It heartened him to know the extent of reinforcements that the Archangel Michael had seen fit to assign to the task at hand. Before they left, Caelen gave orders to Captain Darshan, who dispatched angels to each parishioner's home in an attempt to find those who could still be encouraged to wait upon the Lord and thereby gain the strength they would need for the battle that loomed ahead.

3

REVEREND RAFE RUTHERFORD PREENED before the full-length hallway mirror before leaving the parsonage. He liked what he saw. His six foot frame, lean and trim, was clad in an immaculate shirt and silk tie under a stylish suit that fit his body like a glove. Turning sideways to get a better look, a half smile played about his lips as he patted a stray hair into place. His full white head of hair was indeed his glory! His parishioners loved his hair! They loved him!

All was right with the world and Pastor Rafe was ready to meet both the day and his congregation on this beautiful Sunday morning. He was content in the knowledge that his Heavenly Father held him in the highest esteem and that everything he did was ordained by God for a purpose. Today's services would be no different than all of the past meetings he had conducted. It would be a beautiful and meaningful service and, in his mind, he was already rehearsing the prophetic word that he would give that morning. He contemplated receiving the congratulations of his adoring congregants. *Life was good,* he thought smugly.

In the kitchen, he could hear Eve still rustling around cleaning up the breakfast dishes. Rafe poked his head through the door for a moment, checking his wife's wardrobe for flaws. Dressed in an elegant cream suit with her blonde hair in perfect order, she smiled and waved him out of the room.

He was proud of his lovely wife. She was the perfect woman for him to show off at his side; always dressed superbly and a fine hostess for all of his entertaining. He had chosen his talented mate well. She knew her place, revering him appropriately, faithfully playing the organ in every service, singing with him when asked, and fulfilling the role of a godly mother to their three children in the 45 years they had been married.

A very satisfied man left the parsonage and walked across the parking lot to the church. Unnoticed were the demons that gambolled about his head spewing their poison upon him, nestling in his snowy hair and whispering into his ear. Such was the force of evil about him that it was difficult for Jarah to get close enough to have any effect.

The cloudless, blue sky radiated warmth and sunshine. Shrubbery and blooming flower beds in the forefront of the church caught his eye and he stopped for a moment to take in the pleasing view of the large, imposing church building with its row of impressive pillars setting off the long entryway leading up to the church. More pillars festooned the porch in front of the huge double doors of the main entrance to the facility.

Letting himself in, Rafe made his way quickly past the front counter to the security alarm. Entering his password, he disarmed the system and turned on the lights in the front foyer. Next, as was his custom, he unlocked the doors of the main auditorium and after turning on the lights, he carefully checked the vast room, noting that a paper which he had planted under a chair the day before was still there. His brow darkened perceptibly and his eyes gleamed narrowly.

This is unacceptable, he thought. He demanded perfection and he would definitely have to speak to the cleaning woman about this oversight. She was just not cutting it! He gave little thought to the personal struggles of the woman who barely existed on the meagre pay offered by the church and had to supplement her income with other housekeeping work in order to survive.

Rafe looked about him, observing with pride the high walls of the sanctuary which were painted in three shades of rose and bedecked with colourful themed banners. Rafe's favourite color was rose. It annoyed him when people called it "pink".

A grey carpet with rose flecks covered the floor upon which sat row upon row of padded chairs. Rose-colored curtains adorned the back of the great platform, which ascended, in rising sections, above the main floor of the auditorium. A gleaming ebony grand piano graced the left-hand side of the first level of platform while the opposite side boasted a large imposing Leslie organ and Yamaha keyboard. A massive pulpit of solid oak was placed directly in the center with a large, stunning flower arrangement complimenting its base.

On the second level, directly behind the pulpit, the baptistery tank sat covered with a false floor when not in use. On this and the final third level, a number of chairs sat for the choir. Plywood boxes stained to resemble oak and filled with artificial greenery were placed strategically across the platform in front of the choir loft, to provide a modesty screen for the ladies if they sat down at any time throughout the service.

A number of music, microphone stands and guitar amps completed the platform accoutrements. A set of drums, placed to one side on the main floor level, was surrounded by a sound barrier to protect the ears of the older members of the congregation of which there were many. In fact seventy-five percent of Rafe's congregation was over fifty years of age. He had a way with the more mature members of his church. They loved his refined, debonair manner and brilliant charm, which he lavished freely on all and sundry who attended his services.

Assuring himself that everything was in place, Rafe turned and hurried back past the raised sound booth at the back of the room and out to the vestibule again. The large crystal chandelier twinkled dazzlingly from the lofty height of the main foyer. He rapidly climbed the set of stairs leading to his office on the second level.

Turning the key in the lock, he entered a spacious, well appointed room. His oversized oak desk and comfortable chair were positioned conveniently next to the large window overlooking the parking lot at the front of the church. From this vantage point he could see everyone's comings and goings. The parking lot was still empty, but he knew it would fill fast as service time approached.

The latest in computers graced a magnificent credenza while a large comfortably cushioned couch and coffee table beckoned a warm welcome to visitors. Completing the office furniture was a small glass dining table with four chairs for convenience at tea time.

This was Rafe's haven, the place where he could be himself and not be seen; a private place, where he was not on display unless he permitted entrance. The door, he usually kept locked, only opening it occasionally for imminent appointments with friends or parishioners.

A vast number of demonic creatures had followed the minister, unseen, into the room. Others now tumbled helter-skelter through the walls of the study. They gathered about him in a dense cloud spitting out sticky gobs of dark rancid acid. Tendrils of crimson smoke drifted lazily from the slick gooey substance which dripped from his hair and covered his shoulders.

He sat down at his desk, immediately turning toward the computer which was always left on. A number of new e-mail messages in his inbox caught his attention and he was soon engrossed in them. When all had been answered to his satisfaction, Rafe turned his attention to the telephone, making several calls to parishioners who came only occasionally to church. He wished to impress upon them the vital importance of attending today's service that they might hear the special Word the Lord had given to him to impart to the masses.

Satisfied he had done all that he could to increase attendance for the day, Rafe turned again to the computer, this time browsing a couple of websites. Lust spewed vomit onto his forehead, while an innocuous little demon called Fantasy, stabbed its long sharp talons into his flesh, screaming and laughing in glee, as the pastor found his favourite website. So engrossed was he in the pictures on the screen in front of him, the knock on the door startled him.

A glance towards the window told him that the parking lot was beginning to fill up. An annoyed frown creased his brow as he changed the computer screen with a quick move of his mouse. When he opened the door, the handsome, clean-cut face of his associate greeted him. As was his custom, the younger man was faultlessly attired in an immaculate suit and tie.

Marvin Gates had lasted for two years under the leadership of Rafe Rutherford, which was a boast few could make. His manner and deportment, ever a model of self-effacing meekness, was no threat to the senior pastor, even if he were to curry the favor of the people. Although a talented musician, worship leader and teacher, Rafe used him only for grunt work at the Good Shepherd Church, seldom allowing him in the pulpit. They both knew that Marvin needed the job to support his family of six and that he would keep his place as long as Rafe cared to use him.

Knowing that the pastor hated to be bothered when he was in his office, Marvin greeted him nervously. "We are ready to begin the worship practice, Pastor Rafe," he said apologetically.

"I'll be down in a minute," Rafe replied abruptly, closing the door in Marvin's face. He disliked any interruption when he was enjoying himself, but he knew that he must hurry or the worship practice would run late and interfere with his plans to greet certain of his more affluent parishioners in the lobby before the service.

Rafe turned from the door and grabbed his bible. No time had been spent on study or preparation for his sermon, but he was unworried. Speaking so many times over the years had made it almost second nature. He would draw on experiences from his own life and tell about the wonderful things that God had done through him and because of him. There were always old sermon notes that he could pull if necessary, but this morning was going to be about him and what God had told him to share with the people.

At the foot of the stairs he was stopped by a sweet-faced, middle-aged woman who anxiously inquired if he needed any notes printed. Faith Samuels was Rafe's secretary or more accurately, his right hand. Adored by one and all, she was the darling of the congregation, dispensing hugs freely to everyone who came through the doors of the church. Her warm personality, with its enormous capacity for compassion, was an incalculable asset in offsetting Rafe's exploitive behaviors. She kept him organized and had been with him so long she anticipated his every need. During the week, she often prepared his lunches, at her own expense, to spare him the bother of the short walk to his house.

This morning, he waived her aside saying that he was in need of nothing. Lifting his chin and pasting a smile firmly upon his lips, he entered the sanctuary and made his way to the platform. The worship team, already in place, was practising a song with Pastor Marvin directing from the grand piano. Eve was in her usual spot at the organ.

Taking his place at the keyboard, Rafe slid easily into the song, rattling the keys in his own peculiar honky-tonk style and lifting his rich tenor voice to join with the choir.

Suddenly he frowned and leaning toward the microphone, he tapped it impatiently. "Lenny!" His voice rose a few notches. "My microphone needs to be louder and so does the keyboard. I can't hear myself at all and you know that my voice and keyboard should be heard over the choir and other instruments. I *am* leading after all!"

Lenny Granger, a timid, tired-looking man with a protruding belly, waved apologetically from the sound booth and scrambled to reset the microphones.

"Yes, Pastor R. There ... is that better?" he asked as he frantically turned several knobs on the huge mixer board in front of him.

Rafe, dismissing his efforts with an impatient toss of his head and wave of his hand, turned to the choir. "You just can't get good help these days," he joked, showing his large, pearly white teeth in an ingratiating smile. The choir laughed obligingly and practice began in earnest for the next half hour until Rafe was satisfied with both the song line-up and the execution of the hymns and choruses.

There were six singers this particular morning – three women and two men, most of whom simply sang the melody. The only harmony provided was Mira's rich contralto and a lovely high tenor contributed by her friend Sunni, a vivacious lady with flaming red hair whose personality was as bright as her name. Rafe or Marvin would occasionally add a male tenor part to the mix, in certain songs and choruses.

A tanned athletic-looking woman with short, spiky, blonde hair bounced down the aisle, eyes dancing, begging their indulgence for her late arrival. Mira smiled. Jeanne was another good friend and part of a trio she sang with, which also included Sunni. Their practices were always filled with fun and laughter as they prepared specials to sing at church or retirement homes. One blonde, one red head and one brunette – they giggled and teased one another mercilessly in their attempts to master the various difficult harmonies they would try. Their relationship had deepened over the two years they had been singing together, evolving into what was now a close friendship.

Weekly practice for the worship team was always held just prior to the service. Although choir members were scolded when late, often their numbers doubled as service time approached. This was due in great part to Rafe's desire to have a larger, more impressive choir. He would often ask anyone that he thought could carry a tune to join the more dedicated core members of the group, even as late as five minutes before they stepped onto the platform. He wasn't concerned about whether they had practiced with the others, or even if everyone had microphones, so long as they were properly attired.

It was all about appearance. A big choir gave his ministry an important successful look when recording services. The DVD's and tapes offered for sale in the vestibule each week were popular with both congregants and visitors. Beyond that, Rafe preferred more bodies on stage to back him as he rollicked through the praise and worship time, stirring up the people and better preparing them for his inspiring message which was the uncontested highlight of the service.

When the singing practice ended, Pastor Rafe abruptly left the platform, hurrying to the sound booth at the back of the room. Glancing up, Mira noticed Lenny's downcast expression and flushed features as he listened quietly to what the pastor was saying.

I wish Pastor R. wouldn't be so hard on him, she thought. *He is so faithful and loyal and loves his volunteer work, even giving up time that he might be spending with his wife. I'm sure Pastor doesn't realize how he sounds sometimes.*

Turning, Mira set her music on the stand in front of her and stepped hurriedly forward to take her place in the circle already forming. Eve Rutherford offered a brief prayer and the group scattered quickly, some heading for the restrooms and others angling across the auditorium toward the prayer room to join those already gathered in intercession for the service and the needs of the people.

Mira glanced longingly toward the doors leading to the prayer room. Sunni and Jeanne had already disappeared in that direction. Sighing, she turned and picked up a pile of envelopes, each of which contained a copy of the minutes from the last board meeting and made her way to the vestibule to find the other directors. From experience, Mira knew that they would probably not check their individual folders in the office. With another board meeting looming on Tuesday evening, it would save everyone time if they all had an opportunity to read the minutes before then.

Quickly, she wended her way through the people milling about the hallway and lobby, laughing, chatting and greeting one another with hugs and happy handshakes. Her stomach churned and her head ached.

She wanted... no, she needed to pray before the service. Swiftly, she circled the lobby, passing out the envelopes.

"Thank the Lord they are all here this morning," she breathed softly to herself. She was just about ready to head for the prayer room when she heard a distinctive voice with an English accent calling to her.

"Can you come and sign a couple of checks, please, love?"

Ina Irwin, the church bookkeeper stood at the door of her office beckoning. For ten years she had been responsible for all of the church's accounting and finances. Born in Pakistan and hampered physically with a stiff leg resulting from a bout with polio, she had lived much of her life in England. A virtual bulldog, she ruled the business office with a rod of iron encased in a glove. Although she invariably called everyone either "love", "honey" or "darling", she was a "no nonsense" person who brooked no interference in her job.

Two adorable little faces belonging to her tiny miniature terriers peeped out from between her legs. Living alone as she did, these animals were her babies and wherever she went the dogs inevitably followed. They would spend hours with her in the office, sleeping or playing together, with only an occasional trip outdoors to interrupt her work. They stayed in the office even when Ina attended service.

"Sure thing." Mira followed the diminutive, stout woman as she limped slowly into the small stuffy room that served as the accounting office. The dogs gambolled about her feet until a sharp word from their mistress settled them down to wait and hope for a new playmate.

Mira sighed as she saw the pile of checks inside the folder that Ina handed her. *So much for having any prayer time this morning,* she thought, settling down at a second desk and grabbing a pen to begin the chore. Quickly, she worked her way through the pile, glancing at the backup attached to each check, as she penned her name on the appropriate signature line. Most of them looked pretty standard and she began to have some hope that there might be a little time for the prayer room after all.

Ina shifted uncomfortably behind her desk and cleared her throat nervously. "There is one check in there that you might not like."

"What now?" Mira asked, looking up sharply.

"Joe Dalmer has submitted a second bill for his services in tiling the downstairs banquet hall."

"But we already paid him for everything he has done and more," she protested trying to keep the annoyance out of her voice. "In fact, we've overpaid him just to keep the peace."

"I know we have and I agree that it is just wrong, but he went to Pastor." She rolled her eyes. "You know he's one of the favored ones around here, darling. I didn't know what else to do so I made up the check. I figured you would decide what to do about it." Ina subsided into silence while Mira looked for the billing in the folder.

"$2,500.00? He wants another $2,500.00?" Mira felt the twist in her stomach sharpen while the hand holding the documents trembled visibly. Confrontation was something she usually avoided at any cost, but this she couldn't ignore. It nauseated her to think that she would be forced to question Pastor Rafe about the check.

"I know," Ina agreed indignantly, "it's ridiculous, that's what it is! If you're going to talk to the pastor about it you might as well know also that Joe has only given me one payment of $500.00 on the church van so far. It might give you some leverage. I've been calling his wife, Lucy, every week and she keeps promising payment but nothing ever comes. She claims the van breaks down so often they spend their money keeping it on the road."

"Joe knew when he bid on the van that it was not certified," interjected Mira firmly. "He was determined to have it and he's done nothing but complain ever since. Pastor Rafe already asked the board to forgive $1,500.00 of the price owed because of repairs he claimed he had to make. We've been more than fair with him." She sighed. "I wish we had accepted another bid because I seriously doubt if we'll ever see the rest of the money."

"There's still $3,500.00 owing!" Ina slammed her desk drawer sharply. "You can't write off that kind of money!" Her brow furrowed as she looked worriedly at Mira. "I'll call them again tomorrow, my love, but I don't think it'll do any good." She hesitated. "You're not going to give in on this, are you? Joe's been grossly overpaid already for the little bit of work he did and this has been happening for years. He goes whining to the pastor who gives him whatever he wants because of the private little favors he does for him all the time. One hand greases the other."

"No! I'm not going to authorize it this time... at least not if I can help it," she amended with a groan, suddenly feeling very tired. "I guess I'll have to take it up with Pastor R. I can't just sign the check and let it go. Not this time! It's too much money. Doesn't Pastor realize that this is God's money we're dealing with? It just isn't right!"

"I also need to ask you about the bills you gave me on Wednesday. You said the pastor gave them to you and asked for immediate payment?" Ina's voice sounded strained. "Did you look at what was on the bills?"

"Yes. They're for supplies for the floors downstairs." Mira wondered if she should share with the little bookkeeper the conversation she'd had with the pastor about these same invoices. She decided not. "Pastor R. says they need to be paid right away because one of the bills dates back several months."

"But these are just faxed copies. Where are the originals?"

Mira looked up sharply. "I thought you would have them already. Have you not seen any of them?"

"No, I've never seen these before!" Ina was emphatic. "Joe Dalmer's name is on every bill which means he picked up the stuff. I thought he wasn't going to be involved in the project any more." Her voice grew more indignant. "Since when do staples, wax paper and mesh have anything to do with laying a tile floor?"

"Let me see!" Mira cried, reaching over to take the small pile of papers from Ina's hand. As she scrutinized each bill carefully, she could feel her stomach knot while the hot blood suffused her face and neck.

Pastor Rafe had been very casual about the invoices when he handed them to her after bible study this week, telling her that they were overdue and the company was requesting immediate payment. She had been startled at the large amount of money involved and upset because she hadn't known about the bills. She had asked the pastor why more supplies were needed when the contractor had been given a large check up front to purchase everything required for the job. He had made her feel very small and incompetent when he had angrily asked her why no one had checked with him first, as he had already made a deal with a friend of his to supply everything at a reasonable price.

Mira, horrified at the additional costs which far exceeded the budget, had asked the pastor why he hadn't shared this deal with the board of directors and the bookkeeper. She had tried to point out to him the impossibility of keeping the project on track, without full knowledge and disclosure of his involvement in it, while playing down the fact that the board was supposed to be in charge, because she knew it would only anger him further. He had turned the whole situation around anyway, blaming her again for not having sought his approval for the contractor's payment.

She hadn't calmed down until the thought occurred to her that any unused supplies could be returned for a refund. Her husband, who was lending a helping hand with the project, had refuted this idea, telling her they had run out of tile and more grout and cement would be needed as well. She was further disquieted to learn that the cost of supplies required to lay the tile should have been sufficient for an area three times the size of the enormous banquet hall.

Mira's anger rose as she glanced over the substance of the invoices. "I want you to contact the tiling company listed on these faxes and have them identify what each item is and whether it even relates to a tile floor and Ina? ....Don't pay anything until I approve it!"

"Okay honey." The bookkeeper's voice was sympathetic. She was relieved that the burden was now on someone else's shoulders. "Try not to worry about it, my love." As she looked at Mira's worried expression her heart smote her." I'm sorry. I shouldn't have shown it to you today. You shouldn't be upset going into service."

"I had to know." With sinking heart, Mira finished signing the rest of the checks while Ina went to track down another director for the second signature that was required. As treasurer, it was Mira's responsibility to review and sign all checks, with one of the remaining board members signing as well. Ina had complimented her many times on her diligence and she knew that the other signers trusted her competence and thoroughness so completely that they usually added their signatures without a thought.

This was not the first time that Mira would be forced to question Pastor Rafe about dubious expenditures. A month ago, she had gone to him regarding a second monthly travel expense check that he wanted issued to his grandson, Jonas. Ina had drawn it to her attention, confused over the reason for issuing two payments in the same month.

When she brought the matter up with Pastor Rafe, he had turned on her in fury, accusing her of unfairly persecuting his grandson. Mira had never seen him so angry. Her attempts to point out that Jonas was only there on a three month trial basis and that he was not a staff member only inflamed him further. She had finally fled the building in tears hardly able to drive home after the encounter.

Her attempts to hide the incident from Dan had met with only partial success. He was suspicious and questioning when he noticed traces of tears on her face. Pastor Rafe had called her later to apologize for his reaction but it had seemed superficial; over laden with excuses and justification.

Several more times, Mira had run into problems with money issues regarding Jonas. Each time the pastor reacted strongly. She couldn't help but notice that his treatment of her had changed. It alternated between coldness and outright flattery, keeping her in constant confusion and fear of offending her beloved pastor again.

Now she was in a quandary. She didn't want to face him and risk his anger once more but she couldn't see any way around it. If she instructed Ina to go ahead and cut a check, the other board members would likely sign it without even looking at the backup. There was also the second payment for Joe. The check was in front of her! It would be easy to just ignore it or pretend it had escaped her notice if questioned by one of the directors.

No! She wouldn't do it! She couldn't! It violated her conscience to even think about it! This was her responsibility before God and as she wrestled with her fears she came to the inescapable conclusion that she had no choice but to do what was right. She couldn't compromise her ethics for the sake of peace with Pastor Rafe. God had brought her too far for her to look the other way when it really mattered. For some reason, He had placed her in this position and she determined not to fail Him. Nevertheless, the thought of facing Pastor Rutherford nearly paralysed her with dismay.

A friendly voice interrupted her gloomy thoughts. A slim man with a wealth of greying hair and trim moustache poked his head through the door, a mischievous grin lighting his face. "I hear you need another signature".

Ian Parker was a director whom Mira had worked with over the last two terms. He was a shy, retiring man with an occasional stutter, who didn't say much but had a way of getting right to the point when he did speak. She nodded, not trusting her voice to reply.

Ian grabbed the chair across from her and began to sign the checks that she piled in front of him, with barely a glance at the backup. Excited about a gospel group whose concert he had recently attended with his wife, Jane, he was more talkative than usual, rattling on about the music while penning his name below hers on each item of paperwork.

Answering in monosyllables, Mira managed to finish reading the stack of papers in front of her. She signed the last check and unobtrusively withdrew the questionable documents from the batch before passing it to Ian.

Looking up, she forced a smile. She liked and respected the man sitting in front of her and for a moment debated on whether she should fill him in on what was happening. No, she thought. There was no point in stirring anything up until she had a chance to speak with the pastor. Quietly, she slipped the offending papers into an envelope to be dealt with later. Glancing at the clock she realized, in consternation, that it was already time for the morning service to begin.

Hurrying out the door and through the lobby, Mira rapidly made her way into the sanctuary. Anxiously, she searched the room for the pastor, breathing a sigh of relief when she saw him glad-handing congregants on his way to the platform. There was still time for her to be in her place when the worship team ascended the stage. Swiftly circling the outside of the room, adeptly avoiding handshakes and hugs, she kept her eye on his progress. They reached the front at the same moment. She threw her envelope on the front pew beside her purse and breathlessly took her place in the line-up. They were already starting to move.

4

CAPTAIN DARSHAN HAD A plan. In the early hours of the morning, his warriors had been divided into pre-arranged groups, each with their own assignments to carry out. As the time for morning worship approached, he signalled the largest contingent to follow him.

Boldly they approached the church, swords drawn and shields ready. As he had anticipated, they were accosted before they had even reached the perimeter of the property. A demon of enormous proportions suddenly melted out of the trees and stood barring their way.

"Halt!!" he bellowed raising a wicked looking scimitar which oozed black corrosion like a pestilence. "This is our territory! Leave or be annihilated!" Behind him a horde of evil creatures formed a wedge. The man-like beings appeared perverted - some with claws and extra appendages or eyes, others with suckers for hands; all of them warped in some way by the evil they had succumbed to.

Darshan had six score of his warriors with him. He gauged the power of the enemy carefully. He must engage them long enough to allow Caelen, Valin and the remaining warriors time to breach the sanctuary for the service. He could keep them busy for awhile, he thought grimly. As he raised his sword, white fire blazed from the tip. "Try to keep us out, demon spawn!" he bellowed defiantly.

The wedge of evil began to chant and the demon apparition grew larger until it towered over the group of warriors. Red fire tore from the uplifted scimitar, its force ripping into Darshan's heavy shield. With a deafening roar, the angel warriors leaped to his defence.

A safe distance from the battleground, Caelen and Valin watched as the two forces collided. Cars, streaming down the road toward the church, all passed through the thick of the fighting, oblivious to that which was going on in the spirit realm. Several of Darshan's secret forces slipped through, one by one, in the vehicles. Their appearance had been altered to look human to the evil spirits around them. Swords and shields had disappeared, along with large, imposing statures and they passed through the guards unnoticed, their attention divided with the battle at hand.

The two commanders made a wide circle approaching the church from the rear. In the distance they saw a large black cloud looming. "Vultures!" exclaimed Valin. "Captain Darshan will have his hands full this morning!" The distraction allowed him and his companion to slip unobtrusively by the watchers at the rear of the property. Unseen, they melted through the walls of the church.

In the sanctuary, they saw that only fifteen of the angels had been able to breach the enemy defences. These were scattered throughout the congregation listening to the worship, touching a head or patting a tired shoulder.

Demons were everywhere. They screamed obscenities from the platform. Hooting and shrieking, their contorted black hides capered about in the aisles. Hundreds of tiny imps tormented the worshippers, vomiting and spitting on them, jabbing them with cruel claws, whispering harshly into their ears, making sport of their praise.

~

The worship service was a triumph for Pastor Rafe who threw back his snowy head and played the keyboard with flourish and style. He was in his element, exhorting and exciting some of his audience to a point of frenzy. Davidic worshipers danced their way up and down the aisles, waving banners and scarves enthusiastically. A thin woman in bright, showy dress pranced and weaved her way seductively across the front of the platform, screeching shrilly to be heard over other voices of praise. Waves of emotion surged and ebbed across the congregation.

Suddenly, over the tumult of voices, a strident male voice bellowed thunderously, "Get rid of the abomination in your midst!"

Several people standing near the slender little man with the big mustache, jumped nervously, letting out a started exclamation. Imps and demons scrambled out of his way with shrieks of dismay.

"Thus saith the Lord", he roared. "I, the Lord God Almighty, demand holiness and righteousness! Repent....repent I say, or I will come quickly and remove your candlestick out of its place."

More prophetic words flowed and Mira, in her place on the platform, found herself trembling as she listened. This seemed different from most of the feel-good prophesies that were given in the services every week. She found herself wondering if it was really from the Lord or just another so-called prophet claiming his fifteen minutes of fame. She bowed her head and desperately called on God to reveal Himself to the congregation and speak to them.

Complete silence followed the utterance. It was finally broken by a stylish elderly lady who pushed her way forward, unceremoniously snatching the pastor's microphone where it lay at one side of his keyboard.

Mira groaned, thinking, *Oh please, not again! SIT DOWN! S*he closed her eyes and tried to will the woman away. This was one of those who desired the spotlight and would invariably seize every opportunity to be in the limelight.

Demons chortled and tumbled about in glee, resuming their torment of the saints with impunity. Jealousy stabbed the woman's neck with large, vicious claws, while Competition and Rivalry rode upon her head, gripping her brow with grotesque suction-cup appendages. They screamed obscenities in her ears as she waived her arms and danced about the stage shrilling out her false Word to the people.

Mira strove desperately to shut out the nonsensical ramblings and focus on the Lord. She tried to remember the words that had been spoken but they were already fading from memory, stolen by this incoherent, confused woman. A flush of embarrassment mounted her body, until beads of sweat broke out on her forehead.

From her vantage point on the platform, she hazarded a quick glance around the auditorium. She had a clear and untrammelled view of everyone in the room. Some faces glowed with sincerity while others were merely being swept along in the frenzy of the moment. Her eyes caught those of her husband standing in the doorway at the back. Dan shook his head in disgust and turning on his heel, left the sanctuary.

Pastor Rafe's fingers strayed capably over the keyboard tinkling out another chorus. He was mildly annoyed that he had lost control of the service but was confident that his own pre-rehearsed prophesy would place him back in the spot-light where he deserved to be. Following the song, a few well chosen words with trembling voice kicked off a boisterous wave of approval, signified by the clapping of hands which gave him opportunity to gather his thoughts.

As soon as the noise subsided, someone else started to shout out, but this time Rafe was ready, deftly cutting them off by launching into his own powerful, uplifting word of revelation. This, he calculated, would drive away any remembrance of that ridiculous and frightening Word spoken by the little man with the moustache. It would establish his supremacy, once again, as the true prophet who pleased both God and man.

Bending and swaying, he gesticulated wildly, pacing and prancing, dramatically pointing his finger at the people and proclaiming the favor of God over his ministry in particular and the church property in general. He made it abundantly clear that the Lord's favor was upon the house because he was there. He knew that he held the congregation in the palm of his hand. Several were weeping, many were shouting.

"Woo!" He staggered a few steps and shook himself. "Woo!" The applause increased until it became almost deafening.

"Angels are here!" He proclaimed, the timbre in his voice rising powerfully. "They are surrounding this place. They are here with me on the platform. I can feel their presence." The demons continued their frenzied dance, capering about him, their corrosive spittle dripping down his cheeks.

Triumphal strains of music reverberated ecstatically from the organ. The silver- haired lady who had spoken earlier danced out into the aisle with her partner to join several excited worshippers, who were capering about the front altars and waving their arms from side to side. Tripping daintily over to the edge of the stage, she signalled her desire to speak again.

Mira breathed a sigh of relief when Pastor Rafe refused to relinquish the microphone. His smile was ingratiating as he whispered into the woman's ear something calculated to appease and placate her.

Feeling faintly nauseous, Mira waited restlessly for the gesture that would dismiss the worship team from the platform. Finally their release came with a nod from Eve at the organ. Grabbing her things from the front seat, she made a bee-line for the closest exit and found a washroom where she could splash some water on her face and collect herself.

When she re-entered the sanctuary, the announcements were over and the ushers were already circulating through the audience with offering envelopes. Pastor Rutherford was, as usual, expounding upon tithing or as he liked to say – giving under an open heaven. More and more frequently, it seemed that offering time was an opportunity to pound into the people either the joy of giving, or conversely, the dire consequences or curses they would inevitably suffer should they withhold money from God. He often used graphic illustrations to support his point of view.

Mira found herself becoming more confused over the whole issue of seed faith giving. She knew that prosperity teachers were constantly bombarding the Christian world with messages that wealth and success and even healings would come to the faithful, particularly if they planted a seed offering in their ministry. Pastor R. touted the same philosophy but it didn't seem to line up with the Word of God about how tough things are supposed to get in the end times.

She recalled her wonderful parents who had led exemplary Christian lives. They had tithed faithfully, but in all honesty, it certainly hadn't reaped them the great financial wealth that Pastor Rafe promised to those who tithe. In fact, they had struggled along pretty much the same, year after year, with little or no change in their financial position. There had always been food on the table and the bills were always paid, but the riches and wealth that Pastor R. and the others talked about seemed as illusive as a vapor.

Mira remembered practically making herself ill over the finances of a national conference held at the church. As treasurer, she had felt the pressing weight of her responsibility as the numbers gradually went into the red with all of the expenses that were being incurred. Pastor Rafe had tried to reassure her, relating a personal story which he claimed had shaped his views on money early in his ministry. As a young preacher, he had worried about obtaining enough finances to cover his obligations. Another minister - a mentor - had asked him to look out of the window and tell him what he saw. He told the man that he only saw some people walking by. "Exactly." the older man replied, "That is where your money will come from."

Mira had to agree that his mentor was correct. She had been surprised at the influx of money from the offering plates once the conference was under way. She knew that Pastor R. excelled at squeezing dollars from the people. Ina had regaled her with stories of how he pressured some of the wealthier congregants to give largely, both into the church coffers and to him personally. A word, dropped in the right person's ear, brought a new car, a vacation at a posh resort, airfare tickets and plenty of extra money to spend.

The little bookkeeper had shared with her one day how uncomfortable she was with Pastor Rutherford asking to see the tithing records so that he would know which people to target. One couple, she said, had left the church because they could no longer afford his requests. Mira was sick at heart when she heard this but she was also afraid to face him with her knowledge. It would put Ina in an untenable position and bring his wrath down upon them both. She was afraid that Ina might even lose her job which she depended upon for her survival. No one else knew what she had learned and she wasn't sure what reaction there would be if she did speak up. Council members appeared to be so intimidated by the man that no one dared have a differing opinion regarding any issue.

Someone nudged her with the offering plate that was passing down her row. Mira dropped in her envelope, pushing down the uncomfortable notion that her money was going into a black hole over which she had no control. At least there wouldn't be a second offering today, she thought gratefully. There had been too many of those lately. The people were getting sick of it. She knew that several of the directors had been approached by members complaining about the repeated practice of taking two offerings in one service due to frequent visiting clergy. They were also wondering why their pastor absented himself from the pulpit so often. It gave the appearance that he was disinterested in his flock.

I guess ignorance really is bliss, she thought, trying to quell the gnawing ache in her heart. *Dan is so upset that he has actually told me to stop supporting this work. Should I obey him and risk God's disfavour?* She felt condemned either way. Where was the cheerful giving that had been a part of her life for so many years? Being aware that consistent tithing was one of the requirements of being a board member didn't help at all. It was only recently that she had even given it much thought. Resentment over her pastor's misspending was gradually seeping into her awareness, gnawing daily at her spirit. With an effort, she pulled her thoughts back to the present realizing that Pastor R. had already started his message.

Rafe didn't even open his bible this particular morning. He was on a role, still basking in the glow of his prophetic role in the earlier part of the service. His deep, soothing voice had a calming effect now on the previously exuberant worshippers. Coming down from the platform, he paced back and forth, establishing a personal rapport with each one that met his eyes. Kindness and tenderness oozed forth in his every expression.

He related how God had called him forth, as a young lad, into the ministry and placed a special anointing on his life. Several anecdotes had the assembly alternately chuckling and crying. They heard about his first pastorate and his struggles as a poor boy preacher and evangelist.

Outside, the battle raged between Darshan's warriors and the demon horde. The vultures had descended on them in a black cloud, their ferocious beaks and cruel talons piercing their defences again and again. Angel warriors that had failed to gain entrance to the church joined with them to give aid.

A sudden attack of wolf-like creatures turned the tide in favour of the demons. Striking the fighting mass from both sides, they drove forward with devastating effect, clawing and tearing at their victims in a mad frenzy. The angels spun about, dodging fangs, while desperately trying to keep their footing.

Darshan charged like a madman hacking at any spirit within reach. He knew his warriors were exhausted and was afraid he had vastly underestimated the size of the force they were dealing with. "Flee, on my signal," he howled. The embattled angels fought frantically to open way of escape. Caught in a seething, confused mass of demons and spirit beings, the warriors began to collapse.

A piercing war cry split the skies. Caelen and Valin attacked in unison, their gigantic swords spewing white fire over the roiling throng and splitting the fighting wedge of demons wide open.

"Flee!" roared Darshan, seeing the small gap of hope. His warriors needed no second bidding. They shot through the opening, the sound of the wind rushing through their wings like a thunderclap. The commanders followed when they were sure that every angel had escaped to safety. The demons gave chase, unwilling to release their quarry just as imminent triumph was within their grasp. As the angels increased their distance from the church property however, they soon began to drop off to go in search of other prey.

~

Mira found her mind wandering again as the sermon went on. She had heard it all many times before. Dispassionately observing various reactions about her, it occurred to her to wonder why the name of Jesus was scarcely mentioned. In fact, upon further reflection, she could not remember the last time she had heard Pastor R. preach a sermon based on the Word of God rather than on his own personal experiences. Deep within her spirit a desire to learn flickered. She was desperate to grow in her Christian walk, to develop a closer relationship with her Savior and Lord.

The service eventually wound to a tortuous conclusion with Pastor Rafe pronouncing his gracious benediction. A final song swelled from the organ as he rapidly exited the stage, anxious to bask in the accolades of his parishioners. Dispensing warm smiles and nods of recognition to a favored few, he headed down the large center aisle to take his accustomed place in the foyer near the front door.

Mira quietly gathered up her belongings and making her way into the lobby, she stood waiting for the place to empty so she could have some time with the pastor. Congregants milled about in noisy confusion, collecting children from the nursery and children's church, greeting one another with affectionate hugs and kisses. They crowded the vestibule forming a line, each one wanting a word and warm handshake from their beloved shepherd. The church emptied quickly, everyone anxious to get home to their roasts before they were burned to a crisp.

Finally, the last handshake given, Pastor Rutherford closed the huge front doors and turned toward Mira, a self-satisfied look on his face. He was feeling benevolent this morning, still basking in the glowing compliments of his sheep.

"Wasn't that a great service?" he crowed. "Could you feel the glory cloud that came in and settled over the people?"

Mira hadn't felt anything but she knew better than to say so. She mumbled something that she hoped was non-committal and thrust out her hand with the paperwork on Joe Dalmer. "I need to talk with you about this bill from Joe." Her voice trembled slightly.

Rafe's eyes narrowed and his smile faded. Hungry now, after his great expenditure of energy in the service, he was keen to get to his waiting lunch and afternoon nap. "What about it?" His tone was decidedly short.

Mira, wanting to get it over with, came straight to the point. "Joe has already been paid for the work he did on the tiling downstairs."

"He has done more work since then." Annoyance crept into his voice.

"When?" she asked hesitatingly, wondering desperately how in the world she was going to oppose this payment alone.

"He has been in all week helping Jonathan with the floor."

"What?" She stared. "Who asked him to come?"

"Well, I....Jonathan..." he stuttered. "Well...," he tried again, "he volunteered to help straighten out the mess."

"But the board turned the job over to Jonathan with the understanding that he would be in charge and take full responsibility for it." Mira took a slow, steadying breath and forged on. "We made it clear that we would only be paying him. We do not owe any further payments to Joe. If indeed he has been working on the job, then it is Jonathan who must pay him as a helper, not the church."

Rafe shrugged. "Don't worry about it. I'll talk to both of them and sort it all out." His voice was cold.

"I also need to ask you about the invoices you gave me on Wednesday night."

"Aren't they paid yet? I told you they are overdue and should be paid immediately." His displeasure was evident.

"Why is the company sending faxed invoices? Where are the originals?"

"I don't know," he exclaimed impatiently. "Probably Ina has them."

"No. This is the first time she has seen the charges. We need the original bills," She continued. "Joe's name is on them and some of the items must be for another job."

"No," he disagreed. "I asked Nate, a personal friend of mine, to set up the account for the church so we could get a contractor's pricing and Joe was personally approved by him to pick up the product."

"Well, I've had a good look at the items listed and many of them have nothing to do with a tile floor," Mira stated firmly. "Also the dates are wrong. Joe was not even part of the job for at least three of the invoices so he should not have been picking up anything for the church."

Rafe's jaw tightened imperceptibly. "Give me the invoices and I'll straighten it all out with Joe and Nate. I'll have them tick off what belongs to the church. Good catch on the errors, by the way," he said smoothly.

Mira shoved the paperwork back into the envelope and handed it to him with shaking hands.

"Do you have a song for tonight?" Rafe's voice was silky.

Relief flooded her mind. He didn't seem to be too angry with her or he wouldn't have asked her to sing. "I guess I could pull something that I already know," she blurted out, scarcely realizing what she said.

Rafe walked over to set the alarm while Mira headed for the door. On the steps outside she paused for a moment to take a deep breath in an effort to still her pounding heart. Her knees were still a little wobbly as she headed over to her car, now the only one left in the parking lot.

Rafe followed a few minutes later, walking briskly across the gravel toward the parsonage. He gave no more than a perfunctory thought to the questionable paperwork regarding Joe. His knack for getting whatever he wanted was renowned and this would be no exception. After all, had he not hand-picked his board and council members? He certainly didn't anticipate any problems from them. Unquestioning loyalty he felt was his right and he demanded it from everyone around him. His pride however was pricked and he felt affronted as he reflected that Mira, of all people, should support him without any difficulty. She surprised him with her over-inflated sense of integrity, questioning his actions not once, but several times now! He vaguely wondered if she was going to turn into a problem for him, but dismissed the thought as unworthy almost as soon as it came. His lip curled sardonically. She would bow to his wisdom as they all had. There was no one capable of threatening his authority here.

For a nagging moment, his sense of well-being was disturbed by the memory of a few board members in the past who had given him some trouble. He had ultimately triumphed over them, but it was something he didn't like to dwell on. In any case, it didn't matter since it would take no great effort to neutralize Mira. He quickly pressed the speed dial on the hand-held phone he carried with him and was already deep in conversation as he entered the rear door of his home.

5

It took time for Darshan's warriors to recover from their encounter with the enemy. Caelen and his companion, Valin, conferred with the captain and Jarah, laying careful plans for future encounters. Direct confrontation would have to be avoided at the church due to the magnitude of the Evil One's stranglehold on the place. They were outnumbered a hundred to one.

"Were you able to learn anything in the service?" enquired Darshan, hoping the sacrifice his warriors had made was worth the cost.

The tall commander replied in the affirmative. "There are several hopeful signs among the congregants. Unfortunately, they do not realize their potential to do great harm to the enemy. Because many are elderly and even infirm, they feel their time has past. I want to use several of your warriors to encourage and strengthen them. They must pray for the assembly and the board of the church or we will be forced to resort to another plan. There isn't much we can do without prayer."

Valin agreed with Caelen. "The enemy has gained an enormous foothold in the place," he said earnestly. If we are unable to drive them out, we must save as many as we can. That is our mandate."

"I saw a young man there who is at a crisis point in his life," said Caelen worriedly. "His eyes looked so lifeless that I fear it may already be too late."

"I know who you mean," agreed Jarah. "He is in desperate need of deliverance. The shepherd might have had some influence over the youth but he is so lost himself that he is a danger rather than a help to the lad."

"Dispatch two warriors to his side at once," ordered Caelen. Captain Darshan nodded and singled out two mighty angels to do his bidding.

"The man that gave the prophetic utterance is also in trouble," exclaimed Valin, thinking of the little man with the big mustache. "Jarah, didn't you tell us that he spent a month living at the parsonage."

"Yes. The demon called Lust has spent considerable time working on him. In fact, he was sitting with him throughout the service, whispering into his ear."

"Send two more of your finest to find him. It may be that they will still be able to affect a rescue." Caelen's face shone with resolve and determination. "I want every board and council member and their spouses assigned warriors as well. They will have need of them."

Mira arrived early the night of the board meeting knowing she needed a few minutes before everyone arrived to photocopy the agenda and organize herself. Her stomach began to churn as soon as she turned her car into the church parking lot. Pastor Rutherford was on the phone in his secretary's office when she walked in. Waving a greeting, she slipped by the door into the tiny enclosure that housed the photocopier.

She had barely finished her work when Jack Johnson, the vice-president, arrived with a cheery greeting and accompanying smile. He was a tall man, clean-shaven with keen blue eyes and pleasant features; his close-cropped dark hair was only slightly tinged with grey.

Mira liked the big, tender-hearted man and his lovely wife, Amy. They were a good solid Christian couple, volunteering their help in the Sunday School and more recently taking on the coordination of the Greeters Committee. Quick to respond wherever he saw a need, Jack would often quietly slip a few bills into the hands of those struggling to make ends meet or offer a good used vehicle to some poor soul that could ill afford to replace their old clunker. He liked to dabble in selling used cars but, more often than not, he would give them away or sell them at cost. Although his welding business kept him busy, like Dan, Jack was always offering to lend a hand with various repairs and projects around the church.

Donny Allison blew through the door next, his warm, hearty laugh filling the lobby as he greeted Mira and Jack. He was a well-built, jovial man of forty-something with deeply tanned skin, a receding hair-line and an irrepressible grin that lit up his whole face. For much of his life he had been in the business of moving houses.

To some, he may have seemed a little rough around the edges, but his heart was generous and he invariably brought a cheerful note to every conversation. He had suffered through some hard times and deep valleys in recent years when his wife had suddenly left him for another man. It had taken time for him to work through the hurt and bitterness that settled into his spirit, but eventually he had been able to let it go. Little by little, the spring had returned to his step and now he faced life with the joy of the Lord in his heart.

Gathering up her things, Mira climbed the steps which led to the board room situated just outside the pastor's office. A few minutes later, Jack and Donny followed, accompanied by Ian Parker, who had just arrived along with a distinguished-looking elderly gentleman.

Rev. David Armstrong was a retired minister who had been attending the church with his wife, Ella, for a several years. He had been appointed almost immediately by Pastor Rafe as an elder in the church. Following the last annual meeting, he had assumed the roll of president upon his election to the board of directors.

Just as they were all settling into their chairs, a dishevelled old man in rumpled clothing wheezed noisily into the room. His balding head sported a ring of unkempt, white hair; his full bushy beard was scruffy and untrimmed. Sylvester Zimmer was what one might call a curmudgeon. A perpetually sour, grumpy expression illumined his face. He squeezed himself into an empty chair, his sharp, gimlet eyes missing nothing as they darted around the table.

The other directors greeted him pleasantly, each one being painfully aware of the explosive temper that could manifest without warning at any given moment. They had been privy many times to his ranting stories about his wife, Norma, whom he accused of being sharp-tongued and unloving.

Jack had confided to the others his own personal discomfort when subjected to Sylvester's disrespectful tirades against his spouse. Now he refused to work with him on anything. The old geezer loved to putter about with small projects but he wasn't particularly adept at anything. Poor Jack was often called upon to correct his mistakes.

Norma assisted Ina in the office with the counting of the offering, filing and other light duties each week, so the little bookkeeper had witnessed many of the altercations and interactions between the pair. Although she had a strong personality herself, Ina was sometimes hard pressed to keep the peace between them. Mira had been given an earful on the subject.

Several of Captain Darshan's warrior angels were also present in the room. They had a legal right to be there because they warded those who had prayed and sought the Lord before coming to the meeting. The demon sentries had been forced to acknowledge this right and allow them to pass. Since they were so few of them, they were deemed no threat to the greater forces of evil who took perverse pleasure in mocking and tormenting them.

The group stirred restlessly. The big comfortable leather chair at the head of the table stood vacant. Pastor Rutherford was late again! Although Rev. Armstrong was president, never would he dare to take charge and begin the meeting himself. That would have been construed as a direct challenge of the pastor's authority.

So they waited until, at fully ten minutes past the hour, Rafe finally breezed into the room. The demon-master, Jezebel along with a vast number of lesser evil spirits followed in his wake.

Bringing the meeting to order, the pastor read a short passage from the Psalms and asked Rev. Armstrong to open in prayer. The first couple of items on the agenda, which included the minutes of the last meeting and the financial statements, were disposed of quickly. This done, Rafe announced he would be leaving the meeting early as he had another appointment. Galloping through the agenda, he ignored those items he considered of little importance but gave the full weight of his opinion on anything he felt might affect his own personal interests.

It was obvious to those sitting around the table that he considered the meeting to be a colossal waste of his valuable time. Rafe definitely wanted to be elsewhere. Usually he enjoyed a captive audience and the chance to pontificate. Tonight however, except for one or two things that he wanted to see accomplished, he had no time to listen to the trivial drivel put forward by his minions. He knew that the board, once knowing his will regarding a matter, would follow it to the letter whether they agreed or not.

In particular, Rafe wanted to make it known how unhappy he was with the inept cleaning services of Lorena Hatfield. He had someone else in mind for that job. Joe Dalmer's wife had approached him recently wanting the cleaning contract for herself. The minister had good reason to maintain a friendly relationship with the couple. Joe, a handyman, was always useful and his wife, Lucy, provided him with free alternative healthcare services. The cleaning contract was technically up for renewal but he knew the board was predisposed to continue with Lorena for the foreseeable future.

Broaching the subject carefully, Rafe delicately pointed out, with gentle criticism, convincing evidence of Lorena's dereliction of her duties. Undisturbed by pangs of conscience, he unwittingly exposed his own deceptive actions of planting scraps of debris around the church, with the express purpose of belittling the cleaner's abilities and dedication to her job. Speaking persuasively, he described in glowing terms Lucy's superior abilities, subtly hinting that Lorena had indicated to him that it would be a relief to her to give up the contract and pursue other interests. He continued in this vein until he felt he had made his point abundantly clear and could reasonably assume the board would agree and comply with his wishes.

The other item of interest to him was the update on the tiling of the large banquet hall. To pre-empt what Mira might say regarding those troublesome bills, he launched into a lengthy speech detailing how he personally had given of his time to lug tile for the workers and make arrangements for the best prices for materials.

Mira was confused. *Lug tile! What is he talking about?* She knew that Dan was there almost every day and he had not mentioned anything about the pastor helping. *Would Pastor lie so blatantly? How could he be confused about a thing like that?* Yet she knew her husband would have told her about it, if it were true.

Delicately, Rafe alluded to his desperate need for more help in the church. He was spread too thin and found it difficult to handle everything himself. Pastor Marvin, he suggested adroitly, was a good man but he was disappointed in his commitment. "He just isn't cutting it," he had said sighing deeply.

As he rambled on, Mira listened in amazement as facts were twisted and blame was placed unsparingly upon her for hiring the first crew that turned out badly. Somehow the misunderstanding regarding the purchase of materials was her fault as well. Joe's involvement apparently came at great personal sacrifice and was only done as a special favor for the pastor.

The men sat with their heads down, shifting uncomfortably in their seats, not daring to look up lest they catch anyone's eye. The demons laughed and cavorted, poking fun at the big warriors who listened in silence.

Rafe ended his soliloquy. "If I had just been consulted in everything, there wouldn't be any of these problems to deal with now." *This is hardly worth the effort,* he thought contemptuously. *What a group of spineless wimps!* His lip curled as he rose to his feet.

"Joe and Jonathan are waiting downstairs for me, in order that this may be sorted out and if it is the pleasure of the board...." his voice dripped with sarcasm, "I will request that they speak to you when we're through." He lingered, allowing them to squirm under the full weight of his displeasure.

It was the president who finally broke the silence, his lower lip trembling noticeably. "That would be fine," he quavered. Rafe tossed his head in disgust and turning arrogantly on his heel, he left the room slamming the door behind him.

Sylvester rose to his feet. A cloud of wicked little imps circled his head shrieking hoarsely and spitting. His face was beet red and his voice shook with barely suppressed rage. "I should hand in my resignation right now!" he blustered. "It isn't right, the way he treats Lorena. She *does* need the job! She told me so herself. She knows full well that he leaves things around to see if he can catch her not doing her work properly. She's in quite a nervous state over it."

"Look, why don't we just calm down and start over." Mira spoke soothingly. "We don't want you to resign. Please sit down."

An angel reached out and touched his arm, whispering quietly into his ear. "Well...," grunted the old man, somewhat mollified by her comment, "I don't even know why I'm here anyway. I'm not qualified for this position." But he sat back down in his chair.

"Join the crowd!" laughed Donny. "I don't know what I'm doing either. This is all new to me."

"I wouldn't have let my name stand for the board this year if Mira hadn't particularly asked me to," Jack interjected.

"I know, Jack. I'm sorry I got you into this. Whenever we have a board meeting I feel like I'm a child in school again." Mira sounded frustrated. "I can't even think when he's in the room! I don't get it! I've never had this problem in all of my years in the work force or on any other committee I've served with."

"I agree." Donny replied sympathetically. "I feel the same way. I've run my own business for years and have never felt as intimidated as I do here. I can't figure out what's going on. It's like I can't speak or something." The others nodded in agreement.

Mira looked at Rev. Armstrong. "Really," she pointed out, "you should be chairing our meetings; not the pastor. As president of the board, according to the constitution, it is your responsibility. Pastor Rafe should only be chairing the council meetings."

"Well... yes... I guess I should, but he just seems to take over and I don't like to say anything...." His voice trailed off. They looked at one another in silence, waiting for him to take the lead now.

Finally, Mira spoke up. "I would like to suggest that we go back to the first missed item on the agenda and begin again. Everything has been taken out of order and half of the matters haven't even been discussed."

"That's right," chimed in Donny. "He just skipped all over the place. Why don't we just take them one at a time and make whatever decisions are necessary."

"Maybe we should pray again," Jack suggested looking pointedly at the president.

Rev. Armstrong smiled. "I think that's a good idea." He bowed his head. "Let's pray...Lord, we give you honor and praise tonight and we thank you for your many blessings. We know that we are frail creatures but we also know that you have placed us in this position for a reason. We ask that you give us wisdom and strength to deal with the matters before us and unity with each other that we might all be in one accord. We thank you for these things and ask them in the precious name of Jesus. Amen"

The relief everyone felt after this simple prayer was palpable in the room. The angels grew in stature as the prayer was being uttered, while the demons backed away in fear and confusion. The meeting resumed and business matters progressed quickly with each item being given due consideration. All necessary decisions now seemed to be made with remarkable ease.

Mira shared what knowledge she possessed of the tiling project as concisely as possible. She told how she and Dan had been involved in trying to find a suitable contractor with the limited funds the church could afford. It hadn't been easy but they had finally located a young Christian man, an acquaintance of Dan's, who was both available and willing to take the job on. Jonathan, she explained, had been struggling with finances at the time and needed the work to help support his growing family.

Mira reminded the directors that she had approached the board to gain their approval for him to begin the work. It was at this point, she stated, that Ina became involved, excitedly recommending another private contractor to the pastor whom she promised would give an even better price. Enthusiastic about the savings, Pastor Rafe had supported the idea, so Mira and Dan had stepped back feeling their involvement in the project had ended.

"I think we were all just relieved to save the extra money on a very expensive project," she concluded. "In retrospect, I wish we hadn't agreed so easily."

Rapidly, she summarized the problems that had occurred with the contractor Ina brought in. The written contract had included a promised completion date in order to accommodate the rental of the hall for a wedding reception. However, time dragged on as inexperienced workers were left unsupervised by the contractor. Food disappeared from the benevolent freezers and equipment from the church kitchen. One morning, one of the young men had arrived at work in a drug-induced haze and had to be sent home.

Jack and Donny admitted they were horrified when told by two of the ushers one Sunday morning that the crew was working downstairs during the service. The men had unwittingly stumbled upon them while investigating the noisy sounds of secular music emanating from their boom box. The workers claimed they had permission to work that day as long as they were sufficiently quiet, in order to complete the job as soon as possible.

"We asked Pastor Rafe about it," declared Donny, "but he denied giving his permission. He blamed us! He told us the board is in charge of the project."

Jack laughed ruefully. "I guess we're in a no-win situation. The pastor wants to control every aspect of it but if anything goes wrong, we catch all of the blame."

Mira picked up the tale again. "The whole project came to a screeching halt when the workers ran out of tile," she reminded them. "You know how adamant Pastor Rafe was about handling the arrangements for the original tile purchase personally. He insisted that he could get the best deal and he wouldn't allow us to waste any time conducting a proper price search."

"Yes, I remember him crowing about the great price he negotiated," added Donny. "He told us several times that he had purchased sufficient tile for the job too, but we all know how badly that turned out."

"Dan tried to tell him several times that there wasn't nearly enough tile for the job but he wouldn't listen," replied Mira quietly. "He insisted that he knew what he was doing and that experts had properly measured the area. His error certainly proved to be a costly one with almost six thousand square feet of tile still required."

"Even then, he still wouldn't let us get involved in any of the decisions," put in Ian. "As I recall, he insisted on handling the second purchase of tile from the same source but by then an exact match couldn't be located."

"That's right," rejoined Jack. "We were forced to settle for a product that was as close as possible to the original."

"The delays caused some real problems with the wedding reception," volunteered Mira. "The floor was only partly laid and almost none of it grouted. Ina told me that she and Pastor Rafe ordered the contractor to grout whatever tile he could and hang white tarpaulins to cordon off the area that was still unfinished so that it wouldn't look so bad. I didn't know what was going on until Lorena stopped me, Donny and Jack in the lobby after a service. She was frantic over the state of the floor and told us that the wedding decorators were downstairs attempting to prepare the room over a floor surface that was a terrible mess of dried grout and uncleaned tile. She said that Pastor Marvin had tried to help clean things up apparently working most of the previous night with little success."

"It was too late to cancel the reception," she added, "so they had to proceed in spite of the floor's condition. Of course we had to reimburse the rental fees to a very unhappy bridal couple."

Donny related how he and Jack had stepped in at this point and requested a meeting with the contractor. The man had shown up with several friends and when called to account had brazenly threatened them, cursing and yelling until they were forced to sternly terminate his services.

"Pastor Rafe didn't like the interference," responded Mira quickly. "He blamed you guys for halting the project."

"What else could we do?" replied Donny sounding frustrated.

"We did the right thing," insisted Jack looking around the room. "The pastor never should have gotten involved in the project at all. If we had gone ahead with the guy Mira and Dan found, all of this could have been avoided."

"Well," admitted Mira, "the pastor did finally call us. He asked if Dan would call Jonathan in to finish the project. My husband tells me Jonathan was really nice about it. He had to spend many hours cleaning the mess the other crew left behind, even lifting and relaying a section of tile that had been improperly cemented. Dan helped as much as he could too."

"I just want to see the end of this project." Donny sounded perturbed. "It has gotten totally out of control because every decision we've made has been overridden or interfered with."

The door unceremoniously opened and Pastor Rafe sailed into the room.

"Everything has been straightened out," he stated curtly, whirling past the group toward his office. "Joe wasn't able to be here tonight but his wife came. I had a good chat with Lucy and Jonathan and everything's fine now." He disappeared through the door of his office still talking. "It's amazing, all of the time this has cost me," he hurled back over his shoulder. "And it all could have been avoided, if I had been consulted in the first place."

Suddenly he reappeared in the doorway. Silence reigned and heads drooped avoiding eye contact as he stood behind his chair at the head of the table. "I have Jonathan waiting outside the door. He is willing to talk to the board if that is your pleasure," he said loftily. "Lucy couldn't stay."

"Well....." Rev. Armstrong stuttered nervously. "I think that would be fine." He looked around at the others for support. They nodded silently.

Rafe lifted his chin arrogantly and headed for the door. "I'm late for my other appointment so I will ask Jonathan to come in on my way out." The door slammed behind him as he left the room.

Suppressed air from several sets of lungs exploded around the table. "Whew!" Donny exclaimed. "Well.....isn't that something!" A knock on the door interrupted further comment and Ian rose to grant admittance to the tall young man standing outside.

Jonathan impressed the directors with his forthright manner, setting out in detail the steps required to complete the banquet hall floor. His questions were brief and quickly answered. Mira asked for an explanation of Joe's involvement in the project and what his agreement was with the pastor.

"Well, I guess there was a little misunderstanding about that," he said smiling. "I'm not sure how Joe got involved in the job but apparently the pastor wants him there so I've agreed to use him as a worker and pay him myself."

"I really don't mind," he went on, "the job's still a pretty big one and I can use a helper. I don't think his wife is very happy though." He chuckled. "She just peeled out of the parking lot spraying gravel pretty good. She wanted a large invoice paid by the church but, like I told the pastor, I already paid Joe in cash for the work he's done so far for me."

"Are you saying you actually paid him cash money?" Mira asked incredulously, thinking about the invoice she had seen.

"Yeah. That's what I'm saying," he drawled. "He helped me out some and I gave him a check for $1,000.00 in payment. Then he came back and told me that he couldn't cash it because of some sort of tax problem in his business. It caused me all kinds of problems getting it sorted out. My wife had to re-deposit the check and get him the cash. I felt kind 'o sorry for him, you know. I've had some hard times myself. I gave him a brand new saw too. I thought it might help him out and he said he needed one. Anyway, I had a good talk with Lucy and she understands that he isn't getting any more money for the work. I showed her exactly what was done and I explained right kindly that they shouldn't try to stick it to the church. You gotta always do the right thing in business. If you do, the Lord will bless you for it."

"What did the pastor say?" demanded Mira, choking back a wild desire to howl.

"Not much. He had to make a phone call so he didn't go downstairs with us. I guess he's satisfied that the whole thing is settled."

The directors dismissed Jonathan with their thanks and moved forward with the remaining items of business to consider. After much discussion, they decided that it would be best to implement a proper purchase order system at once, thus eliminating any further confusion in the purchase of supplies and contracting of laborers.

"Pastor Rafe will need to be informed about the new system as soon as possible," suggested Mira. "How will we do that?" She trembled at the thought of the wrath they would bring on their heads if he disapproved of their decision.

"Draft a letter from the board," said Donny resolutely. "Not that he will pay any attention to it." He grinned at the others.

Jack's face looked serious. "I think it has to be done. A strong reminder that the financial and business aspects of the church fall under the board's legal mandate should also be included in the letter. Everything of a business nature should be left in the hands of the board."

"That's true," added Ian. "Pastor Rafe's involvement should be kept to spiritual matters only. Everything else he touches gets messed up." Everyone seemed in agreement and all were satisfied that the letter, although unpleasant, would conclude the matter.

Mira suggested they tackle the problem of the church van payments still owed by Joe Dalmer.

"It sounds to me as if we're never going to see the money," said Donny with a laugh after she had filled them in.

"I agree," replied Jack. "Why don't we forgive the promissory note and call it quits. At least that way it will end our association with the Dalmers. It seems like every time that man or his wife get involved in a project, there are unexpected complications."

"It's a lot of money but, after what we just heard, I think it would be best to take the hit and get clear of them," agreed Ian. "We just need to be certain that this latest invoice Lucy is flapping about gets included in the deal."

"Yes," Donny rejoined. "Make them sign off on that invoice. Otherwise she may come back again for payment on it after the note is forgiven. It would be just like them."

"The old van wasn't worth anything anyway," growled Sylvester. "I wouldn't have given you two cents for it."

Mira was relieved that no one dissented. She promised to draft a letter to the Dalmers informing them that the van note would be forgiven if they would sign a release form freeing the church from any obligation for the work Joe had done on the floor. The proper motion was quickly brought forward, followed by a unanimous vote from the directors.

The only piece of business left was the cleaning contract for the church and parsonage. The directors decided the issue speedily being of one accord in their desire to continue Lorena's cleaning contract until the end of the year.

Sylvester beamed. "That will be such a relief to her."

"I would like to suggest that we have a prayer time together before we leave." Rev. Armstrong's voice sounded stronger now, more sure of himself.

For the next half hour, they prayed aloud and wept before the Lord, asking for wisdom, guidance and direction. They held up one another's burdens as each one shared their struggles and what lay heavy on their hearts. Holding hands in a circle of unity the aged reverend breathed a final benediction.

The warrior angels drew themselves to their full height. They appeared to pulsate with light. Imps and evil spirits withdrew howling and shrieking in impotent fury.

"I've never seen a board or council meeting where we had prayer like this and I've been on the board quite a few times and a council member ever since I came to this place." Sylvester's gruff voice sounded tender. "When I first started coming, I needed help and I shared that with the pastor. He made me an elder almost immediately but I never did get the help I needed." Tears stood in his eyes. "I shouldn't be an elder," he blurted out, "and I know it."

The others looked at one another helplessly. No one knew what to say or how to lessen the old man's misery. Impulsively, Mira gave him a warm hug.

"We all love you, Sylvester," she said seeing him in a different light now with this new vulnerability showing. She cleared her throat. "You know, tonight has been special for me too. I feel a unity here that I haven't felt before. Things are different somehow." She turned to the other men. "Don't you feel it?"

"Yes – absolutely - me too." The answers came rapidly and with conviction.

"God is doing something awesome here." Jack spoke reverently. "I don't think we'll ever be the same."

"I think it's the prayer. Maybe we need to have more of it," Donny said excitedly.

"I would like to see us have an old fashioned Jericho march through the basement," Jim said shyly. "What do you think?" As they looked at one another, he continued. "I think it was wrong of that crew to work here on Sunday and even though we didn't know about it until it was too late, we are still the legal governing body of this church and we need to set it right. There was swearing and taking the Lord's name in vain. I think we need to repent and cleanse the place with prayer."

"We have been plagued with one thing after another, this last few months. I think you're right on," replied Donny emphatically. "Count me in." The others chimed in as well making it unanimous.

"Let's set a date and time then," Mira interjected practically and after a brief consultation of schedules, they settled on an evening the following week.

"Do you think the pastor will come?" asked Sylvester.

"I'll tell him what we've decided to do. Surely he will be behind it," said Mira happily. With hearts light and joyous they turned out the lights and made ready to leave.

The angels looked fearsome and eager, strengthened by the very promise of prayer as they accompanied the directors from the building.

6

The week passed without incident and on the appointed evening, the directors gathered together again. Once more their assigned warrior angels were permitted entrance without conflict.

Mira informed the men that Pastor Rutherford had declined their invitation to attend, sighting a prior engagement. They quickly pressed forward with the business items on the brief agenda she submitted, until the final item was reached.

Apologizing for taking the extra time, Mira brought forward a request from the bookkeeper. A frustrated Ina had asked her on the preceding Sunday to please ask the board for instruction on how and when to pay the pastor's grandson. Knowing this was a sore spot with Pastor Rafe, Mira had given it a good deal of thought. No monitoring system was in place to ascertain whether Jonas was present simply to attend a service or if he was actually working. A time sheet would surely offend him and his grandfather, she thought, so after much agonizing, she decided to call it an accountability sheet. Surely the pastor could not object if they asked his grandson to document his trips and have a staff member approve it.

In order to bring a clear presentation of the matter to the board, Mira was forced make a difficult decision. She would have to tell the members about the altercations between her and the pastor over his grandson.

As simply as possible, she related the circumstances and problems she had experienced. These not only included the matter of the second check for Jonas but also an issue with the petty cash fund which had been used for a youth project. Money had been taken by Pastor Rutherford without providing a chit or receipt. He had been highly incensed when reminded that proper paperwork was needed in order to satisfy the auditors and Mira had been accused of having a vendetta against his grandson.

The directors were not happy to hear of the treatment the treasurer had received at the hands of the pastor. Jack and Donny wanted to confront him immediately. Horrified that she had made matters worse, Mira pleaded with them to let it go. "It's over now," she said anxiously. "I'd rather not stir things up with him again. I just needed you to know how delicate this matter is. It will require careful handling because the pastor is very sensitive when it comes to Jonas."

One by one the directors shared the complaints they had heard throughout the congregation as well as their own opinions regarding the ministry of the pastor's grandson. It quickly became apparent that there were deep problems that needed to be addressed. Many of the older members of the assembly were upset over both Jonas' body piercings and his behaviour during the worship services. None of these things had been discussed openly because of fear of reprisal from Pastor Rafe.

Jonas' marriage to his fiancée had taken place a couple of months after they came. However, both before and after the wedding, the pair had been noticeably absent for much of the five months since he had been introduced as the new youth minister so many were wondering where he was and what he was doing.

"Do we even need him?" asked Rev. Armstrong. "I haven't seen any consistent ministry or growth among the young people."

"I say forget about the accountability sheet. I think we should just suspend the travel honorarium," Donny said decisively. "It doesn't make any sense to have a youth meeting one week and then nothing for three or four weeks because he doesn't show up. Let's face it, if you did that on a regular job, you'd be fired." He laughed. "I'd certainly fire him if he worked for me. I can't believe we let him get away with it this long. It was supposed to be a three month trial period. Right?"

Mira nodded.

"Well, we've given him five months and it isn't working. I move that the travel honorarium be discontinued immediately for lack of performance." Donny's motion was quickly seconded and to Mira's surprise the vote was unanimous.

The group promptly adjourned to the large banquet hall in the basement where they spent the next hour in prayer together, walking through the rooms and anointing the doorways with oil. Demons flew this way and that, in confusion and turmoil, in an effort to escape the sweet incense caused by the prayers of the saints. More angels poured into the basement as the demons were driven out. A spirit of unity and peace prevailed among the directors and when they had concluded their evening, they all felt they had been in the very presence of God.

As they gathered up their things to leave, Mira spoke up hesitantly. "Someone will have to inform the pastor of our suspension of Jonas' travel honorarium. I think he should be told as soon as possible, but I will be away this Sunday. I have been asked to lead worship at another assembly. I don't really want Pastor Rafe to learn of our decision when he sees the minutes or he will surely blame me. Out of courtesy, he should be told in person."

The men looked at one another in consternation. Fear floated through the door and tried to spray his corrosive vomit over the group. The angels quickly countered the attack.

"Maybe the President should tell him," Mira finally suggested looking at Rev. Armstrong. He looked up startled, terror written on his face. She felt sorry for him. "Or," she hesitated, "perhaps the Vice-President could do it or maybe the better plan is for the two of you to go together?" She looked at Jack appealingly.

"Why don't we all do it together on Sunday morning after the service," said Donny bravely. The men readily agreed to this plan knowing that strength comes in numbers and unity.

~

Rafe was in high spirits the following Sunday. The service had gone smoothly with a visiting evangelist bringing the message so he had not had to exert himself in the least. He enjoyed more and more the meetings that required minimal effort for maximum return. His pulpit was covered for the next six weeks at least, he thought smugly. Special speakers were always calling hoping for some extra funds. They would certainly give him a much needed break. He could take a few speaking engagements himself if the opportunity arose and make a little extra money on the side.

Rafe worked his way through the congregation, smiling and shaking hands. As he neared the back of the sanctuary, he noticed several of his board members huddled together in a back corner. *That's strange,* he thought suspiciously. *I wonder what's going on.* Changing direction, he headed straight for the group, smiling ingratiatingly as he approached.

It had happened that only four of the directors were present that morning and they had been quietly discussing how best to approach the pastor and break the unpleasant news regarding their decision to suspend Jonas' honorarium. Sylvester was suspiciously absent. He rarely missed a service but this morning he hadn't shown up.

As the pastor approached them Donny glanced up. Seeing him coming, he nudged the two men standing on either side of him and spoke a quiet word. Their nervousness was apparent as they turned to greet the pastor.

"What's going on?" Pastor Rafe's tone was honeyed. "It almost looks as if you're having a board meeting." His lips smiled but his eyes narrowed warily.

The men squirmed uncomfortably looking at each other in awkward silence, waiting for Rev. Armstrong to take the lead. The old man looked petrified, his chin wobbling noticeably.

Fear and Intimidation twined leathery coils about the director's heads. They hurled flashes of green corruption with abandon. The golden shield of a warrior inserted into their midst took the brunt of their attack. He drew his sword while another angel leaped to his aid. Together, they managed to drive one of the demons away.

Gathering his courage, Donny stepped forward, blurting out their message. "On behalf of the board, we would like to inform you that we have suspended Jonas' travel honorarium for lack of performance."

Rafe's jaw dropped in surprise. "We'll see about that!" he gritted from clenched teeth. Color rushed into his face as his ire rose. He threw out his chin aggressively. "That was an illegal meeting," he blustered furiously. "I'll have this board fired by the council!" Turning on his heel he strode angrily away from them.

"I ... I guess he took that pretty well." quavered Rev. Armstrong.

Tense faces relaxed and the men even chuckled nervously, surprised by the old man's unexpected humor and ridiculous statement. They dispersed quickly without further comment, shaking hands and scattering in several directions in search of spouses and friends.

When Donny headed for the door the crowd had thinned out considerably with only a few still milling about. Rafe intercepted him in the main lobby. "Do you want to tell me what this is all about now?" His color was still high but his voice was quiet and controlled.

"It is just as I said. The board voted to suspend your grandson's travel honorarium. He hasn't been around and the three month trial period is long past. People have been complaining about his appearance and his attitude when he *has* been here." Donny hesitated and then forged on. "We are not happy about the way you have treated Mira either." He deliberately kept his voice low so as not to be overheard. He looked squarely at the man. "We will not allow you to treat her disrespectfully."

"Just what has she told you?" Rafe's voice trembled with anger.

"She told us what happened over a second check that Jonas never should have received and about several other incidents that have occurred, all of which have involved you in matters that concern your grandson. We will not allow her to be intimidated or mistreated," he said firmly.

"I knew it! She's behind all of this!" he said furiously. "Well, I want you to know that your board meeting was illegal. I was not properly informed."

"You were told about the meeting and declined to attend. You didn't ask us to postpone it," Donny replied icily.

Rafe's voice shook with the effort it took to keep his tone modulated. He didn't want this overheard by any stray parishioners. "I was not told that my grandson was on the agenda," he ground out between clenched teeth. "I will take this to the council and either they fire the board or I will leave."

"Perhaps that is the best way to handle it then." Donny snapped brusquely, closing the interview by walking out the door.

Pastor Rafe turned away to greet David and Ella Armstrong. He beckoned the elderly man to follow him into the front office alone. A host of demons accompanied them.

~

Python slithered silently through the basement walls of the church. He sniffed the air sensing that something was amiss. "What'sss been going on?" he lisped harshly.

"Your Eminence," responded the Jezebel demon-master. His nose wrinkled in distaste. "Those wretched board members had a prayer meeting down here and they anointed the whole place with their loathsome oil. We've been working hard to get rid of the stink of it but you can still smell it!"

The serpent's tongue flicked out, tasting the insult in the atmosphere. It made him uncomfortable, a feeling he didn't appreciate. His enormous head weaved back and forth, red-rimmed eyes searching the enclosed space for a victim he could torment. "What of our noble Passstor?" he prodded, gazing at the black, evilly distorted face of his compatriot with an unblinking stare that was almost unnerving to the lesser demon.

"No problem there," snickered Jezebel with false bravado. "He does whatever we want." The demon drew himself to his full height and puffed out his cheeks importantly. "Our forces were well able to drive back a full division of angels that were dispatched against us." He wanted to rub that in the face of the great serpent. After all, it was his forethought and defence plan that had saved them from allowing six score or more of the despicable heavenly warriors access to their territory.

The serpent seemed mollified by his news so the demon-master offered another tidbit destined to put him in the good graces of his superior. "We have the young drummer ready to sell his soul to Lucifer. He dabbles in witchcraft and Satanism and is almost ready for us to spring our trap." His laugh was ruthless.

"Yesss!" The serpent seemed delighted. Its huge head bobbed hungrily. "Our Massster will be pleasssed when I report thisss. You have done well. Sssee that you don't fail and make a fool of me!" His unspoken threat hung in the air.

"I will not fail our master," the spirit replied with a self-satisfied, evil grin.

~

Mira walked through her door to the strident ring of the telephone. She was surprised to hear Rev. Armstrong's voice on the line. *Something must have happened when the pastor was told about the travel honorarium business,* she thought as she braced herself for what might be coming. She hadn't attended the Sunday night service and two days had passed since then.

The initial pleasantries over, the old reverend cautiously broached the real reason for his call. "Ahhh ... I guess you know that we ... uh ... that is, we told Rafe.... er, Pastor Rafe, that is, about the suspension on Sunday."

"Yes. I figured you had told him." She hadn't wanted to think about the pastor's reaction to the news.

"Oh yes. We told him." He chuckled dryly but there was no mirth in it. "Well.... I guess I should tell you that he asked me and my wife to come into the office for a talk." Mira felt her heart lurch but made no comment choosing instead to wait for him to continue.

"He wasn't very happy, but I guess that's to be expected. He says the meeting wasn't legal because he didn't receive notice."

"He did receive notice." Mira could hear the waffling in his voice. "I told him myself."

"Well... he says that matter wasn't on the agenda or he wouldn't have allowed the meeting."

Mira's lips tightened. "He has no authority to stop a board meeting. The notice is merely a courtesy and what's more any board member can bring up any item they wish under *"New Business"*. We were perfectly within out right to address the issue. In fact, Ina needed our direction on it. The matter of the travel honorarium should have been raised long ago."

"Well... he's pretty mad. I think we're going to have to give in sooner or later."

He's going to cave in. This is totally ludicrous. We are nothing more than a puppet board! She took a breath to calm herself. "You can certainly call a board meeting and revisit the issue if you wish."

"What's your honest opinion about what the others will do?" he asked.

"I honestly don't know," replied Mira. *I hope they won't all give up this quickly,* she thought. *I wonder if I should commit myself. Oh, why not....., my goose is probably cooked now anyway.* "I only know that I will not recant my vote," she said with all the firmness she could muster. "I'm not sure about Sylvester. I think the others will stand behind their vote but I can't be sure. I guess the only way to find out is to call the meeting."

"Well..... maybe we should just let it be for awhile until the whole thing cools down."

Mira felt sick as she hung up the phone.

~

Familiar spirits whirled about the unkempt dirty-blond tresses of the young man who made his way down the street in a drug-induced haze. Black hatred filled his heart toward his parents and those other so-called Christians that had tried to influence his life. Condemnation dogged his steps and Bitterness, Resentment, Wrath, and Rebellion were his constant companions.

God has never done anything for me, he thought contemptuously as he aimlessly wandered the downtown core of the city. *I think it's time for me to try Satan.* He had dabbled in certain satanic ceremonies already, doing his best to copy the things he'd read about in a book he'd stolen from the library.

As he walked, his anger and resentment grew to enormous proportions driving all sane thought from his head. He could hear the voices, the harsh whisperings in guttural tones, prodding him, asking him to do unspeakable things. He veered into a bar and sat slouched over a beer for awhile, contemplating what he meant to do, waiting for the voices to command it.

The two angel warriors couldn't get his attention. He was too far gone. "If only we could force him to listen," one of them said sadly.

"You know that we cannot do that," responded the second warrior. "They have choice. He must choose to serve either the Lord God Almighty or the fallen one. He knows the Word but in his rebellion he refuses to repent and bow the knee to the One who can save him."

"Perhaps he may yet yield," the first angel replied doubtfully.

~

It was with some trepidation that Mira went to bible study that night. She had deliberately timed her appearance with the start of the service to avoid running into Pastor Rutherford. Seeing the beckoning hand of Ina as she passed by the business office, she turned aside.

"There are checks for you to sign, my love," the bookkeeper said smiling up from her desk.

Sylvester, seated behind the spare desk, was already signing the documents. His greeting was barely a grunt and he wasted no time on civilities. "That Donny isn't fit to be on the board," he snarled as soon as Mira pulled up a chair.

She crooked her brow inquisitively. *Whoa, the pastor sure got to him. He's fit to be tied!* Ignoring the statement, she grabbed a pen and started to work her way through the batch of checks.

Infuriated by her silence, the old man threw out his jaw aggressively. "He had no right to say anything to the pastor." He sounded cantankerous. "I thought we decided the president and vice-president were going to set up a meeting with Pastor Rafe to break the news."

"Actually, I don't think that was completely decided on, was it?" Mira intentionally kept her tone pleasant and unruffled. "I think the idea was to let Pastor Rafe know before I gave out the minutes. Everyone was understandably nervous and I'm sure Donny stepped forward because no one else was saying anything."

Sylvester wasn't ready to let it go. "I always had a bad feeling about Donny anyway. He isn't board material."

"This board business is all new to Donny," Mira replied in an effort to placate him. "Does it really matter that it wasn't perfectly handled?"

"Well I just guess it matters to the pastor!" he snorted. "He's just as sorry as can be that he ever approved Donny's name to stand." He glared at her, his temper escalating.

"Look, he may be a little rough around the edges sometimes, but he has a warm heart and a generous spirit. He also runs his own business so he has the necessary qualifications. The pastor certainly thought so just a few months ago. What's changed?"

"Well, I'll just tell you that he isn't happy with him now," he fumed. "What's more, I could have told you all along he was bad news!" He thrust out his chin belligerently, his face turning beet red. "Anyway, the

Lord spoke to me as I was meditating at Tuesday morning prayer meeting and you wanna know what He said?"

Mira was done trying to humor him. She just signed her name as fast as she could, wishing herself away from the sound of his voice.

"God told me that things are gonna change around here." The old man's voice rose shrilly. "God's gonna clean house! People are gonna leave – maybe a whole bunch o' them," he paused for dramatic effect. "But He told me He's gonna have a remnant left – those that want to follow His will."

Now Mira was exasperated. *He means that for me and the rest of the board,* she thought, her cheeks growing hot with anger. *How dare he carry on this way in front of Ina? It's both unprofessional and unconscionable! Boy, has pastor ever done a number on him!* Throwing caution to the wind, she put as much sarcasm into her answer as she could muster. "I too believe that God is going to clean up His house," she said, speaking slowly and emphatically, "But it may not happen the way you expect."

With this last thrust, Mira fled from the office, hiding out in the ladies restroom until she was sure the old man had gone into service. Ina was still at her desk when she returned.

"You okay, honey?" the bookkeeper asked sympathetically.

Mira tried to force a smile. "I apologize for that tirade. You shouldn't have been subjected to it." Her anger was still roused.

Ina laughed outright. "I've seen much worse than that! By the way, the pastor had him in his office alone on Monday for more than two hours."

"I figured as much."

They chatted for a few minutes until interrupted by the sudden appearance of Sylvester's wife, Norma. After a brief clarification of some minor filing issue, she turned toward Mira with pursed lips and sour expression. "Boy, that Donny is really something, isn't he? I don't think he should be on the board," she said disagreeably.

"Norma, Donny didn't do anything wrong." She was furious that Sylvester would drag his wife into board business. "He's a good man trying to do a difficult job, as we all are." Mira was just starting to realize that the pastor was a force to be reckoned with. She rose from her chair, excusing herself on the pretext of going into the service which was now in full swing.

Worship was over and Pastor Rafe was in the middle of the announcements when she entered the room. She attempted to slip unobtrusively into an empty seat at the back. Catching her eye, Rafe lifted his chin haughtily. "I would like to take this opportunity to applaud the faithfulness of a man who serves tirelessly in this assembly for little or no thanks. I am talking about Sylvester Zimmer. Would to God we had more board members and elders like Sylvester," he said with an oily smoothness. "There isn't anything he won't do for me." The old man beamed at the unexpected flattery while Mira ducked her head to fumble with the pages of her bible.

The study that evening was a repeat of Sunday with Rafe sharing again the multitude of prophetic words that he maintained had been spoken over both his own life and that of the Good Shepherd Church. As his talk drew to a conclusion, he told them of a man who had come to him earlier in the day, compelled to share a vision or dream about a five-story-high Jesus he had seen by the greenhouse out on the main road. The gigantic Jesus was waving a steady stream of cars down the road and into the church parking lot.

"This place is about to explode," Rafe thundered dramatically, "and Satan will do everything in his power to stop it!"

Mira wondered why Jesus would be pointing the people to a church. Was He not the only way? Shouldn't it be the other way around – the people pointing the way to Christ? Somehow it just didn't sound right. She sighed. Why did Pastor always take to heart these wing-nut prophesies and yet would not heed any of the serious Words that were given?

When service was over, she hurried out the door hoping to escape any interview with the pastor, but she was not quick enough. He made a bee-line for the lobby smoothly intercepting her flight.

"Did you know there's a letter for you in the office?" he asked her pleasantly. She mutely shook her head allowing him to usher her into the secretary's office. He closed the door firmly behind her.

Fear and Intimidation were already there, waiting in anticipation. Two tall warriors flanked her on either side.

An impression of a spider catching a fly in its web flitted through Mira's mind. *What's the matter with me,* she thought impatiently. *He's just a man. It's not like he's going to eat me or something! Get a grip, girl!* She smiled as he handed her the envelope. *That's odd! It's just a bank statement and Ina usually gives those to me. It was just an excuse to get me in here alone!* Her heart started to thump painfully in her chest.

"I'm really disappointed in Donny." Rafe's jab was careful. "He's just not board material. I never should have allowed him to be nominated and now we're paying for it. I thought he could be trusted but now I'm sorry I ever recommended him"

Funny how incompetent he became the first time he disagreed with you. Same words as Sylvester used – not board material – what are the chances of that!

When she didn't respond, his eyes glittered dangerously. "Where were *you* in that board meeting? Why didn't you have my back? I trusted you!" His voice was shaking slightly. "That was an illegal meeting." He glowered at her, his jaw set sternly. The look on his face and the determination in his eyes frightened her. "I'm going to call a meeting with the whole council and either they will fire this board or I will quit," he threatened dramatically.

"The meeting was not illegal." Mira had no idea where her courage came from. "I notified you myself."

"That was not on the agenda that I saw." He was growing enraged.

"The matter came up under *"New Business"*. Board members are allowed to raise any matter under *"New Business"* in any meeting. The decision was made by the whole board and it was unanimous. We were all in complete unity in that meeting no matter what Sylvester might claim now." Her mouth was dry, her heart pounding. She backed slowly toward the door.

Rafe's face was so contorted that Mira thought she was seeing a demon. "Yes, I admit I had a long chat with Sylvester and he told me that he felt tremendously pressured by the rest of the board to vote the way he did. He said that he noticed that Ian was squirming too and believes that he felt pressured as well."

"I don't believe that for one minute," cried Mira indignantly. "It was the best board meeting I have ever attended. We prayed together, cried together and were all in one accord."

He tried another approach. "I've always thought of you as family," he said sentimentally, allowing his voice to tremble slightly. One tear spilled down onto his cheek and he turned so she would be sure to see it dribble down his face.

Mira opened the door and backed into the lobby. “I’m really very tired,” she said, trying desperately to keep her voice from shaking. “I need to go home now.” Turning, she fled from the building.

As she drove away from the church, Mira sobbed her heart out. Her love for her pastor had not diminished but her respect for him was certainly damaged. The two warriors that accompanied her used their considerable power in an effort to give comfort and encouragement.

7

She finds herself looking down upon a large public building full of activity. People are streaming in and out, laughing and talking, oblivious to the world around them. As she takes in her surroundings, she becomes aware of two young men who are casually approaching the structure. They are very pleasing to look at, striking in appearance with attractive faces and stalwart bodies. The wind ripples lazily through their blond curly hair as they move closer. Now she notices the heavy backpacks they carry, the harnesses of which strain against their brawny shoulders.

They seem familiar to her somehow. A fleeting hidden memory niggles at the back of her brain and she shivers with sudden dread. Unexplained mind-numbing fear overtakes her, holding her riveted to the ground. She opens her mouth to scream but finds her throat as empty as the wind.

Helplessly she watches their steady progress toward the unsuspecting throng milling about below. Unexpectedly, they turn in her direction and halting their steps, they stare at her with bright eyes and laughing faces. As she returns their gaze, her heart leaps against her ribs and she can feel the sweat trickling slowly down her neck and back. Overwhelmed with suffocating horror, she cannot move or even draw a single breath.

A wild scream fills the air. "Run! Run for your lives! They are not what they seem to be!" She realizes the screams are hers, coming in quick ragged gulps. She is running toward the building as if in slow motion, every step a laboured effort. Arms waving, shrieking her terror at the people, she strives to capture their attention. No one turns to look.

In desperation, she glances over to where the two men are standing. As their eyes meet hers, they undergo a terrible transformation. Their faces suddenly blur into snapping, snarling wolf-like creatures, enraged and dangerous as trapped animals in a snare. Blind unreasoning fear turns her suddenly away from the building and she rushes headlong through the open field to the shelter of a deep, dark, wooded area.

There seem to be a few desperate souls running with her now. Tripping over roots and falling on the uneven ground, she runs until her throat is dry and her muscles ache for relief. Suddenly, she stumbles into a clearing. Her strength is gone and, come what may, she cannot run any further.

"Quick", she gasps as others stagger from the trees and collapse panting on the ground. "Form a circle. Start a fire." A pile of dead branches and leaves are swiftly piled in a large heap as everyone works rapidly together with almost superhuman effort.

"They are coming and they are many," she shouts, barking out another order. "Everyone grab a firebrand and form a circle. Put the little ones and those that are weak and hurt in the centre for protection. Do not let even one of the demons past the perimeter. We must hold our ground."

A shadowy savage pack of wicked slavering creatures close their circle about the little group waiting for an opening; an opportunity to strike...

Mira jerked upright in the bed panting and flailing her arms. She could feel the terror of her pounding heart. She squeezed her eyes shut in dismay. Beside her, Dan lay undisturbed and unaware of her torment. She didn't want to think about what the dream might mean.

The young man in the bar leered companionably at the barmaid, a young girl with pierced eyebrow and nose. *She might be worth pursuing,* he thought hazily. The voices inside his head were screaming and he couldn't concentrate. "Do it now! Do it now! They betrayed you! Only Satan really cares about what becomes of you. You can gain all power through him."

Laughing insanely, he stumbled to his feet groping in his pocket for some money. Throwing it onto the counter, he lurched out into the night, intent on carrying out the demands of his master. Demons cavorted gleefully around him, feeding his hungry spirit with rage, envy, self-pity and violence as he careened down the street.

The little house was just around the corner. Sitting down on a nearby curb, he watched the place, shaking his head in an effort to clear away the fog. When he could no longer stand the searing pain in his brain, he heaved himself to his feet and tottered over to the door. He heard diabolical laughter all around him as he pounded his fists in fury on the only obstacle separating him from the inmates inside.

A middle-aged man opened the door. Grabbing him by the throat, the young man threw him back against a hallway railing. This was a house that he knew well. As a little child, his parents had brought him here for bible studies. The owner, now an elderly woman, had been like a grandmother to him for years. He noticed a knife was in his hand. It vaguely surprised him.

Violence stabbed him brutally in the forehead with a long venomous claw. He exploded into murderous rage. "Where is your God now?" he screamed, his muscular arms hammering a fist into the frightened face in front of him. Hatred raged like vitriol through his veins. He stabbed the blade with vicious abandon into the upper torso of his victim. Even when the man lay still and unresponsive upon the floor, the young man found he couldn't stop. His cruel blows rained down upon the man's head and chest repeatedly while he sadistically kicked the body over and over again. Blood spurted everywhere.

He looked up and saw the white, terrified face of the frail, old woman who used to teach him about Jesus. A phone was gripped in her hand. In blind rage, he grabbed the receiver and bludgeoned her over the head until she fell limp in his arms. He searched the house for the remaining tenant but found the rest of the place empty. Sitting down in the entryway, he casually examined the body of the man he had stabbed to death. He smeared some of the blood onto his fingers and licked them, giggling maniacally. His eyes were flat and lifeless.

~

Two days passed before Mira received a phone call from Pastor Rafe. He started by asking her if she had heard about the young drummer from their worship team who had been arrested for the murder of two people. She was horrified to learn what had happened.

"Apparently he was searching for his parents that night in order to kill them," the pastor told her. "He thought his victims might know where they were." He seemed unconcerned.

Mira hadn't known the young man well, but her heart was pierced to know that he had attended the Good Shepherd Church and yet had completely lost his way.

"Do you realize that is the third murderer we've had in our congregation in the past three years?" Pastor Rafe mumbled as he munched on a sandwich. "There was the usher who took the life of his girlfriend," he recounted. "He beat her to death with his bare hands. Then there was the young man from Jamaica. He killed his pregnant girlfriend. Both of them call me from prison once in awhile," he admitted, "but there isn't much I can do for them. This boy voluntarily gave himself over to the devil. His father rose up against me, you know. He was one of those who tried to get rid of me six years ago."

Mira was horrified. It sounded as if he blamed the young man's mental state on his father's insubordination toward Rafe. As he continued to discuss the event, she sensed his overall satisfaction and belief that those who opposed him would suffer untold agonies, perhaps even death as a result of their rebelliousness. *I guess he's sending me a clear message,* she thought bitterly.

Rafe eventually got around to the real reason for his call. He told Mira that he had been talking to a prophetess, Lana Vanderwood, who had insisted that he not go into any more board meetings until she had opportunity to meet with him. The woman apparently had a Word from the Lord to deliver. Or so she claimed.

Puzzled, Mira listened as he made her aware that Lana was one of a small group of prophets who met with him each Saturday morning in order to speak into his life. Recently, he claimed, some of them had been urging him to take a sabbatical for an extended period of time.

From the ensuing conversation, Mira suspected that their messages must be in conflict with one another, causing confusion in his mind. It struck her forcefully that he wavered back and forth, like the waves of the sea, sometimes endorsing the idea as a good one and other times refusing to even consider the notion. She couldn't help but wonder if it had really been Lana's idea to put all board meetings on hold. More than likely, she thought to herself, it was his idea, perhaps for the express purpose of waiting them out until the next annual business meeting when the mix of the board would change as three directors fulfilled their terms? That would make more sense.

It came as somewhat of a surprise to Mira when he immediately contradicted what he had just told her by requesting that she call a board meeting. "No agenda," he said resolutely. "I just need to address the board before the Sunday service. Please make sure that everyone will be in attendance."

In spite of her confusion over the mixed messages he had given her, Mira agreed to call the directors and set up the meeting. She felt it might help clear the air between the pastor and the board.

The atmosphere was subdued as the board gathered together in the little room outside the pastor's office. For once, he didn't keep them waiting long. He timed his entrance perfectly with the arrival of the last person not wanting to allow them time to whisper behind his back. Rafe had given a great deal of thought to this encounter. His pride demanded that his will be supreme but he would rather accomplish his purpose without a battle.

Divide and conquer! It had always worked for him in the past and he was determined to make it work this time too. Sylvester hadn't been difficult to win over and he was confident that Armstrong would fall in line as well. That only left three directors to pressure because, in his arrogance, he didn't count Ian. The man was too quiet and timid to challenge his authority alone. Mira hadn't succumbed yet either but she would submit when the others did.

Donny was the only real threat of the bunch. If Rafe had known how headstrong he was, he would never have manoeuvred him onto the board in the first place. It bothered him that Donny was against him now. He had been such a generous donor and willing servant. Too bad! It was a shame to lose both the monetary gifts and a willing worker. He had already set into motion the groundwork for getting rid of him, but that was only a precautionary measure at this point, on the off chance that tonight was a failure.

Greeting his directors with his most ingratiating smile, Rafe spoke at some length regarding his calling and ministry. Not wanting to waste an opportunity to pontificate or impress, he went on to tell them about an offer he had received from some prominent affluent men who treasured his wisdom so much that they wanted to pay him $450.00 per hour to advise them once a month. His little laugh of embarrassment contained just the right mixture of humility and modesty.

He followed this story with another. Recently, he and Eve had been invited by a wealthy couple to spend a couple of days on their yacht. He shared how grateful he was for the opportunity to get away and seek the Lord as he was very troubled by recent events. God had spoken to him during this time, he claimed tremulously, and the message had been just one word – *hoarding*. He felt the Lord was saying that the church was hoarding money and they needed to loosen up and spend it for the furtherance of the kingdom. He reminded them of the vision of the five-story-high Jesus.

Rafe studied the faces of his directors thinking that by now they should be ready for what he considered the crux of the meeting. His deep, expressive voice sounded quite contrite as he extended his heartfelt apology for his reaction to the news about his grandson, but his pride would not allow the apology to stand alone. He stressed his disappointment in the board's decision, delicately pointing out the magnitude of their offence and his undeniable innocence. If they had only waited and come to him, the whole matter would have been cleared up. It had been *he* that had urged Jonas to take the summer off and wait for the fall to start up the youth ministry again and he alone must take the blame. If only someone had asked!

Rafe admitted his reaction to what the board had done had not been very Christ-like and the feelings it had stirred up in him had surprised him. Now God was requiring him to ask their forgiveness and make things right. The Lord had told him, *"Son, you must set the example and take the high road here."* With trembling voice, he told them how impossible it was for him to serve communion on Sunday unless he was reconciled with his board.

He looked at Donny with soulful eyes. "Brother, I don't know why you are so angry with me." His voice shook slightly. "I would just like things to be as they were before all of this trouble."

Donny looked Rafe squarely in the face. "When I first came on this board a few months ago, I thought you were the best thing since sliced bread. I have given generously out of my heart to this church and to you personally. I don't regret anything I've done because I did it unto God and not for man. At your request, I have taken people into my home and kept them for months at a time at my expense. You made promises to me! You told me that I would have help with them but after they were dumped at my door, I saw no help. Not long ago, I stood in the lobby of this church and told you that I was struggling in my business and did not have food for my table. You offered me not so much as a dime. I've laid out thousands of dollars at your request but you didn't offer me even $20.00 for food. Now, I have been told that I am not board material. Why? What has changed since April? I was good enough then."

Rafe was seething by end of Donny's speech. He hadn't wanted anyone to know how he had used the man and now the cat was out of the bag for sure. He had to minimize the damage, but one thing he knew for sure, Donny would definitely have to go!

"I don't know the incidents you are talking about, but I'm more than willing to sit with you so we can work our way through them. You seem to have a lot on your mind. Why don't you come and talk it over with me in private?"

"I don't know if I'm ready to do that yet," Donny replied brusquely. "I need some time to work this all out in my own mind first."

"Take all the time you need. I'm here when you want to talk." Rafe looked at him plaintively. "I really want my friend back."

He closed the meeting down quickly after that, wanting to cut off any further revelations. The shock, registered on the faces of those around the table, told him plainly that Donny's unfortunate disclosures had hurt him somewhat. As he worked his way around the room, embracing each member, he gazed soulfully into their eyes, trying to get a sense of whether he had accomplished his purpose with any of them.

Rafe really didn't want to bring this to the church council as he had threatened. Better to contain the damage here at the board level with only the six of them involved. The directors, after all, were part of council, with two of them, David Armstrong and Sylvester Zimmer, also serving as his only elders. That left only four deacons outside of this circle to round out the full council. He was pretty sure of them but perhaps he'd better not risk it if there was another way. Not yet anyway. He had another course of action he could take if this didn't work out.

The day after the board meeting, Rafe called Mira and asked her to set up a full council meeting for the following week, after the Wednesday night bible study. He had no intention of raising the matter of his grandson, he told her meekly, as he gave her the agenda. He just needed to address camp meeting issues as it was fast approaching.

Sunday services came and went with the vision of the five-story-high Jesus being trotted out in both. The usual little group hoorayed and shouted, believing that something big was about to happen.

Mira was alone again, Dan refusing to accompany her. The story of the giant Jesus was getting old now and it was starting to irritate her more and more. *What's the matter with me,* she thought. *I'm starting to dislike even coming here. I love a lot of the people dearly but I'm drying up. I need to hear the Word of God again. I need to hear about the real Jesus. He's seldom mentioned anymore except to be used in some ridiculous vision.*

Maybe that's what is wrong with Dan, she reflected glumly. He had gone willingly with her when she had led worship at the other church. A thought came unbidden to her mind. A dear friend of hers, a lovely Christian lady who had left the church some time ago, had confided that her spirit was dry and unfed due to the lack of teaching from the Word of God. Mira had been sure her friend was mistaken but now she wondered. *Could she have been right? I think I'll start keeping track of the times that the bible is used and preached from.*

By the time the last council members arrived for the meeting, Jack and Donny had the chairs all arranged in the fellowship hall. They had even moved a table to a more convenient location for Mira who would record the minutes. Good natured bantering passed between the men as they took their seats and waited for the pastor to come from the front office.

Tormenting spirits hopped gleefully from one to another of the members, afflicting them wherever they could find an opening. Their deadly poison was spewed throughout the room with abandon. Tall angels stood by, their faces severe, deflecting as much of the corrosive liquid as they could with their shields. They were under orders not to engage the enemy directly so they suffered in torturous silence.

Phil Schmidt, a jolly rotund little man was regaling the others with his delightful dry wit when Pastor Rutherford entered the room. More demons came with him overwhelming the heavenly beings by their sheer vast number. The warriors were hard pressed to keep their cool.

Bringing the meeting to order, Rafe stepped easily into his role as chairman steering them skilfully through the usual devotion and opening prayer. He disposed of the first few items on the agenda quickly, moving on to tackle the more important ones. However, progress was too slow for his liking, so forgetting the agenda, he skipped ahead to his own pet projects and upon these he waxed eloquent, ignoring the rest. The allotted time disappeared all too rapidly.

From her desk at the front of the room, Mira could watch the faces of each of the men that made up the church council. Jack Johnson, the vice-president of the board of directors, was fiddling nervously with a now partly crumpled letter that was one of the purposely shelved items. Donny looked decidedly bored and Ian was nearly half asleep. He would have to leave shortly for his night shift. Phil Schmidt squirmed impatiently while Sylvester, his forbidding demeanor grim, glared helplessly around the circle. The president of the board, David Armstrong, who was completely marginalized by the pastor at every turn, simply looked bewildered. Frank and Pierre, both deacons, sat with their heads down, eyes fixed on their agenda as if they feared it might disappear at any moment. Rob Samuels, Faith's husband looked tired and ill.

Mira glanced up sharply as Pastor Rafe started to talk about the youth ministry wondering where he was headed. He spoke in glowing terms of the capable management of his grandson. Even though they had not conducted any services all summer, he assured them that Jonas was in touch with many of the young people by e-mail every day, developing real relationships with them.

"A bonfire and wiener roast brought out fifteen youth," he said rubbing his hands in glee. "This is phenomenal growth. I realize that some of the older people don't like the body piercings, but after all, isn't it results that count?" he said smoothly, "I asked Jonas myself to remove his earrings but he laughed and said that I need to get with the times." He chuckled. "I guess I can be a little old-fashioned sometimes."

Well, wasn't that clever? Mira thought as she looked at the men's countenances. *The deacons have no clue what's been going on or that he's manipulating them with half truths and lies. Does he not realize that he just told us that his own grandson has no regard for his authority, either as senior pastor or his grandfather?*

Rafe gave no opportunity for comment and no one would have dared to say anything even if he had. Next, he passed out copies of a proposal to purchase some used television equipment at a cost of $129,000. The directors looked dazedly at the figures. This was the first they had heard of it.

"Some have been urging me to resurrect my television ministry," Rafe said eagerly. "Many have prophesied that I will be a voice to the nation once again. This proposal is a tremendous opportunity to acquire everything we would need, in order to fulfill God's mandate in my life. It is a once in a lifetime deal and they are offering it to us because they are friends of mine. We have to make up our minds quickly as all of this equipment will be replaced shortly. They are even willing to train our own technicians for three months at no extra charge."

Ah ha! Here it is! thought Mira. T*hat's why he told us at the board meeting the Holy Spirit doesn't want us hoarding money. It was to prepare us for this! I wonder who these friends of his are and if he's getting a cut-back for setting up this deal!* Aloud she said," Pastor, it's a lot of money. What if the equipment is worn out? None of us have any expertise with this kind of thing."

"These are honorable men. I know them well," he insisted, faint color tingeing his cheeks. "They wouldn't sell us defective equipment."

"That may be, but this is still a huge undertaking," exclaimed Rob. "They mention in this letter that the main auditorium may need major renovation in order to make it more conducive to television taping. That would add considerably to the cost. Alternatively, they suggest building our own studio. Again, that expenditure would be extra. We should also consider that we don't have anyone qualified to run the equipment so we wouldn't have any idea if we were being taken or not."

"They are willing to take three months of their time to train our people," flashed Rafe.

"Do we have anyone who wants to volunteer their time for that?" asked Rob doubtfully. "All of our current volunteers are stretched to capacity. I can't think of even one who could spare the time for this. This document states that they must be paid in full as soon as the equipment is delivered. What do we do if it turns out to be faulty or worn out?"

Donny chuckled dryly. "I'm no expert, but even I can see that this proposal has a lot of holes in it. If you look at the fine print, they don't provide all of the cabling either, so that will be extra. Furthermore, after the initial training period, they are going to charge us for technical support. I wouldn't touch this with a ten foot pole."

"Donny is right," acknowledged Mira, relieved that he had spotted the inconsistencies so quickly. "This is a huge commitment! Even if we should consider starting a television program, there would have to be careful research and price comparisons. We couldn't possibly just accept the first quote submitted."

Rafe ground his teeth in fury as he watched his prized plan go up in smoke. "This is a one time deal and if we lose it we may never be offered this opportunity again."

"They always tell you that to get the sale," laughed Donny, unimpressed with the pastor's reasoning. "Perhaps it's for the best anyway. I'm sure not comfortable with their proposal. Are you sure these are friends?" he asked, unable to resist the dig.

Rob suddenly remembered something. "Do you recall back a few years ago when we tried videoing the services in order to upload them to the internet?" Some of the men nodded. "We were supposed to get the networking services free of charge." He snorted. "The next thing we knew, we had a bill of $65,000 to pay for technical support. We managed to negotiate it down to something like $35,000 but it turned into a really ugly legal mess before it was all over. We sure don't want to go through that again!"

"I just gave you the proposal to pray over and consider." The pastor's voice sounded brittle. "I still think it's a good deal."

Coming back to the agenda, Rafe revealed some changes he wanted to make in the camp meeting schedule. This year he had half-heartedly announced that he was cutting back the usual full week of special meetings to just half a week. The truth was, he would rather have cancelled the annual event altogether. There was enough on his plate at the moment and he really didn't want to be bothered.

With camp meeting, came the added responsibility of boarding and entertaining the special guest speakers in the large five bedroom parsonage. Of course, Eve handled most of that with Faith's capable help and normally, it was a wonderful opportunity to ingratiate himself with the evangelists. There was always the possibility of gaining a future opportunity to speak in their pulpits.

He looked around the circle. "I've received confirmations from the two speakers I wanted. They will fill the Wednesday through Sunday slots. I know it's late for adjustments, since the meetings start in just a few days, but it's been difficult for me with all that I've had to do, especially with the renovations going on. I'm tired," he ventured choosing his words carefully. "I really need help. Pastor Marvin is a good man but he hasn't been able to lift as much of the day-to-day burden as I had hoped."

Recent events had changed Rafe's mind about the camp meeting. A slight alteration might just do the trick and bring most of the board back into the fold. He threw out his surprise with a masterful stroke. "I would like to extend the camp meeting to the full week and bring in Grace Benning to do the first part of the week."

Mira froze. Grace was her sister-in-law. She had preached many times at the church and was well liked and accepted by the people. A year ago, she had resigned her pulpit in a church on the east coast to go into full time evangelism. *This is meant to disarm me,* she thought, immediately seeing through the manipulative move by her pastor.

"Everyone likes her", Rafe continued, "and the Lord just impressed upon me that she should come." He smiled benevolently at Mira. "What do you think?"

"I guess you could ask her," she choked, struggling to keep her tone neutral. *Won't that be uncomfortable with things the way they are between the pastor and the board,* she thought dolefully.

Mira liked Grace and above all respected her ministry. Every time she had heard her speak, she had been impressed with the fiery woman of God, who expounded scripture with a unique and fresh view. Although she knew they would all benefit from the teaching, she wasn't sure that she wanted her sister-in-law here in the middle of the current mess.

Rafe had been confident that he would obtain his council's approval with ease and they didn't disappoint him. He was about to close the meeting when Mira raised her hand. "Jack Johnson has a letter that he wishes to read." She nodded encouragingly at the vice-president who cleared his throat nervously and smoothed out the crumpled piece of paper clutched in his anxious grip. An angel whispered comfortingly into his ear.

The letter had been written by his wife, Amy, who wished to share some things that she felt the Lord had impressed upon her during one of her prayer times. In it, she strongly urged the council to outline a proper job description for Faith, the pastor's secretary, including prescribed hours with proper lunches and breaks to conform to the labor laws of the land. Council members shifted uncomfortably in their seats as Jack concluded the letter. Mira waited with bated breath for Pastor Rafe's response.

"I'm sure we all love Faith and know that much of what she does falls under her own ministry of "*Helps*". Since the hour is late, I think we should adjourn the meeting so that all these good folk can go home to their spouses." He smiled benignly around the circle. "Sylvester, will you close the meeting in prayer, please."

Council members barely spoke to one another as they scattered swiftly to their vehicles.

8

Grace Benning arrived at the Grant home just before camp meeting began. Although her preaching schedule was a heavy one for the first few days of the week, Mira and Dan enjoyed what moments she could spare, benefiting much from her wisdom in spiritual matters.

Ina Irwin talked Dan into volunteering his cooking talents at the church for the lunches catered there each noon hour throughout the week. These were meant to provide an opportunity for those attending the meetings to enjoy a delicious home-cooked meal at a reasonable price. Putting aside his animosity toward the pastor, Dan entered in with a right good will and the small banquet hall downstairs was filled every day as the people took advantage of both the good food and the fellowship with one another.

The speakers received a special invitation to dine at the parsonage along with a few other guests each evening following the service. Mira was included among those invited as it was her vehicle that transported her sister-in-law back and forth to the services each day. Although she found the situation uncomfortable due to the issues still pending between the board and the pastor, she swallowed her feelings and tried to be as inconspicuous as was possible under the circumstances.

Camp meeting was a mixture of different personalities in the pulpit. Pastor Rafe seemed happy with Grace's preaching. She kicked things off from Sunday to Tuesday, bringing a series of powerful messages to which the people responded in droves, filling the altars, weeping and waiting before the Lord. Lives were challenged and changed in spite of evil spirits trying to manifest and disrupt the flow of God's Spirit.

Grace was followed by a renowned teacher from Wales, small in stature but mighty in his knowledge of the Word of God. From his lips many deep truths from scripture were taught and expounded upon.

The final speaker was an aged lady with delicate features and an abundance of snowy white hair swept high above her broad forehead. Although she leaned upon a cane, and seemed frail and weak, the stories of her life were filled with faith and promise.

The number of angel warriors increased exponentially in the meetings as the week progressed and prayer increased. Caelen and Valin were encouraged by the response of the saints and the captain was able to infiltrate his whole division into the sanctuary by the end of the week.

Even with this marked success, each meeting still held enormous challenge. The stranglehold the demon-master had upon the pastor and certain members of the congregation appeared to be unbreakable. The sheer number of imps, unclean spirits and demons was so vast their presence was made known to even the dull of spirit.

A couple of strange women appeared in the services, disrupting those around them with loud hissing noises as their bodies shook spasmodically in their seats. When the Word was being preached however, the Spirit of the Lord was so strong that those sitting nearby either ignored the distraction or moved to another seat. Strategically placed warriors stood protectively by them, keeping the evil horde at bay.

Hitherto, Mira had never seen or experienced chaos, disorder and confusion of this magnitude in a meeting. As the week progressed, the manifestations of unwelcome spirits and demonic power trying to regain control over the services seemed to escalate to gigantic proportions. Her spirit felt violated by it and she was mortified that her sister-in-law should witness such disgraceful activities. Other board and council members grew concerned as well. They wondered why the pastor made no move to stop it.

Grace was also surprised that Pastor Rafe made no move to control what was happening. Instead, he hid behind the keyboard during the altar services, playing and singing as if oblivious to what was transpiring around him; distaining prayer, either for himself or anyone else.

As the meetings progressed, Mira became increasingly uncomfortable with the amount of time taken from each service to promote the sale of books and audio sermons. Grace and the little man from Wales barely said anything about their products but the old lady went on at great length, sometimes taking half an hour of the speakers' time to talk about the subject matter of her books.

Mira didn't see the necessity of going through the same procedure each night with more or less the same people attending. She couldn't help but notice how the Englishman fidgeted, anxious to be turned loose to bring the Word of the Lord that burned in his heart. One evening, the minutes of advertisement ticked by slowly until almost an hour and a half had transpired since the beginning of the service. The people were tiring and still the man of God had not been called to preach. By this time Mira found her cheeks hot with shame as she squirmed uncomfortably in her chair.

Why doesn't Pastor Rafe cut off this nonsense, she agonized.

The old lady finally took her seat and instead of turning the remainder of the evening over to the speaker, Rafe called out a young man in the audience to come and sing. At this point, Mira thought she would surely explode. She could almost feel the deflation of the little man beside her.

"*This is beyond rude*!" she seethed, as she watched a slim, effeminate-looking young man simper to the stage to give Pastor Rafe a hug. More time was taken while the pastor oozed over the stranger. The song he chose to sing was a popular worldly piece, altered slightly to give it a Christian slant.

In spite of all of this, the preacher still managed to bring a powerful word to the people. Mira found a place of prayer at the altar that night, prostrating herself on her face before the Lord as she, with broken heart, sobbed and repented over wrong attitudes. She prayed constantly for her husband, her pastor, the board and the church. The other directors also frequented the altar, crying out to God for wisdom and help, both in their personal lives and for the situation they found themselves in as board members.

Late in the week, Pastor Rafe approached Mira requesting an update on the camp meeting finances. She reminded him that both Ina and Norma had been helping Dan in the kitchen every day and therefore had not yet counted the offerings. Rafe did not want to hear it! He insisted that a full update be provided prior to the evening service.

Mira was puzzled. "Pastor, what difference will an update make in the size of the offering tonight? People will only give what they can afford, regardless of what has come in to date." She reminded him that the congregation was pretty much tapped out even before camp meeting had begun, with all of the recent second offerings that had been requested. Many of them lived on fixed incomes and they only had so much to give.

"Get me the numbers by tonight's service," he snapped. "I need it so that I know how much pressure to put on the people for money so that the expenses will be met." Mira had been embarrassed to go to the two tired women, still toiling in the kitchen after a long day, and tell them she must have the figures.

Faith worked every day of the camp meeting. She was at the church during her regular office hours, present in every service and over at the parsonage until the wee hours of the morning, serving and cleaning up after the guests.

One morning, Mira found the secretary with suspiciously wet eyes in the office. Inquiring what was wrong, she learned that Faith had asked the pastor if she could come in one hour later than her usual time for the rest of the week. She was bone tired and it had been well past one o'clock in the morning by the time she had arrived home the prior night.

"Why not just go home early?" Mira asked sympathetically.

"I'd love to, but I can't leave Mrs. Rutherford with all of that clean-up every night," Faith replied forlornly. "I just can't do that to her."

With a little more digging, Mira found out that Pastor Rafe had haughtily denied the request, asking Faith who would answer the phones for that hour if she were absent. She was utterly incensed for her friend. "No employee should be subjected to this kind of inhumane treatment without consequences. As Christians, I believe our standard should be higher than that of the world. God expects us to treat our employees well. This is unacceptable." Surely, she thought, Pastor Rafe could readily see the obvious - that Faith was nearly ready to drop in her tracks!

But Faith wouldn't hear of any interference on her behalf. She was afraid that if anything were said it would only make matters worse for her and she didn't dare jeopardize her job. She couldn't afford to lose it, she had told Mira weeping.

Mira told her not to worry about her job. "Slaves don't get fired," she said sarcastically.

That had brought a glimmer of a smile through the tears but she still saw a haunted look in Faith's eyes. The woman confided, in a rare moment of candidness, how hard it was for her husband as well. He had to come home to a cold supper every night that had been prepared in the morning before she left for the church. "Pastor Rafe just doesn't seem to understand," she had ended unhappily.

No, Mira mused thoughtfully, *he doesn't understand anything except what he wants!*

In spite of the problems Mira encountered throughout the week, when the final evening of camp meeting came, many of the saints and the board members in particular, found themselves embracing and speaking words of encouragement to one another, strengthened by their communion with the Lord. Peace and comfort came to each one as only God can give. Warring angels protected and supported them. The confusion that had been felt earlier in the week lifted, leaving in its place peace and a resolve to stand for integrity no matter what the cost.

"Things are heating up!" Caelen spoke quickly, aware that his time was limited. The commanders had arranged a brief meeting to update one another on their progress.

"Yes, there is more trouble coming," agreed Jarah. "The Evil One's forces gain in strength and power daily while many of the saints sit by unaware that a battle rages for their very souls."

"Some of the board have caught the vision and are praying," interjected Valin, his eyes shining with hope.

"Yes. That is encouraging," rejoined Caelen his countenance brightening also.

Jarah looked glum. "If only more of them would seek the Lord. The place is full of weak, anemic Christians who pray little and fast even less. Many have lost their first love. Some dabble in forbidden sin. Others are too distracted by the cares of life to bother getting involved. They go through the motions but any real power is as far from them as the east is from the west. They have no understanding or knowledge of who they are in Christ, so they sit passively by, doing nothing at all. Complacency has made great inroads. Many of those who could be great warriors in the fight are more interested in temporal matters than in their spiritual welfare. They do not hear the call of the Spirit."

Captain Darshan sighed heavily. "It makes our battle harder. We need the prayers of the saints to win this warfare. They need to put on the whole armor of God in order to withstand the attacks of the enemy. Many precious souls hang in the balance. If only we could do more!"

"The enemy has such a foothold," groaned Jarah. "We cannot seem to shake it loose no matter what we do."

The captain looked discouraged. "Caelen, we lost the battle with the young drummer. He has utterly sold himself to the devil."

"What of the other one you were watching– the little man with the moustache?" inquired the commander anxiously.

"A scandal brews and is about to break over his head," he replied gravely. "He gave in to his lustful desires and molested a young boy."

Caelen shook his head sadly. "I fear immeasurable damage has been inflicted upon the child then. It will be a long and difficult road for him. And the man? What has happened to him?"

"His actions are now being called to account," responded Darshan gravely. "It won't be long before it becomes public knowledge. There does seem to be some promise for true repentance however. At least he has shown regret for his behavior and has been greatly humbled. Time will tell whether or not he is truly sorry for what he has done or whether it is a case of being sorry he was caught."

Jarah let a sigh escape through his teeth. "When the covering of the church is so damaged, it affects the entire flock." His fiery beard quivered in indignation.

"Still, we must keep trying," cried Valin, his dismay rising. "There has to be a way to reach more of them and encourage them to fast and pray."

"There are a few – a remnant." Hope shone like stars in Caelen's bright eyes. "We must strengthen those and try to awaken the others." He drew himself to his full height. "We have been given a strong assurance that some will be saved out of this battle. Even so, it is the Lord's strong desire that *all* would be preserved."

Darshan nodded crisply a fierce passion taking fire in his eyes. "Then we must save all we can and trust that not one soul will be lost to the Lord's enemy of those whom He has called to be His own," he said resolutely. "My warriors are committed to seeing this battle through to the end."

"Amen to that!" responded Valin with a glad cry.

Serious consultation followed this exchange as the angels developed strategies and laid out plans for warfare. At the meeting's conclusion, the heavenly commanders vanished into thin air, evaporating like shooting stars blazoned across a darkening sky, each determined to carry out his mission.

Mira dropped the wet pot back into the sink and hurried to answer the telephone. Ina's greeting was hesitant. "Darling, I think I need to tell you something I heard today."

"What's wrong? You sound upset."

"I had to take Nathan to the airport. Do you know who I'm talking about?"

"Certainly," she replied, curious to know what Ina was about to reveal. "It's the young man from the Caribbean; the minister who's been staying at the parsonage with Pastor and Mrs. Rutherford for the last few months."

"That's correct. He's been working part-time for a Christian school in the area."

"What about him?"

"Well my love, on the way to the airport he shared some things with me that I think you need to be aware of. He's been in the country on a one year visa but the school wants him to sign a full-time, two year contract. In order to get the visa extended, he has to return to his own country after which he can turn around and come right back, in a couple of days. He told me that Pastor Rafe gave him a letter which he's going to give to immigration stating that he is a volunteer at our church. That will speed up the process."

"What?" Mira cut in. "I haven't seen any letter."

"Well, that's the thing, darling. I thought the board was the legal entity of the church and I know the pastor doesn't have any signing authority. Another thing...," she paused, "I think he used the church seal on the letter as well."

"What is he thinking?" Mira shook her head in disbelief.

"I wish that were all I had to tell you," replied the worried little bookkeeper. "Pastor Rafe has been making his little side deals again. According to Nathan, when he starts his new contract, his pay check is going to be routed through our church. In other words, the school will pay us and we will pay him. But get this – he said he doesn't want any deductions taken. He wants it all to appear as honorariums or travel expense because he's supposed to be a volunteer for us."

"What?" Mira cried with rising excitement. "We can't do that! That's illegal!"

"I know it is, my love. I can't imagine why the school is going along with it but he says it's all arranged between them and Pastor."

Mira spoke crisply. "Ina, you call me the first minute you see any check from that school or receive any kind of request regarding wages for Nathan. You are not to deposit any money on his behalf."

"Okay, Honey." She sounded relieved. "I wouldn't have processed it without asking anyway. I just thought you should know what's coming. There's more," she said hesitantly. "It's no big deal but I thought you should know."

"What is it?"

"For some reason, Pastor wants to keep the church seal. He came asking for it again the other day. This time I told him you had it, so the next time you're here, you had better take it home with you for safe-keeping."

"What on earth does he want it for? It can't be for Nathan's letter because he would have taken that with him when he left."

"I have no idea but I would guess that it's to add an official note to some deal he wants to make."

"I'll get it from you on Sunday. What else?"

"Pastor has been trying to designate his tithes to his grandson, Jonas. He wanted me to go ahead and issue him a church check. Darling, I don't think Jonas knows that his travel allowance has been suspended by the board and what's more, I don't think Pastor wants him to find out. He says there shouldn't be any problem since he's designating the money for it. Of course I said I couldn't do it without permission from the board. I used the memo you gave me with the directive to suspend all further payments as back-up."

Mira thought rapidly for a moment. She could hardly fathom her pastor being so sneaky and underhanded. "What did you do about the tithes?"

"I held them back from the deposit. I told him that I couldn't do it that way."

"Good girl!" she cried. "You are absolutely right. It's against the law to designate money to a relative and funnel it through a charity. I wouldn't have signed the check in any case. What did he say?"

"Well, my love, he was certainly upset with me but he finally let me deposit the tithes in the general fund like always. He said that he'd pay Jonas out of his own pocket until he gets this thing settled. You know he's never going to let it go until he gets his way."

After Ina hung up, Mira's head reeled over the grave import of the information she had been given. No he wouldn't let it go! He was too stubborn for that! But the other matter...why would Pastor break the law for this man? Surely he would not put them in this position! The board was legally responsible for the every financial decision and it would be their reputations, not his, on the line over this. Why had he taken this man into his home in the first place? At the very least, it was an unwise thing to do, she thought dismally. Christian circles are small and a little gossip can run wild. People never forget! I'm sure they remember there was an indiscretion with a man years ago. Surely, it behooves him to avoid the very appearance of evil! What about his wife? Eve is either very naïve or oblivious as to how it must appear to others. Good grief! She had left the two men alone for a whole month when she went to visit family in another state. Mira knew that questions and whispers had been circulating for awhile as people became more uneasy but no one had the nerve to say anything to Pastor Rutherford.

She had to remind herself over and over that she trusted her pastor just as she always had. But did she really? His behaviour of late made her question everything she knew about the man. She had always thought him a man of God, a man of good character, upright and honest in all of his dealings. She had to admit that recent events had shaken her to the core of her being.

The insistent ringing of the door bell brought her reverie to an abrupt end. Trio practice was tonight! She had almost forgotten! The conversation with Ina had driven it right out of her head! Mira flew to the door to greet Jeanne, the first arrival.

"What's the matter with you?" Jeanne asked bluntly after she had settled down on the couch. Mira was never able to hide her feelings very well, especially from those who knew her best.

"I just received a phone call that was kind of upsetting," she replied hesitantly. "It's just some board stuff. I'm sure it will work itself out."

"Humph," grunted Jeanne. "Lately you seem to have more than your share of board stuff." What's going on? Or can't you share it? I'm not trying to pry or anything. I just don't like to see you upset all the time."

"What do you mean - upset all the time?" Mira laughed ruefully. "Am I that transparent?"

"To me you are," Jeanne replied candidly. "Where's Dan?" she asked, changing the subject.

"He's gone out. You know Dan." Mira chuckled. "He thinks we'll have a better time if he disappears for awhile. That must be Sunni," she added, glancing out her window and seeing a car pull up to the curb.

Following the arrival of the last trio member, the women entered into their rehearsal with enthusiasm and laughter. Two hours disappeared rapidly as they chatted amiably and sang until their voices gave out.

Before they knew it, Dan was poking his head through the doorway, a cheerful grin illuminating his face, signalling the end of their practice. They hugged one another warmly as they said good night, Mira's two friends giggling and kibitzing their way to the door which she finally closed on their antics. Returning to the kitchen, she found her husband whistling while he prepared a batch of fries.

"Singing always makes me feel great!" she chattered happily. "Music is so powerful. It has a way of lifting the spirits no matter how badly one feels. I think it has to do with praising the Lord." Her heart felt lighter and she was able to put aside her concerns for awhile as she went about her household chores.

9

As summer gave way to the crisp days of autumn with its blazoning panorama of color, Mira found the pressures of her position at the church increasing. Sleep fled from her. Troubled in spirit, she tossed and turned each night, unable to find rest, as she prayed constantly for wisdom to deal with each crisis as it arose.

The other board members were suffering as well. Suddenly, Donny's business was flagging financially. Although plenty of jobs were available, nothing seemed to be coming his way. Sometimes, he told them disconsolately, it felt as though he were walking under a black cloud. Distracted and worried over the affairs and goings-on at the church, he was finding it difficult to concentrate on business matters.

Jack admitted that he was not sleeping properly either and his health was starting to deteriorate because of it. His wife, Amy, would pace the floor at home for hours, crying and praying for the pastor and the leadership.

Ian walked into the church one Sunday morning to find himself replaced as head usher. To add insult to injury, he was told of his termination by the chap who took his place. A relative newcomer to the assembly, the man was completely oblivious of the furor he had unwittingly created as Rafe's pawn. Ian didn't blame him. How could he know that he was being used by the pastor to accomplish his purposes?

The story took on a life of its own, flying among the congregants at an alarming pace. Many grew increasingly upset and even angry over the pastor's appalling treatment of one who had devoted many years of untiring voluntary service. Of course, Pastor Rafe, when confronted directly, denied any involvement in the decision and tried to cast the blame on Pastor Marvin, but it was clear to many that he had orchestrated the whole thing.

The following Sunday, Rafe, thinking to put an end to the mutterings and gossip but still unwilling to rescind his appointment, gave his own version of the story from the pulpit. Ian had wanted to quit the position for some time, he stated authoritatively, and was actually very happy to be replaced by such a capable man. He asked the congregation to give the new man their full support and allowed them to believe that Ian wanted to step back and take a well deserved rest from the position.

Many were appeased by the speech, not once thinking to question if there were any truth behind it. But there were some, with first-hand knowledge, who were dismayed by the blatant lies spoken from the pulpit. One of these, who served as a volunteer audio technician, immediately left the church with his family, adamantly refusing to return unless the pastor apologized or stepped down. That his pastor would use subterfuge and lies to gain his own way was simply too much for the man to handle. Discontent over the leadership was now rapidly becoming an unmanageable problem.

Rafe had grown accustomed over the years to use his position and pulpit to add veracity to his statements. His ability to fire wicked darts at his board and council in such a way that he couldn't be held accountable was formidable. A practised thespian, he possessed an extraordinary gift for portraying himself as the poor victim of every circumstance.

"My God, when will you take me out of this place of obscurity and deliver me from this rebellious people," he thundered one fateful morning as he paced the platform. Many of his attacks passed over the unwitting heads of the people but seldom missed those they were aimed at.

Faith called Mira shortly after the Ian incident with the news that Pastor Rutherford had decided to have a meeting the following Saturday morning, for all those involved in leadership or ministry in the church. The attendance of all council members was mandatory. As with most of Pastor Rafe's ideas, it was a last minute thing, thrown together and poorly organized.

The morning of the meeting, Captain Darshan was present with as many warriors as he could filter in past the demon sentries. Security had been tightened and only those angels who had a legitimate right to be there were allowed to pass. In pairs, they flanked the sides of the saints who had some kind of prayer life.

The small banquet hall was full when Mira arrived for the meeting. Unseen by the human world, Caelen and Valin warded her, fiercely safeguarding her from the slime and corrosion the demon hordes were vomiting upon the unprotected. She found an empty seat at a table near the back of the room with Phil Schmidt and his wife.

Rafe was in his element. He controlled every aspect of the meeting with obvious relish. After requesting the opening prayer from Rev. Armstrong and sharing a brief, dry reading of scripture, he moved on quickly to business. He intended to use this opportunity to solidify his grandson's position and this he did at length, painting a glowing picture of growth in the youth department and attributing its success to Jonas' style and rapport with the teenagers.

His leadership looked at one another in bewilderment knowing they had not seen any evidence of the growth he spoke about. They were all aware of the two teenagers who came on an irregular basis when forced into it by their parents. Beyond these, they didn't know of anyone else in that age category who attended a regular church service.

Phil's wife leaned over and whispered into Mira's ear. "I hope that Jonas isn't on staff and receiving a salary?" Her voice was tense, even a little belligerent. Mira assured her that such was not the case and the woman settled back with a sigh of relief.

Rafe, rubbing his hands together gleefully, moved blithely forward with his agenda. He was ready to show his board that he was way ahead of them. "I have a new vision for the church," he stated proudly. "God has given me this vision which I am now prepared to share with the leadership". His secretary rose at his command to distribute the documents he had requested her to prepare beforehand.

The directors fumed in silence as, for the first time, he revealed his extravagant, irrational ideas to expand existing ministries within the church and add some twenty others. None of the plans had ever been submitted or discussed with the board and council or even hinted at. They all felt like fools as they listened along with everyone else.

Included in Rafe's grand new vision was a brand new youth center, a retirement village, a Christian school, a conference center and several other ministries. At the close of his grandiose speech, he triumphantly unveiled a model for a prefabricated gymnasium for the youth with a flourish and turned the floor over to an acquaintance obviously there to sell his pitch.

Following the salesman, Rafe finally threw open the floor for comments. The leaders stirred restlessly, looking at one another for courage, each hoping someone else would take the lead.

Several warrior angels bent and whispered in the ears of their charges while imps and demons flew back and forth, spitting thick black gobs of corrosion over the heads of the leaders. The heavenly beings used their wings and shields to cover as many as they could but try as they might, they were spread too thin to protect such a large number. They were forced to concentrate heavily on the saints they warded. Two brave souls struggled apologetically to their feet after several nudges from warriors standing over them.

Dora Golding, a former board member who had suffered wounds of her own during her terms on the board, nervously questioned the viability of trying to start all of these ministries at once. She reasoned that Women's Ministries was currently the only stable ministry in the church and suggested that a wiser course of action might be to concentrate on revitalizing the youth and children's ministries which were floundering.

Rob Samuels immediately concurred with her viewpoint. "We already tried to have a school here and it didn't work out. The Men's Fellowship program has been dropped completely for several months now because there is no one willing to step up and lead it; not since the last leader left. I recommend that once our existing ministries are on a firm footing, then in a year or so, we might press forward with something else."

Mira applauded Dora and Rob's courage to speak with such honesty, especially after the pastor's complimentary youth report. Heads nodded and a murmur of agreement buzzed throughout the room. More than one voice whispered that it would be foolhardy to try to implement all of the programs at once. Volunteers were in short supply with many wanting to step back and take some time off due to discouragement and burn-out.

Rafe was unbending and did not make any attempt to hide his disappointment in his leaders. "God has great plans for this place," he told them loftily, reminding them of the five-story-high Jesus. "Where is your faith," he questioned, berating them as if they were children. "As leader and shepherd here, this is my call! God spoke to me directly about these plans and I will not go against what He has told me to do. I intend to carry out His will."

He appointed Pastor Marvin the task of implementing each of the ministries listed in the document. "It will be his job to find the volunteers to get the job done and there are plenty to draw from," he said adamantly. His listeners felt the cutting rebuke and slunk lower in their seats, shifting uncomfortably and becoming increasingly restless.

Rafe, gauging the effect of his speech on his audience, felt the time had come to be a little more gracious and magnanimous toward his leaders. In a complete about-face, he now lavished them with praise and flattery, masterfully preparing them for his last little surprise. "I want you to know how much I prize the opinions of the church leadership," he said smoothly. "To that end I am going to ask each of you to fill out a survey form which has been prepared by our dear former board member, Dora Golding."

Thanking Dora for her excellent work, he asked Faith to hand out the forms, requesting that they be returned at the end of the meeting. The leaders looked at one another in consternation as they received the thick surveys.

"Do you want quantity or quality?" It was Lenny Granger's voice from the back of the room. "These look as if they require more than a one word answer."

"Of course we want quality answers." Rafe smiled benignly. "We want total honesty. You don't even have to sign your names unless you want to. We welcome your comments - good and bad." He hesitated. "I guess we could give you a week. Why don't you hand them in to either Faith or Pastor Marvin by next week-end. That will give everyone plenty of time to fill them out. Maybe Dora would be willing to summarize them for us by the next leadership meeting." He looked smilingly in her direction. "I want to have these meetings regularly from now on because we value your input."

People scattered quickly after they received their surveys, anxious to get back to their weekend chores. Mira ran into Ian, Donny and Jack chatting together in the parking lot.

"So... whaddya think of all that baloney we heard this morning?" Donny laughed as the others shook their heads. "I just don't get it. Who does he think is going to volunteer to carry out these grandiose plans of his?"

"I don't know," Mira replied flatly. "Pastor Marvin sure has his hands full. A month ago he confessed to me that most of our volunteers are stressed and tired ... burnt out. They're stretched now to the max and they don't want to take on anything more. We don't even have enough Sunday School workers for the kids and the nursery isn't properly staffed. The Children's Ministries leader is talking of quitting if she doesn't become a paid staff member but Pastor Rafe certainly won't allow that. Pastor Marvin says we're going to lose her if we don't do something soon. Some of the children's workers left a few months ago. They simply disappeared, never to return. Why? Who knows! Pastor says they either took offence unnecessarily or they're controlling and manipulative."

"Controlling and manipulative!" Donny snorted derisively. "We all know who is controlling, manipulative." They nodded their heads in agreement.

"Well, I know a few people who wouldn't mind helping out but they're pretty unhappy with the current leadership," admitted Jack with a sigh. "They all seem to be waiting to see what's going to happen before they commit themselves,"

"Jane and I are hearing the same thing," chimed in Ian. "It seems like everyone is in waiting mode, and it has to do with the top leader. No one wants to work with the man. I feel sorry for Pastor Marvin."

"He looks utterly exhausted. I sure hope he doesn't quit over all of this extra work that's just been loaded onto him. If we lose him, we've lost a treasure. He really cares about the people." Mira blinked back the tears that rose to her eyes and struggled to swallow the lump that rose suddenly in her throat.

"Amy and I have talked about leaving," offered Jack quietly. "I don't know how much more I can take. I feel I should step down from the board. I'm not much good anyway."

"Oh Jack, don't even think of it, please," Mira cried. "We need you! We all need each another. I truly believe that God has placed each of us on the board for this time. Man had nothing to do with it, even though the pastor might think so. God sets up the governing bodies for good or for ill. I've wanted to throw in the towel too at times. Let's face it - who needs this? But somehow, in spite of everything, God has kept me here. I just don't feel released to leave yet. If it should come to that, I think we should all step down together, as a unit, but only after we know there is nothing more to be done. I think God has a purpose that He is trying to accomplish. I believe He wants integrity brought back to the church and right now, we're the vessels He's using to bring about His purpose in this place. The people ... they don't know what's going on here. Besides, the bible says when you don't know what to do, just stand. I think that's what we're supposed to do. Just stand, and don't allow anyone to intimidate or sway us from doing what is right. Keep the standard of integrity high for as long as we are called to do so. I really don't think it will be much longer. I somehow feel that something will happen by the end of the year. I don't know if that means December or the board year which ends at the next annual business meeting in April. I only know that I feel it strongly in my spirit. We'll know what to do when the time is right."

"Wow," exclaimed Jack contemplatively. "I guess I never thought of it that way. I'm willing to hang in there for awhile longer. I just hope it all ends sooner rather than later. I'm tired of all of the dishonesty and the wicked dealings here. I don't live that way and I never thought stuff like this would happen in my church."

"I have to say I'm disappointed in Pastor," he continued earnestly. "I really thought he was the best thing that ever walked on two legs and I certainly never dreamed of going through this kind of thing in a church.

You kind of expect it in the business world but it catches you totally off guard with fellow believers.

"I was thinking of walking away too," admitted Donny, "but I've changed my mind. I'm in it until the end. Let's see this thing through."

"Me too," said Ian firmly.

Tears stung Mira's eyes. She felt the strength of unity that bound the four of them together even though she was unsure of where Rev. Armstrong and Sylvester stood in the matter.

Mira and Jeanne walked at a brisk pace along the woodland trail on a bright October afternoon. The air was crisp and clear and the women enjoyed the sound of the dry leaves crunching underfoot. A flock of birds circled and swirled overhead in a futile attempt to organize their long flight southward. A large gaggle of Canada geese, honking raucously, waddled down the slope of the riverbank that bordered the pathway. The gurgling sound of the swift moving current brought a measure of peace and tranquillity to Mira's troubled heart.

"I haven't seen much of you lately," began Jeanne interrupting a lengthy silence. "Have you quit going to church?"

"No. I needed a bit of a break from all the stress the board has been under, so I've been going with Dan occasionally to another church." She hesitated, wondering how much she should say. "You know that he hasn't sat through a service at our church for a long time. He seems to really like the pastor's preaching at this other place. In fact, Dan's like a different person when we go there, sitting at the front, entering into the worship. I hardly know him."

"Maybe you should think about making a switch then, for his sake."

"I have thought about it," Mira replied soberly. "I just can't shake off my responsibilities at the Good Shepherd Church. The good news is - I think it will be over soon, one way or another. I've certainly done a lot of praying about it lately, seeking the Lord for wisdom and discernment. I have to admit - I really do like this other church and I've been fortunate to have opportunity to built up a relationship with the people, over the past couple of years, by leading worship there every five or six weeks. I like the pastor and his wife very much and the transition would be much easier than if we had to find a brand new place. Sometimes I almost think the Lord may be preparing me for it by opening a door to this new place so that I won't be totally lost if I do have to leave our church. The thought of it still scares me though. I've been attending Good Shepherd for almost fourteen years. I love the place and the people."

"I know you're not a church hopper," Jeanne said warmly. "You've given your best to the place. You have a lot of friends there who really love you."

"Do you really think so?" Mira asked forlornly. "Sometimes I think it would be best if I just walked away and other times....I can't even imagine it! I would miss it all so much! It's been a huge part of my life; even more so since my retirement from the work force. It means everything to me. It's pretty much my social life too." She smiled at her chum. "I really don't want to have to make new friends."

"Well ... you won't lose me no matter what you decide." Jeanne kicked a stone out of her path, embarrassed at her unusual display of sentimentality. "You aren't the only one to notice things aren't right in the pulpit, you know."

"What do you mean?" asked Mira, her voice sharpening with apprehension.

"I've been coming to this church for over ten years now. Pastor Rafe married me and Manny. I love Pastor but we've had our share of grief from getting involved with him."

She stopped walking and faced her friend. "I think there are some things you need to know. Manny and I lost our life savings over a money scheme of Pastor's. We got involved in buying some shares because he said it was a good deal. The guy we bought them from was a minister friend of Pastor's, so we trusted him. Well... it turns out he defrauded a lot of people and ended up in jail over it. The company he started went down the tubes and our shares plummeted overnight to nothing. Manny thinks that Pastor Rafe had inside knowledge of what was about to happen because the church sold their shares just before the stock fell and were able to pay off the building and the parsonage and still have money in the bank. But there were some of us that lost - big time!"

"Oh Jeanne, I had no idea! I know the man you're talking about. As a matter of fact, he just got out of jail recently. Pastor Rafe wanted to let him set up an office in the church with a free phone and computer. The board only found out because we had to pay an invoice for the cabling that was installed in the downstairs office he was assigned to use."

Mira sighed. When she had asked him about it, Pastor Rafe had denied giving his permission for the use of the office and equipment but the proof was on the invoice. It had the man's name on it! Even Ina, who had known all about the deal, had said nothing to her. She wondered if it was because the bookkeeper had served as the man's accountant. It was hard to comprehend Ina's continuing friendly relations with the man who had nearly landed her in prison for complicity in his fraud. She shuddered at the thought of all the checks she had signed in the past two years for items or services that neither she nor the board had prior knowledge of.

"The directors put their foot down and refused to allow him an office", she told Jeanne. "Even though Pastor said he trusted him, we didn't know what the man would be doing, so it was too great a risk. Pastor doesn't seem to think these things through! What if he should target the membership again for investments?"

"Manny would be livid if he found that criminal was getting a free office in our church," replied Jeanne, her eyes widening at the thought. "He didn't go to church for quite awhile after it happened. He still gets angry when he thinks of it!"

"I don't blame him! I would be beside myself! I'm surprised you still want to attend this church after what happened!"

"That isn't the only scheme Pastor Rafe has brought into the church. There have been a number over the years." Jeanne chuckled but there was no mirth in it. "Let me see...there was the jewellery pyramid ploy. You know, sell jewellery and sign up others to sell for you and you'll make a fortune. Selling health food products and really expensive vitamins were two more that made the rounds. Those that got involved invariably hit up all of the church members to buy from them. It doesn't seem right somehow! Church should be a safe place to attend; free from all that garbage! Even Eve was trying to sell stuff to people and of course, you feel obligated to purchase from her."

"I didn't know too much about it," replied Mira. "I only heard rumors. I guess Dan and I weren't on Pastor's favored list. Thank God for that!" she added gratefully. "But I do remember one time he tried to get us to attend a meeting on a Thursday night at the church. It was a pyramid scheme involving putting pills into your gas tank. It was supposed to make your gas go further." She laughed. "Give me a break! That scam was going around years ago! I told Pastor Rafe not to go through with it. I was afraid some of the members might get taken in by it and lose money and I told him so. When he couldn't capture my interest, he tried to get my son-in-law to attend. I'm so glad Jason had enough sense not to go."

"People have been so hurt by these schemes he's promoted," said Jeanne earnestly. "Some, like us, have lost thousands of dollars. He always seems to come out alright though. I know the Samuels have lost a lot of money too. They trust him completely. I'm afraid Manny has been roped into his latest scam."

Mira looked stricken. "Oh Jeanne, there's more?"

"You bet there is! Another minister "friend", recommended by Pastor, told a bunch of members that if they donate money to a certain charity, they will be issued tax receipts for amounts anywhere from three to ten times as much as they invest. It's supposed to be completely legal," she added doubtfully.

"But that doesn't sound right. I'm sure it's fraudulent. Come to think of it, I saw something about that in the news! The government is now auditing people all over the country for that very thing. They're going to have to pay back the tax refunds they received."

"I know. Manny is attending meetings about it now. I don't know what will happen. They're still claiming its legal and asking for even more money."

"Manny won't give them more, will he?" cried Mira aghast.

"I don't know. Probably! He's so gullible! I don't even want to know about it this time! After we got married, he told me about a lot of scams and fraudulent schemes endorsed by the pastor and yet he still gets sucked in! One time, Pastor Rafe told the congregation that the Holy Spirit woke him up in the middle of the night, instructing him to help a family in the church that couldn't pay their mortgage. Their house was going to be repossessed. Pastor laid a real guilt trip on everybody, telling them that if they were real Christians, they would give the money required to purchase the house in order to keep the family from being evicted. He asked everyone to cash in their retirement savings and put mortgages on their homes to raise the necessary funds and he promised that their checks would only be held by the bank as collateral for a short period of time and not cashed."

"And they believed that?" Mira asked incredulously.

"They believe anything he tells them! Of course the checks were cashed immediately! When the people tried to get their money back, they were stalled until they threatened to go to court. This went on for more than two years. One poor guy gave $2,500 and when things got rough for him financially, he tried and tried to get it back. He ended up losing his apartment and had to sleep in his car but the pastor sure didn't jump to help him! He had to threaten legal action before he was finally reimbursed."

"Didn't the family pay back the mortgage?"

"The man was a friend of Pastor's and the president of the board at the time. He decided that it was gift from God and he didn't have to pay it back."

"You've got to be kidding!" Mira's eyes went wide with shock and disbelief.

"No, it's true. There are still a few congregants around who know the story. Everyone felt sorry for the wife and kids, but the board was finally forced to evict the family and sell the house to recoup the money because the guy refused to pay anything. Many were hurt financially over it and, as a result, left the church never to return."

"A pattern that seems to repeat itself every few years," groaned Mira.

Mira decided at the last minute that she would go to the midweek bible study. Her decision was based more on the fact that Ina needed her to sign checks than for any other reason. As she pulled into church parking lot she could feel her stress level escalate.

"Heavenly Father, please protect me," she prayed as she ascended the steps. "Give me clarity of thought and oh Lord, please give me wisdom and discernment. Help me."

The two angelic warriors following her smiled at one another, growing more splendid and magnificent as they expanded to gigantic proportions. The demon sentries patrolling the doorway stepped back uncertainly. These two looked much too formidable to pick a fight with.

Mira's stomach did flip-flops as she opened the front door hoping the main lobby would be empty. A sigh of relief escaped her lips as she saw only the accounting office was illuminated. Ina greeted her cheerily, the terriers rushing to the door to gambol excitedly about her feet, each vying for her attention.

"Stop that!" admonished the bookkeeper. "Two terrors, that's really what they are," she said, laughing at their antics. She handed a folder of checks to Mira along with a pen. "Thank you for coming in, darling. I really wanted to get these finished."

"Anything new, Ina?" Her voice was strained. "What about the invoices from the tiling company? I haven't seen them resurface since I gave them to the pastor."

"Oh, I have them." Ina grinned. "Pastor gave them to me. He says he had Joe and Nate mark what they felt belonged to the church but I checked the dates of the invoices and they don't agree with the time period that Joe was working here so I haven't cut a check for them yet. I won't either, my love, unless you say so."

"Let me see what was marked." With heads together, they poured over the invoices checking the dates against the two tiling contracts. "There may be one invoice that is legitimate," Mira declared. "I'll check with Jonathan and then give my approval for that one, but not the others."

"Okay, my love." Ina took a deep breath. "I think I might know what the rest of them are for."

"I'm listening."

"I think it's possible that the other supplies could be for the pastor's personal condo."

"What condo?"

"He's purchased a condo with Johanna Hanes."

"Go on!" Mira raised her eyebrows. "Why on earth would he do that?" She knew the elderly spinster well as she had attended the church for many years.

"I heard Pastor took her out of the nursing home where her relatives had put her and then they bought this condo together, each paying half. Johanna is supposed to live in it until she passes away and when she dies, he gets the condo. Pretty sweet deal for Pastor, if you ask me! Johanna's niece and nephew are so mad that they are thinking of suing. The thing is - she has Alzheimer's, which is why her family placed her in a proper facility in the first place. I guess she was getting so senile and unmanageable they could no longer care for her themselves and of course, they couldn't allow her to stay by herself unattended. They were just about to have her assessed when the Rutherfords inserted themselves into the picture and took control of the situation."

"Apparently, Pastor convinced her to give either him or his wife her Power of Attorney," she continued, "taking it away from the family. After that, it was easy for him to remove her from the home, which he managed to do before the assessment made it to court. Then he fired the lawyer that was handling her affairs and got his own lawyer to take over. You know how frail Johanna is and she thinks the world of Pastor and Mrs.R. After he got rid of her lawyer, he instructed the new attorney to issue legal notices to all of her family members forbidding any contact with her on threat of lawsuit."

Mira was stunned. "Surely, there must be another explanation for this," she stammered, turning white. "Pastor said something to me not long ago about helping Johanna to buy a condo, but he definitely did not say anything about being part owner. He told me that sometimes pastors have to go beyond the call of duty. He asked a couple of church members to take her in until her condo was ready."

"I know all about it, darling. They were really concerned about her welfare because she has deteriorated to the point that she doesn't know enough to take her medication. She isn't even aware that she's purchased the condo. She thinks she's still looking for a place."

Mira interrupted. "Oh Ina, I remember one night when I was at the parsonage with Grace after a camp meeting service and someone called. I overheard Eve tell the pastor that he would have to send someone over to the condo because Johanna couldn't remember what the number of her place was, so she couldn't get past the security system. It was around midnight. Pastor Rafe was miffed about the interruption at the time and wondered why they were called about the situation at all."

Mira hesitated while gathering her thoughts. "You know what? I remember Pastor telling me that he was helping Johanna out by overseeing the installation of all new ceramic and hardwood floors for her place. I didn't really think much about it at the time." She took it one step further. "Do you think the flooring materials on these invoices were purchased for the condo floor and that perhaps Joe was the one he had install them?"

"Why else would Joe be picking up flooring supplies, my love? He runs a stucco business. When work is slow, he tries to pick up odd jobs doing renovations. I'd bet my bottom dollar that's what these invoices are about." Mira stared at her in consternation.

"Lorena came to me a couple of weeks ago with an invoice for cleaning the condo too," Ina continued. "She said that Pastor asked her to bill the church. Of course I told her that we couldn't pay a cleaning bill for his personal condo. She claims that he told her that it was a fair exchange because she still owed the church for a couple days cleaning from her last contract."

Mira grunted. "I knew that whole thing would cause problems." She frowned as she chewed on the end of her pen. "I didn't feel right about it at the time. Mrs. R. cancelled her services at the parsonage four weeks in a row. She claimed that Nathan was doing the cleaning for free board so she didn't need her."

"Lorena should have been paid for the month anyway," replied Ina. She has a contract with the church, so we are obligated to pay her even if she isn't used."

"I know. Pastor Rafe was very angry when he found out how the contract was worded. He didn't want her to have the money if she didn't do the cleaning and he made a really big deal out of it. Lorena was crying and extremely upset."

"No wonder," exclaimed Ina indignantly. "She couldn't afford to be shorted that way on her contract. She depends on it to live."

"I should never have left it with the pastor and her to sort out between them. I knew better," cried Mira. "He told me that it was all settled between them and that she agreed to do some extra cleaning at the parsonage for Mrs. R. You know... some of the stuff around the house that doesn't get done in normal cleaning, like windows and closets. Eve and Lorena were supposed to coordinate the times between them and when her hours were completed, she would then submit them for payment."

"Technically, we should have paid her the money first anyway. A contract is a contract," said Ina resolutely.

"Yes, we should have." Mira sighed. "At the time it seemed like an amicable arrangement. It appeased the pastor and Lorena insisted that she really wanted to do the work for the money. I thought it was all settled! It never occurred to me that Pastor would use her to his own advantage this way and of course, I didn't know about this whole condo business."

"It isn't honest," Ina declared. "I'm disappointed in Pastor." She paused. "I guess I should have expected as much though. I've seen and heard too much over the years. He takes whatever he can get. Do you know he even took money out of petty cash once for an inhaler? He said he got an allergy walking across the church parking lot so the church should pay for it."

"You're kidding!"

"No. It's true, honey. I've seen more garbage than you would believe."

"Then why do you stay, Ina?" queried Mira, looking at her intently.

"He's the only pastor I've ever had," she replied. "I came to know the Lord under his last pastorate so that's where I attended church and I've just stayed with him ever since. I moved here after he took this church because I wasn't really happy after he left. I guess I've really put him on a pedestal and it's not easy to accept that he isn't honest sometimes or that he has hurt a lot of people. I really do love him, you know, so I forgive him every time he does something that makes me see red."

She fiddled self consciously with some papers on her desk. "I'm afraid to go anywhere else so that's why I stay. The devil you know is better than the one you don't," she confessed hanging her head with embarrassment."

"I have felt pretty much the same way," Mira admitted quietly. "I thought this was the only church for me but Dan isn't happy here and I don't know how much longer I can stand it either, knowing about all of this stuff and unable to do anything about it. You know I've been leading worship at another church every five or six weeks for the last couple of years. I really feel the presence of God when I go there. Pastor Rafe has always claimed that there is no other place that is as good as this church. I wonder...." She paused for a moment and then continued. "I'm not sure I believe him any more. I think there are many good churches out there and good pastors too. It might take a little time to find the right fit but I'm starting to think that it's worth the effort."

"Oh, honey, please don't even think of leaving," Ina cried. "I don't know what I'd do without you. I can talk to you about these things and at least keep my sanity. Do you know that I have never felt that Pastor values me at all? I went through a very difficult time last year and he never once asked me how I was doing or if he could pray for me. Not once!" A tear slid down her cheek.

"Oh Ina," Mira exclaimed, "I'm so sorry. I didn't know."

"Don't get me wrong, I'm committed to the church family here but it would be nice to have a pastor who genuinely cares about his flock instead of using and manipulating them to his own advantage. It's been heart wrenching to see so many people that I love walk out of my life and become a memory. Leaders and associate pastors never stay long. They are given positions without authority and used like puppets to do his will."

"I know what you mean. I thought Pastor was the best of the best and never really found out the difference until I became part of this board." Mira's voice broke. "I'm so tired of putting out fires all the time. I feel the heavy responsibility of my position and I want to do what's right, but oh Ina, it would be so much easier to just quietly leave." She covered her face with her hands, her shoulders heaving.

Ina rose from her chair and limped over to give her a warm hug. "Never you mind, my love," she said, patting Mira on the shoulder, "We'll get through this together. I'm used to his yelling at me but I know it bothers you. He hollered at me the other day because I didn't put through a personal phone call to him while he was in a meeting."

"That's something that really angers people," Mira replied, looking up earnestly. "They come to see him about their problems and he totally demeans them by taking phone calls and looking at e-mails during their appointment time. They can be crying their eyes out and he'll take a call right in the middle of it. It's so rude! If he hears his e-mail signalling a new message, he actually turns away to read it and, more often than not, he'll send back a reply instead of giving his full attention to his visitor. I know because it's happened to me, more than once."

"I can't even get an appointment with him at all!" Ina sat down heavily in the chair across from Mira. "One time," she confessed, lowering her voice confidentially, "I wanted to talk with him about some things, so I made an appointment with his secretary and took a board member with me as a witness." Fire flashed from her eyes. "NOTHING was accomplished! He talked all around my issues and when it was all over, nothing had changed! He will NEVER admit to any wrongdoing whatsoever! That's something you will never see! EVER! Don't bother to even go there! He'll just skate around the issue – around and around – until he tires you out and you leave with your problems unresolved."

"I know what you mean," agreed Mira. "The worst of it is that he really believes everything has been resolved – just because he talked with you!" She looked at the little bookkeeper, tears welling in her eyes. "I don't want to talk about him but I am so frustrated. I don't know what to do!"

"I know darling. It's hard to hear him from the pulpit telling us how much he loves us all and then he treats us shamefully at times. I'll tell you something else! If you ever cross him, he will dig you from the pulpit. That just seems wrong to me!"

"It isn't right, Ina. It's an abuse of power," Mira asserted vehemently. "I fully expect that the directors will take some verbal blows from the platform before this is over. The truth is - I hate to even step through the door these days." Putting her pen away, she rose. "Well, there's no point stalling any longer. I'm off to service. Remember? Pastor said that he wanted to share his vision for the church tonight and also some personal direction."

Maybe he's going to take that sabbatical that his prophets have been advising, she thought. *That would certainly take some pressure off the current situation. Oh God, please let it be true!*

"Yes, my love, I remember." Ina murmured. "If he really shares anything new, I'll be the most surprised person here!" She chuckled. "He's used that little trick for years! Every time he wants to get the numbers up on a Wednesday night, he'll tell the congregation that he can only share his heart with family." She rolled her eyes. "And as we all know, family isn't the Sunday morning crowd. Real family comes to the midweek service."

"You have to admit, it works though. Like fools, they come, because they want to be thought of as family. It's a guilt trip! Anyone that comes only on Sunday is made to feel like a second-class Christian."

"Well, I doubt if they'll hear anything more than the usual drivel. I wish it were different, but seriously darling..." She crooked her brow at Mira. "We both know how unlikely it is that he will say anything life-changing."

Mira grimaced at the truth of the bald statement. She slammed the partially opened drawer shut, punctuating her foul mood. Grabbing her purse, she headed into the lobby and down the hallway, slowing her steps to accommodate the limping bookkeeper. Together, they joined the service already in progress.

10

Rafe really wanted some time off. He had debated for a week or more the merits of playing the sabbatical card or merely taking an extended vacation. In both of the last board and council meetings, he had subtly prepared the way by announcing how exhausting it was to carry all of the church burdens himself. He was positive that he could stave off any further crucial meetings until closer to the annual business meeting in the spring. A long vacation was just what he needed to get out of the line of fire for awhile but he knew he couldn't afford to give the board any further ammunition against him. Perhaps the better plan would be to try a short vacation first and then extend it into a sabbatical if the directors proved problematic. He did not want any further dealings with this board. The next one would be stacked more favourably and then those remaining would fall into line when they found themselves outnumbered.

As Rafe faced his Wednesday evening crowd, these thoughts were uppermost in his mind. It pleased him that a great number of his flock had turned out to hear what he wished to impart and it was certainly very inspiring to see how they esteemed him, hanging upon his every word.

"A major shift is coming to the church and the order of things will be changed," he proclaimed, shifting easily into the booming voice he often used when delivering a prophetic utterance. "The Lord has told me to go back to my original calling. He wants me to take up my Elijah mantle again and get the people ready for the coming of the Lord." He spoke persuasively about the need for an affirmation directly from God and not from man so that all would move from being children of God to sons of God.

Mira wondered what the difference was and then felt ashamed for questioning his Word from the Lord. Perhaps the deeper meaning had escaped her.

"I'm going to share something very personal with you," continued Rafe, his voice softening suddenly with tender emotion. ""These are things I can't share with the Sunday crowd. They wouldn't understand. You are the ones I can share my heart with – my family." He spread his arms wide as if he would encompass them all in his embrace.

Ina rolled her eyes in Mira's direction and it was all she could do to stifle the giggle that rose unbidden to her lips.

"My ministry has always been the most important thing in my life. For the last while, my wife hasn't made any secret of the fact that she would like to retire. After all, we aren't getting any younger. Of course, she *is* older than me." He chuckled as he always did whenever he teased his wife publicly about her age. Eve reddened in embarrassment.

"When she first broached the subject, I thought to myself, *"Give up my Ministry? If I have to choose between you and my ministry, you can hit the road, baby!"* There were several sharp intakes of breath throughout the crowd. Eve squirmed uncomfortably in her chair and dropped her head.

"It's true! I'm not perfect!" Rafe admitted, a gentle smile playing about his lips. "Of course I didn't tell my wife how I felt, but God did have to deal with my attitude on that one. My ministry has always defined who I am. I would be lost without it! When I told the Lord this, He said to me *"Son, you need to get your priorities straight."* Our Heavenly Father disciplines those He loves but after I had repented for my attitude, God showed me that He is not finished with me yet. He just wanted me to be willing to give it up so that He could bestow a greater calling upon my life - my Elijah mantle, in even greater measure than before!"

Rafe waxed eloquent, knowing he had his audience in the palm of his hand. "I have always known that I was called to be a prophet, but now God has told me that the end of my ministry will be even greater than the beginning and He will accomplish this great work in me. I'm being transparent because I feel we need to be real with one another. We all need more transparency. We need an intimacy of prayer. Perhaps I might even need to pull away for awhile. We need to ask ourselves if God wants a whole new team brought in."

Mira gasped. *Whew, that's pretty blatant,* she thought. *Maybe he will come right out and say that he wants to get rid of the board.*

"Either we will lock in and freeze or we will prepare for a paradigm shift in direction." The words rolled masterfully from Rafe's tongue. "The church is going to change as we know it. God is bringing together those of like mind and spirit."

God help us all then. Profound sadness filled Mira's heart. She heard empty words completely devoid of God's Spirit; mindless rhetoric and political manoeuvring carefully veiled in spiritual language.

"There will be shakings and strippings that will make us uncomfortable," he thundered powerfully. "Repentance is needed for the idolatry in our hearts."

Amen to that, Mira reflected soberly.

Suddenly, Pastor Rafe did the unexpected. He opened the floor for comments and stepped to one side of the podium. Mira waited expectantly. *There must be someone here he has carefully prepared ahead of time to speak.*

A stout little lady in a bright pink jacket rose from her seat in the front row. Two gigantic warriors moved to shield her from the wicked looking darts that Fear and Intimidation were poised to throw.

"I have a Word from the Lord for the pastor which God gave me during a recent period of prayer and fasting," she said in a trembling voice. "It isn't something that I want to say but I feel that I must be obedient to my Lord." She faced Rafe bravely, her face crumpling as a sob momentarily tore at her throat choking her speech. "Restoration is needed for you, Pastor. You must get alone with God – away where there are no phones. You must set aside an extended period of time to seek His face. I love you Pastor and this is hard for me to say because it sounds like a rebuke." Tears were running down her face and dripping from her chin by this time.

Other eyes were wet and Mira felt a lump rise in her own throat. *This is real,* she thought brokenly. *God is trying to send a message here. This was certainly not prepared!* She could sense the sincerity in the woman's voice. Stirred to the depths of her soul, she sent a fervent prayer of her own heavenward. *Oh Jesus, please speak to him.*

A golden glow materialized around each of the heavenly beings. Their size appeared to increase as the glow became a flame that pulsated with white light. Brighter and brighter they grew with each word spoken. Demons shrieked with impotent rage but fell back, one upon another, until they were pushed almost to the door.

Still weeping, the woman sat down. One of the prophets, part of Pastor Rafe's Saturday morning circle, jumped to his feet. "There is going to be a shift – a new alignment of this body of believers," he proclaimed. "We have been living on milk for too long and we are in desperate need of a vision for the church. I believe people from this assembly will be used all over the world but they fear to move. The Lord is saying that the pastor needs to take a sabbatical of at least three months."

The demons were getting bolder again. They pressed forward, claws extended, licking their misshapen lips in anticipation. Their advance ground to a halt as a third person stood to confirm the first two Words spoken.

She was a peppery little woman, unpredictable at times, but always loving and loyal toward her pastor. "It is time for us to move on to the real meat of the Word of God," she declared. This body is full of unbelief and self-idols. We are doing our own thing and robbing God of His glory. We defile ourselves! It is serious and dangerous! God wants to dwell in us."

She looked directly at Pastor Rafe. "Pastor, you can't hear from God because you are too busy doing other things. You need to take the time to hear what He has to say; both to you and to the church."

Another woman quickly followed her, proclaiming the same message that the pastor should be released by the congregation to spend time before God. Silence followed this final pronouncement. Rafe seemed uncertain. Jezebel leaned over his shoulder and whispered comfortingly into his ear. A host of demons rushed forward forming a wedge, chanting frantically, but their momentum was broken. They had lost their control over the people.

Shaking off the feeling of doom that settled in his heart, Rafe ended the service without further fanfare. With solemn faces the people quietly disbursed to their homes, none lingering to chatter with one another as was their usual custom.

The next day Lucy Dalmer called Mira about the flooring invoices, insisting they be paid immediately. Mira explained patiently that the dates didn't match the times Joe had worked for the church and therefore she could not authorize them.

Shortly after her conversation with Lucy, Nate called to add his own plea for payment. Mira went through each invoice with him also and explained what she knew about the whole situation. Nate eventually agreed with her analysis and told her he would collect the money from Joe for the items purchased. He was in tight spot, he told her, because it was his name and account that had been used.

About an hour later, Pastor Rafe called. He sounded upset. "Just pay the invoices," he demanded heatedly. "I trust Joe Dalmer with my life. He would never be dishonest or take the church in any way."

"I beg to differ with you," stated Mira calmly. "The invoices are not for church materials. They are for some other job he had on the side."

"I thought Joe and Nate checked off the items that belonged to the church," he fumed.

"I saw the checked items, Pastor, and they don't add up. Joe was not working for the church on those dates and most of the items do not relate to a tiled floor. Only one invoice appears to be ours and I have given authorization for that one to be paid, but the rest I will not authorize."

"Then I guess I'll have to pay it out of my own pocket!" He was livid with her now.

Mira took a deep breath and tried to be patient. "Pastor, you surely cannot expect the church to pay for it."

"I know those materials were used on the floor downstairs," he said furiously.

"I don't see how they could have been." Mira tried to hold on to her temper. "As I said, I have checked each invoice carefully."

"Well... I'll just have to get everyone together in my office and sort this out!"

"That's a great idea, pastor. You meet with Nate and Joe and call me when you have them there with you. Perhaps we can get this straightened out, once and for all." Several hours passed before the phone rang again.

"Uh... Mira, this is Pastor." Rafe's voice sounded distant. "I have you on speaker phone and Joe and Jonathan are here with me."

"Where's Nate? I thought he would be there also."

"Well, uh...he was willing to leave everything in our hands."

"Okay... let's see if we can get this settled then." Mira went through each invoice again and explained in detail why she felt the majority of the supplies were not used on the church job. Jonathan agreed with her analysis with one small exception; some grout Joe had picked up for him.

Mira quickly agreed to pay for the grout. "I will authorize the payment for this one item and instruct Ina to cut a check tomorrow. Other than that, are we all in agreement that no other payments will be made by the church?" She wanted clear affirmation from each one. "Everything else is Joe's responsibility," she repeated. "Do you agree, Joe? Jonathan? Pastor?" She heard three separate voices concur with the arrangement.

"Then this matter is concluded. There should be no further invoices from this company billed to the church. This is the end of it! I want to be certain that everyone understands this." The three men assured her that everything was completed satisfactorily. She sighed as she hung up the receiver. "I truly hope this is the last I ever hear of it!"

This did not prove to be the case, however. The very next day, Lucy called, insisting angrily that the invoices be paid in full. Mira was fast losing her patience with the woman. One more time she carefully went over what was being paid and why, only to be told that the church still owed Joe for the invoices.

"Lucy," she said determinedly, "you have to understand that this matter was resolved last night. Your husband agreed with the resolution and assured me that there would be no further request for money. There is nothing more I can do. The matter is finished!"

More protesting followed with a lengthy speech recounting the great blessing the Dalmers were to the assembly and how much they had sacrificed in time and money. After she had heard about all she could stand, the woman finally hung up.

Mira paced the floor allowing the conversation to replay itself over and over like a tape recorder in her head. Her thoughts raced in turmoil and confusion. "I just don't get it!" she cried aloud. "I thought this was finally settled and done with. Everyone agreed!" She was so angry she could feel the blood pounding in her ears.

Valin reached out and touched her shoulder softly, while Caelen spoke words of comfort and peace into her spirit. Throwing herself down on the couch, Mira took a few deep breaths in an effort to calm down. Tears of anger and frustration coursed down her cheeks. *I need to pull myself together before Dan sees me like this,* she thought with a sigh. *I should probably pray about it but I sure don't feel like it!* Although she couldn't see the warrior beside her, she suddenly felt an overwhelming compulsion to slip to her knees.

Burying her face in her arms, she wept. "Oh Lord, I am so angry and upset! I know I'm not handling this the way I should, as a Christian. I came so close to losing my temper and shouting at her. Even though that didn't happen, I know that my tone wasn't very nice." She cringed as she remembered her shortness with Lucy. "God, I really need your help," she wailed. "Please help me to love people as I should because I sure can't do this on my own. I know I'm without excuse. I guess I need a lot more patience! Please forgive me for my attitude and help me to be kind and loving and patient. I do love you, Lord and I want to be more like you. It's just so hard sometimes! Please give me wisdom and help me to walk daily in love and forgiveness."

Mira stayed on her knees for quite awhile, sobbing out her woes into the ever listening ear of the One who always loves and forgives. When she rose to her feet, her whole countenance had changed. It shone with renewed peace and gentle calm. She felt as if she had been ministered to by angels.

Popping her favourite CD into the stereo, she hummed along to the music as she resumed her household tasks. Glorious strains of worship and praise filled the room lifting her soul and spirit to new heights. She found herself immersed in praising her Savior – the One who had redeemed her from her fallen state and changed everything in her life.

By the time Dan came through the door, she was back to her usual sunny, serene self. What a difference praising the Lord had made in her attitude, she thought humbly. She found she didn't have nearly as much trouble loving Lucy now as she had earlier. Smiles softened the faces of the two formidable commanders who had watched Mira's struggle over her nature.

~

As autumn leaves twisted and tumbled in their blaze of glory, Mira found herself making her way more frequently to the new church where she occasionally led worship. Her husband seemed happy there, entering into the services with enthusiasm. They liked what they saw of the ministry of Pastor Holman. He preached sermons based on the Word of the God, which pierced like a double-bladed sword into their spirits, bringing great change in both of their lives.

It came with a price however. Although Mira was always careful to inform Pastor Rutherford whenever she was going to be away on a Sunday, she found her excuses were wearing thin by the time the first flutters of snow covered the crisp brown leaves with a blanket of white. She and Dan had just returned from a peaceful weekend spent at a cottage on a nearby lake. Scheduled to lead worship at Holman's church the following Sunday, Mira had called Pastor Rafe to let him know that she would be absent from the morning service.

Rafe was not amused and he told her so in no uncertain terms! It was not right that another pastor should ask her to lead worship in his church without asking him for permission. Mira was confused and told him so.

"Pastor, why are you so upset?" she asked. "This is the ministry that God is leading me into. You have always told us and even prophesied that those in our church will touch the nations. You should be delighted for me and supportive of my ministry."

Rafe would not be appeased. "It's wrong of Dave Holman to ask you to come so often. Some would accuse him of sheep stealing. I'm thinking of calling him about this!"

"Please don't do that!" Mira answered sharply. "I can assure you that he has never once even so much as hinted that he wished me to change churches, nor would he. He is a man of integrity."

"Well, uhh....I'm sure he is, but I'm just saying, there's a matter of protocol here and he should know better. Most ministers would ask for permission to use someone who attends another church."

"Really? I didn't know that," replied Mira calmly. "So... you *ask* then before you use anyone to sing or minister at our church?"

Rafe ignored the thrust. Changing the subject, he asked if the trio could sing in the Sunday night service. Mira told him that she would contact the others and find out if they were available.

Replacing the receiver thoughtfully into its cradle, she wondered if she should set up a meeting with Pastor Holman and his wife, just in case the pastor should decide to go behind her back and talk with him. *It's queer how upset Pastor got. He doesn't think anything of stealing someone from another congregation. He bribes them with positions to lure them away from other assemblies to our church. Does he think I'm too stupid to know that? Everyone knows it, for goodness sake! Obviously he feels that any ministry I have is second-rate. I guess he believes he is so far above everyone else that our ministries or God's call on our lives must take second place to his will.*

Upon further reflection, Mira decided to wait and see how things developed before saying anything to Pastor Holman. Truthfully, she was feeling a strong pull to the other assembly, partly because there was no stress put on her there. Her ministry was accepted; the people showered her with love and, for the first time in many years, she was hearing the Word of God preached. It was like a banquet feast to a starving person. She had to admit that she didn't really want to give it up.

As she so often did these days, Mira went to her knees to pray about the matter. "Lord, I don't know what to do. Things are in a terrible turmoil at church and I know I have a responsibility as long as I am on the board. I don't want to let anyone down, including you, Lord. I know you placed me there for a reason and I'm trying to do what is right, but I can't help thinking that you could be preparing me for another assembly. Is that it, Lord? Do I need to walk away? You know how much I care for the people. This has been my church for almost fourteen years. It's hard, Father! What should I do?"

No answers came to Mira as she waited on God hoping for a definite Word. She prayed again for wisdom and discernment as well as love for her pastor. "Father," she cried, "I'm going to put this into your hands. Please Lord, you be the one to close the door here if you want me to leave. I have to be sure! You be the one to open all the doors in my life and to close the ones that are necessary. Thank you, Lord. I know that you have my best interests at heart as well as a plan for this church. Whatever it is Lord, I want to be part of it, but only if that is Your will."

Two silent listeners ministered reassurance and comfort to Mira. "We must aid her," said Caelen to his companion. "She has need of a safe haven now. Let us visit this Pastor Holman and see what manner of man he is."

"I have heard good things but a visit wouldn't hurt," agreed Valin.

~

Mira was worried about Dan. Although her husband wasn't one to complain, she knew when he was in pain. Following a particularly restless night in which he had tossed and turned, moaning in agony for most of the night, he finally reached his breaking point. He could stand it no longer.

"I think you'd better call the doctor," he panted, the sweat standing thick on his brow.

Dan's visit to their family doctor brought a quick referral to a specialist in urology who ordered an exhaustive round of tests. The diagnosis was a blow, as devastating as it was unexpected.

"Sir, I'm sorry to tell you that you have cancer of the bladder."

The "C" word! Mira's heart leaped with fear! Her mind, numb with shock, scarcely took in the remainder of the interview as the doctor explained the treatment options to them. She had lost several members of her family to the deadly disease. Her own beloved mother had wasted away, eventually losing the battle for her life on Christmas day of all days. *I can't stand to go through this again?* she thought dazedly.

Scarcely a word passed between them as they drove home. Dan felt as if he had been kicked in the teeth. Forced to face his own mortality, his attempt to wrap his head around the news seemed futile in the silence of that half hour drive. Mira quietly wiped away the tears which forced their way down her cheeks, not wanting her husband to see her panic and dismay.

When the interminable ride ended, Dan disappeared into the bedroom and throwing himself on the bed, he turned his face to the wall. "If anyone phones, tell them I'm sleeping," he called out.

Sensing that he needed to be left alone for awhile, Mira unplugged the phone and quietly left the house. She needed some time herself to process the news. Driving to one of her favourite trails down by the wide rambling river which coursed through their city, she spent the next few hours hiking in solitude. She wasn't ready to share this terrible thing with anyone except her Lord. To Him she poured out her heart in an agony of tears.

The miles flew by as she pushed herself to the limit of her strength in an effort to quell the overwhelming terror that was trying to take control of her mind. Hours were spent alternating between pleading and bargaining with God or sobbing with dread and despair. She had no knowledge of the two heavenly beings who kept pace by her side.

Finally, completely worn out, she collapsed on a park bench overlooking the water. The river was running high and the sound of the rushing current seeped slowly into her consciousness, inexorably bringing with it a measure of quietness.

Valin gestured slightly with his hand. A daring little mite of a chipmunk scurried across her foot, stopping directly in front of her to see if she had any offerings. She smiled down at him in spite of the wrenching pain that racked her chest.

"Aren't you a feisty little thing?" she asked aloud, reaching into her pocket for a tissue to wipe away her tears. "You're pretty adorable, but I guess you know that." She laughed now at his begging antics, wishing she had some food to give him.

Looking around her, she noticed the scampering squirrels storing their tiny treasures and dainty tidbits for feasting upon during the cold winter months. A large flock of birds suddenly rose from the trees, swooping and circling high above her head. She fancied they might be trying to decide if today was a good day to wing their way south. The splendour of fall colors engulfed her senses, while the smell of dried leaves and damp earth filled her nostrils.

What a gorgeous day it is! She wondered why she hadn't noticed earlier. She bowed her head. "Father God," she prayed, "I have given myself to you and I know that You care for me as a father cares for his child. Our times are in your hands and you know what is best for our lives. I ask you for Dan's healing from this terrible disease. Please make him completely well again. Help me to put my faith in you alone. Give me peace in this whole situation, Lord. I love you and I want to serve you with all of my heart, no matter what circumstances I find myself in. I ask you to take away all fear, in the name of Jesus. I thank you for your love and your faithfulness to me."

Mira returned to her car in a different fame of mind from that which had driven her from her home. Her eyes drank in the beauty of God's creation and peace reigned in her heart. Hope swelled in her breast for the first time since she had heard the news of her husband's illness. She knew that God was her strength and help in this time of trouble.

The angels ministered strength and peace to her spirit. They would continue their unceasing watch over her life with the knowledge that she would need their aid even more in the days to come.

Dan's treatment program was scheduled to begin immediately. The urologist had tried to prepare them for the first procedure, which would be extremely painful without anaesthetic. This would be followed by a lengthy program of six weeks of chemotherapy followed by six weeks rest after which it would begin all over again.

Mira contacted family and friends, requesting prayer for her husband. She found much needed strength in their faithful support. Calling the church, she shared the news with Faith, who promised to put Dan on the prayer list and to let Pastor Rutherford know.

The night before the first procedure, just as they were getting ready to retire for the night, Pastor Rafe called and asked to speak to Dan. Mira was surprised and relieved. *Better late than never,* she thought. Finally, Pastor was showing an interest in her husband! She felt grateful that he thought enough of them to call and pray before the procedure. This gesture would go a long way in softening her husband's heart toward the man. These thoughts were uppermost in her mind as she handed the phone to Dan.

The call was brief. Pastor Rafe wanted Dan to come over to the parsonage immediately to replace the batteries in his security system. Dan, in disbelief over the request, refused to go out at that hour and told him to call the security company to come and take care of the problem. The conversation came to an abrupt end when the pastor realized that he was not going to be able to persuade him to come.

Mira's heart sank as her husband related the reason behind the call. "How could he do that?" she exclaimed angrily. "He knows you're having surgery tomorrow morning and he expects you to go over there at this hour because he can't replace a battery!" she cried.

"That's who he is. It's always about him and what he needs or wants," replied Dan flatly. "I don't know why you're so upset. I certainly didn't expect anything from him."

Mira's protective instincts rose. "How about a little common decency? Is that too much to expect from our pastor? I don't know anyone who would call at this hour and expect you to drop everything and come running at his beck and call. It's a half hour drive one way! And you with surgery in the morning! Did he even mention it?"

"Of course not! I doubt if he even thought of it. I'm not that important to him."

After taking his last dose of pain medication, Dan slept heavily, for which Mira was thankful. She dozed fitfully throughout the night, alternately praying and listening to her husband snore.

The first procedure went well and for the next five weeks, once per week, Mira drove Dan to the hospital for the painful bladder washes. She continued to believe and pray for his complete healing, asking the Lord for a good report from the doctors at the end of the first six weeks. At that time, they would re-evaluate her husband's condition before beginning the next round of chemotherapy.

11

Mira wasn't sure why she agreed to go to the women's breakfast. It wasn't being held at her church and she had no particular reason to attend. The invitation had come out of the clear blue from a woman she barely knew; someone she had met briefly at a similar function a few months earlier.

Mira had been the speaker then, sharing her testimony of deliverance from depression. She could still recall her nervousness as she faced the packed room but, in spite of that, God used her story to touch a number of women that day. Several had been so affected they bolted from the room in the middle of her talk. At first, she was afraid that perhaps she had offended them, but later learned this was not the case from the assigned counsellors who found them crying in the hallway. Each had returned, and at the close of the meeting, had come to her to unburden their hearts and ask for prayer.

So many hurting women; Mira's heart went out to them. She felt a special connection to those who walked with heads down, shuffling through life with no hope; every day a misery. Various opportunities had opened for her to speak both in her own church and others. She had appeared as a guest on Pastor Holman's radio broadcast following a talk she gave at his monthly church breakfast. In February she was booked to speak a Valentine's banquet. God was continually surprising her with open doors and opportunities to share His abundant love and compassion and in this she found her greatest contentment.

The anguish Mira had experienced of late over the unethical practices of her pastor had cut her to the quick. On the one hand, she had to admit that God was using her in an unprecedented way to touch the lives of hurting women. On the other however, were growing difficulties and storms within the church and the recent heavy blow of Dan's illness. It was all too much to process and she found herself struggling daily with feelings of inadequacy that hounded her, regarding duty and loyalty to the pastor and the board. So much time and effort was expended on fixing problems and putting out unnecessary fires, caused by the inappropriate behavior of Pastor Rafe; time that was robbed from her precious husband who needed her.

In her heart of hearts, Mira knew that she had come too far to turn back now, but there were times when she wished with all her might that she could turn back the clock, wiping out the past few months. She desperately wanted to see her pastor as the nearly perfect icon she had once adored.

Entering the building with halting steps, Mira debated with herself whether to go or stay. *I should be at home with Dan,* she thought ruefully, wishing she hadn't promised to come.

An invisible warrior leaned over and whispered soothingly into her ear. *Well,* she thought, *I'm here now anyway. I guess I'd better at least check it out.* Valin nodded brightly and smiled encouragingly at Caelen.

Following a couple of women, Mira descended the stairs and found the banquet hall which had been rented for the ladies' breakfast event. *I can slip away quietly as soon as the meeting is done. Look on the bright side, girl. Who knows? Maybe the speaker will be so good that I'll want to arrange for her come and share at one of our meetings. At least I'll have this opportunity to hear her and decide.*

The woman who had invited her suddenly materialized from a side room and greeted her with a warm hug. After a few introductions, even though she still felt a little out of place among so many strangers, Mira found herself actually enjoying the laughter and chatter, as the ladies mingled and helped themselves to the buffet. The atmosphere was light and carefree, a pleasant change from the anxiety that tormented her spirit whenever she darkened the doors of her own church.

From the time the speaker started until she ended, the Holy Spirit's presence was evident in the room. There didn't seem to be any of the constraint that Mira felt in her own church. At the conclusion of the message, an invitation was given to come forward for prayer. She hesitated, fighting an overwhelming urge to step forward with the others. Finally, acquiescing to the tug of the Holy Spirit, she slipped into place at the very end of the line.

When the speaker reached her, she stopped for a moment and reaching forward, she took Mira's hands in hers. Mira started to tremble as she felt a strange surge of power sweep through her body.

"You are like a person in waiting," the woman proclaimed without hesitation. "It is as if you are in a waiting room filled with people. You are wondering if you should step up and take a number. You aren't sure if it will be worth the wait or whether you should just leave now. You should take the number and await your turn. Go to the wicket! There is an executive position there, a job to do. What you are called to do will be made clear to you in time. You won't be kept waiting for long." Following a brief prayer, the woman turned away to minister to others who had just joined the line.

Stunned, Mira stumbled back to her seat. She scrambled through her purse for a pen and something to write on. Someone handed her a piece of paper and on it was written everything the woman had said. Her hands trembled as she looked over the words that had been spoken. It was amazing how wonderfully they fit into her current situation. This was the confirmation that she needed. It was something to hold on to!

Mira dropped her face into her hands and wept out her thanks and praise to her heavenly Father. She hadn't realized how much she needed this affirmation from the Lord. New resolve poured into her spirit, bolstering her sagging strength, steadying her nerve. She knew, beyond a shadow of a doubt, that God wanted her to stay and see the church situation through to the end. The uncertainty she had been grappling with lifted in that hour. She was in the right place, at the right time, and God would take care of the details.

November days gave way to the hustle and bustle of the holiday season. Christmas parties abounded and Mira found herself busy with preparations for the final Women's Ministries meeting of the year. She threw herself whole heartedly into the thing, supervising each detail, wanting it to be perfect. The end of the year was fast approaching now and she wasn't sure if she would be here another year. She was living month to month, almost week to week. Perhaps the New Year would see her entering a new phase of her life. As exciting as that was to contemplate, a certain sadness and nostalgia sometimes overwhelmed her, leaving her teary-eyed and heavy hearted.

The annual Christmas banquet at the church, she decided to skip because Dan refused to attend the event. He would not be a hypocrite, he had told her, and pretend that everything was alright. It hadn't helped that this year the entertainment highlight of the evening would feature the musical talents of the pastor and his extended family. Instead, she and Dan hosted a fun evening of games, laughter and song with a few of their closest friends.

The banquet was not the only occasion that Mira had to deal with during the holiday season. Mrs. Rutherford instructed Faith to send the customary invitations to all council members and their spouses to attend a Christmas party at the parsonage. This had become an annual event over the years and it was generally accepted that everyone invited would attend. When Mira showed the invitation to Dan, he refused to even think about it. He wasn't the only one. Some of the board members spoke to her also about being very uncomfortable with the party's location. In the end, they refused to go to the pastor's house and pretend that all was well.

Faith eventually confided in her that only two or three had accepted the invitation. "I feel badly for Eve," she told Mira.

"I do too. I doubt if Mrs. R. is aware of what has transpired lately or how badly her husband treats council members so she won't have any idea why they won't come." Mira paused. "Faith, I can't ask Dan to come. I'm not sure he would anyway, even for me! He already told me that he won't go."

"I really don't have a choice," sighed Faith with a crestfallen face. "I'm expected to be there to help with the food and the clean-up. Eve wanted me to prepare some games too." She looked worn. "I told Pastor that I just can't do games this year. I haven't the heart for it." A tear slid down her cheek. "Rob doesn't want to go either. He said it would make him feel like a hypocrite."

Later, at the mid-week service, Mira was chased down by Pastor Rafe as she was making her way to the door at the end of the service. "We've decided not to have the usual council Christmas party," he told her. "Apparently there are too many that can't make it for one reason or another. Faith and Ina were thinking that we might have a party at the Steakhouse Restaurant instead and include all of the leaders and volunteers. What do you think?"

Mira peered at him out of tired eyes. All of the worry over church affairs and her husband's health were taking their toll. "What about the money?" she asked. "Something of that magnitude would need a board meeting to approve the expenditure. Do you have numbers and prices?"

"You could call the board members for permission," he suggested, smiling archly.

"No, I can't." replied Mira tartly. "I'm exhausted! It would require my spending most of tomorrow on the phone, back and forth between board members, trying to get approval for another last minute affair. I haven't even got prices to give them. It's simply too late to even think of it!"

"Don't worry about it," he replied soothingly, seeing her agitation. "I'll handle it myself. I'll make all of the calls or get the office staff to do it. I understand there's a special deal on that night so it shouldn't be very expensive.

Later, Mira heard from Ina that the party had indeed been transferred from the Rutherford home to the restaurant. She assumed that permission must have been obtained from the other board members, so she said nothing about her altercation with the pastor. Dan even agreed to go because it wasn't being held at the parsonage as did most of the council members.

The evening was at least partially successful, with church leaders and volunteers having an opportunity to enjoy one another's fellowship. The only hitch to the evening occurred when the dessert menus were handed out. Pastor Rafe quickly intervened, asking everyone to refrain from ordering. "My wife and I would like to invite you all to come back to the parsonage for dessert and coffee," he said smoothly.

Annoyed council members saw right through his ploy. He was trying to manipulate them, using his wife and the other volunteers, in order to force them to comply with his desire to end the party at his place and thereby save face.

"It's still about winning," Dan grumbled. "He always has to win."

Mira had to admit that it seemed like the pastor always managed to get his way. No one quite knew what to do after that, so everyone quickly dispersed with the majority returning home. Most had no desire to attend the little gathering at the parsonage except for an unwitting few.

Ina told Mira later that the expected special was not offered during the holidays. "I pulled the pastor aside to quietly tell him, but it was too late to do anything about it," she confided. "I asked him not to make any scene but to let the people order what they wanted since it was supposed to be for volunteer appreciation. I was so embarrassed when he told everyone not to order dessert or coffee. It wasn't right to do that, especially since not too many returned to the parsonage."

"I'm sure he didn't care about the money," Mira responded. "It was probably the only way he could think of to force us to at least finish the party at his place. Maybe Eve had some unpleasant questions when so many refused to come there in the first place. Did Pastor ever call the board for approval on the party expenditure?" she asked out of curiosity.

"Not that I'm aware of."

"I didn't think so. I wonder how much it will cost."

"It'll be more than we thought but the pastor said that he has permission, according to the constitution, to spend $600.00. He suggested that I let him know how much extra the bill was and he might put some in to cover the excess."

"Wait a minute! There is nothing in the constitution that gives him permission to spend anything without board approval," Mira observed dryly. "We had a conversation about the party last Wednesday night and he promised me that he would take care of getting permission from the board. I might have known better," she added bitterly.

"Are you sure about him not having authority to spend any amount under $600.00?"

"I'm absolutely certain! Hoo boy! I'm not going to enjoy raising this issue at the next board meeting.

The week before Christmas, Faith called Mira with the news that Pastor Rafe was insisting on a full council meeting in two days. "I know it is short notice," she said apologetically, "but you know how he is. He's getting ready to go on vacation right after New Years Day and I guess he has some things that he wants to clear up. He wants to talk to you as well. I'll try to get him on the line for you."

In a few moments, Mira heard Pastor Rafe's deep voice greeting her. He came straight to the point. "As you know, I've been trying to persuade Grace to come and work with us for the better part of a year now. I urged her to consider it when she was here during the summer camp meeting." He paused. "I really need someone in place for the first week in January. Do you think she would come?"

Mira was stunned. She knew that he had mentioned something to her sister-in-law about coming to work with him but had just assumed it was so much hot air. When Grace asked her about the invitation, she had told her that she didn't think it a good idea. Too many ministers who had tried to work with him had come and gone. Many of them had started out on a voluntary basis, in good faith, with the promise of a salary when the numbers increased. That time had never come for them. Either the goals had been changed or they had fallen out of the good graces of the senior pastor. In any case, they had all left with a bad taste in their mouth.

"I...I really have no idea," Mira stuttered. "There would have to be a contract or she couldn't even consider it." *And that will be the end of that!* She thought cynically.

"I don't think that will be a problem. I'll ask the council myself. Do you think she will come?"

Whew! He's really serious about this. Mira's thoughts were racing. "I guess you'll have to ask her to find out. It's really short notice!" *Fly by the seat of your pants just the same as always,* she reflected derisively.

"Would you mind giving her a call? I really need to know her answer before the council meeting the day after tomorrow."

"I'll call her," she replied. "I'll ask her to call you with her answer as soon as possible."

Mira felt dazed as she hung up the phone. *I certainly hope she says no.* Anxiety filled her heart and a sick feeling in the pit of her stomach made her want to lie down. *He will tear her apart! It's like leading a lamb to the slaughter. She doesn't know what she is dealing with or what position this puts me in. Here I am, almost ready to walk out! I can't very well do that if she comes. How would it look to everyone if I leave just as my sister-in-law is coming on board? Maybe she won't come.*

But Mira's hopes were soon dashed. She had several conversations with her sister-in-law in the two days following her phone call with the pastor. It seemed that Grace grew more excited each time she spoke with her about the possibility of coming. Mira was strong in her warning to insist on a written contract. "Do not even think of coming here without it," she declared firmly.

After much soul searching, she decided to share some of the things that had been occurring between the pastor and the board. "We are all on the verge of walking out or at least four of the six board members are," she told Grace, as she divulged her despair over her pastor's integrity. "Please think long and hard about this! Pray about it!"

"I have been praying about it," Grace had insisted. "Even your brother is in agreement that I should come. I really feel that this is in God's plan for my life right now."

"But I thought you wanted to travel evangelistically," faltered Mira miserably.

"I've spoken with Pastor Rafe about that and he has agreed on an arrangement that will allow me speak in other churches once per month."

"Get it in writing!"

"Mira, did you ever think that perhaps I can be of some assistance in calming things down between the board and Pastor Rafe? Maybe that's why God is leading me to come." Grace pleaded. "You sound as if you hate the idea! Do you think I'll be that much of a failure?" Blunt as always, she was trying to understand why Mira didn't want her there.

"Of course not!" Mira's voice held the hint of tears. "You just don't have any concept of how he destroys people; especially those who work for him. I've heard some things and I know first hand what he's like to work with now. You can't trust anything he says!"

"I've preached for him many times," Grace insisted, "and he has always treated me well. He even refers to me as his daughter."

"Daughter!" Mira snorted. "He doesn't mean a word of it! You just disagree with him once and see how much of a daughter you are! I know you think you've worked with him in the past, but you were only here for a day or two as an evangelist. He can be very gracious and charming in public. It is totally different working day in and day out with the man. You'll see that I'm right!"

"Even if that's true, he's not going to be around at all for the first month and if everything goes well, he said he may take three whole months," she reasoned. "So it's not as if I'll be seeing a lot of him. I've requested a four month contract so I'll only be there until May 5th. I told him that I need a few days to finish up some business here, so I can't come until the end of the first week of January. You know, Mira, it's been a lifelong dream of mine to come and work with Pastor Rafe. I grew up listening to him on television. He can't have changed that much. I'm sure everything will work out just fine. He even told me that I can use the parsonage when he and Mrs. R. are in Florida. I thought that was really gracious of him to allow me to use his home. I won't even be a bother to you at all. I can get an apartment when he returns or he had some suggestions of people I could stay with."

"Well," Mira sighed, "I guess you'll have to find out the hard way. Who knows," she added, "maybe it will work out if he really takes the sabbatical?"

She felt rotten after ending the conversation; sick with worry. Dan didn't make her feel any better when he heard. "Is she crazy?" he roared. "Why would she want to work with that liar? She'll be sorry, mark my words!"

"We must be even more vigilant from now on." Caelen's voice was compelling as he instructed the other commanders. "Jezebel has the ear of the pastor and he works tirelessly day and night to pervert and distort his thinking. Unfortunately, the man has given himself so completely over to his own lusts that even the most skilled of us cannot pierce the shell of pride and superiority that encompasses him."

Jarah looked discouraged. "I speak to him constantly but his ear is attuned only to the whispers of the enemy. He rarely reads the Word, only opening it to grab a quick verse to bolster his own thoughts and ideas. He will not wait upon the Lord but spends his time in unholy pursuits. By his own will, he gives the Holy Spirit no access."

"Python extends his power daily also," added Captain Darshan. "My warriors are hard pressed to find a foothold anywhere. He is slowly squeezing the life out of the people."

"We are not giving up though, are we?" asked Valin, a troubled expression on his countenance.

"Never!" replied Caelen fiercely. "We will not surrender so much as one of the Lord's chosen lambs!"

"The shepherd is growing more desperate in his attempt to gain control over the legal governing board of this assembly," Jarah warned. "Failing that, he will use every skill he possesses to rid himself of them."

"Then we must surround them constantly and give them our full protection and aid."

Captain Darshan nodded fiercely at Caelen's words. "We will not fail them."

12

MIRA READIED HER TABLE for the council meeting. She had prepared two agendas, one for council and one for the board meeting which would be required to approve the resulting paperwork for Grace, if the council vote was favourable.

A small band of angels, led by Captain Darshan, warded council members along with the mighty Caelen and Valin. Demons of all sizes filled the room, capering about the aisles, brandishing their evil weapons and screaming hoarsely at the warriors, trying to provoke a fight.

Rafe, for once, bypassed his normal pontificating and delays and came straight to the point. "I am tired out," he announced, sighing delicately. "In fact, I'm really completely exhausted. I feel that I need to take a much needed break immediately following New Year's Day."

After whining about his unrelenting work schedule to enlist their sympathies, he adroitly underscored his lack of vacation time. "I haven't had even one real vacation in fifteen years." He proffered the falsehood shamelessly, knowing that he wouldn't be challenged.

The council members sat in silence, each one wary of becoming the target of his evil glares or worse - his considerable verbal skills. They knew he would annihilate them if they dared to disagree. Besides, the lie would almost be palatable if it meant that he was going to be gone for awhile. Their countenances brightened at the possibility of the long awaited sabbatical.

Mira jotted down a reminder note for herself. She would check with Faith on exactly how many days of vacation Pastor Rafe had taken in the past year. If memory served her correctly, she surmised the figure to be fairly substantial, but she wouldn't risk saying anything without proof in front of her. They were all prepared to let the statement pass but, for her own peace of mind, she wanted to know the exact truth of it. There had been so many lies and half-truths of late that it seemed every statement he made must be verified.

Scarcely daring to breath, they waited for his sabbatical announcement, hoping against hope for a lengthy reprieve from dealing with him at all.

"I know there have been some who have been urging me to take a sabbatical," Rafe began tentatively. "Although I would like to do this and feel that God has called me to do it, I don't feel comfortable leaving the church with Pastor Marvin in charge. I don't think he will be able to hold the crowds while I am gone."

"That's true, pastor." It was Phil Schmidt that spoke. "The numbers always drop when you go away."

"I know," he replied, sighing loudly. "You all know my feelings regarding Pastor Marvin. He's all right as an assistant but he just wouldn't cut it as a senior pastor. He doesn't have what it takes." He paused for a moment and cleared his throat. "I would like to ask someone else to come; someone who has the required preaching skills and is also well liked by the congregation. I know you will agree with me on my choice." His smile was oily and smooth. "I am talking about Grace Benning."

He looked at Mira, his face beaming, before continuing. "After all, who could we possible find on such short notice that could preach any better than Grace?"

"Would she be willing to come?" asked Rev. Armstrong timidly.

"Yes, she is willing. As a matter of fact, I have a letter here from her that I'd like to read and a proposal for you to consider."

At this juncture, Mira raised her hand for recognition. When the pastor nodded at her, she stood to her feet, clearing her throat nervously. "Gentlemen, I would like to excuse myself from these proceedings. Since Grace is my sister-in-law, I feel that it would be unethical of me to stay. I want everyone to be free to consider the proposal and vote openly without worrying about my reaction or opinion."

Rafe was surprised. "Oh, I don't think it's necessary for you to leave the room," he said with a smile. "Everyone here loves Grace. That's no secret." He looked around jovially.

"It's the right thing to do," Mira insisted gently, but firmly. "If one of you gentlemen would please come and get me when this motion has been decided, I would appreciate it." She was already moving toward the door.

As she paced back and forth in the lobby, Mira prayed. "Father, let your will be done here. If she is not meant to come, then please close the door on this. But if it is your will Lord, please protect her and don't allow her to be hurt. Father, help me and the rest of the board to stand steady. Give us strength to bear whatever burden you place on us. I ask these things in the name of Jesus and I thank you for the answer."

The two commanders, who shadowed her constantly, walked at her side as she strode nervously back and forth, speaking quiet words of comfort and strength all the while.

Mira heard Ian's footsteps coming down the full length of the corridor. He poked his head around the corner, a big grin on his face. "We're ready for you," he said beckoning her back into the meeting.

The pastor appeared smug as they entered the room. "She took a unanimous vote," he declared, his delight evidenced by his broad smile.

Was there ever any doubt? Mira thought weakly as she took her place again. *I have a feeling that he usually gets what he wants, one way or another.* Suddenly she felt as if the strength had been drained out of her.

Rafe seemed anxious now to conclude the meeting. "I had originally planned to leave right after New Year's Day. In fact, my wife has already purchased her airline ticket, but apparently Grace can't come until January 5th, so I'm going to delay my own departure slightly. I really feel I should spend a couple of days with her here before I join my wife in Florida. For now, I will only be taking three weeks vacation. I don't feel that I can take a sabbatical until I know for sure that the church is doing well. So we'll try this and when I return at the end of January, we'll see about maybe taking the three months off that many have suggested."

Rafe cut short any further discussion, dismissing the deacons promptly so the directors could deal with the details of Grace's contract. His spirits were high as he excused himself from the room on the pretext of making an important phone call. He even took time to chat jovially with the deacons in the hallway, as they were donning their winter coats and boots. When the last man was gone, he entered his secretary's office, congratulating himself on his successful evening. He could hardly wait to wing his way southward to warmer climes leaving the freezing weather to his subordinates.

The Jezebel spirit stood next to Rafe in the office, one of his claws resting familiarly on the pastor's shoulder as he made his call. His course voice whispered constantly into the ready ear of his victim. A host of smaller demons settled like a black cloud over his head. They yowled and gibbered obscenities at the man, spewing their venom with abandon.

Rafe reluctantly cut his phone conversation short, promising to call again later. It wouldn't do to leave the directors alone together for too long, he thought. The demons followed him as he left the room, tumbling over one another in their haste, each one wanting to be closest to their prey.

The board meeting was in full progress when he entered and took his place. The minutes of the last director's meeting had already been dealt with and Mira was just raising the issue of the Christmas party expense.

"I can explain that," Rafe announced easily. "Faith and Ina thought it would be good idea to honor all of the volunteers with an appreciation dinner. We usually have the Christmas dinner for the council members and their wives, but this year, there were only a few who could make it... although I noticed that most were able to come to the restaurant," he added viciously, the color rising in his cheeks. "My wife was devastated when she found out that hardly anyone was coming. You know, when the...uh... when the queen invites you for dinner, you don't refuse to come."

Mira stared at him and then looked at the circle of men in disbelief. They showed no reaction. *Had he really said that? S*he almost questioned her own hearing. *Soooo...that would make him the king, I guess,* she thought wryly. *Wow! I wonder if any of the rest caught that!* She made an effort to concentrate on what he was saying.

"....so we didn't know about the special not being valid during the holidays and when I saw the bill, I put in a couple of hundred dollars of my own money to help cover the excess expenditure. You all know that I have authority to spend up to $600.00 without approval."

Mira cleared her throat. "I have a copy of the constitution here and as far as I'm aware, there is no such clause. I certainly can't find it, if it exists. One could also argue that, even if it were true, you could spend thousands of dollars with no accountability whatsoever as long as you kept each bill under the prescribed amount. Of course, that wouldn't be ethical." She paused. "The board is responsible to the government for all expenditures. Pastor, you told me a week ago that you would call each of the directors to ask for approval for this expense. Did you call?"

"Well...no, I didn't," he admitted sheepishly. "Faith and Ina thought it was a good idea to include the volunteers and with the special, it wouldn't have exceeded the $600.00."

"But we've already established that you have no authority to spend any amount without board approval," she reiterated patiently. "You told me that you would call and you didn't." Turning to the directors she asked for confirmation. "Did any of you receive a phone call on this matter from anyone?"

"The only phone call I got was to invite us to come to the party," said Jack. Everyone responded similarly.

The color of Rafe's face deepened a shade. "I didn't think I had to ask permission," he blustered angrily. "Just wait until everyone hears that this board won't even give the volunteers who work so hard all year a lousy dinner."

"And who will tell them what is said in a closed board meeting?" asked Mira coldly.

"Well....these things have a way of leaking out."

"Yes, I'll just bet they do." Mira gripped her temper firmly. Making an extraordinary effort to keep her voice steady, she wearily repeated the criteria for obtaining the board's approval for spending. *He just doesn't get it!* she thought despairingly. *It doesn't matter what I say or how I phrase it, he just doesn't get it! What is the matter with him!*

They went round and round going over the same ground several times with no headway being made. The knowledge, that issues like this would resurface again and again, caused Mira's frustration to increase as she listened to her pastor deny, blame, bully and threaten.

Rafe glowered darkly. "In my forty five years of ministry, I've never had a board like this one," he said accusingly. "I want to know who supports me here."

Mira felt her heart turn over. *He's going to ask us to raise our hands!* "God!" she pleaded silently, "don't let him do that!"

He turned on her sharply, as if he could hear her thoughts. "Haven't I always been there for you?" he snarled. "Haven't I walked with you through your deepest valleys?" She hung her head without reply.

"I want an answer," he said heatedly, his mouth twisted in a grimace.

Mira slowly raised her eyes. Her mouth was dry and her heart pounded. Fear and old pain overwhelmed her, nearly blinding her to the presence of the others in the room. All she saw was the accusing, distorted face of her once beloved pastor bending toward her, disgust written plainly on his countenance. *He's going to reveal everything that I shared with him the day I nearly took my life,* she thought despairingly. *I have to stop him!*

"Yes," Her words were mumbled. She felt aggrieved and forsaken.

"What did you say?" His voice grated harshly on her tender spirit.

"Yes," she said a little louder, struggling past the nausea in her stomach as bile rose up in her throat. She felt as if she was sliding back to those bleak, dark days of her life.

Every demon in the enclosed space of the room turned toward Mira, concentrating the force of their exertion on this new vulnerability they sensed in her. Chanting desperately, they tried to find a door of access as they crowded closer, forming their formidable wedge of power.

Leaping forward, Caelen drove the scalding white shaft of his sword into the hulking bulk of the demon of fear. All of the vast might of heaven howled silently in his limbs. His thrust brought howls of anguish from his victim. Molten greenish vapour sizzled from its distorted hideous flesh.

Catching a glimpse of Shame attempting to slide in surreptitiously from the side, Valin whirled about, fire blazing from his blade. With his lips pulled back from his teeth, he charged the demon head on, taking him down in a bone-crushing grip all the while hacking at the blood-sucking limbs that tried to encompass him. Captain Darshan dove into the fray with a roar. Several more warriors leaped to defend his back.

A single thought struggled to the forefront of the whirlwind swirling through Mira's mind. She grasped hold of it.

It wasn't Pastor Rafe that helped me. It was God that brought me out of the pit I was in! It came to her with startling clarity that she had given her pastor far too much credit for her miraculous recovery from her devastating depression. It dawned on her that there had been many friends and family who had stood by her. Faith was one who had called almost every day to encourage and pray with her. Pastor Rafe had tried to take credit even for that! He had only come to see her once, although she had spent weeks in hospital. Come to think of it, whenever he had called, there had always been something he wanted from her. No! Any credit for her recovery belonged to God alone. He had pulled her out of her pit and set her feet on solid ground again, enveloping her in His great love.

It's too late now to say anything, she thought dispiritedly, her body drooping in discouragement again. *He'd just tear me apart anyway.*

Rafe had turned on Donny. "Didn't I help you when you were going through your divorce?" He had completely forgotten that he had been on the verge of asking for a vote of confidence.

The unseen battle raged on as the warriors struggled to keep the air around the council free of the demon horde.

Realizing the utter uselessness of trying to make any further point regarding the expenditure and desperate to keep the pastor from ripping Donny apart, Mira unexpectedly interrupted his tirade, bringing a motion herself to approve the invoice. She looked appealingly at the men for a seconder and Jack quickly complied. She blessed his sensitivity. A quick vote ended the matter and they all breathed easier feeling that a crisis had been averted.

The demons cautiously drew back, their aching, jaundiced eyes promising hungry retribution. Angels ringed the circle of council members, their visages stern and uncompromising; weapons drawn and shields ready.

Mira continued to pray silently while the pastor prattled on with some irrelevant nonsense. She wondered about his reactions when things didn't go his way. The confusion that had filled her mind slowly dissipated allowing her to think more clearly.

Suddenly, it was as though a light bulb lit up inside of her head. *He doesn't seem to be able to grasp or understand what I was trying to say. No, that's not right. He's a very intelligent man and he understands it alright – he's just incapable of accepting it! That's it! Why haven't I seen it before? He doesn't understand the connection of any consequences to his actions. He's a complete narcissist!*

Mira tried to remember the traits of a narcissist from a psychology course she had taken years ago. *It fits! He is totally self-centered without any remorse for his deeds, unreliable, undependable, manipulative, insensitive, and controlling. He always has to be right! He has to win! He doesn't listen, because he doesn't care! He must control everything and he will never, under any circumstance, admit fault. He has no conscience, so he's probably a sociopath as well.* She took it a step further. *Surely, there must be some spirit connected with this type of personality or maybe even several.* Rafe was back on track again, so she abandoned her musing for the present.

Grace's contract was straightforward and swiftly dealt with. She had presented a letter of expectation which was shared and approved without controversy. Mira again offered to leave the room but was asked to remain by the directors.

The last item on the agenda was the cleaning contract which would expire at the end of the year. Several bids had been submitted for the board to look at. Sylvester seemed happy to report that although Lorena had submitted a bid, she had branched out and taken on other contracts, which didn't leave her sufficient time to handle the demands of the large facility.

For her part, Mira was relieved to hear that the cleaning woman had other income sources. She had shared with some of the board what Ina had told her regarding Lorena's unpaid bill for cleaning the pastor's condo. Jack had been so incensed with the unfairness of the situation that he had insisted on paying Lorena the money owed to her by the pastor out of his own pocket.

Mira had been present when Jack gave her the money, even adding a little extra to the total because she had waited so long. Lorena had promptly burst into tears and had thanked him profusely for his thoughtfulness and generosity. Privately, Jack had told Mira that he didn't think the pastor would ever pay her and he couldn't sleep at night thinking about it.

The directors were all relieved to see that Lucy Dalmer had not submitted a bid. In all good conscience, none of them would have voted in favor of it had she done so. After some discussion, a bid was accepted and voted on.

The meeting wound to an end with Sylvester asking for the floor. The directors shifted uneasily in their chairs, knowing how long-winded his bluster could sometimes be. Mira felt a prick of anxiety as he rattled on, talking about his own ministry in past years. Warming up to his subject, he related a story of a young, inexperienced Christian man, who had assisted him in a Drop-In Center. The youth, although enthusiastic about the work, had seen evil spirits in everything, Sylvester said sneeringly. It had eventually ruined the ministry which had to close its doors.

Mira was starting to sweat. She thought she knew where he was headed with this. He had said some things in the office that day when he had talked about Donny in such derogatory terms.

Edging menacingly closer to the perimeter of angels, the demons were becoming bolder now. Their lantern eyes narrowed in anticipation. The warrior angels watched in tense silence, ignoring the brash jibes of the enemy. As if answering a call, more evil spirits began pouring into the room. Jezebel seemed to increase in strength and height, feeding upon the attitude and words of the disgruntled old man. Strife and Jealousy dove forward and finding an opening they thrust dripping daggers into Sylvester's neck.

The angels turned to counter the move but were too late to save the old man. Demons attacked from every side, driving the heavenly warriors back from their warding positions, overwhelming them with the viciousness of their assault.

Suddenly, Sylvester turned toward Jack. "You're always talking about evil spirits here and evil spirits there," he accused, jabbing a finger at him. "I'm sick of it! You see spirits in everything!"

Mira was flabbergasted. She had felt certain that it was Donny he was after.

Donny was already on his feet. "I've had just about enough of you," he said in disgust. "We should be supporting one another not tearing each other apart. Jack is a good man and I won't sit here and hear him maligned."

"You...you..." spluttered the old man, shaking his finger at Donny. "You are an evil man."

"Evil!" Jack roared. "You shut up! I will not listen to this! You are the one that is evil! You badmouth your wife to everyone who will listen. I've tried my best to work with you and all you do is complain. You told all of us that you aren't qualified to be on the board. Why don't you resign then?"

"*You* resign!" Sylvester was practically incoherent. His scraggly white hair stood on end. "You're not wanted here! And you....." he choked, turning purple and shaking his finger again in Donny's face, "you had no right to tell the pastor about the decision on Jonas. It was supposed to be the President and Vice-President that told him."

Mira caught the smirk on Rafe's face. *He's enjoying this,* she thought in dismay. "Actually that decision was never made," she interjected quickly, jumping to Donny's defence. "It was discussed generally after the meeting, if you recall."

"That isn't the way I remember it!" Sylvester stuck his big chin out aggressively. His moustache twitched threateningly.

"Does it even matter at this point?" replied Mira trying to placate the old man.

"It matters to me," he insisted belligerently.

"I....I think we had better adjourn the meeting," Rev. Armstrong stuttered. He stumbled to his feet, lips trembling. "I don't think we're going to accomplish anything now."

Mira bent over her books, hands shaking as she struggled to fit them into her bag. She wanted to wail but held herself together with pure brute force. Her face felt like a frozen mask. Looking up she caught Jack's eye. He walked over to grab his papers from the chair he had occupied. "I'm done," he said hollowly. "I'll give you my resignation this week." Mira could see determination in his stony face and it broke her heart. In a sweeping motion, he grabbed his paperwork and headed for the door.

In the midst of all of the confusion, Pastor Rafe had disappeared. Following the others down the hallway, Mira fumbled with her boots and coat, her scarf falling from nerveless fingers. Dazedly, she noticed the pastor had reappeared. He was talking with Jack in the lobby. She passed by them quickly, nodding her farewell, unable to trust herself to speak.

As she reached the door however, a sudden impulse turned her around. Walking over to where the two men stood, she reached out and touched Jack's shoulder timidly. "Please, Jack!" she implored. "Don't resign! Please! We need to stick together and see this thing through. We can't do it without you. If we go, let's do it together!" She didn't care that the pastor was standing there. Turning, she fled from the vestibule, tears coursing down her cheeks.

Grace is walking into this mess? she thought frantically as she drove out of the parking lot. *I want out of here!* She wailed out her brokenness to her Lord. "God, help us!" she cried. "Please! Help us!"

~

The battle for supremacy raged on in the spirit world. Captain Darshan and his warriors fought desperately for their survival. As the tide turned slowly and inexorably against them, it seemed that nothing could save them from being annihilated. Caelen signalled frantically and an angel immediately withdrew a silver trumpet from his robe and blew a loud blast. It lingered in the air momentarily. The demons froze in surprise, disturbed by the unusual sound.

The dark void around them started to shift ever so slightly. It began to grow brighter. White fire erupted through the walls of the building. Angels poured in from all sides to help their exhausted comrades. With their pure fire they absorbed the foul corruption spilling outward from the fray. Wielding dangerous swords, they drove back the enemy, throwing them into confusion and disarray.

With a loud cry, the captain signalled the withdrawal of his men. Flanked by the new recruits, they were able to affect an escape from the battle. The demons howled in twisted rage and torment as their prey vanished from sight.

~

Rafe went through the building, turning out lights and locking doors. He was pleased with the blow up tonight. It would make his life easier if he could shake up this board and he felt that he had made good progress in the meeting. Without Jack, Donny would likely quit and Mira wouldn't stand on her own against him. She would come around and she was still too useful to be lost. She just needed to know her place, once and for all.

Jonas was on his mind as he locked the doors of the church. Slipping and sliding on the icy parking lot, he wended his way slowly toward the house. His grandson still didn't know about the board's action in suspending his travel allowance. Rafe was too proud to say anything about the matter, as he felt it reflected on his ability to run the church as he saw fit. Also, he wasn't about to admit to anyone that he was accountable to his board. The very thought of it was utterly obnoxious! With every fibre of his being, he refused be accountable to anyone!

He was, however, running out of ideas. His attempt to have the suspension lifted through David Armstrong had failed. The old fool hadn't done a thing! He had tried his best persuasions on each of the board, both collectively and separately, with only partial success. Two weren't enough! He needed to sway at least one more to his side but the remaining four were proving surprisingly resistant. He had been sure that Ian would resign when he was replaced as head usher. That would have thrown out the balance of power. The idea he had about designating his tithe had been brilliant, but he wasn't prepared for Ina's stubborn refusal when had tried to bully her into issuing a check to Jonas. They just weren't cooperating with him at all.

Stingy with his own money, Rafe chafed at paying his grandson's travel allowance out of his own pocket. He would have to find a way to resolve this quickly. He was banking heavily on Grace's coming. She would settle down Mira and the board would then fall into line. After all, Grace was a nobody, a little farm girl from Maine. She would be so grateful to him for this wonderful opportunity that she would be willing to do almost anything to please him. He had to admit that she could preach well. She would keep the numbers up while he was away and he would eventually have everything he wanted. He would keep a careful watch from afar on things and return if she became too popular. That wouldn't do at all! Of course, he thought brightly, she would prove an excellent scapegoat, if needed, to take the blame for any problems or failure in the future.

He smiled grimly. It was too perfect really; a win-win situation. He would have his nice long rest in the sunny south at full salary and April was coming ever closer. This board would change significantly at the annual business meeting. He was already planning who he would keep and who would be dumped. He could afford to wait them out if he had to, but he really thought things would be made much easier for him with the advent of Grace.

Yessiree! Three glorious weeks of vacation; a quick trip home to ascertain the situation and off again for three months! Life was good! He was smiling as he stamped his boots at the back door of the parsonage.

13

Christmas came and went, its demanding activities leaving Mira little opportunity to dwell on the internal issues of the church. Jack called her the day after the board meeting and told her that he had prayed about resigning and talked it over with his wife. He would stay on the board for the present anyway. Mira was content with the decision. She thanked him warmly, assuring him that she didn't believe it would be for very long, perhaps only until the annual business meeting in April. Jack seemed satisfied with that.

Mira and Krysta both took part in the beautiful candlelight service on Christmas Eve singing a duet together. The service also featured many other singers from the choir and congregation. The following day was spent with family, exchanging gifts and enjoying a traditional roast turkey dinner with pumpkin pie.

Mira was glad she would have a couple of weeks to prepare for Grace's arrival. She needed some time to process the happenings in her life over the past month or two. Her husband still had one more treatment before his assessment which was scheduled for the first week of January.

Perhaps her thoughts were too full of these things as she headed downstairs one evening to watch television, a plate of food in her hands. Distracted for a moment, she missed the last step and was thrown to the floor wrenching her ankle severely. The plate went flying; food plastered the walls and floor, some of it landing on top of her. The pain in her ankle was excruciating and Mira screamed with agony as she lay on the floor. Dan rushed to her side, crying out when he saw her rapidly swelling foot.

Panting and faint, she lay on the cold tile, willing the pain to pass between gritted teeth. A lump, the size of an orange quickly rose on her ankle. "I think I may have broken it," she told her husband. "I'll have to go to Emergency."

Somehow, the two of them managed to get her standing. She held onto a chair while Dan went to find her a cane that he had used for an old injury. He returned to find her trying to clean up the mess of scattered food, crying and hobbling back and forth between the laundry room and the bottom of the stairs.

The ride to the hospital seemed interminable. "Oh God," Mira prayed, "please give me favour and let this be as quick and painless as possible." She groaned as she hopped into the ER, leaning on her cane. The room was full of people waiting to be seen. *It'll take me at least six hours, by the look of it,* she thought dismally.

To her surprise, she was processed almost immediately. The admitting nurse was friendly and helpful, giving her an ice pack for her ankle and ordering x-rays immediately. The news was good! There were no broken bones, but Mira was ordered to stay off the leg for a few days and the doctor gave her a prescription to manage the pain. In less than an hour, they were on their way home, praising God for his goodness and favour.

The first week of January was normally a busy time, kicking off the traditional week of prayer and fasting at the Good Shepherd Church. Dan however, was insistent that Mira rest her foot, so she was unable to attend any of the services.

One piece of good news brightened her world considerably. Dan's tests came back clean. There was no sign of any cancer cells. Mira was ecstatic! God had answered her prayer! Dan would still have to be tested every three months, but for now, all was right with the world!

The week-end brought her sister-in-law, Grace, who settled into their spare bedroom with minimal fuss. The day following her arrival, she went over to the church to spend her first day with Pastor Rutherford.

Arriving home late for the evening meal, her glum face warned Mira that something had happened already.

"I don't know why Pastor told me that I could stay at the parsonage while he and his wife are away," she confided unhappily. "He's now saying that he has a house guest and that it is not available to me after all."

"Uh huh." Mira was unsympathetic. "I hate to say I told you so, but... I told you so."

Grace laughed. "By the way, just who is this guy that's staying with him?" she asked curiously. "He didn't mention him when he first offered me the parsonage to stay in."

"He's a minister from the Caribbean, who has been staying with the Rutherfords for months. I think he's divorced and had some kind of falling out with the church where he was associate pastor. He's working as a French teacher in a Christian school here in the area. He hardly ever comes to church, which is strange. Maybe he attends the church that the school is connected with."

"The Caribbean! It's pretty hot there! How strange that he was running around the parsonage with shorts on when I was over there talking with Pastor. It's freezing! For goodness sakes, it's the middle of the winter!"

Mira looked at her oddly but offered no comment.

"Pastor Rafe should have told me about him before I came," Grace said disappointedly. "Anyway, he set up an appointment for tomorrow with one of the ladies of the church who has an apartment in her basement. He says it has a small sitting room as well as the bedroom. It sounds nice and I guess I'd be comfortable enough there."

She sounded so forlorn that Mira relented. "Never mind, Grace. You can stay here until you find the right place. We don't want you pressured into accepting something that you might not be happy with."

Her face brightened at once. "I really appreciate it. I miss Dale and the boys already. It will be nice to be with family this week."

Grace didn't see much of Mira and Dan that week. Pastor Rafe absorbed hours of her time the first couple of days. In fact, he was with her right up until the very hour of his departure for the airport.

After he was gone, her calendar quickly filled with appointments as she stepped into her new role in the assembly, sharing duties with Pastor Marvin, who seemed delighted to have her on board. She hadn't known what to expect of the young associate and was relieved to find him very easy to work with.

Pastor Rafe had told her that the two of them would be sharing the responsibilities equally however he also made it crystal clear that he expected her to be in the pulpit every Sunday morning as it was the main service of the week. He told her that the numbers usually suffered whenever he was absent and that Pastor Marvin wasn't a strong enough preacher to hold the crowds. When she had asked him about their mutual arrangement of giving her opportunity to go out and preach somewhere else once a month, Rafe refused to allow it while he was away.

"What about on a Sunday evening when Marvin is scheduled to preach?" she had inquired, bewildered at the sudden change in her arrangement.

"No", he had answered, in a tone that brooked no argument. "I want you there for every service while I'm gone. You should preach some of the night services too. I don't find Marvin very good with altar calls. I want you there to oversee these things."

That meant the speaking responsibilities were not at all equally divided. Grace was uncomfortable with the arrangement, worrying that Marvin might misunderstand her role at the church. She didn't want him to feel pushed aside.

She was also disappointed that Rafe was reneging so early on their contract, but she didn't want to make a big issue of it just as she was starting a new job. It would only affect the first month anyway, she thought, so it would better to swallow it and press on. Once he returned from vacation, she would be able to pursue her evangelistic calling.

The end result of her two days of association with Rafe left Grace in an uneasy state of mind and spirit. It suddenly occurred to her that he had met with both her and Marvin separately and she couldn't help but wonder what his purpose was for doing so. Since he had confided in her privately that he didn't think much of Marvin's abilities, it was natural for her to speculate regarding the instructions given to Marvin before he left. How long did she have before he would think less of her? The more she saw of Marvin the more she genuinely liked the man. His quiet steady manner offset her own exuberant personality well and she felt they would make a good team, if left alone. She thought he might be a little too self-effacing with Rafe. Perhaps he would fare better and gain more respect if he stood up to the man once in awhile, but she kept these thoughts to herself.

The month of January flew by. Grace's days were filled with appointments and church business. She left the house early and came home late. A couple of weeks after her arrival, she confided to Mira over a late night cup of tea, that she had scarcely had the time to look for a place.

"Small wonder! You're always on the go." Mira laughed. "I'm glad I don't have to keep up with you."

"I have been offered a basement apartment by one of the church members. It's really nice. I guess I'd better call the woman tomorrow."

Mira looked closely at her. "Look Grace, why don't you just forget about the apartment? You're not any trouble to us at all and I don't want you going home at night to an empty place. I don't think it would be good for you."

Tears welled up in Grace's eyes. "Do you really mean it? I would far rather stay here, if it's alright with you and Dan."

"Of course it is. Dan enjoys the cooking. The highlight of his day is getting up a supper that you will enjoy." They both giggled. Grace knew that Mira hated to cook. She had often said that she would starve if it wasn't for Dan's love of cooking. Mira could manage warming something up in the microwave but that was pretty much the extent of her talent in that area. Dan often teased her that she couldn't boil water.

"Thank you, my friend." Grace's voice was full of relief. "I'll call the woman tomorrow and tell her that I won't need the place after all."

Mira found that she enjoyed the company of her sister-in-law. They had never had opportunity to spend much time together, living so far apart. She had always held a deep respect for Grace as a preacher but now, for the first time, she was getting to know her as a friend. She liked what she saw. Grace walked the talk. She didn't represent herself any differently at home than she did in the pulpit. She was a "real" person. No show, no glitz, no putting on airs – just a genuine woman of God who lived and breathed the Word from every pore.

Mira felt she was being taken to a new level just by her association with this woman. New hope was born in her heart for her pastor. Nothing seemed impossible when the Word was being preached with such power. She noticed a difference in the board and council members. Heads were held higher these days. The altars were full every service with repentant sinners and saints alike, weeping their way to a new found freedom in the knowledge of God's great love toward them.

The new pastoral team worked together in harmony and love. Grace openly shared her heart's calling with Marvin and the office staff. Members swamped the office with requests for appointments now that they had someone who would listen and pay attention to their struggles and issues. There was a prayer time every morning with the staff. Ina and Faith were overwhelmed with the changes.

"It's so wonderful! If only it would last," they wept. "But it will all be gone as soon as pastor comes back."

Grace assured them that this wouldn't happen. "I won't let it. Besides, don't you think that Pastor Rafe will be delighted with the changes?"

They looked at one another and shook their heads. "It will all go out the window when he returns," they said dolefully.

Grace sat down with Marvin later in the day and asked him about the earlier conversation in the office and the staff reaction she had observed. "Why are they so discouraged?" she asked him forthrightly. I can't help if I don't know what the issues are."

"Sadly, what they said is true." Marvin hung his head.

"But why should that be? Surely Pastor must want change. He must want things here to improve. I don't know all of the problems yet, but he did share some things with me and he truly seems to want change. I think he just doesn't know how to go about it."

"I don't know about that." Marvin sounded suddenly tired. "I've tried to talk to him many times. He just doesn't hear! Most of the time, I can't even get an appointment with him. I have to e-mail him to get his attention. He seems to respond to that, at least some of the time. Ina and Faith know him pretty well. They've been here over ten years, while I've only been here a couple of years. Mind you, they tell me that I've lasted longer than any other associate pastor he's ever had. I started out as a volunteer doing anything I was asked. Then I finally went on staff with a part-time salary last year. He persuaded me eventually to move to full-time and I only lasted three months the first time. I found I had no life! He wanted me here every day from nine to five plus every service. There was no time for my family. I couldn't handle it so I went back to part-time. Then my wife had to take some time off work in the fall, so I asked to be reinstated to full-time again. We needed the money." He sighed, "I try to let most stuff roll off me now and not take things so much to heart. It doesn't pay! The more you give, the more he wants and nothing is ever good enough."

Marvin dropped his head into his hands. "It's true, what they said this morning. Once he gets back, prayer will go out the window. I know I can't seem to maintain my prayer life when he's here. He just saps the strength out of you." He looked up at Grace. "You know what? This short period of time, since you came and we've been working together, has been the best of my ministry here."

"I really enjoy working with you too, Marvin," she replied fervently, not knowing how to respond to all he had told her. Optimistic by nature, she was just beginning to realize the depth of the issues the leadership was facing. After pondering the thing in her heart, she decided to meet it head on.

"I want to have a nice breakfast at the church for all of the Council members and their spouses," she told the staff, after their prayer meeting the next day. "I think it's important that I formally meet them and get to know who they are. Can we do it?"

"Sure we can, my love," declared Ina thoughtfully. "I'll ask Dan to help me with the cooking. It will be really nice; I promise." The bookkeeper's excitement grew as she started to plan the menu and decorations. "I'll even do up some proper invitations," she offered enthusiastically.

Mira was pleased with the way her sister-in-law was received by the congregation. They flocked about her after service, warmly praising her sermons. More importantly, the altars were full each Sunday, with eighty five percent of the congregation responding. A couple of snowstorms affected attendance slightly, but outside of those occasional blips, the numbers were steady.

Mira knew that Pastor Rutherford would only be interested in the size of the congregation and the amount of money taken in, so these things she carefully monitored. Offerings were up, attendance was starting to climb and a few were returning to church who had been absent for some time. One of those couples told her in the lobby after a service that they were delighted with the preaching. They wanted to know if Grace would be staying on, as their daughter was now showing an interest in attending church for the first time. These were things that gladdened Mira's heart.

Her own life was being enriched as well. The Word was doing its work in her heart, teaching her, bringing repentance where needed, and strengthening her for the days ahead. For the first time in many months, she had hope. Hope that things would turn around. Hope that the church would come into her destiny and do great things for God.

The only glitch in the month occurred when Pastor Rutherford called, insisting at the last minute, that a friend of his take the pulpit the following Sunday morning. Mira was annoyed to find him meddling with the church scheduling from a distance. She felt it showed a lack of trust in and respect for his colleagues. It was also too late to change the advertisement in the newspapers, which incorrectly announced Grace as the speaker. It appeared that his arm was long and his will still paramount and for Mira's taste, her sister-in-law had capitulated too easily, to the interference.

"Things are improving at the Good Shepherd Church." Caelen was conferring with the commanders of the heavenly host. They stood in a dark alley between two towering skyscrapers in the city, many miles from the besieged church building.

"Yes," replied Jarah, a pleased expression on his face. "The two associates work well together. The very atmosphere of the place has changed. If this could just continue...."

"Don't get too comfortable," ejaculated Captain Darshan. "The other one will return soon enough."

"I know," sighed Jarah. "He calls the church constantly. He's really still running things, only at a distance. He has his spies who keep him well informed."

"Interesting!" exclaimed Caelen. "He is supposed to be taking this time to seek the Lord," he added dryly.

Jarah shrugged uncomfortably. "Word is that he is busy with other things and has no time to spend with the Lord. The Jezebel spirit controls him completely. Our forces cannot get close enough to him to be of any effect. The further he delves into spiritual wickedness, the more unreachable he becomes."

"Still, we not give up or abandon him," Caelen replied.

"No," echoed Valin. "God forbid!"

As the night hours passed, the commanders strolled through the city streets keeping a watchful eye out for listening ears as they planned for the coming days. In the wee hours of the morning, they concluded their meeting and dispersed, melting silently into the shadows of the surrounding buildings.

The day of the council breakfast dawned clear and cold. Spirits were high as the members and their spouses sat at the beautifully appointed tables and helped themselves to the bountiful supply of deliciously prepared food. Ina and Dan had outdone themselves and by the time Grace was ready to address the group, they were relaxed and contented as any well fed crowd could be.

Sylvester managed to create a moment of tension when he slouched into the buffet line behind Jack, asking loudly if he was going to deign to say "hello" to him. The briefest of hesitations preceded Jack's gracious greeting. Satisfied with this response and unaware of the resulting twinkle in Donny's eye, the old codger thereafter ignored them both. His futile attempts at conversation were then limited to his wife and those who sat next to him. Following this unfortunate incident, the breakfast progressed as smoothly as anyone could hope for.

After reading from the scriptures and praying, Grace imparted briefly her vision for the church, opening her heart to them without reservation. She wanted to hear about their hopes and dreams, showing obvious interest in what each one had to say. Her warm, down-to-earth, caring demeanor released them to share with one another struggles, frustrations, discouragement and disillusionment as well as expectations for the future.

Both Grace and Mira listened in amazement to the outpourings as one after another of these downtrodden saints gained the courage to verbalize what each one had been holding in the secret places of their hearts. Things they hadn't dared to say came spilling forth. Mira waited, trying to quell an impelling urge to speak of what she was seeing and feeling. Finally she could contain it no longer and she spoke, tentatively at first, and then more boldly as she progressed.

"It does my heart good to hear this today. I just felt I had to say something about it. Do you realize that this is the first time I have heard council members speak honestly and openly about the problems we are facing in this church? And there *are* problems...I think we all realize that. In fact, I think we can all agree that this church is in crisis." Her voice rose passionately. "Why do we sit with our heads down in our board and council meetings, saying nothing, meeting after meeting? Why do we have such a problem speaking up? Am I the only one who finds it difficult? I don't think so! Not from what I've heard today. You all know what I'm talking about." She looked around while several heads nodded their agreement.

"In our meetings, I sometimes feel like I'm a child in school again," she continued. "I'm unable to articulate any meaningful dialogue. It's like there is a spirit of intimidation in the room and I find that I can't even think. What is wrong here! This is the most refreshing experience I have had with council so far. I know the wives are here too and maybe I shouldn't say anything. I know our council meetings are supposed to be entirely confidential, but our spouses have a right to know what we deal with on a regular basis." Her head drooped in discouragement, her eyes lowered to the table in front of her. "Please forgive me, if I'm wrong."

"You're right!" It was Rob, Faith's husband who spoke. "It's been like this for years! No one dares to say what they really think. I, for one, am sick and tired of it!" His voice cracked. "I feel of no more importance than a rubber stamp. Let's face it guys, that's all we're good for! What's the point of trying to serve here? You have no say! Any opinion that differs from Pastor's is treated like so much garbage. We've all been dancing around the main issue. It's the pastor! I'll say it! There is a lack of integrity in our pulpit! How can any church move forward with the kinds of things that are going on here?"

He paused a moment and then continued. "Guys, come on - we all know it can't go anywhere! How can we expect to accomplish all of these great things that we've been talking about today until we have integrity and honesty in the pulpit?"

He looked at Grace and Marvin. "I'm not talking about you," he said. "God bless you for what you're trying to do here! This is the first time in a long time...I can't even remember how long, that we've heard the Word of God preached in the pulpit. Usually it is just stories...stories about the pastor's childhood and life. I'm drying up! This is great, right now, with the two of you preaching, but what happens when he returns. I can't go back to what we had!"

Heads around the table nodded their agreement, some looking at one another with sheepish expressions. "I feel the same," came from several mouths at the same time.

"But what can we do?" quavered David Armstrong. "We can't touch God's anointed. I guess all we can do is pray. Maybe we could have a prayer meeting."

Rob snorted. "Something more needs to be done! We sure can't go on like this! I'm about at the end of my rope! For ten years I've been putting up with this garbage! I'm not growing in the Lord. I need to be fed the Word of God constantly just to cope with everyday life. We all do! Unfortunately, no one will risk mentioning anything about the mess we are all in, much less doing anything about it, because anyone who tries will be ostracized by the pastor. Unless we all stick together, we might as well forget it! I've seen too many board members crushed to believe that it can ever be any different. We need to pray for this board," he went on. "They are having a difficult time here. I wouldn't want to have their decisions right now. I'm only a deacon and to be honest, I don't even know what that means or what I'm supposed to do. I've never been trained! I'm just flying by the seat of my pants!" His voice trembled as he self-consciously ducked his head.

"I feel the same." It was the gruff voice of Sylvester. "I shouldn't even be on the board. I'm not qualified for the position. I've wanted to quit several times but Pastor won't hear of it."

"From what you're all telling me, the main problem here seems to be the senior pastor then." Grace spoke quietly into the silence that followed Sylvester's speech.

"That's right, but what can we do about it?" Rob sounded utterly discouraged. "No one can confront him on the issues. I've tried! He'll get out of it! He just skates around the problems but never looks at them or deals with them. And what's more, he'll bury you in the process. *You* will be the one made to look like an idiot."

"I can see there are some deep issues here and you have legitimate concerns," replied Grace earnestly. "Maybe I'm an eternal optimist, but I truly believe that there is always hope and you do have some options available to you. I just need to be clear that you are definitely all on the same page before I make any suggestions." She looked around the table. "Can I ask each of you to identify whether you feel that Pastor Rafe is the main problem here?" As she went around the circle with her question, each one responded in the affirmative, Sylvester and Phil adding that, as much as they hated to say it, it was true.

"I would like to begin the healing process by sitting down with Pastor Rutherford and having an open, honest discussion with him regarding your concerns." she said frankly. "Pastor Marvin and I can do that together, so that no one on council will be centered out or feel threatened. Would that be something that you would like us to do?"

Agreement was unanimous although most didn't hold out any hope for significant change. "I think a council meeting should also be set up as soon as Pastor Rafe returns. We will meet with him first so that he doesn't have any surprises and after that, everyone should sit down together and deal with the issues, one at a time."

Rob spoke grimly. "This is all well and good as far as it goes, but if we're going to get anywhere, someone other than Pastor Rutherford should chair the meeting."

"I don't see why that should create a problem," Grace replied.

"I doubt if Pastor will allow it," Marvin interjected quickly.

"I don't think he will agree to it either," Rob murmured, "but unless that happens we might as well all stay at home because nothing will be accomplished."

"Who would you want to chair the meeting?" asked Grace tentatively.

His reply was firm. "Either you or Pastor Marvin." Several voices joined in agreement.

Marvin shifted uncomfortably in his seat. "I'd rather not unless the pastor asks me directly."

Jack looked at Grace. "Then would you agree to chair the meeting? I think it should be one of you pastors."

"I don't mind, if that is really what you all want." She looked around the group as heads nodded vigorously. Even old Sylvester chimed in, adding his gruff approval to the others.

"Do you really think a council meeting will make any difference?" Mira asked the question that was on everyone's lips. "We've been dealing with this for a long time. He won't take kindly to being questioned about his actions."

"I will fully prepare him," Grace promised. "I see it as a first step only to resolving issues that have been festering for a long time."

"I'd like to ask a question since we're being honest."

"Go ahead."

"Who is preaching on Sunday?"

Grace reddened slightly. "Well, actually it's a missionary from the Ukraine that is going to be speaking."

"How did that happen? Are you not advertised in the paper as the speaker?" Mira was relentless. I *might as well get it all out, since we're being open, honest and direct*, she thought.

"Yes....." Grace's voice trailed off. "We didn't find out until yesterday that Pastor Rafe had booked him for this Sunday," she admitted truthfully.

Mira cut in quickly. "This is just one more example of his control and manipulation." Her cheeks flushed as her frustration level rose. "First he tells you and Marvin that you're in charge and then he pre-empts your plans and substitutes his own at a whim. Just how often does he call the church?"

Grace looked at Marvin for help.

"He calls every day," put in Faith quietly, "sometimes several times a day."

Mira was just getting warmed up. "I've been asked by church members if it's true that he's on a sabbatical. Talk about confusing! He told us in the last council meeting that it's definitely a vacation and then he tells the people that it's a sabbatical. If you and Pastor Marvin are supposed to be in charge, why is he still running everything from Florida. He doesn't give two hoots about any of your plans nor does he care that the church looks foolish for advertising a different speaker."

"I know that you have put forth some legitimate complaints here today," Grace admitted in a straightforward manner, "but I would ask you to look at the position that we, as associate pastors, have been placed in as well. It wouldn't be fair to cancel the speaker now. It's too late for him to find another engagement. I know I wouldn't want anyone to do that to me, if our roles were reversed. I understand that things are often done without planning or foresight here and I promise that we will work to change that. However, for tomorrow, I would respectfully request that you not put me in the position of either going against what the senior pastor has arranged or treating our guest shabbily. I apologize to all of you for this unfortunate circumstance but for this occasion, I think the best thing is to just go ahead with the pastor's plan. It would be too disruptive to do anything else for tomorrow's services. Will you do that for me?" she asked pleadingly.

Mira felt badly that she had put Grace on the spot and acquiesced readily to the request. After bandying about several alternatives, none of which were viable because someone would inevitably get hurt, everyone agreed to leave it alone. With the noon hour almost upon them, Grace closed the meeting in prayer.

Willing hands quickly cleared the dirty dishes and leftover food from the tables. Renewed hope beamed from the countenance of every worker. Good natured bantering filled the kitchen as the breakfast dishes were washed and dried. Expressions of joy, hope and an air of excitement pervaded the atmosphere. All of this transpired simply as a result of each one being afforded an opportunity to voice their opinions to someone who appeared to value them. And this was one time they didn't have to worry about suffering any dire consequences as a result of it.

14

Mira popped her head through of door of Faith's office, her bright face grinning from ear-to ear. "Hi Sunshine, how ya doin'?"

"Hey you!" The secretary's face lit up. "I'm doin' great. What about you?"

After a few minutes of cheerful banter, Mira casually asked Faith if she kept a record of the pastor's trips.

"Sure, I do," she replied. "I have his calendar right here. What do you want to know?"

"I would like the actual dates that he's been away for the last year."

Faith looked surprised. "Is there any special reason?" she asked.

"No, not really," Mira replied casually. "We'll need the information shortly for reviews and I wanted to get an idea how many vacation days staff members receive. Ina has filled me in on everyone except the pastor. She says that he gets upset if she asks him about it."

"Okay. Just let me find January of last year." She flipped backwards in her appointment book. "Let me see....uh, fifteen days from January to February 2nd....here's eight days at the end of April...five days in May." She turned some more pages. "I don't have the actual dates, but I know he went to Texas in the summer for a few days....maybe four or five.

Mira jotted down the information as Faith continued to leaf through the book. "Didn't he go away right after that and spend some time on a yacht with friends?" she interrupted, nibbling thoughtfully at the end of her pen. "I know he told the board all about it some time ago."

"I think you're right.... but I don't seem to have it written down here. It probably happened during the week and if he didn't tell me....." her voice trailed off.

"That's okay. He told us it was two days. Anyway, it doesn't have to be exact. I seem to recall that he was gone a couple of times this fall. Do you have those dates?"

"Yes, he was gone in September for five days and of course there was the trip to California in November. That was ten days. I'm sure there were more days taken in the summertime but I was away on vacation myself so I have nothing to verify it with."

"This is good enough for what I need. Thank you." Mira looked at the numbers on her notepad and did a quick total in her head. Erring on the lower side where she was unsure of the numbers, she could count forty nine days of vacation. *Interesting,* she thought. *Forty nine days last year that I can prove and yet he claims that he hasn't had a vacation in fifteen years. I wonder if anyone else has ever checked.*

To Faith, Mira said nothing but she was deep in thought as she drove home from the church. As soon as she arrived, she went into her office and pulled out the financial records that she kept on file for the year. This time, her interest lay in another direction. She searched the accounts, one by one, until she found the money paid to visiting speakers.

Quickly she compiled a list of all the guest speakers used in the church that year. It was easier than she had thought. She could tell from the payment dates exactly who had filled the pulpit on any given Sunday. In total, she found that a special speaker had filled in for the pastor forty two times during the year. That included mid-week services as well as Sunday. Added to that, she learned that there had been fifty one second offerings taken.

She whistled as she leaned back in her chair with the paper in her hand. *I knew he hardly been in the pulpit this year, but I honestly didn't know it was this bad,* she thought. *I wonder what happened to the surveys that were filled out at the ministerial meeting in September.*

She found Dora Golding's number in her directory and picked up the phone. "Hi Dora," she said when she heard her voice on the line. "Listen, I was just wondering whether you ever finished the summary of the surveys that were passed in at that ministerial meeting we had in September.

"I handed that in in the last week of November," Dora replied chuckling. "To tell you the truth, I'm surprised that Pastor allowed it at all. You could have knocked me over with a feather when he asked me to prepare the survey in the first place. I was even more surprised when he didn't ask for any changes. It was a pretty all-inclusive, comprehensive survey and boy did it ever get some comments!

"What do you mean?" Mira asked, her curiosity getting the best of her.

"I mean that there were some pretty open and honest remarks. Some were almost brutal! In fact, I would say eighty five percent of them were. I doubt if my summary will see the light of day! To tell you the truth though, I don't think he's even read it yet. Faith has trouble getting him to read anything. If it isn't sent by e-mail, he's not interested. Sometimes, I wonder what's with him and that e-mail. He spends most of his time either on the phone or on the computer."

"Yes, I know," agreed Mira with a laugh. "That's pretty common knowledge. He has even admitted himself that he has a phone addiction. He doesn't seem to want to do anything about it though."

"Yeah, when he wants to show the people that he's being vulnerable with them, he talks about this problem he has with the phone." Dora chortled. "What a crock! It's not like he's ever going to do anything about it! Too bad he won't get transparent for real and actually repent for the terrible things he does."

"You must know quite a bit. You were on the board for several years."

"Too long!" she snorted. "I took my fair share of blows and have the battle wounds and scars to show for it!"

"I know you told me that when I let my name stand for the board but I honestly didn't think it would happen to me," Mira replied. "I really thought I knew him and that he would never hurt me," she added.

"Well, I did try to warn you, my dear. Anyway, let me know if the surveys surface. I put a lot of work into them – many hours – and I'd like to see that summary go to the council if you can swing it. Maybe we can get come change around here then. God knows, it's sorely needed.

"I'll do my best, Dora."

"Okey-dokey. Give my best to your husband."

"I will. We'll chat soon."

Mira sat awhile deep in thought. *She knows more than she's willing to share. I wonder what sort of things she dealt with during her terms on the board.* She sighed deeply. *Too bad board members won't share with the new ones coming on. It would save us all a pile of grief. But then,* she thought grimly, *they probably wouldn't get anyone to serve at all.* The more she pondered the matter, the more determined she became to demand that the survey summary and results be brought to the council.

Frigid temperatures and blowing snow dominated the last week of January. Then the weather cleared and Mira turned her thoughts to the council meeting that was set for the first Saturday morning in February. Pastor Rutherford was expected to return from Florida with a definite direction for the church. More than one council member was calling for the results of the surveys and speculation was rife regarding the sabbatical that everyone felt the Lord had called the pastor to.

Pastor Rafe arrived home the day before the expected meeting. His two associates were closeted in his office for more than five hours, divulging the various issues that had been discussed at the council breakfast. Grace even went so far as to tell him how many would vote against him if a non-confidence vote should be taken. He was also apprised of council's desire to see the results of the September survey.

When their meeting was over, both Grace and Marvin were satisfied that there would be no surprises in store for him. They had been completely open, determined that he be entirely prepared for the meeting that would take place the following day. Marvin was surprised that he had not objected to giving up his usual place as chairman.

A dozen of Captain Darshan's best warriors were able to infiltrate the confines of the council's meeting room. Dimming the brightness of their appearance and sheathing their heavy swords, they looked vulnerable and vastly outnumbered against the great horde of evil spirits that crowded the room. Some of the demons jeered and cursed at them crowing over their obvious impotence. Most simply ignored them, not considering them worthy of notice but rather giving their attention to their potential victims.

Council members stirred restlessly waiting for Pastor Rafe to arrive. Even irrepressible Phil, with his limitless supply of jokes or anecdotes, sat silently staring at the agenda handed around by Mira.

Rafe hurriedly pulled into his parking space in front of the church. He spoke quietly into the phone at his ear as he scrutinized the cars in the lot. The muscles around his eyes quivered involuntarily and he gnawed his lower lip in anticipation of what he knew he had to face.

As he entered the building, a cold wrath was beginning to intensify within him. Keeping his manner deliberately unhurried, he doffed his coat, hanging it on a rack in Faith's office. The computer screen caught his attention. He debated for a moment whether to succumb to the overwhelming desire to check his e-mails and decided to forego the pleasure in order to put this unpleasant task behind him as quickly as possible.

The Jezebel spirit sprang to his side, its surprising swiftness belying the enormous bulk of its body. Green spittle oozed from the corners of the creature's malformed mouth. A crooked claw clung to Rafe's arm.

Grace stepped into the lobby just as he was heading for the small banquet hall downstairs. Two giant unseen warriors kept pace with her, warding her body from attack. Her face still carried traces of tears from her own private prayer time with the Lord.

For some reason the very sight of her irritated Rafe. *She wants to usurp my place here,* he thought resentfully. *She doesn't have a clue who she's dealing with!* His lip curled sardonically as he thrust his chin into the air. *She's way out of her league!* He looked her over contemptuously as she preceded him down the stairs. *I'll put her in her place,* he thought with a sneer.

Immediately upon entering the room, Rafe took his place at the head of the table with an air of authority. Opening his bible, he read a few verses of scripture followed by comments as was his normal practise. Baffled by his nonchalance, the members sat stiffly in silence, exchanging bewildered glances and wondering at what point he would step aside and allow Grace to take the chair as they had requested.

But Rafe had no intention of relinquishing the chair position to anyone. He pontificated at length reiterating the history of the church property, pointing out various deeds of deceased owners of foreign culture who had been in some way connected with the building.

Mira found her face getting hot and she dug her nails into her palms in an effort to quell her rising indignation. If someone didn't say something soon, the whole morning would be wasted.

Finally, with a flourish, Rafe announced that the survey summary would be presented by its preparer, Dora Golding, who had graciously consented to come and explain it to council. Mira was sent in search of Dora who was involved in a meeting with the benevolent committee in another corner of the building.

"How's it going", Dora whispered as they walked down the hallway together.

"Badly," acknowledged Mira. "He's been going on and on about dead people and irrelevant nonsense for almost an hour. If we don't do something soon, everyone will be too exhausted to care."

Dora's presentation was thorough, leaving scope for very few questions. A pregnant silence followed her dismissal from the room. Desperation flickered over the faces of the group around the table.

Finally Rob took a big breath and broke the silence. "From what I can see in this summary, the main problem seems to be you, pastor."

"I don't think that is true," replied Rafe defensively. "There are only a few derogatory comments and I don't care what church you go to, there are always a few disgruntles. Besides, this is only a small representation of the whole church. Only a few members even turned them in." He looked at Rob triumphantly.

"These surveys were really only distributed at the leadership meeting. The comments here are taken from twenty one of your leaders, not the average attendees," Rob stated insistently. "These are the people who volunteer regularly and give largely of their time and effort to this place. Let's face it," he continued, "only the leaders and staff here really know the inner workings of the place anyway, so their comments should send a message. What I'm seeing are discouraged, frustrated, burnt out, hurt individuals that don't feel valued or appreciated. They don't want to start all of these new projects that you introduced at the leaders' meeting. They want the children and youth ministries stabilized first. Seventy one percent of your best workers feel that the church has no goal or direction and only a scant few believe that their individual concerns are being dealt with. Your workers are tired and many won't get involved until some changes are made. That sounds to me like a church in crisis."

"Well, I don't see how that should be my fault!" Rafe was indignant. How dare anyone question his ability! "I set up these surveys with Pastor Mark and Dora for the purpose of finding out where we're at. It was supposed to be a constructive exercise and now you're using it as a weapon against me. I told everyone, even from the pulpit, to be honest. We should go through them and deal with each issue scripturally."

"We are trying to deal with them, pastor, but it would appear that you do not want to take any responsibility for anything written here. What do we do with that? What about all of the comments that are directly related to the way you treat people?"

Rafe changed his tactics. "It seems I'm expected to do everything," he quavered trying to gain their sympathy. "I'm trying to handle everything but I can't do it all by myself."

He went on at some length justifying and excusing, skating around the damning evidence that he now wished he had never permitted in the first place. "I never thought when this survey was brought out that it would be used as a tool to get rid of me. I guess I'm just like the poor old grey mare that outlived her usefulness and now that she's too old she's only good for the glue factory." He allowed his chin to tremble. The tears he had hoped to squeeze out weren't cooperating. Every ounce of his control was needed to squelch the hot anger that boiled beneath the exterior.

"I have to tell you that I am in shock from this attack on me. I went away to take the sabbatical that the Lord has called me to and that everyone has been telling me I should take and I return to find an insurrection brewing." His voice rose heatedly. "I came in here totally unprepared for this, except for a caution that the Holy Spirit gave me just as I was pulling into parking lot of the church."

Rafe's voice deepened automatically as he slid into his prophetic role. ""Son," the Holy Spirit said to me. This meeting isn't what you think it is." He just gave me the word "*insurrection*". Another prophet called me today as well and gave me warning of the same thing."

"STOP!" thundered Ian. "YOU'RE A LIAR! I don't believe for one minute that you heard from the Lord or that there is any prophet. It's just more lies! Tell us the name of the prophet!"

For a split second everyone sat immobilized in stunned silence, gaping in disbelief at the normally mild-mannered man, who rarely opened his mouth during a meeting. Although he suffered from a mild speech impediment, sometimes stammering when he spoke, there was certainly no semblance of a stutter now.

"I can't do that!" Rafe flashed back. "It's confidential!"

"Pastor, if you can't name the prophet, then how can we be expected to judge the prophesy?" asked Mira. "If the prophet is unwilling to allow his name to be used, then how can we be expected to believe his Word."

Enraged, Rafe stumbled to his feet. "Is that the way everyone here feels?" he roared.

No one spoke. Even normal breathing was suspended.

"I want to know how each person here feels about me." he spluttered angrily. When no one volunteered any comment, he turned to Marvin and asked him to pass out a piece of paper to each council member. "I want everyone here to write down whether they want me here or not and what their reasons are for the way they feel," he ordered.

Marvin scrambled to obey. He was about to leave the room to go in search of some paper, when Mira signalled him. She tore a few sheets from her notebook and mutely handed them over. While they were being passed around, Grace asked the pastor to step outside into the corridor with her and Marvin. Rafe glowered at her darkly.

"I must speak with you – NOW!" she insisted decidedly, her face white with distress. Rafe motioned her impatiently toward the door. Marvin followed reluctantly. At a signal from Caelen, Valin melted through the door behind them.

Mira sat with pen and paper in hand, trying to decide what to write on the sheet. There was no question in her mind as to what her vote was going to be, but he had asked them to write their reasons. Her stomach was doing crazy flip-flops and her mind was confused and blank. Something felt wrong about all of this but she couldn't put her finger on what it was. Donny was feverishly writing, filling his paper fast. Mira tried desperately to pull her thoughts together.

Caelen bent over and spoke insistently into her ear. His gigantic wings covered her back, holding at bay a number of demons who were trying to get her attention.

At that moment, the door opened and Marvin re-entered the room. Leaning over Mira, he whispered into her ear. Quickly pocketing the offending slip of paper, she excused herself and went in search of her sister-in-law whom she eventually found in the washroom throwing up. Grace's face was ashen as she stumbled out of the stall, her hair plastered against her neck and forehead which dripped with perspiration.

"I had to confront him over the lie he told," she gasped. Leaning against the wall, she sobbed and sobbed. "He lied in there, Mira! He lied, right to my face!"

"I know, I know," Mira replied soothingly. "He tells lies all the time." She gave her sister-in-law a comforting hug. "I guess you believe me now, huh?"

"I never thought he would lie so blatantly," she panted. She seemed as dazed as she was upset. "I asked him why he lied and he denied it. I told him everything, Mira. He knew exactly what he was facing when he walked into that meeting today. Marvin and I spent over five hours with him yesterday and we withheld nothing." She looked at Mira aghast. "How could he use the Holy Spirit like that? It is downright blasphemy!"

"He does it all the time. Don't worry! I don't think anyone in there seriously believes that a prophet told him anything! Furthermore, I'd bet that no one believes the Holy Spirit cautioned him either. He's adept at using a religious covering and false prophesies to give weight to his own agendas and wishes. I wish it wasn't so but I've seen enough this last few months to last me a lifetime!"

"Mira!" Grace looked stricken as a thought occurred to her. "He intends to make me the sacrificial lamb here," she cried. "I just know it! He means me to take the fall for this! I think that's why he asked me to come. He expected me to settle the board down and if I couldn't, then he would have someone else to take the blame for the church's problems." She looked miserably at Mira. "He thinks I'm just a poor little farm girl that doesn't know any better. He's been using me all along."

"You've done nothing wrong." Mira patted her shoulder. "You know that I wasn't very happy when you agreed to come because I was worried that you were walking into a hornet's nest. But Grace, I truly believe that God brought you here. You don't know how much help you've given us. You've preached the Word without compromise. We've been starved for it! The people are hungry to learn about God, instead of hearing a continuous stream of stories about Rafe. It might be true that he asked you to come – begged you even – but God's hand was in it." she said warmly. "No second guessing! You knew that you were in the will of God when you came and whatever happens here, God will take care of you. You'll make yourself sick if you carry on like this!"

"I already did," she confided unhappily. "I came in here and threw up right after I spoke with him. I don't know what's wrong with me. I've never done that before. Do you know what he said?"

Mira shook her head.

"He said that I didn't use the word "*insurrection*". That's his reasoning! He claims he didn't know what he was facing because I didn't use that word. Is he delusional?"

Mira laughed. She couldn't help herself. "Delusional? Maybe! Crafty? That's a definite *Yes*!"

While Grace splashed some water on her face and neck, Mira asked her what to do about the papers. "I'm confused. If this is meant to be a vote then we should write a simple "Yes" or "No" but I don't think he means it to be a vote. I think he wants to find out who is for or against him. That's the only reason I can think of to explain why he wants us to clarify what we think of him. What does he intend to do with the papers when he has them?"

"Don't fill it out! You're right! He didn't ask for a vote! He just wants to know who is against him. Don't put anything in writing. He will only use it against you later. There's no purpose to it except for him to determine which members can be swayed and manipulated and which ones to cut loose." Grace patted her face dry and headed for the door.

As they re-entered the meeting room, Mira glanced around, looking for the pastor.

"He told Pastor Marvin to call him when we were done," Jack volunteered seeing her gaze sweep the room. "Is everything alright?"

"Everything's fine." She forged ahead quickly, wanting to address her concerns while the pastor was still absent from the room. "I would like to ask whether or not you are all as confused as I am about what we are doing with these papers?" Seeing several heads nod, she continued. "Is this a legal vote? If it is, then the ballots should be simple – Yes or No. Why are we being asked to write down personal opinions on the spur of the moment? It doesn't feel right to me."

The response was immediate from all sides. "Me either." "I don't know what to write." "I have no idea what we're doing with this exercise."

"I thought it was a vote," said Donny.

"I don't think he means this to be a legal vote. I think he wants to use what we write to divide and conquer this council," Mira stated boldly. "He hasn't answered any question or responded to any of the issues that we've put before him. We need to decide what we're going to do because if we hand him these papers, he will approach each of us separately and deal with us according to what we have written."

"She's right!" It was Jack who spoke. "This is just more of the same tactics we've seen in board meetings for months. Why can't he just sit down and talk about the issues and problems here?"

"Why is he even chairing the meeting?" asked Ian. "I thought Grace was supposed to chair this one." Everyone looked at her questioningly.

"I thought I was too," she replied slowly. "I came prepared to do that, but he just took over. I thought at first maybe he would just do the opening devotional and then turn it over to me, but obviously that didn't happen."

"Guys....he never had any intention of letting anyone else chair the meeting," put in Rob. "He wouldn't be able to control it and he is never going to relinquish his control here. I knew he wouldn't. He can't! It isn't in his nature!"

The door opened abruptly and Pastor Rafe strode into the room, head held high, leaving the group to wonder if he had been eavesdropping outside the whole time. As he took his place at the head of the table, the fire in his eye didn't bode well for the council.

"Have the papers been collected?" he asked Marvin.

"Uh...no, they haven't, Pastor," he answered timidly. "It appears there's some confusion over why you want them and how they are going to be used."

Grace interrupted. "There seems to be some confusion over whether this is a vote of confidence or not," she said quietly.

He snorted in derision. "Of course it isn't! A vote wouldn't be constitutional. There is a process that you all seem to have ignored. It appears that you have been conspiring behind my back while I was on the sabbatical that many in this church wanted me to take. My pastoral staff...." he threw Grace a look of utter contempt, "told me that this was going to be a reconciliation meeting. It was supposed to be a time when we would look at the issues and know how to solve them, not to have something thrown at me....like....it's over for you buddy."

"Pastor," Rob interjected, "we've been trying to bring out issues but you keep denying and justifying. You haven't been willing to talk about any of it,"

"I've always been willing to sit down in a reasonable manner and go over anything that I need to," he replied, his voice rising. "What I object to is being ambushed like this!"

Mira raised her hand. Rafe glared at her but she spoke out anyway. "Pastor, I think we should clarify that the last month has not been a sabbatical. It has been a vacation." Seeing the look of anger and disbelief on his face, she quickly continued before he could interrupt. "You called me from Florida one evening and when I asked about the noise in the background, you told me that you were having a new dock put in and a number of other renovations done. You also said that you hadn't been able to get the rest you wanted because of all the work going on there. Don't you recall telling us all before you left that you were going to take a vacation because you were so tired?"

Her voice trembled with emotion. "Are you telling us now that you took time to wait on God? Do you have direction for the church? Everything I have heard today sickens me. So far, you have not once admitted even the slightest fault. This church is in crisis and you only seem to care about yourself! All I hear is justification, anger and defence. I don't hear any repentance at all. If just once, you would admit to any of this...any little thing at all...just one thing even.... you know we would rally around you instantly! We all love you Pastor, but the way you treat people is just plain wrong! You are not honest in your dealings! I wish it were not so but we are at the point where we can no longer turn a blind eye to it. We're responsible to the people of this congregation!"

She dropped her head into her hands as the tears flowed freely down her cheeks. "You just don't seem to get it! What's the use!" she choked miserably.

Rev. Armstrong spoke timidly, his chin wobbling visibly. "I think maybe we need to have some prayer meetings," he stammered.

Rafe interrupted the old minister disdainfully. "I would like to think about the sabbatical that's been suggested." he said, smoothly changing the subject. The members looked at one another in bewilderment, suspicion plainly written on a number of faces. Experience had taught them that he was not apt to capitulate easily unless he had another plan.

With practiced skill, Rafe shifted the focus of the meeting, expertly moving the group's attention away from the survey, talking persuasively about his exhausted state, justifying his need for a time of rest. Several times, he mentioned the multiple requests of those who had recommended a sabbatical period. He actually sounded reasonable! "I can go now with confidence, knowing that Grace and Marvin are an excellent team doing a great job." He proffered the lie effortlessly "I would like to think that after all of the years I've given to the work of the Lord, and the church here in particular, you would extend me that much courtesy."

"Well..." Rev. Armstrong put in tremulously, "I think we should give the pastor what he's asked for."

"What period of time are you talking about?" asked Rob doubtfully

"I would like to take a sabbatical until the end of March. That would be three months. I'm even willing to give up my salary so that no added strain will be put on the church to carry three full-time pastors."

"I think that is a very generous offer," replied David Armstrong not daring to mention that the first month of the period he was suggesting had already been taken as paid vacation.

Silence followed his statement. The members looked at one another for some sign of support. Mira could almost taste the fear and frustration emanating from each of them.

Pastor Rafe rose stiffly to his feet. His color was high and his voice shook with suppressed anger. "I think it might be better if I were to leave so that you can discuss my proposal. I feel it is a fair request. I'm not asking for much after fifteen years of service." He headed for the door, closing it firmly behind him as he left the room. His footsteps echoed down the hallway and faded into the distance.

Mira struggled with the lump in her throat and angrily brushed tears from her eyes which would come in spite of every effort to hold them back.

"What do we do now?" The question hung in the air.

"Well, I think we have to give him what he's asking for," offered Rev. Armstrong timidly.

"We can't kick him to the curb like they did at his last church," put in Phil. "He's asking for the sabbatical that everyone wants him to take. I think we have to give it to him."

"I feel he's just going to wait us out until the annual business meeting." Donny sounded frustrated. "Notice that he is returning before the meeting even though three months sabbatical should take him through to the end of April. He knows the mix on the board of directors will change at that time."

"I think he should be given a formal letter from the council requesting a follow-up meeting to address the issues," Rob insisted. "He is dodging everything we bring up. He doesn't seem to realize that we have a crisis on our hands here. If something isn't done there is going to be a split."

"I think there will be a split no matter what we do," agreed Mira. "There are quite a number of people that are going to leave if he doesn't resign or at least address these issues. I was really hoping that the survey results would bring some accountability but he refuses to take any responsibility for anything."

"We must have another chairman if we even try to have another meeting," said Rob. "He simply cannot chair a meeting that is primarily about his own actions."

"I agree with Rob," responded Jack. "We need to let him know that we want Pastor Grace to chair the meeting and we need it in writing." He looked at Mira. "Would you mind drawing up the letter?"

"I'll do it today so it can be given to him tomorrow at church. When does he leave for Florida again?"

"Not until the thirteenth," Pastor Marvin replied. "He said he has some business to take care of before he goes."

"Then let's set the meeting for the twelfth," rejoined Mira.

Relieved to be released, the council members rapidly dispersed. Rob Samuels lingered to chat with some of the directors, while Mira gathered up her papers.

David Armstrong approached her hesitantly. "We need to settle the matter of the pastor's grandson, Jonas. It's been dragging on too long. It might make the pastor feel better about things if we cleared it up. He asked me to call a board meeting to settle it."

Sylvester gruff voice rose above the chatter. "Yes, it's high time it was looked after. I know the pastor wants the travel honorarium reinstated."

No doubt, thought Mira grimly. Aloud she said, "Then I guess we need to deal with it. Why don't we just go ahead and set a board meeting for a time when we know the pastor is here – like Wednesday night?"

"I think we need to have some prayer if we're going to tackle him on that subject," said Jack. The others nodded in agreement.

"Pastor Grace is speaking that evening, so Pastor Rafe will be free for the meeting," said Mira thoughtfully. "We could set a half-hour for prayer first before we take care of business. It shouldn't take long with only the one item to decide. Afterward, if there is time, we can join the service. We might even be able to take in some of the message." Everyone seemed content with the plan in spite of their misgivings regarding the contentiousness of the issue they must decide.

15

ON SUNDAY, PASTOR RAFE shared from the pulpit that he now felt that he could comfortably go away for an extended sabbatical because he knew the church was in excellent hands with the associate pastors on staff. Mira delivered the letter containing council's request to have Grace chair the next meeting. In the afternoon, she e-mailed the pastor informing him that a board meeting had been set for Wednesday night at 7:00 pm, at Rev. Armstrong's request, to settle the Jonas matter.

After he received the agenda, Rafe called wanting to know what the half-hour prayer meeting was all about. Mira explained that the directors felt a time of prayer beforehand would be beneficial for all of them. *I'll bet he doesn't come until that part is over,* she thought. *I don't think he can pray for more than five minute....at least I've never seen it, but maybe this time will be different.* She emphasized that it was part of the meeting, probably the most important part.

"But the midweek service is at 7:00 pm and you should all be in attendance," Rafe objected irritably. "Why not schedule it either before or after the service?"

"Jack and Donny have businesses to run," Mira explained patiently. "They can't come early and they refuse to stay afterward, risking a late night because both have to get up at the crack of dawn. It just makes more sense to do it this way since we all really want the half hour of prayer before we begin. We can change the meeting to Thursday evening if you would rather. That would mean an extra night for everyone, which seems rather silly since there is only one item on the agenda except for the prayer time which, I'm sure you'll agree, is sorely needed." If only he would join them, she reflected, they might be able to sort this mess out.

"Can't you just pray upstairs in the service and meet when it's over for a few minutes?" asked Rafe, stubbornly refusing to capitulate.

"Maybe we should just change the date," suggested Mira shortly, quelling the urge she felt to accede to the pastor's wishes. She knew Donny and Jack would be upset if she agreed to his request. They might even refuse to attend. "We all thought this was the best solution since your time is very limited before your return to Florida to begin your sabbatical. Pastor Grace is speaking in the service, isn't she?"

Rafe was annoyed. He had always found it more effective to have meetings after a service. Members were more pliable and easy to manipulate when tired out and anxious to leave. However, he definitely did not want the meeting pushed to Thursday. He already had plans for that evening that he would not change for anyone!

"I'm busy Thursday. I guess it will have to be Wednesday then." His tone conveyed his displeasure.

"We will be meeting downstairs in the small banquet hall," Mira informed him. "That way our prayer meeting won't be disturbed by anyone."

"Why not use the boardroom outside of my office? No one will bother you there."

Mira didn't want to tell him that Jack and Donny had both refused to meet there. They had particularly requested that the meeting room be changed because they felt intimidated and shut down in the board room. The very atmosphere seemed bound by evil spirits.

"We decided it would be better to be close to the kitchen so that we could have easy access to water and coffee should we wish it," she explained lamely.

"Well...I'll have to start the service so I may be late for the prayer meeting."

Mira doubted that he would show his face at all but said nothing. In the two days leading up to the meeting, she prayed constantly, weeping bitter tears, for God's will to be done in the life of her pastor and for strength and wisdom for the directors.

It was a subdued group that met downstairs in the church on Wednesday night. Besides Caelen and Valin, only nine warriors had accompanied Captain Darshan past the devilish guards patrolling the meeting area. A larger force of angels attended the bible study upstairs in the fellowship hall, filtering in two at a time with a few of the praying saints.

The pastor was nowhere in sight when the board members opened their meeting. Distant strains of music filtered down from the worship service above as they paced the floor, calling on the Lord to give them wisdom and understanding. Each one prayed aloud as the Spirit of the Lord led and when the half hour was finished, peace had settled into their hearts, even though there were traces of tears on their cheeks.

Pastor Rafe hurried into the room just after they had taken their seats. Without apology or explanation for his absence during prayer time, he took immediate control of the meeting. He seemed in a hurry to get the thing over with, quickly launching into his own version of his grandson's involvement in the youth ministry. He justified Jonas' frequent absences saying that it had been his idea to stop the meetings until the fall.

"It has always been a dream of mine to work with my grandson." Rafe allowed his lower lip to tremble slightly. "But I am willing to submit myself to this board and let you decide whether that is best or not. Jonas has built up the young people from two or three to fifteen in a mind-boggling short period of time. They have a rapport with him and some are e-mailing him on a constant basis. I don't think anyone could have done a better job and I take full responsibility for his absence all summer."

His volume escalated slightly. "If anyone had asked me, I could have told them that he would be starting things up again in the fall. So, that's pretty much the whole story and I will leave it to you folk to decide whether he goes or stays." Dead silence followed his speech. The directors looked at one another waiting for someone to take the lead.

"Well... I guess we should take a vote on it then," offered David Armstrong weakly. His chin wobbled nervously as he looked helplessly around the table.

Mira hitched uneasily in her seat. Something should be said before the vote, she thought anxiously, vainly hoping someone else would speak first. When no one did, she cleared her throat and took the plunge. "I would like to clarify a few things before we vote on this matter." Her voice shook in spite her efforts to keep it steady and her heart thumped wildly as she looked at Pastor Rafe's stern visage.

"Pastor, we did not lightly suspend the travel honorarium for Jonas, nor was it done strictly because he was absent this summer. When he started in April, he came for a couple of weeks and then disappeared for two or three weeks. He was back for a week and gone for five and yet you asked us to pay him twice for travel in May. He had already received his full compensation for that month when you requested the second check. You were angry with me for questioning it. That is my job, Pastor! You intimated at that time that Jonas thought he was on staff. Where did he get that idea? He was brought in on a trial basis and has never been paid more than a travel honorarium as you well know and yet you were outraged and tore a strip off me when I reminded you of it."

Mira saw that he was about to interrupt, so she pushed on, scarcely drawing a breath. "We, as directors, are at fault in this matter as well." Rafe's face brightened. He could almost taste victory.

"We were wrong not to insist on interviewing Jonas before he was given the position of youth leader. As a board, that was our responsibility. We abdicated it because we love you and we trusted your judgement. Also, we know that you were bound and determined to have him and no one wanted the battle that would ensue if we denied you your wish." *In for penny, in for pound,* she thought. *I might as well get it all out on the table.*

She forged on. "Pastor, you told us yourself that Jonas refused to remove his body piercings at your request. Not only is he refusing to come under your authority as senior pastor but he is disrespecting you as his grandfather. As far as his building up of the young people to fifteen, anyone could get that many to come to a Saturday night wiener roast. Although fellowship is necessary and good, it does not translate into changed lives or more young people in the church. There has been no increase visible among the young people and everyone knows it." Rafe's eyes narrowed and his jaw tightened imperceptibly.

"The congregation are, for the most part, elderly," Mira continued. "They do not like the earrings and some have complained about Jonas and his wife talking and laughing all through the worship portion of the services whenever they are present. A committed leader should be entering into the worship and setting an example for the young people to follow. On the contrary, Jonas acts as if the songs are too old for him to bother with. He drums on the back of the seat and looks extremely bored at the whole thing. The fact of the matter is, if this board had conducted an interview, we would never have given him the position. *You* would have turfed him out of here long ago yourself, if it was anyone else but your grandson. You would *never* put up with the kind of attitude or absences that we have all witnessed."

"Well," sputtered Rafe. "I have always been harder on my own children then on anyone else." He went on to justify and excuse Jonas' behaviour while continuing to laud his great accomplishments.

Ian bolted from the table in the middle of his oration. "This just makes me sick," he said in disgust. "It makes my stomach churn." He disappeared into the kitchen, where he stayed until the pastor had stopped speaking. Then he rejoined the group at the table carrying a tray of water glasses for each of them.

"Pastor, I need to say something." It was Donny who spoke. Mira held her breath, wondering what was coming. Sometimes Donny could be very blunt.

"Why is it that whenever we are in a meeting, I feel totally intimidated by you? I am a business man and before I gave my life to the Lord, I travelled in some pretty rough circles. I've stood toe to toe with a man who wanted to kill me with a knife and never flinched. But here, and in every board meeting that I've been in so far, I've been totally shut down. I feel like I can't even think. My stomach just churns."

"Same here." "Me too." Everyone was nodding in agreement.

"Well, I don't know why that should be," bridled Rafe. "I've always done my best to include everyone." He took the floor again in an effort to bully and bribe with flattery the members who would ultimately decide the fate of his grandson. The directors were done speaking and simply waited him out. There was nothing more they could say.

Rafe left the room confident that he would have his way. He knew his power of persuasion and was certain that he already had Rev. Armstrong and Sylvester in his pocket. All he needed was one more person. That would tie the vote. If that should happen, the chairman would have an extra vote, according to the constitution, to break the tie.

David Armstrong's chin was vibrating visibly. "I guess all we have left to do is vote," he said timidly.

Caelen touched Mira's shoulder and spoke quickly into her ear.

A sudden inspiration struck her. "You do know," she said slowly, catching a glimpse of Sylvester fidgeting at the end of the table, "that you can abstain from a vote if you choose."

The old man leaped at the idea. "Really?" The relief on his face was palpable. "I think I'd like to do that."

"That's fine," replied Mira. "I vote against reinstating the travel honorarium for Jonas. Nothing said here this evening has changed my mind."

"I vote "No" too," came from Ian, Jack and Donny, almost simultaneously.

"Well...." stuttered Rev. Armstrong, "I guess that pretty much finishes it then. There's no point in my voting at all." He seemed relieved. "Rafe wants to know tonight what we decided so I guess I'll have to go and tell him." He cleared his throat nervously.

"Do you want us to go with you?" asked Jack sympathetically.

The old man looked alarmed at the prospect. Mira wasn't sure if he was more frightened of taking the bad news to the pastor or of having Jack accompany him.

"No, there's no need, I can tell him myself."

"Let us know how he takes it," said Donny with a grim chuckle.

"I dread the council meeting!" Mira threw her writing materials into a bag and headed for the door. In the hallway she met Grace who had come in search of her.

"Meeting over already?" Mira asked.

"Yes, look at the time. How come you took so long? I thought it was to be a brief meeting."

Mira laughed outright. "Come on, Grace. You know Pastor R. Do you really think he's capable of being brief?" she snorted. Her sister-in-law grinned but made no reply.

It was the next day before Mira heard from David Armstrong. There wasn't much to tell, he said. He had drawn the pastor aside and quietly told him that the board had voted against reinstating the travel allowance. Outside of a curt nod, Rafe had shown no sign of his true feelings regarding their decision.

Mira could feel the storm clouds gathering as she hung up the phone. She was relieved that she was booked to lead worship at Pastor Holman's church next Sunday morning. That meant she wouldn't see Pastor Rafe until the council meeting on Monday evening and Tuesday, he was scheduled to fly out.

Cloudy skies and flurries threatened the forecast for Saturday. Mira was scheduled to speak at a Valentine banquet that evening in a small town about an hour and a half away. Krysta accompanied her, along with her husband and sister-in-law. The occasion was heightened with excitement for Mira, who was delighted to have an opportunity to include her daughter in her ministry. Krysta would be singing both a solo and a duet with her mother.

They left early for fear a storm might hamper the drive. In an effort to quell the butterflies she felt churning inside, Mira played a worship CD as they navigated the roads. The weather was better than predicted however and they arrived an hour ahead of schedule. Snow showers were just starting to fall as they turned into the church's parking lot.

Sick with nervousness, Mira paced the lobby of the church between the banquet hall and the restroom. Grace finally took her aside and calling Krysta, they prayed together for God to take control of the situation and use them to do a work for him. The final hustle and bustle of the preparations for the banquet swirled around them as they dedicated the evening to the Lord.

An apologetic sound technician timidly interrupted their prayer, requesting a sound check and their background accompaniment CD's. Mira nerves steadied as she plunged into the last minute preparations. Couples were streaming into the hall now, laughing and chatting, shaking the snow from their coats.

The evening went by in a daze. Krysta's solo brought tears to the eyes of many and a proud glow to Dan's face. Once Mira began to share her testimony, she forgot about herself and words poured forth as she allowed the Spirit of God to speak through her. At the close of the meeting, she found herself praying for people with an authority and anointing unlike any she had ever experienced. At one point she raised her head and saw her husband and daughter praying with someone and found she wasn't surprised by it. It seemed a natural thing for them to do.

A thick, sparkling blanket of snow covered the world in quiet softness as they left the building that evening. Mira felt as if she were stepping on clouds. The long drive home seemed as nothing compared to the glorious feeling inside of her. God had used her as an instrument in His hands and she knew she would never be the same again. The terrible reality of the chaos at the church faded into insignificant babbling for a few precious hours.

Surrounded by demons, the angelic forces, led by Captain Darshan, seemed pitiful by comparison, numbering a scant twelve, plus the two commanders. Gurgling sounds, snarls and hissings filled the air, as a multitude of black misshapen forms careened through the room

Council members came together with a suppressed eagerness to finish the task they had started. Once again, Pastor Rutherford took charge in direct defiance of the letter he had received requesting a different moderator. He tired the members out with irrelevant ramblings while their precious allotment of time dwindled away. Eventually, their eyes seemed to glaze over as they lost interest and focus. Grace and Marvin were side-lined as silent observers, having been ordered to be seen and not heard, unless spoken to directly.

Eventually Rafe's meandering lecture wound to a tortuous conclusion. "The survey results," he observed gravely, "are skewed by a few disgruntles who are determined to find fault with me. They were intended to be used as a tool to highlight weakness in the administration, rather than as a reason to get rid of me."

With calculating coldness, he blind-sided the directors with an announcement to council that Jonas had been dismissed as youth leader as a result of the board's actions. He related how hurt his grandson and new wife had been when they heard how much the board hated them. "They wanted to know the names of the directors." Rafe regarded them coldly with fixed, icy malice. "Of course I didn't give them any names," he hastily added. "I guess I should have introduced them to the directors when they first came but, in retrospect, I'm glad I didn't because now they don't know who it was that gave them the axe." He looked appealingly at his deacons. "I don't know what will become of all of the young people that Jonas was helping and mentoring but I guess the board didn't give that any thought through all of this process."

Rafe's voice quivered with indignation and resentment. "I have to say," he said brusquely in hard tones, "that this is the worst board I've dealt with in all of my forty five years of ministry. I have been deeply wounded by their actions. I'm sure we'll find a way to work through it all, but I can't help but say that this all could have been avoided if you had just showed a little patience and support. I am the shepherd here and my only thought is for the sheep. I want to do what is best for them."

Mira could feel the heat rising, suffusing her face and neck. David Armstrong dared not lift his eyes from his hands which trembled uncontrollably. Sylvester glowered uneasily while Jack and Donny seemed to shrink into their chairs. Ian looked fixedly at his agenda never once glancing up.

Their agony ended when Rafe eventually subsided into silence. Phil Schmidt spoke up immediately, as if on cue, suggesting that the pastor should be accorded his requested sabbatical until the end of March. Rob Samuels asked for *"sabbatical"* to be defined as complete rest with no involvement in church affairs.

Relieved that things seemed to be progressing without further discomfort, Rev. Armstrong addressed council, eagerly persuading them to accommodate dear Pastor Rutherford who had served the church so untiringly for fifteen years. "He deserves the honor and respect of this council," he said, his chin wobbling noticeably.

No one dared to stand in opposition since they had all, at some point, encouraged the sabbatical. The vote was taken with unanimous results. Pastor Rafe was to have his sabbatical. Most of the members simply wanted him gone so they could have some peace and quiet for awhile.

A warning screamed in Mira's spirit. Try as she would, she couldn't shake the feeling that they had done the wrong thing. As she walked out to her car, she saw several of the men chatting together in the parking lot. She joined them to find out their reaction to the meeting and to share with them how disturbed she was by the outcome. "If this is the right thing to do," she said worriedly, "then why do I feel so rotten. I feel sick inside – like we did the wrong thing."

"I think he's buying time," said Jack who felt as uneasy as the treasurer. "He wants to wait us out. That is probably why he's chosen the end of March. He knows that if he can just make it to the annual business meeting, he'll be able to get rid of us and start over with another group."

Mira looked startled. "Of course! That's exactly what he wants and we played right into his hands! What can we do now?"

"Well, what's done is done. We can't turn back the clock," he replied. "But I sure don't like it!"

"Don't worry," laughed Donny. "He hasn't gone on any sabbatical. It's supposed to be complete rest and no involvement in the church, right?"

"That's what he said."

"You all know he won't do it. He can't help it! He'll be calling the church every day, same as usual. I heard him say he's coming back in the middle of March to go on a mission trip with that guy he had filling in while he was away. Some deal they have going. Mrs. R. is supposed to go too. So he's not on a sabbatical. Never going to happen!"

"You're right!" agreed Jack. "He would never relinquish control of the church like this without a fight. He has something in mind and we had better be prepared for it!" He looked at Mira. "He has said several times now that we are the worst board he's ever had. I find that hard to believe! Is there any way we can find out if he's had any issues with other boards?"

Mira chewed her lip thoughtfully for moment. "I know there were problems with another board five or six years ago," she said slowly. "It collapsed completely.... of course the pastor said they were in the wrong."

"Like we're in the wrong? Sure thing!" replied Donny sarcastically.

"I did see a binder in the archives once," volunteered Mira, "which bears the name of John Schilling, the young associate minister who was at the center of that board's big issue, whatever it was. It might shed some light on why they went to pieces. There are also books, filed by year, that contain the minutes of all of the meetings held by past boards. I don't know what's in them, but I do know that it was Dora Golding who virtually created most of the books and files. She had to sort through piles of paperwork in boxes, including lawyer's letters and so on, from that old mess. She told me that she worked on it throughout her whole term. In fact, her appointment as a director was made when that other board collapsed. She's been fairly open with me about wounds that she received at the pastor's hand during her term. She actually apologized, after my election, for recommending my name to the pastor as a possible board nominee. She told me that I didn't know what I was getting into. I sure didn't have any idea what she meant at the time."

"I know it's a lot to ask, but would you be willing to have a look through the files and see what you can find?" asked Jack.

"Sure! It'll take some time but I suppose I could take them home and go through them, one at a time. I have the keys to the archive room so the staff needn't know anything about it. As members of the board, we have the right to see all of the archive files anyway. I just wouldn't want the pastor to know about it. I wouldn't put it past him to destroy files if he were to find out our interest in them, particularly if there is anything damaging in them."

"Good, that's settled then. I have a feeling that we aren't the only board that has dealt with some of these integrity issues."

~

Valin looked solemnly at his companion. "The woman is about to learn some things that will shake her to the very core of her being."

"Undoubtedly she will suffer severe emotional distress when the credibility of her pastor is shaken even further, but she is stronger than even she realizes," Caelen replied. "Although her dilemma will terrify her for a season, she has been prepared for this moment and in the end, I believe she will not crumble. She has come too far for that."

"What of the others?"

"I feel that at least three will stand with her. The other two...." Caelen's voice trailed off, doubt plainly written on his face.

"We must redouble our efforts to reach them in time," Valin exclaimed.

The other commander nodded distantly. His focus seemed to have shifted elsewhere. "They are in a far better position today to deal with this, than they were when elected last April," he said with finality.

16

The next day, Mira busied herself with her Women's Ministries' executive team making preparations for their annual Valentine banquet, which was to take place that evening. Even though it was potluck, it still required a fair bit of organization. The banquet hall was painstakingly decorated with brightly festooned hearts and ribbons of red and white, while tables were attractively set with beautifully themed centerpieces.

The event was well attended by both couples and singles alike. Several long buffet tables groaned with a vast display of culinary dishes, as each one vied to please the crowd with their offering. The worship, Mira handled herself, with the help of Pastor Marvin, who served as pianist for the evening's festivities.

This year, they had booked a husband and wife team to sing and share their personal testimony and from the comments Mira received afterward, she felt that the event was quite a success. Even so, she was glad when it was over. Filled with a mixture of joy and sadness, she couldn't shake the feeling that she wouldn't be here much longer. Perhaps this would be the last ladies' meeting she would preside over. After everyone was gone, she went into the archive room and picked out a couple of binders to take home with her.

For the next three weeks, Mira combed through the records and files of the church. As she delved into the special cases and official board books, an undeniable pattern quickly emerged. Letters of censure, issues of control, manipulation and unethical practices, pointed directly at the senior pastor. These had all been somehow swept under the rug or shelved by past councils. Many names that surfaced were familiar to Mira and her questions about their sudden disappearances from the church ranks were now being answered.

After she had waded through most of the books and files, she settled down one evening to read a thick binder she had saved for last. It was labelled *"John Schilling"*. Mira knew very little about the associate minister who had left in disgrace some six years ago. Pastor Rafe had accused him of being one of those who was after his pulpit. He claimed the man had come to the church with an agenda to oust him as senior pastor, in order to take the position himself.

Cold beads of sweat broke out on her forehead as she digested the details of a serious charge of immorality which had been levelled at the senior pastor by the younger minister. Several times, John had refused Rafe's efforts to seduce him into becoming involved in a homosexual affair. He had even written a letter, asking the pastor to stop his harassment and get counselling. When this went unheeded, he had been forced to approach the board and council to apprise them of the situation, which was growing increasingly uncomfortable. The agony he suffered, as a result of bringing the matter out in the open was apparent from his letters and writings.

Numerous testimonials, from well respected men of faith, testified to the moral integrity of John, while only one letter, from a man who appeared to be morally suspect, supported Pastor Rafe. The board had been divided by the pastor; broken down with manipulation, harassment, lies and defamation of character. Two of the directors had lost their health over it. One of the elders, a retired minister of stellar reputation, had tried to mediate the situation but, in the end, he had finally thrown in the towel and left. According to the documents, he had burned several letters which would have been severely damaging to Pastor Rafe. There were also allegations of improprieties between the pastor and a young boy who had attended the Christian school operated by the church for a brief couple of years.

Most of the names were familiar to Mira and things began to fall into place as she remembered the sudden departure of many of the board and council members during that time. Gone! They were all gone! She vaguely recalled the undercurrents that had washed over the congregation during the time of John Schilling. She had been removed from most of it, spending weeks in hospital hardly able to lift her head, suffering from the major depression that had nearly taken her life. The young man had been almost a stranger in her world. She had seen him around the church a few times, but he had only lasted three months, so she had no opportunity to get to know him well.

Mira's heart ached for his wife and children. John had uprooted their lives to come and serve as an associate to Pastor Rafe and he counted heavily on the job. They had suffered great humiliation unjustly, as well as financial ruin. Unable to pay their rent, they were forced to leave their apartment with no alternative in place. A dear couple, who left the church at the same time, had taken them in for several months, until John was able to support his family again.

Accepting what she was told by her dearly loved pastor, Mira hadn't delved very far into why all of these people had left. Most of it had been kept rather hush-hush. Now however, her eyes were being opened. She was beginning to comprehend the reason why so many willing workers and leaders in the church had disappeared and why the Christian School had been summarily closed for no apparent reason.

A new board had been appointed. After a three month cooling-off period, a statement had been read to the congregation of the Good Shepherd church in a Sunday morning service. Mira remembered the day well. She had been glad at the time that her adored pastor had been exonerated of any and all charges and that he had the confidence of the board and council. The document was worded carefully so that the charges were unclear and it was only now, in reading the statement carefully, that she realized he had not been exonerated at all! John had simply been unable to prove what had transpired between him and the pastor.

As she pondered over the documents, Mira clearly saw inconsistencies in Pastor Rafe's denials and testimony. He seemed to have no problem maligning the young man's character, twisting and rationalizing conversations, always with his own image in mind. She knew what story he was telling people privately about the incident and it sickened her to the very core of her being. Her mind spun and her stomach revolted at the thought of sharing this with the rest of the board. They would have a hard time accepting that their pastor could be capable of this degree of deception. If she had not worked with him this past year and seen his unethical, dishonest conduct with her own eyes, she would not believe it herself. But her eyes had been opened.... slowly, a little at a time and so had theirs.

Knowledge is powerful tool, she thought grimly. *With what I already know about the pastor, his pathological lying, his manipulating of people and circumstances, it isn't any great leap to draw a conclusion from what I've read tonight. I wonder if I should make a copy of this file. Hard proof is better than just my words or thoughts.*

Sleep fled from Mira that night. She tossed and turned, unable to stop her mind from returning to the terrible documents. The hours ticked slowly by. Finally she left her bed in frustration and, making herself a cup of tea, she settled down to read her bible at the kitchen table. A few minutes later, she heard the spare bedroom door open.

"Why are you still up?" Grace asked, her voice showing her concern.

"I just couldn't sleep. Too much on my mind, I guess." Mira's voice trembled slightly.

"What's wrong?"

Tears welled up in her eyes in spite of her effort to restrain them. "I found out some things tonight about Pastor Rafe. I brought home a binder from the church archives and now I almost wish I hadn't read it." She started to sob. "He's guilty, Grace. I know it in my heart."

"What's he done now?" inquired her friend. "It can't be that bad!"

"It's what he did six years ago that I learned about tonight. I truly didn't know that he was capable of being so evil."

"Whoa! Wait a minute! Maybe you'd better tell me about it. I can't help if I don't know what you're talking about."

Mira took a deep breath. "Several years ago we lost quite a number of congregants – good people - leaders and volunteers. I just found out why they left." She went on to explain what she learned in searching the archives and particularly what was contained in the last binder she had just read.

"Dan is right," she ended woefully. "Pastor Rafe is a wicked man! I know that's an awful thing to say but it's true." Tears coursed down her cheeks.

Grace patted her hand sympathetically. "I really don't know what to think. I had so much respect for the pastor when I came. I used to listen to his sermons when he had a television ministry and I thought he was wonderful. It's always been a dream of mine to work with him but now I'm not so sure. I've heard that it was a serious incident of sexual impropriety that got him fired from his last church. It basically devastated his ministry at the time. When I told a friend of mine that I was coming here for four months, she asked me if I was sure that God had called me. She said that Pastor Rafe has caused much devastation in his former pastorates. I didn't believe the stories, Mira. I couldn't!"

"Well, for myself, I believe what's in these books. It all makes sense, especially after all of the unethical things I've seen for myself over this past year." Mira looked desolate. "Some friends of ours tried to warn us about this but we didn't listen. Or at least I didn't! At Krysta's wedding they saw Pastor Rafe flirting with a gay waiter. I was sure they must be mistaken but that wasn't the only occasion. They claimed they had witnessed him acting inappropriately with visiting men in the church. They left because they couldn't stomach it! I didn't want to believe that such a thing could be true! He married my daughter and son-in-law!" she wailed covering her face with her hands.

Grace looked a little dazed. "You didn't know any of this then, Mira," she comforted. "You can't beat yourself up. I can hardly believe it myself."

"I remember something else too. Another friend told me quite awhile ago that she was having a real struggle over this very issue. She needed to know for sure if Pastor Rafe was dabbling in an immoral life-style and still preaching in the pulpit. She went so far as to follow him one night when he left the parsonage. He went to the home of a known homosexual man and spent the evening. She left the church at the time but still visits occasionally. He seems to have such a hold on people that even when they know of his immorality, they still are drawn to him. I really loved and respected him, Grace and now I feel totally betrayed!"

"I understand how you feel but, if this is really true and he is dabbling in wickedness, then we need to pray for the man more than ever. His very soul is at stake." She looked suddenly stricken. "How awful it would be if his eternity is spent in a place of torment after devoting his life to the gospel of Jesus Christ. This is such a serious thing! He's not a young man and he doesn't have a lot of time left. Most of his life is now behind him. How terrible if he goes to his grave unrepentant! We need to pray as we've never prayed before!

~

Desolate over what she had learned and desperate for advice, Mira sought a meeting with Pastor Dave Holman and his wife, Emma. To them, she poured out her heart, omitting nothing of the terrible dilemma the board was facing. "I just want to do what is right!" she cried, wiping away fast falling tears. "We all do!"

Openly, she shared her personal struggle over whether to walk away from the church, or stay and see it through to a conclusion at the annual business meeting. "I love the people," she wailed, "but I find it harder and harder to go to church there. My husband hates it! He won't even attend, when Pastor is there. Yet, I still don't feel a release to leave." She looked at them miserably.

The pastor and his wife listened intently, asking a question from time to time, and where possible, imparting a wealth of wisdom and advice. Their deep concern and love was apparent to Mira. She couldn't help but notice the difference between them and her own pastor. She knew she was only important to Pastor Rafe if she could produce and be of service to him. But this couple! They really listened and seemed to care! She wasn't accustomed to being heard or valued and she tucked it away in her heart to ponder over, in the dark days ahead.

~

Saturday brought a pleasant break from church affairs for both Mira and Grace. At Krysta's invitation, they attended a women's breakfast, a special event, hosted by a non-denominational Christian group and catered at a local hotel. Krysta had been asked to share her own personal testimony at the meeting of how her encounter with a real God had changed her life's direction.

When they arrived, the room was packed with women, some of whom came merely for the fellowship and others who were desperate to find out if God really cared about them and their needs. When her time came, Krysta spoke easily about how God had revealed himself to her one night in her bedroom; how He had changed her life and given her new purpose and a hope of eternal life beyond this life's journey.

The women responded readily to come for prayer at the end of her little message. Profoundly stirred, Mira wept before the Lord, praise and thanksgiving welling up in her heart over the change in her only child.

The final days of February ended with a blast of arctic air that brought blizzard conditions with a mixture of drifting snow, sleet and freezing temperatures. There was little that could be done outside beyond the clearing of driveway and sidewalk, so Mira devoted the extra time to finishing the task of sorting through the data stored in the archives of the Good Shepherd Church.

Copies of information she thought relevant to the board's decision-making process were made before returning the borrowed binders and books. Some of it was so explosive that she hesitated about whether she should share everything in its entirety. However she knew that Rev. Armstrong and Sylvester, in particular, would probably balk in disbelief if she didn't present hard evidence of what she had learned.

The weather had cleared by Sunday, so the trip from Mira's place to the church across the back roads was no longer hazardous. Heading into Faith's office, she threw her tote bag onto the floor and collapsed into a chair with a grin. She had a surprise planned for the morning service. The associate pastors and the board of directors were going to present the faithful secretary with flowers and a gift in the morning service, to commemorate ten years of service to the congregation of Good Shepherd Church.

"How's it going, Sunshine?" The secretary got up from her chair and gave Mira a warm hug. When their greetings were over, Mira settled back for a chat.

"How did you weather the big storm?"

"We did okay once I got home but I have a confession to make." Faith's eyes looked concerned. Mira just raised her eyebrows questioningly. She knew the ethics and loyalty of the secretary were beyond question so it couldn't be anything too devastating.

"You know when the storm started on Thursday?"

Mira nodded. "I think it's the worst we've had all winter. I sure stayed put, I can tell you."

"Well, I don't know if Pastor Grace told you or not, but after lunch that day, the snow started to fall fast. The wind was just whipping across the parking lot and we were all starting to get really concerned about making it home."

"I don't wonder," replied Mira. "I heard a radio broadcast that said the police were warning everyone to stay off the roads and portions of the highway were completely closed. Everyone was being sent home from their jobs. I hope you went home."

"Well, that's just it. We all decided to leave at two o'clock but Pastor called just as I putting on my coat. I wish I hadn't answered the phone," she added worriedly.

"Why was he calling?" Mira asked curiously. *He's not supposed to be calling,* she thought. *He's on sabbatical and he promised that he wouldn't be calling or trying to run the church during this time that he was away.*

"He always calls in every day," replied Faith, "in fact I usually hear from him several times a day. He likes to know what's going on." She lowered her voice conspiratorially. "Don't tell anyone I said this, but sometimes I think he just wants to check on the staff to see if they're here. I can't think of any other reason why he calls so early every morning and again right at five o'clock. I think he wants to make sure we don't leave early."

Mira threw up her hands. "You've got to be kidding!" she said in exasperation. "You're the most honest person I know. What! He doesn't trust you after ten years?"

"I guess not," she replied softly. "Anyway, I told him about the big storm and I said that we were all just about to leave when he called."

"So what did he say?" Mira was really curious now.

"He asked me to stay until five o'clock."

"What! For heaven's sake, why?"

"He said he might need to call me at five o'clock for a phone number," she said meekly.

Mira snorted. "And I'll just bet you stayed!"

Faith's eyes twinkled. "No I didn't," she admitted sheepishly. "He told me to stay overnight at the parsonage if the roads were too bad but that would mean Rob would worry about me being there. Besides, Nathan's there. I can't believe he would even suggest it! I guess I'll have to take the consequences when he gets back." She laughed. "I'm real brave with him so far away. But Mira, I truly didn't want to stay there, even if it weren't for Nathan. I don't sleep well in that house for some reason," she confessed. "I don't really know why." She hesitated for a moment. "Sometimes I think I hear things...noises...I don't know..." Her voice trailed off.

"You shouldn't have to stay there unless it's a dire emergency or something. I'm glad you had enough sense to leave."

"I probably wouldn't have, if it hadn't been for Pastor Grace. She insisted that I go home. She said that my safety was more important and that nothing was so imperative that it couldn't wait. The phones were pretty dead all day anyway," she said defensively.

"You did the right thing, Faith, and if the pastor tears into you over it just refer him the board. You work for us, not him."

"Ohhh, I wouldn't dare tell him that!" The secretary looked horrified. "He would make my life miserable!"

"No doubt!" muttered Mira tightly. "I truly don't know why you put up with the way he treats you."

"I know, but I love working here," she replied. "Not so much for him but I love the people. I used to cry and cry when he'd say something that hurt or demeaned me but I am getting tougher."

"Yeah, sure you are," snorted Mira, knowing her friend had a tender heart and a gentle spirit.

"No - really! I've stood up to him a few times. Once I actually slammed some papers down on the desk and walked out." Mira laughed in disbelief.

"It's true!" she said breathlessly. "I told him that I had just had it and I was done! I said I was tired of him sweeping things under the rug all the time and not dealing with anything. He had been really mean to me that day, blaming me for something that was his fault and had nothing to do with me, so I left. I drove around for awhile and then I spent the afternoon at a friend's house. We had some tea and talked and talked until I felt better. I knew I had to come back to the office because there was a wedding appointment for the next day that had to be entered into the pastor's date book so I didn't have any choice."

She laughed in embarrassment. "I sat in my car and waited until he left for the parsonage before I went in. Mrs. R. called me that night at home. I know he got her to do it because he knew I was upset at him. Rob called me on my cell too. Pastor had called him trying to find out where I was."

Mira looked at her speculatively. "I'm willing to wager that no one, except maybe your husband, has a clue what you've been through this past ten years. No wonder Rob feels the way he does about Pastor."

"We've seen and heard way too much." Her eyes welled with tears and her voice shook. "It's just the way he treats people, Mira. I don't think he means to," she added loyally, "but the truth is, it's always about him. Everything is always about him! I used to take care of his house all the time when he and Mrs. R. went away. Once, I had to stay there for three weeks in the coldest part of the winter. I was sick the whole time and their old dog, Toby was pretty much at death's door. He kept dirtying the carpet and leaving deposits on the kitchen floor, but I couldn't leave him outside in the cold. I could hardly crawl from the couch to the bathroom myself. The Rutherfords returned from their Florida vacation and almost immediately left again; this time to take a group to Israel for eleven days. So I had to stay at the house again. When they returned from that trip, Pastor asked me to prepare dinner for them as soon as they walked in the door."

A tear spilled over onto her cheek. "I actually wrote Pastor and Eve a letter afterwards. I find it easier to put things in writing because I get too emotional when I talk and sometimes I leave out the most important things, because I get so tongue-tied. Anyway, I told them that I was happy to look after their house from time to time, but I just couldn't do it for that length of time again. It isn't fair to my husband. He runs a business, so all of those nights that I was gone, he was alone at our place with no hot meal waiting for him after a long day on the road. I mentioned that I don't sleep well at their house either. I was so exhausted by the time they returned from the second trip that I was sick for a month. I had to clean their house and mine as well. Grocery shopping had to be done for both places because of living apart from my husband. I guess it seems like a small thing to get upset about, but I was really disappointed when Pastor asked me to make dinner that night. It would have been really nice if he had offered to go out to dinner instead, as a thank you for taking care of the house. Rob and I would have even paid our own way. I was just so worn-out and unwell. I wasn't feeling like myself at all," she offered apologetically.

"What was their response to your letter?"

"They didn't understand at all. Even Eve said that Rob could have come and spent his evenings there with me. But he didn't want to, Mira. His computer and business phone are at our place, so it would still mean running back and forth every evening. They don't seem to realize that it takes almost a half hour to get home in this weather. I guess they just don't stop and think."

"From what I've seen and heard, pastor really doesn't care about anyone other than himself!" said Mira sharply. "It's always about him and his needs and wants!"

"I don't mean to complain, truly I don't," replied Faith anxiously. "I just have no one to talk to. If I say too much to my husband, he gets all upset and I certainly can't share this with any of the church people. I shouldn't even be telling you."

"Why not? Everyone needs someone to share things with. I'm surprised that you haven't had a complete meltdown before now."

"Like I said, I'm starting to stand up for myself." Faith gave her a shaky smile and with an apology, she hurried out of the office to prepare the overheads for the song service.

Mira ducked out to the car to smuggle in the big bouquet of flowers she had bought to present to Faith later in the service. She adroitly hid them under a seat off to one side of the sanctuary. Worship practice had already started as she quietly slipped into place.

The presentation to Faith occurred after the morning announcements. Besides the flowers, Mira had purchased a beautiful crystal statue of the Good Shepherd holding a lamb so that Faith would have a memento of the occasion, but the real gift from the board of directors was the approval of another week of vacation for her. They had quietly agreed on this after the pastor had left for Florida, knowing that he would probably object if he knew about it. He hadn't even wanted to pay her for the statutory holidays, so they figured another week of vacation might make him positively apoplectic.

Together, Pastor Grace, Mira and Rev. Armstrong made the special presentation overwhelming Faith with the unexpected gifts and attention. Parishioners surrounded her after the service extending their love and warm congratulations. It was obvious that everyone loved her. Her kindnesses and compassionate, friendly nature reached into the hearts of all who knew her. She was one who possessed a great gift for making people feel loved and special and now it came back to her from the very ones whose lives she had touched.

Grace preached a powerful message that morning. As people streamed to the altar for prayer, she felt a strong urge to call the whole assembly to corporate prayer for the church and the leadership. Many responded, staying behind to weep at the altars, calling on God for wisdom, unity and direction for the assembly and praying one for another.

The response was so heartening, Grace felt encouraged to ask the people to support a season of prayer and fasting. This, she believed, was desperately needed to break the strongholds of the enemy over the pastor and the church and find new direction. That very evening, she threw out a challenge to all those who were really serious for a move of God. Requesting a commitment of one month, she asked the congregants to fast one meal each Sunday afternoon and spend the time in prayer for the leadership.

Still she didn't feel that this was enough. The urgency for prayer was so heavy upon her that she could scarcely stand it. Setting aside her busy schedule, she announced that the sanctuary would also be open all day Wednesday for people to come and pray, even if only for a small portion of the day.

All of the board members frequented the altar that Sunday, praying and weeping together, as they searched for answers to the dilemma they found themselves in. As Mira sought the Lord an unnatural calm seeped into her spirit. She still had no answers but she felt strongly that she would soon be sharing with the rest of the board what she had found out. After the service as people were milling about the lobby, donning coats and boots, she joined Jack, Donny and Ian who were talking together in a corner.

"I think the surveys provided invaluable feedback from the leadership but personal letters will carry more weight with council," Ian was saying.

"Well, I've decided that I'm going to write a formal letter to the board to go on record with my own personal complaints," replied Mira, joining the conversation. "If any of you are willing to write letters, please let me have them in time to circulate them to all of council in advance of the next meeting."

"I know of several who would be willing to write letters," volunteered Ian. "Both of our sound technicians have now left the church, along with their wives, but I think they might be persuaded to return if Pastor Rafe leaves permanently. I believe they might be willing to write a letter stating their complaints and why they decided to leave."

"Good," exclaimed Mira. "Would you feel comfortable asking them?"

"Sure, we keep in contact on a regular basis."

"We need hard facts – preferably an exact number of people who will definitely leave if there is no change. I made a list of people that have indicated to me that they are on the verge of leaving and there were thirty. Of course, one never knows for certain how serious they are. The only thing I know for sure is that Dan and I will definitely go if the pastor stays and I am willing to put that on paper along with my reasons. My husband would have left long ago, but I just haven't felt released by the Lord yet. I've prayed and prayed about it and the only answer I receive is to wait a little while longer. In my spirit, I feel that I will be finished here as of the annual business meeting. I have no answer from God on how it will go or what will happen, just that it will all be over by then. One more month, gentlemen...we will only have to stand for one more month. After that, it will be over and in all likelihood, we will be leaving"

"I feel the same way," said Jack. "My wife and I have talked it over and prayed about it and we have decided that we will leave as well, if the pastor stays. We're willing to write a letter to that effect," he added. Ian and Donny both promised letters as well.

"I think there is something else we should do," added Jack. In the constitution, it says that in order to bring a complaint against the pastor on the basis of immoral, unethical or unscriptural conduct, it must be in writing and signed by the member bringing the charge. If a complaint is brought on the basis of perceived ineffectiveness of his ministry, it has to be in writing with specific details and facts supporting the complaint and signed by three active members. If we're really serious about holding the pastor accountable for his lack of integrity, lying and so on, then we need to do this if we are going to be in line with our own constitution."

"What about Rev. Armstrong and Sylvester Zimmer?" asked Ian.

"Can we trust them to keep their mouths shut until we're ready to present the letter?" asked Donny. Doubt was written clearly on his face.

"We only need three signatures and there are four of us here," replied Jack. "Let's not even ask them. I think it would make them uncomfortable. We're either ready to back up what we've said or forget it and walk away."

"I'll prepare the letter," promised Mira. "I'll touch base with each of you during the week about the content so that we are all in agreement over the wording. It'll be ready for our signatures on Sunday. I will also summarize the issues that have arisen from the surveys so that they will be presented clearly and concisely. The pastor will not address anything that is longer than a page or two. By the way, Faith told me the other day that the he is flying in next Friday."

"So much for his sabbatical," grumbled Jack. "I thought he was supposed to stay away until the end of March."

"No, he is coming back in order to go on that mission trip he had planned. He's going to spend a week here first and then Mrs. R. is flying in, so they can go on the trip together. Maybe we should go ahead and set up a council meeting for the week that he's here."

"Might as well. He's broken the terms of the sabbatical anyway," Jack observed.

"Things are going to get nasty," exclaimed Donny. "He won't just leave that's for sure. He's going to put up the fight of his life,"

17

PASTOR RAFE LEARNED ABOUT the council meeting the next time he called the church. A request from council for a change of chairperson had caused him to grind his teeth in fury and determine in his heart never to let it happen. His associate pastors both admitted to receiving a request to be present. He could feel a showdown coming!

Rafe had no intention of being pre-empted from either his position as chair or as pastor. They might as well have waived a red flag in front of a bull. He tore up the phone lines every day trying to learn what he could about what the board might be planning. Catching wind of the letters starting to pour in from leadership and members alike, he became more determined with each passing day to stall their intentions until the annual business meeting.

Seeds of doubt and suspicion were carefully planted in the minds of as many parishioners as possible. In a desperate attempt to break the unity of the board, a carefully crafted campaign was started against Donny Allison. If he could manage to discredit him then it would break the impasse of the four directors who were standing solidly in his way. The two old men, Sylvester and David Armstrong did not worry him in the slightest. They could be bullied into anything.

After a few judiciously placed calls, he dialled the church and asked to speak with Marvin and Grace. "There have been two serious complaints against Donny Allison," he told them. "I've requested letters from the parties involved and you should get those in a day or two. When you have them," he ordered, "I want the two of you to ask Donny to come in to the office to address the allegations. He is to be placed under discipline."

After the call was terminated, the two associates looked at one another in consternation. "What is he up to now?" Grace asked curiously.

"He's got something in mind, that's for sure!" replied Marvin. "I think there's something in the constitution about a board member having to vacate his position if he's under discipline."

"That's it!" she said in disgust. "What an underhanded thing to do!"

"That's the way he works! Think about it! He tried to get rid of Ian by pulling his head usher position. That didn't work, so now he's getting desperate because he's running out of time. If he can divide the board, David Armstrong carries an extra vote in case of a tie. He'll go after at least one more."

"Is there anything we can do about Donny?"

"Well.....we don't have to do anything until we get the letters so let's just wait and see."

~

After a day had passed, Rafe called again asking if they had talked to Donny.

"No, Pastor," replied Marvin. "We haven't seen the letters yet. We can't do much without them."

Later in the day, the young associate told Grace that a letter had been hand-delivered to the church. "It's pretty bland really," he said, handing it to her to read. "Not much substance; certainly not enough to put him under discipline," he added.

"The pastor must have really put on the pressure to get this." Grace looked sober. "Does he seriously expect us to haul him up on charges because he said something about the pastor's conduct?"

Two more days passed before the second letter made its appearance. It was written by a young man who had worked for Donny briefly.

Marvin showed the second letter to Grace. "I have had serious problems with this guy myself," he confided. "He played the drums here in the church for awhile - off and on. I stopped him at one point because he sent an unacceptable e-mail to one of my daughters. It was pretty graphic! At the time, I told him that until he was fit for ministry he couldn't play with the worship team. Of course, his mother went running to Pastor Rafe and he insisted, over my objections, that I put him right back on drums the very next time he came. He spent several months living with the Rutherfords at the parsonage, you know."

"Really?" queried Grace. "How interesting! So we're supposed to take this young man's word for what happened between him and Donny?"

"If we don't do something, Pastor Rafe will do it himself when he returns on Friday," he replied ruefully.

"Fine, let's call Donny in."

~

Grace phoned Donny Allison immediately to set up an appointment with her and Marvin at the church. Always anxious to please, Donny obliged, dropping into the office the same day. He laughed heartily when he heard the content of the two letters.

"The pastor must be really desperate," he chuckled. His manner was honest and direct as he shared his side of the incidents in question. Things hadn't worked out with the young man who had written one of the letters. The youth was unreliable as a worker and belligerent to Donny as his boss, so he had been forced to let him go.

"Well, there doesn't seem to be anything to that letter other than vindictiveness over being fired but, regarding the first letter, I have to say that I don't think it was wise to say what you did about the pastor to two of the congregants," Grace said when he was finished.

"You're right. I probably shouldn't have said anything. I'm sorry for that and it won't happen again," Donny replied.

"You need to be aware that if anyone else reports any inappropriate comments regarding the pastor, you could be brought under formal discipline and have to step down from your position on the board," she said pointedly.

"Yes, I understand completely." He looked at them soberly. "I'd like to thank you for your patience with me," he added. "It's my first time to serve on a church board and there hasn't been any teaching or assistance. I've just been thrown into it without any guidance whatsoever."

Marvin laughed openly. "No one gets any guidance here. You just fly by the seat of your pants and hope that everything works out for the best."

When Donny had shaken their hands and left, Grace let out a sigh of relief.

"So....what will we tell Pastor Rafe when he calls?" inquired Marvin curiously. "We didn't put him under discipline as ordered."

"We're in charge while the pastor is on sabbatical...right?"

"Yes...."

"Well, we dealt with the complaints. Donny has apologized for any inappropriate behaviour and has promised that it won't happen again. End of story!"

Marvin laughed aloud. "You know the pastor won't be happy with that."

"No, I don't expect he will, but he'll have a hard time resurrecting these charges again. Besides, you know as well as I do, that this whole thing is bogus. It was trumped up to further Rafe's agenda to divide the board."

Grace was right about the pastor's motives. Rafe was furious when he returned from Florida and learned that Donny Allison still wasn't under church discipline. He was loath to completely abandon his plan to discredit the board member. In fact, he would have had no qualms about destroying the man utterly if he could. His face was a study as he questioned the associate pastors angrily in his office.

"Pastor," Grace said bluntly when he had finished his tirade, "it wouldn't look very good for your reputation if the elders and council found out that you solicited letters of complaint against Donny. One of the parties involved is morally suspect, according to your own associate pastor."

"What do you mean by that!" Rafe snapped.

"He sent sexually graphic e-mails to one of Marvin's teenage daughters, Pastor. Of course that would all have to be disclosed if there should be a disciplinary hearing. Marvin and I thought it best to talk to Donny and elicit an apology. We didn't feel that any further action was warranted."

Rafe slammed the door of Marvin's office so hard the window rattled. Grace could scarcely suppress a grin.

"You have to admit, that we are certainly in a most interesting position right now," Marvin said with a quiet smile.

"What do you mean?

"Where else could you sit on the sidelines and watch this kind of drama unfold right before your eyes."

She smiled. "I guess I never thought of it that way."

~

Wisps of black smoke eddied about the banquet hall. A sickly smell of sulphur and attar pervaded the atmosphere. Lidless, red-rimmed eyes regarded the assembled demonic force with a cruel malicious hunger. The enormous head of Python swivelled dangerously close to the apparition of Jezebel, flicking its treacherous forked tongue as it weaved and bobbed; a mesmerizing, nightmarish atrocity.

"You are losssing control of the board." Fetid breath and glittering eyes swept by the bristling huge black beast. The air was charged with fear and rage.

Jezebel abhorred the great serpent's supremacy which he coveted for himself. "We will triumph," he asserted with more confidence than he felt.

"If you cannot even control the puny woman than how will you dominate the ressst of them?" Power emanated from even its smallest movement.

Sweat glistened on the evil black countenance of the demon as it shifted its feet nervously. "Oh, Great and Mighty Ruler." He bowed obsequiously before the monstrous spirit. "She and three men pray constantly." He spat out the words like a curse. "They are protected day and night by the Holy One but we will find a way to subvert them. If not, we will utterly destroy them!"

"The Massster will not be pleasssed with you if you fail!" hissed the serpent savagely. The warning brought an icy chill of foreboding to the heart of the lesser demon and a stronger determination to succeed – nay, to surpass the expectations of his master, Lucifer, Prince of Darkness. He would prepare his army of demons carefully for the next encounter with the angels of light.

~

Rafe positively strutted into the council meeting on Saturday morning. Jezebel stalked dangerously beside him, a wedge of demonic power following in their wake. A small band of a dozen warriors, had gained legal entrance with Captain Darshan and the two commanders. They only partly shielded the members, brushing aside many of the poisonous darts of the enemy, who constantly searched for a weak spot to breach their defences.

Taking his place at the head of the table, Rafe opened his bible with a flourish and read scriptures carefully chosen to bring as much guilt and shame as possible down upon the heads of his despised board. Not being in the mood for prayer, he asked the old reverend to do the honors after which, ignoring the agenda, he skipped over the survey report to the fourth item listed as "*Members Letters*".

Rafe knew well the content of the letters they were about to discuss and was prepared to dismiss them quickly as so much garbage from a few disgruntles. He was upset that Mira had dared to copy and distribute them to all of the council members and pastors in advance of the meeting. They outlined a litany of complaints and issues which pointed inexorably to the senior pastor. A common thread appeared to be his inherent dishonesty, broken promises, shameful behaviour and the way he manipulated and intimidated people. Five additional letters had come in after the others had gone out. These Mira now circulated explaining that they had only been received in the last couple of days.

The color heightened on Rafe's face as he scanned the content of the new letters. "I think it unfair to spring these letters on me without giving me time to go through them and deal with them myself," he said indignantly.

Mira answered his impatient query in a calm, steady voice. "I did leave an envelope containing the first set of letters for you with Faith. She said she would give them to you before this meeting. Did you not receive them?"

"No," he replied cunningly. "I haven't seen any letters." The lie came readily to his lips. His look of bewilderment was practised and perfect.

Mira was prepared for his denial. "I have another full set here with me," she said as she serenely handed him the extra package she had prepared with this very moment in mind. Her heart lurched wildly as she caught his furious gaze but her voice remained cool, betraying not the slightest tremor of intimidation. "I would suggest that they be read so that everyone can be made fully aware of their content, particularly since five of them are new and have just been handed out."

Jack responded quickly to her lead. "I think that's a good idea."

Rev. Armstrong turned to Pastor Rafe. "Before Mira reads these letters, I would like to ask you if you would share your intentions with council regarding your own future and that of the church. You've had a chance to get away and rest. What has God told you?"

Rafe stared at him groping for an answer. "Well... I don't know really," he finally stammered. The question had startled him, especially coming from the aged minister, who rarely said a word unless requested to do so. He felt a smidgeon of control ebbing from his grasp. When had the old man slipped out from under his thumb? "I haven't really had a chance....." He struggled for the words, hating the elder for making him look foolish, well aware that everyone in the room expected an answer, especially since he had asked for the sabbatical at the last meeting. He knew that the "exhausted" card probably wouldn't fly a second time.

David Armstrong gestured vaguely with one frail hand. "So...what you're saying is – you haven't heard from the Lord and you don't know what you're intentions are for the future.

"No... I really don't know anything yet," he replied his tone growing mildly irritated. He wished fervently that the old goat would shut up.

Rev. Armstrong cocked an eyebrow at Mira and shrugged. "Well.....I guess you can start reading, if you're ready,"

With heightened color, Mira began the first letter, keeping her eyes glued to the page, afraid to even glance up to see the pastor's reaction. When she had finished reading all of the letters, Jack hastily signalled his wish to be heard. Needing a little time to think and consider his response, Rafe surprisingly turned the floor over to Jack with a silent nod.

This gentle man; usually so quiet and retiring, boldly read the full summary of issues arising from the surveys that Mira had diligently prepared. He did not conclude until he read the letter of complaint, signed by the four of them earlier in the week. Scarcely taking a breath, Jack then brought a motion that Pastor Rutherford be released from his duties at the church to pursue his own interests. "We are requesting your resignation, Pastor," he finished. Immediately, Donny seconded the motion. A moment of stony silence followed this surprising turn of events.

Rafe's ire was apparent when he spoke. "I have no intention of resigning," he snarled, his deep voice shaking with suppressed rage. "I've already called one of those that wrote a letter to try to resolve the issue of him and his family leaving the church."

So he did get the first seven letters! Another lie! Mira pursed her lips thoughtfully as she watched the play of emotions flicker over the pastor's face. *He's really incapable of telling the truth – even about the simple things.*

"These are full of untruths," snapped Rafe, grasping the pile of documents and shaking them in the air. He separated a page and threw it on the table. "This letter from the sound technician, for instance – he left because he was upset over Ian's replacement as head usher. All of these so-called letters were written by a few disgruntles. They don't represent what the majority of the people want here."

What about my letter, thought Mira. *Am I just a "disgruntle" too?*

"I am the shepherd here and these sheep love me," ranted the pastor. "This is just a well orchestrated attempt to get rid of me." His eyes narrowed with suspicion. "I would like to hear from the associate pastors and where they stand in this situation," he said sardonically, clearly daring the younger ministers to stand against him.

Marvin cleared his throat nervously as he stood to his feet. "I actually spoke to Ron, the sound man that left," he said cautiously. "He indicated to me that the head usher problem was not the main reason behind his leaving. He felt that Pastor Rutherford didn't care about him or his family and he wondered what the pastor did with his time because he seemed to have no time for the people of his congregation."

He looked at Rafe apologetically. "I'm just telling you what he told me," he reiterated uneasily. He tried to grasp for something more positive. "Uh....I noticed that one of the letters said something about your being "burnt-out". I think that could be important."

Drawing a ragged breath, Marvin threw out one last comment. "The last thing I will say is that I know of churches that have encountered serious problems with large portions of the congregants leaving. Whenever this kind of thing happens, the church usually suffers as a result, sometimes irreparably."

Rafe crucified Marvin with a look. He would deal with him later, he thought, his eyes burning with remorseless rage as demons howled about his head like a boiling cauldron. He waved a hand haughtily at Grace, indicating it was her turn to vindicate herself.

She rose to her feet reluctantly, feeling a little like a hunted animal at bay. "I believe that I came here in the will of God," she said thickly, her voice rife with feeling. "Since coming, I have learned that every leader in this church seems to leave burnt-out and devastated. We all need to speak the truth to one another. The situation here involves hurting sheep. The Good Shepherd, Jesus, who is our example, said that He would lay down his life for the sheep. What we need to do is to look at the core of the problem. I, personally, find it offensive to continuously refer to these wounded sheep as *"disgruntles"*. It is the council's duty to give honor to those who work among the sheep, but also they need to look at the state of the church and the future direction. At a recent breakfast meeting with the council and their spouses, every single person who attended, stated individually, that the pastor had not been a shepherd for the past year. The letters are merely a reflection of hurting sheep. I believe that this church is in crisis. The attendance numbers will bear that out. I checked back in the records and they have been falling consistently over the past few years. That's really all I have to say," She felt as chilled as if icy water had been poured down her back.

Rafe had been thumbing through his bible while Grace was speaking. His voice rang out in stentorian tones. "Ecclesiastes 10, verse 4: *If the spirit of the ruler rises against you, do not leave your post; for conciliation pacifies great offences."*

"What do you mean by that?" interjected Rob quizzically. "What is the context of the passage? I'd like some clarification."

Except for the sneer that played about his lips, Rafe's features were blank and controlled. Rob's question he simply ignored, pushing ahead with strident, unrelenting sureness. "Someone told me about a dream they had recently," he proclaimed. "In it, the Good Shepherd Church was left desolate with *"Ichabod"* written over the door." He stared pointedly at Rob. "That means, "*the glory has departed*"," he rasped sardonically in an effort to humiliate the deacon.

I will make him sorry for this, Rafe thought. *I will make them all sorry.* His face was the pale grey color of cold ashes. Jezebel maintained a firm grip on his arm whispering gutturally into his ready ear.

"Pastor, we have been trying to tell you that this church is in crisis." Mira's voice shook with passion. "You will not listen to us! There are, at minimum, thirty people who are on the verge of leaving."

"I don't believe it!" he interrupted angrily. "Give me names!"

"I won't do that!" she snapped, her voice brittle. "You would badger the life out of them! Frankly, I believe the number is much higher, perhaps as many as fifty, but one cannot be sure until it actually happens. Perhaps some may be persuaded to change their mind; however, I can say with some assurance, many will not. Those will definitely leave if things don't change here. We don't know the authors of the survey comments, but we do know they are your leaders here and the vast majority are obviously unhappy."

"There will always be those who agree and those who disagree," interjected Phil Schmidt blandly.

Mira had found her voice and refused to be intimidated. "Pastor," she said bluntly, ignoring the deacon's interruption, "you have not admitted even the slightest fault." She pounded the table in front of her in frustration. "If we could see any repentance...anything at all, we would rally around you." Her voice cracked and she faltered, blinking away the tears that gathered in spite of her. "Instead you call us *"disgruntles"*. You dismiss our letters as insignificant. You haven't called me or any of these gentlemen sitting here, many of whom have written letters."

"We've had enough discussion," put in Jack. "It's time for a vote to see where everyone stands."

"It has to be by secret ballot then so that everyone feels free to vote their conscience," said Mira, tearing some sheets from her notebook as she spoke.

Rafe rose to his feet. "I'll leave," he sneered furiously. Pastor Marvin can call me when you're done."

The demons attacked with the savageness of a hurricane, titanic and monstrous. Captain Darshan responded with a penetrating bellow to arms. His own commands sounded as mad as a gale. Swiftly the creatures girdled the company, their oddly proportioned limbs and hairy, deformed torsos dancing like greased lightening around the tall shining warriors. Vitriolic fluid flung from the misshapen spirits spilled over them, its torrent shredding their garments, burning large gaping holes in their shields.

Caelen and Valin fought valiantly against the relentless force of evil, wielding their powerful weapons with purpose in a horrific fusion of unearthly metal and flesh. Miraculously, the angels were able to hold the line of defence.

The vote proceeded quickly, unhampered by the physical presence of Pastor Rutherford. The two associate pastors counted the ballots, the result of which was seven in favour of the pastor's resignation and two opposed. Marvin called the pastor's extension from the phone in the kitchen with the news that they were ready. The rest of the little group waited in silence, dreading the sound his footstep in the hallway.

Rafe's manner was confident as he strode across room to where the two young pastors were standing. Marvin stepped forward quickly communicating the result of the vote. "I guess this means that the council is calling for your resignation," he said.

"I will not resign!" Rafe's nostrils flared ominously. His voice shook with passion. "This is worst board I've had in forty five years of ministry." With curled lip, he thrust his chin arrogantly forward and turning on his heel, he left the room again as quickly as he had come. "Marvin, I appoint you as the new chairman of the meeting." He threw this over his shoulder before he slammed the door.

Caelen felt the resolve of the demons crumble around the edges. Confusion reigned within their ranks. Stumbling and cursing, they withdrew to the far perimeters of the room. One by one they began to disappear through the walls, like candles being snuffed out, except that the room brightened rather than dimmed with their passing. The angelic force began to pulse with an unearthly, dazzling light. Torn clothing and battered shields were instantly cleansed and made new; every trace of filth and destruction erased.

The discussion which followed Rafe's exit had a relieved air to it. The thing was done! Now all they had to do was follow it through. They discussed how to proceed in a proper and right manner, showing mercy to the pastor.

Marvin recommended that the board contact a lawyer to make sure that the church constitution was being followed correctly and to receive advice on a proper settlement package and any other legal matters that might arise from the situation. Mira suggested that perhaps the wisest choice would be the lawyer who had been instrumental in helping the church draw up their constitution, since he was already familiar with it.

Grace asked the council what their pleasure was regarding the positions of the associate ministers. "Do you wish for us to stay for the present or should we step down at this time as well?

"Definitely stay," was the overwhelming response. Not a dissenting voice was raised.

They were almost ready to call it a day, when the kitchen phone rang. Pastor Marvin hurried to answer it. After a few minutes, he re-entered the room with the news that Pastor Rutherford had requested that the council stay awhile longer. "He would like you to meet with Tom Storey and Dora Golding," he reported dutifully. "They are apparently on their way over." He wondered briefly if he should reveal the rest of what Rafe had told him. He shrugged. *Why not!* "Pastor Rafe wants the whole meeting thrown out and declared unconstitutional," he told them.

Council members knew Tom and Dora fairly well; in fact the latter was related to Phil Schmidt. Tom and his wife had left the Good Shepherd Church several months ago and it was widely known that they were now frequenting another church in the area. The real reason for their leaving was still a mystery to council but, since both Tom and Dora had been instrumental in the drafting of the constitution, it seemed a good idea to stay and listen to what they had to say about the morning's events.

Since it was well past the lunch hour, Mira called Dan and asked him to pick up some food for the council members. It was almost two o'clock and no one had eaten since breakfast. Tom and Dora arrived almost the same time as Dan. Willing hands soon laid out the meal in buffet style and for the next half hour, council members ate with relish, chatting and laughing with one another until most of the food had disappeared.

Dan left immediately following the repast and Rev. Armstrong called the meeting back to order, welcoming their guests. Mira quickly briefed the two new participants on the morning's events and the results of the vote. Council told the pair that ideally they would prefer that the pastor resign so that he could be properly honoured with a celebration party for his years of ministry and a generous severance package. However, if Pastor Rutherford was not inclined to submit to this then the only other option possible at this point would be the termination of his employment.

"I don't think he will ever submit to the board," declared Rob Samuels. "He's an authoritarian. It has to be his way or no way!"

Tom suggested that mediation between the pastor and the board would be the best way to approach an agreeable settlement. The mediators would have to be agreed on by both parties, he said, and it was his hope that the termination could be worked out amicably. "I think the pastor might be willing to have me and Dora mediate but we would like time to think it over and pray about it. How would that sit with council?"

The members were relieved. They felt it would take a lot of pressure off the situation and let a third party take the brunt of the pastor's anger. They all hoped that it might minimize manipulation of the process and anticipated problems in the pulpit as well.

"Mrs. Rutherford wants to retire," volunteered Rob. "She's been talking about it for several years now."

"Actually, Marvin and I have had people ask us if the pastor is retiring," put in Grace. "When he spoke to the people just before he went away, he intimated that he wanted to go into a global ministry, so many of them think he's pretty much done anyway."

"I've had several conversations with Pastor about his retirement," added Marvin. "I believe he has some idea of changing his title to bishop. He wants to maintain his ties with the church but he doesn't want the day to day pastoral routine, hospital visitation, counselling and so on. What he'd really like, I think, is to travel and speak in various churches whenever he wants. But he still wants the authority and the control of the church here."

"Nice life if you can get it!" chuckled Donny.

"That's not going to happen," said Mira. "It would give him total control but someone else would be doing all of the work! No! That's not right!"

The discussion heated up as each one volunteered their own bit of information on what they knew or had heard around the church. They all agreed that the last thing anyone wanted was division in the assembly. Notwithstanding, their convictions were strong that a change in the role of the senior pastor was necessary for the health and growth of the assembly.

"I think that this meeting has come as somewhat of a shock to Pastor Rutherford," said Tom finally, after hearing a number of suggestions on how they should proceed. "I would like to propose that the pastor be given a couple of days to process this meeting and everything that has occurred."

He further urged them to set up three mediation meetings to address the various complaints and concerns raised. "We need to be cognizant of the requirements of the constitution and proceed properly and in order. The by-laws of the church allow for mediation in circumstances such as these - where the board and council have reached an impasse with the pastor. Before you terminate his employment, if that is what you truly wish to do, you need to exhaust all other means of reconciliation."

"I don't honestly see any meeting of the minds here," replied Rob. "He has no intention of resigning! I can assure you of that! The only way to handle this is to fire him!"

"Well... I'd still like to see you follow the proper mediation procedures set out in the constitution," said Tom. "Then everyone can feel assured that they did everything that could possibly be done before considering termination of the pastor's employment. The people may not understand if he is suddenly ousted from the pulpit. They would want to know the reasons behind it. You could very well cause the split you are trying to avoid. What about allowing the two of us to meet with the pastor in order to communicate the results of our meeting together? He requested a meeting with us anyway as soon as we are finished here."

"We can set the mediation dates up and see if he agrees to them, but what if he doesn't?" asked Rev. Armstrong. "What if he wants nothing to do with it?"

"We won't know unless we ask," replied Dora. "We'll certainly do our best to reason with him and I think he might calm down a little if he has some time to think about everything, particularly if you're right about him wanting to retire anyway – whatever *"retire"* means to him," she added ruefully.

"We can go ahead and set up the dates but they have to be before the annual business meeting on April 11th," said Mira.

"You won't be able to do anything until the end of March," put in Grace. The pastor flies back to Florida on Monday and doesn't return until his mission's trip with Mrs. R. I don't think they return from that until the 29th of March.

"Why do all of the mediation meetings have to be scheduled before the business meeting?" queried Tom.

"The mix of the board will change after that meeting and then we will have three new people who have no idea what's been going on or what we've been through. We'd have to start all over from scratch."

"That's exactly what he's hoping for," declared Donny. "I know my term is up and he will make sure that my name is left off the list of nominees."

"Same with me," affirmed Ian.

"Yeah, mine too," said Sylvester. "I don't think I want to stay on the board after this term anyway. My health isn't the best....." His voice trailed off.

Tom looked at his date book frowning. "That doesn't leave any time at all. I suppose we could set up the first one for the last day of March. It's a Saturday so we wouldn't have to worry about the time element as much as if it were an evening meeting. Ideally, there should be a week between each of the meetings to allow time for everyone to process the results. Maybe we should change the date of the annual meeting. I certainly don't want the pastor to feel like he's been railroaded through some fast meetings for appearance sake. Mira, could you ask the lawyer when you meet with him? You might be able to have a member's meeting after church on Sunday in order to extend the deadline."

"I'll ask the lawyer when I meet with him but I'm pretty sure that we can't change it," said Mira flatly. "According to the constitution, it has to be before April 15th. We've already pushed it to the limit by scheduling it on the last possible Wednesday before the deadline. Also, we're required to give thirty days notice to the members in order to call a special meeting. I don't know about anyone else but I've just about had it with this whole thing. I can't go on for another couple of months. Let me rephrase that. I don't want to go on for another two months. I want this over with!"

"I understand that this has been difficult for all of you," said Tom soothingly. "I just can't help but think that there's a way to get around this date issue."

Jack raised his hand. "I don't feel right about going against the constitution," he said with worried look. "If there's trouble at the annual meeting, anything this board has made a decision on could be nullified because we improperly changed the date. It's too great a risk!"

Tom seemed annoyed. "Well...for now, let's schedule the three meeting dates to fall before the 15th. They can always be changed if it turns out that we can delay the annual meeting. How about adding April 2nd and 5th? At least that gives a couple of days of rest in between. I still think it is too rushed though."

"There's one more thing," Rob interjected. "We should request that the pastor please not take the pulpit on Sunday. He won't be able to resist using it for political purposes. If he should say anything publicly.... well, the split would happen sooner than expected."

"We can't keep him out of his own pulpit," objected Phil. "That just wouldn't be right."

"Dora and I will address your concern regarding his use of the pulpit," replied Tom, looking at Rob. "I think it might be wise not to agitate him too much though. We don't want him to get his back up because that wouldn't be good for the process or the church body. All we can do at this point is ask him to use discretion. We can stress that angering his council now would be counter productive."

It was past the dinner hour by the time everyone packed it in. Mira was absolutely drained, but in a great measure, she found relief in believing the hardest part was over.

18

ON SUNDAY MORNING AFTER church, Rob Samuels told Mira that Pastor Rafe had ordered an emergency meeting with his elders and deacons for Monday morning. Upset over the lack of a proper notice, he had refused to attend. "I'm going to write a letter of objection to the board," he said heatedly. "It's totally illegal. We're supposed to have proper notice!"

After Rob left, Mira spotted Jack and Donny chatting with a scruffy looking, white-bearded man in the corner of the sanctuary. She recognized him as Kyle Gibbons, a friend of the pastor's. *I wonder what he wants,* she thought suspiciously. He came so infrequently to the church that she hadn't any chance to know him or his wife personally.

Drawing the directors aside, she indignantly blurted out the latest news. "It's just more of the same type of manipulation," she seethed. "He's likely going to stack the elder board and then try to fire the directors or at the very least outvote us in a council meeting. He needs more bodies to be able do that."

After the treasurer left, Kyle ambled back over. "I'd like to have a chance to talk to the board," he requested, smiling amiably at the two men. "I feel I could be of some assistance in helping to mediate the current situation. I know Rafe pretty well and I'm told there may be some misunderstanding between him and the board. I've had some experience dealing with this sort of thing and I really believe the pastor may be suffering from burn-out. If he could just take a year off, he'd come back rejuvenated and everything else would work itself out."

"You're mistaken," replied Donny affably, but firmly. "There is no misunderstanding. We understand him very well, but I don't think that you do."

"You have no idea what we've been through with that man for the last year," added Jack.

"I know him well enough to believe he has the best interests of the church at heart," the man answered crisply.

"I disagree," replied Jack, "but I'm not going to argue the point with you. This is neither the time nor the place." They started to walk away from the man.

"Wait a minute!" Kyle grabbed Jack's arm to stop him from leaving.

Jack shook off the man's grasp. "I don't want to talk about it! You don't have clear understanding because you haven't been on the board."

"I think we're done here," added Donny.

Kyle, however, continued to harass the two men, following them through the lobby and out onto the front steps, repeating his request to meet with the board, most insistently. The directors adamantly refused to participate in further conversation.

Mira was headed for her car when Rob hailed her again. "I'd like to ask you if it would be possible for my wife to take a few days off from her secretarial duties. With Pastor Rafe back, she's under so much pressure that she's finding it almost unbearable," he said. "Could you just talk to her?"

Mira retraced her steps and found Faith alone her office just getting ready to leave. "Rob's worried about you," she said cutting straight to the point. "I want you to know that if you need to take some time off, until all of this mess is settled, please feel free to go ahead and do that. With pay, of course," she hastened to add. "I know it must be tough for you right now."

Faith's eyes filled with tears. "It's just awful," she confessed. "Pastor gets so angry with me when I question him about what is going on. I can't help it though," she cried. "I'm remembering things that I've heard – even from other ministers that have passed through. I've never allowed myself to believe anything bad about Pastor but now I don't know what to think. I've been asking myself - Is everyone lying, except him? I can't believe that any more. There are just too many."

She got up and checked the hallway, closing the door and turning the lock, before she returned to her desk. "Sorry, but he has a habit of sneaking up on you when you least expect it. You know that I haven't been back for very long from the little vacation I took at Pastor's place in Florida. I spent a week there at Mrs. Rutherford's invitation. Pastor Rafe wasn't there until the last couple of days before I left to fly home and I'm grateful for that. He was so angry when he arrived. He talked about the council meeting and he told me that my husband is an evil man. He said that Rob is leading the pack against him."

She dabbed ineffectively at the flow of tears that ran down her cheeks. "I know that my husband is honest and honourable, but I'm so confused about everything. The more I hear, the more confused and upset I get. The other day, Pastor Rafe and Pastor Grace talked together for almost two hours in the fellowship hall. Pastor Grace came into my office afterwards and told me how Pastor seemed to encourage and support her ministry. She seemed relieved and happy. After she was gone, Pastor Rafe came in and he told me that she was a matriarchal witch. Who am I supposed to believe!"

"Matriarchal witch!" snorted Mira. "If there is any witchcraft going on here, it certainly isn't Grace. She lives what she preaches!" She could see that conflicted loyalties were nearly tearing Faith apart. It disgusted her that the pastor would put his secretary in this position. She was such a loyal, compassionate person and something like this would devastate her. As she sized up the situation, it didn't surprise her that Rob was concerned for his wife's health. "Faith, take the time off," she urged. "Stay away until after the annual business meeting if you like. You're too valuable an employee to lose."

Faith twisted her hands uncomfortably. "Will the rest of the board be upset if I'm not here doing my job?"

"Of course not! We owe you an enormous debt of gratitude for what you've had to put with the last ten years. This is the least we can do for you! You told me yourself that you didn't get paid for your statutory holidays the first few years you worked here. Good grief, girl! Take all the time you need! The board will understand that it is essential for you to get out of this pressure cooker situation right now.

"I think I just need to get out of the line of fire for a bit. When Pastor is here, he gives me no peace. His daughter even called me the other day, demanding to know what is going on. I guess he must have told her something. I said I didn't really know but then she asked me outright if he had done it again!"

Mira looked at her curiously. "What do you mean – done it again?"

"I think she wanted to know if he had done something sexual because that's what got him fired from his last church. She sounded very upset and angry. She said, "If he's done anything again, we're all done with him. I'll get my mother out of there and send her to my brother's place on the west coast." I just told her that I thought there were some issues between him and the board and I didn't know anything else."

"Whew!" Mira said weakly. "I sure didn't expect that! She thinks he's guilty of sexual impropriety because she believes in his guilt the last time he was caught - and she's family!"

Rob opened the door putting an end to the conversation. "Ready, Hon?" Faith nodded, not trusting herself to speak. "I'd like to find out what options, if any, my wife has available to her, if the board should leave and the pastor stay," he asked Mira nervously. "Surely there must be something after ten years of service."

"I will add it to the agenda of the next board meeting," assured Mira. We'll put a package into place, just in case it's needed."

Rob thanked her as they left the building together.

~

On Monday morning, Mira was sitting quietly in her robe reading her bible at the kitchen table when the phone rang. Pastor Rafe asked her if she could come immediately to the church to take the minutes for an elder-deacon meeting. She grinned when he mentioned that Faith wouldn't come and do it.

Throwing on some clothes, she grabbed her purse and notebook and drove to the church. She didn't see the two commanders who accompanied her.

In the office, Ina told her that the elders had just come over from the parsonage where they had been invited for a cozy breakfast with the pastor and his wife.

Mira groaned inwardly. *Pastor sure hasn't wasted any time. I wonder how much lying, manipulation and twisting of facts he's already accomplished, before this meeting has even begun.* "I guess I'll know soon enough!" she muttered as she reluctantly ascended the stairs. She deliberately chose an empty seat at the opposite end of the table from the big chair normally occupied by the pastor.

Phil Schmidt was laughing with Pierre over a joke. The men seemed relaxed and either unknowing or uncaring about the pastor's agenda. Old man Zimmer was the exception. He barely acknowledged her greeting as he glared out from under bushy, white eyebrows. *He's changed his mind! He won't meet my eyes.* Rev. David Armstrong's chin wobbled nervously, but his warm hug and the kiss he left on her cheek seemed friendly and genuine.

Pastor Rutherford's appearance from the doorway of his office was silent and swift. He had no intention of leaving Mira alone with the men. She might learn too much! His silky greeting sent a shiver up her spine.

From his position behind Mira's chair, Caelen felt the air turn icy cold. His companion, Valin, winced noticeably as an involuntary chill knifed sharply through his being. The Jezebel demon-master entered the room and stood behind Rafe, towering over him like a hidden menace, frogs spilling like bile from his gaping maw. Abhorrent shadowy spirits, passing through the walls at will, hissed mockingly at the two commanders who transmitted sharp warning signals to Captain Darshan and the half dozen warriors who accompanied him.

The angels stolidly watched with impassive countenances the demonic forces that instantly surrounded them, railing at them with threatening gestures and false bravado. Their unresponsive stance further infuriated the enemy, who hurled even more terrible epithets with vicious, unwavering malice.

Taking his seat at the head of the table, Rafe leaned forward, staring directly into Mira's eyes. This was the opportunity he had been waiting for – a chance to separate her from those other idiots! He looked forward, with great anticipation, to the prospect of intimidating and breaking down the treasurer's resistance. He could almost taste victory and it was sweet!

"The Holy Spirit gave me a message for you," he intoned, his expressive voice deepening automatically. "He woke me in the wee hours of the morning and your face came up before me." He paused to build the suspense, watching her as a cat watches a mouse before it pounces. The men barely breathed, hanging on every word, eagerly awaiting his revelation.

Yes!" he droned, smiling gently at her. "I saw your face and then the Holy Spirit told me just one word - "*Deceived*". He showed me that although your heart is in the right place, two men are deceiving you. Your mind has been so confused by them that you are unable to think clearly."

Mira's large blue-grey eyes were expressionless. She knew he expected a reaction from her, but she was determined not to give him one. His Word from the Lord was completely false but if she questioned it openly, he would convince the elders that she lacked spirituality. *Now I wonder who he is referring to... Donny, for sure! Jack? ...maybe ... or perhaps it was her husband.*

Rafe was disappointed. He had been certain that if he could separate her from the other rebel board members, she would be as putty in his capable hands. He was prepared to use every tool at his disposal to force her into submission - persuasion, bullying, spiritual intimidation. Whatever it took! She would bend to his will, eventually! It perplexed and unsettled him that she gave no outward indication of what she was thinking. In vain, he waited for a sign that would signal which approach would best accomplish his purpose.

Mira's long lashes barely quivered as she continued to watch him in unblinking silence. Rafe found that stare disconcerting. When no response was forthcoming, he repeated his carefully concocted message, emphasizing its grave import. He knew how to be convincing and was confident in his ability to sway his listener.

"My mind is perfectly clear," Mira said dryly, when he had finished. She refused to engage him in conversation. Picking up her pen, she readied her note pad for the minutes. Her throat felt parched and her stomach churned with tension and nervous dread. She was beginning to wish she hadn't come. Curious to find out the purpose behind the meeting, she had thought her safety lay in numbers, figuring he would surely be on his best behavior before so many witnesses. Her escape from his clutches this day would not be accomplished without difficulty, she thought uneasily, as she prayed for wisdom.

Rafe's eyes narrowed. This wasn't going to be as straightforward as he had anticipated. He had figured if he could get her away from Jack and Donny, she would be easy to manipulate. "Well... I'm just telling you what the Holy Spirit told me," he ended lamely. Her white, stern face made him strangely uneasy.

"Where are the associate pastors?" countered Mira, changing the subject abruptly. There was something in his eyes that caused the bile to rise up into her throat, nearly choking her. She reached for a glass of water and swallowed slowly, trying to collect her scattered thoughts. Deep inside, she was praying desperately, "God, please give me clarity and wisdom." Determinedly, she pushed back the fear that tried to grip her heart and mind. "I thought pastoral staff was supposed to be present at elder meetings."

"Uh.... I think they're in the building....uh... would someone go and find them?" he ordered." Inside he was fuming. The last thing he wanted was either of his associates present to witness what he desired to accomplish. Still, it wouldn't do to alienate Mira just when he was sure that, given a little time, he could gain mastery over her.

Pierre jumped to do his bidding and while he was absent from the room, Mira asked where Rob was. "Well....uh....he's not feeling well," Rafe stuttered. "I offered to have him connected by telephone to the meeting but he wasn't well enough even for that."

Liar! thought Mira. Her temples throbbed as blood suffused her face. She knew that Rob wasn't ill and that he would be e-mailing a letter of complaint about the lack of notice given for the meeting. A desperate attempt to discredit the board of directors, he had called it, and he refused be a part of it. "Where is the agenda for the meeting?" she asked.

"Uh...well... actually," he stammered, "I think it's in Faith's office."

"Oh?" Mira let the question hang compellingly in the air.

Rafe grimaced, his hands twitching revealingly. He hated her for making him appear incompetent. "Uh.... yes. Well... actually, you know, Faith was supposed to take the minutes for the meeting, but she seems to have taken the day off."

Dead silence! Sylvester's chair creaked noisily causing the old minister sitting beside him to jump nervously. They all seemed relieved when the door opened to admit Grace and Pierre. The latter advised Rafe that Marvin would follow shortly.

Mira felt sorry for her sister-in-law. There had been no opportunity to warn her in advance. She saw Grace's eyes widen as they flickered over the little group and suddenly met hers. Rafe had no alternative but to admit that he had called an elder meeting. They both knew that he had done so without informing either of his associates.

Defiantly, he plunged forward with his hitherto hidden agenda. The men had been called and he was determined that he would accomplish his purpose. "One of the letters, presented to council two days ago, was pressured from the couple who wrote it, by three of the directors," he stated maliciously. "I called them about it and they are sorry that they were so harsh. They will be re-writing it and the new version will be watered down considerably. I might as well tell you that I'm talking about Lenny Granger and his wife."

Mira wrote studiously in her notebook. A fire was growing inside of her, gnawing at her belly. *Pressured? We didn't pressure anyone! He's trying to make these men think that we are persecuting him and he'll lie or do whatever it takes to get rid of us! How utterly contemptible!* She knew only too well that he was practised at making blind statements that could not be verified during the course of a meeting. He relied heavily on the fact that, most of the time, no one would check the veracity of his assertions, but would simply believe whatever he told them.

You can bet I'll certainly check it out! Quickly scribbling a reminder note, Mira thought about her last conversation with Lenny. Before the Grangers left the church, he had spoken with Mira, asking her why the directors didn't remove Pastor Rafe from his position. His letter to the board had been scathing! *How could Pastor possibly think he will recant what he has written? I don't believe it for a minute!*

"The board may be able to pressure a few disgruntles into doing their dirty work for them but I want you know that many letters of support for me are now starting to pour in." There was a self satisfied smirk on Rafe's face as he turned toward Marvin who had just taken his seat. "How many letters have we received so far?" he asked.

Marvin cleared his throat nervously. "Actually, Pastor, I haven't seen any yet." He sounded almost apologetic.

"Well, they're coming," stressed Rafe belligerently. He felt as if some of the wind had been taken out of his sails and wondered fleetingly why he had the bad luck to have an associate who wouldn't lie or exaggerate for him when he needed it!

"The council meeting that was held last Saturday was unconstitutional, making any decision null and void," he declared, his mouth set and his eyes determined. *I'm on solid ground now,* he thought smugly. "Both Tom and Dora were shocked and upset over that ungodly meeting and they agree it was totally unconstitutional." He looked at Mira triumphantly and waited, as if he expected a reply. Knowing he meant to belittle her and the board in front of the elders, she continued to write on her pad, ignoring his bate.

Rafe was forced to move on. "I want to clarify with the elders and deacons an allegation made by Ian Parker who called me a liar in that meeting," he said indignantly. "I shared with the members that a prophet had warned me of an insurrection brewing. Several of the board didn't believe me."

Mira interrupted his tirade. "As I recall, we requested the name of the prophet and were told it was confidential." It was a struggle to keep her voice even.

"Well, I want everyone to know that the person who gave me that prophesy has agreed to come here today in order to speak to you all." Rafe sounded jubilant. "He will repeat the Word he was given first-hand." He glowered fiercely at Mira.

A curious calm settled over her spirit. "Who is it?"

"It's Matt Billings," he answered shortly.

The look on Mira's face clearly indicated her thoughts for Rafe turned on her, suddenly enraged. "How dare you roll your eyes at me!" he snapped, his tone hard and vicious. "You had better wipe that look off your face right now!"

Mira wanted to laugh and cry at the same time. The corners of her mouth twitched precariously close to mirth but the grimace hid a wildly thumping heart within her breast. *Frauds!* She wanted to scream that they were both frauds!

Rafe sent Marvin downstairs to bring Matt up to join the meeting.

Mira sat silent, toying with her pen and thinking over what brief history she knew of the man. He was a close friend of Rafe's – too close! The pastor had originally brought him in to set up the computer system in the church. Ina had confided in Mira several times that she suspected him of snooping in the files for confidential financial information either for his own purposes or to report to the pastor. She had requested Mira's help in changing her password for that very reason. Matt's business practices were also questionable. Ina had complained numerous times about his unreliability and his padded bills. Nothing had ever been done about it because Pastor Rafe always vouched for his hours and no one else knew what he was doing up in the pastor's office for hours on end. Mira had tried to retain the services of another computer technician but had been stymied at every turn by the pastor.

Matt entered the room with an arrogant swagger. A cloud of satanic creatures encircled his head gibbering gleefully in a frenzy of madness. They mewled and howled as they caught sight of the angels. The man stopped behind Rafe's chair enjoying his protection and confidence as he delivered the Word he claimed to have heard from God.

"I was sitting in my car weeping and the Spirit of the Lord told me that Pastor Rafe is special. He said that He loves Pastor very much and has a purpose for him that is not complete yet. He told me there would be an uprising against the pastor because they don't see the good in pastor's life. I am to give you a warning that if this wonderful man of God is let go, this church will fail."

Rafe easily picked up the thread now. "After Matt received this Word, he left a phone message for me to call him. I heard this prophesy just minutes before entering the council meeting in February."

Grace interrupted with a question. "Matt," she queried, looking him square in the eye, "isn't it true that you were in the office, just prior to that council meeting, asking questions about what was going on in the church? You spoke to both me and Ina, as I recall, so you must have had some prior knowledge about problems or issues in the church or you wouldn't have asked.

Matt's face grew red. "I did not have any prior knowledge about problems in this church," he insisted heatedly. "The first time I knew about anything was the day the Holy Spirit spoke to me."

Rev. Armstrong suddenly joined the fray. "Young man, I do not believe for one minute that you heard from the Lord. I think you already knew or were told about the problems between the board and the pastor."

Matt leaned over Rafe and shook his finger in the elderly man's face. "The Holy Spirit revealed some things to me about you too," he snarled, his face turning purple with passion.

"Oh? And what would they be?" asked Rev. Armstrong settling back with a twinkle in his eye.

"Matt, I think you might benefit from some reading material on prophetic words and what is really spoken by the Lord versus what is flesh," interrupted Grace earnestly.

"I don't need to read any books," came the cross reply. He moved irritably towards the door. "I came here in good faith to share with you people what God told me and you act like you don't believe me!" He sounded outraged.

"Matt," can I ask you a question?" Mira smiled, deliberately keeping her tone light and friendly, but her eyes crinkled with amusement. He nodded rather sulkily. "You seem to have a problem with Pastor Grace? I only say that, because I seem to sense some hostility in your attitude towards her," she said innocently.

"Yes, I have a problem with her," he snapped. Leaning across the table, he shook his finger at Grace. "The Holy Spirit has revealed some things to me about you too."

What did He tell you?"

He glared at her belligerently. "I'm not ready to share that yet!" he choked.

"Well, I guess it can't be very important then," she replied, the corners of her mouth twitching.

Matt gurgled something unintelligible and stormed out of the room, slamming the door behind him. A multitude of imps followed him, rushing to maintain their stranglehold upon the man and sustain the madness that comes from serving their master.

Rafe's face was a study. His triumphantly staged scenario had not gone at all as he had planned. His young friend had made a fool of himself and Rafe in the process. Now he watched helplessly while Mira briefly shared what she knew of Matt's shady business practices. He knew he would have to try to minimize the damage.

"I've known Matt for many years and he's honest," he blurted out defensively. "He just has some time management issues because he's so busy. You have no right or basis to accuse him of dishonesty," he insisted, confronting Mira directly.

"I can only speak about what I know from the office staff here," she replied stubbornly. "Both Ina and Faith have told me that he is unreliable and untrustworthy. Rob Samuels worked with him on a project to put a monitor in the nursery and run telephone and computer lines to the basement offices and his opinion is the same. Matt's business practices are shoddy. He has sold us inadequate, outdated computers. What is more, his word is completely unreliable. When we experience problems, he sometimes takes days to respond. Furthermore, he sold us a piece of junk that he represented as a new monitor. Rob had to force him to replace it by withholding payment."

Rafe was embarrassed. He hadn't counted on Mira answering back. At an impasse, he swiftly moved to change the subject. "These so-called letters that have been written against me are nothing but a well organized plot to get rid of me," he blustered. "They are a pack of trivial nonsense."

Mira half rose to her feet. Tears burned the backs of her eyes. She could bear no more. "Trivial," she cried passionately. "Is that what you think of all of those letters – mine included? Is that all you think of us? These are genuine concerns expressed from the congregation here, especially your leaders." She pounded the table with her fist in total frustration. "How dare you call them trivial!"

"Smite the shepherd – scatter the flock," boomed Rafe with a dramatic flick of his wrist and contemptuous toss of his head.

Rev. Armstrong interrupted. "Well....I think we all agree that this church is in serious crisis and has problems that need to be addressed. We shouldn't just ignore these letters and the concerns they raise."

Rafe threw his hands in the air, his fury evident. "What would you do, given the same set of circumstances?"

"I would have resigned long ago," replied the older man with a quiet air of dignity.

"You mean to tell me you would let a few disgruntles run you out of your church?" Rafe asked, his voice rising shrilly. "Well, I won't let a small handful of people dictate to me what I should do!"

"I would like to speak, if I may," said Grace rising from her chair. Rafe's nod was brusque. "I accepted your invitation to come here under the assumption that although there were serious problems, reconciliation between the pastor and the board was a possible scenario. Both my husband and I felt a strong witness that it was God's plan for me to come. I am an open, honest and direct person and I will not substantiate any untruths or lies. I will not be blindly loyal to anyone but God."

She had everyone's full attention now. "I realize that my reputation will, in all probability, be damaged in this area. I know that Pastor Rutherford no longer trusts me because I will not compromise the truth. Since I have come, I have tried to wait on the Lord for His direction. I have preached the Word, listened to the hurts and problems of the people and tried to help them get healed up from their wounds. I feel I have worked well with Pastor Marvin and I respect him as a pastor."

Marvin nodded, his eyes glistening with unshed tears. Grace continued, her voice trembling with emotion. "God chooses how to use each vessel and He can use me in any way He pleases. I am committed to serving Him no matter what happens to me." As she took her seat again, one or two surreptitiously wiped away a tear, while others blew noisily into their handkerchiefs.

Mira broke the silence that followed Grace's speech. "I would like to know what the purpose of today's meeting is."

"Uh...well... it was called to deal with the slate of nominees for the board of directors," replied Rafe. "The annual business meeting is drawing near with the election...."

"May I please have the list of nominees for the records then?"

Rafe's color heightened perceptibly. The knuckles of his slim, manicured hands whitened as he gripped the edge of the table. "Well...uh.... actually, I don't have the list with me. Uh...I think it's in Faith's office." He was uncomfortably aware of how foolish he looked. If there was any single thing that Rafe could not endure, it was being made to look like a fool. Furious over the direction the meeting had taken and outraged that each of his plans had failed miserably, he grasped for control with a vengeance.

"Well, you might as well know," he said with a sneer. "The purpose of this meeting is to disqualify Donny Allison as a nominee. He spoke out of turn to some congregants telling them that the board should get rid of me."

"Donny may not wish to let his name stand after serving on the board this past year," snapped Mira, jumping to his defence. "I certainly wouldn't blame him if he didn't! If you are attempting to get him fired from the current board, then you will have to take it to the whole membership and there would have to be a seventy-five percent vote against him in order for you to accomplish your goal. What kind of shenanigans is this anyway! Donny isn't even here to defend himself! He may be a little rough around the edges sometimes but at least you know where he stands. He speaks his mind and is honest. He has been very generous to both the church and to you personally. The board members know exactly what I am talking about," she said, looking pointedly at Rev. Armstrong and Sylvester. "It is small wonder that he might be a little hurt or bitter over his treatment by the pastor after all he's done for him, time and time again."

Rafe was enraged to the point where he was no longer careful. He didn't want the elders to hear what Donny had shared with the board. If that were that to happen, his image with them could be tarnished and that he would not stand for! He was determined to turn the tide in his favor. "Jack Johnson practically attacked poor Sylvester in a board meeting, even calling him evil," he ranted. "He had no reason or basis for a comment like that!"

Mira perked up her ears. *So Donny isn't his only target.* She moved swiftly to counter the allegation. *Sorry Sylvester, but you know very well that's not how it happened.* "Jack said nothing, until Sylvester attacked him for a lengthy period of time, accusing him of not being spiritual enough and poking fun at his beliefs."

"Sylvester tried to resolve the matter between him and Jack so that he could take communion. Sylvester apologized, but Jack didn't," stated Rafe gleefully, feeling positive that he now had the upper hand.

Mira knew it was a falsehood but she didn't have Jack there to disprove what the pastor had said and Sylvester sat like a lump with his head down, refusing to meet her eye. "It is unfair to say anything against Jack since he is not here to defend himself," Mira said firmly. If there is an unresolved issue between the two men, then they should come in and meet with Pastors Marvin and Grace and sort it out in a proper biblical manner. I don't believe that Jack would be unforgiving if Sylvester apologized. He isn't that sort of man," she said stoutly.

Rafe decided to bring the meeting to a quick conclusion. He hadn't accomplished even one of the things he had purposed in his heart to bring about. The next time, he would know to exclude Mira. He had thought it a stroke of genius to include her in the meeting but his brilliant plan, to get rid of Donny and Jack and swing her over to his side, had utterly failed. He would have to think of another way...

19

WHEN SHE LEFT THE board room, Mira went straight into another meeting with the church's auditor to go over the financial records which had to be ready for the annual business meeting. One of the concerns highlighted, which came as no surprise to the treasurer, was a dramatic decrease in the total income for the prior year. The last quarter had been particularly low. The auditor warned her that something would have to be done if the trend continued and wondered if she had any idea why this had happened.

Mira kept the internal strife issues to herself. She hoped that by next year someone else would have the headache. In any case, there was nothing she could do about it. It appeared highly unlikely that Pastor Rafe would choose to do the right thing and resign. She groaned at the thought of trying to deal with the congregation if he didn't leave amicably.

When she finally left the building, Mira was exhausted. Four and half hours of precious time had been squandered on the illegal elder/deacon meeting and she was sick with worry over the headway accomplished by the pastor, during his breakfast with the men.

As she drove home, she prayed for wisdom and guidance, giving Caelen and his companion an opportunity to minister strength and peace into her spirit. By the time she reached her door, she felt convinced that God was in control of the situation and that this turn of events wasn't taking Him by surprise at all.

Mira's next course of action was to check on the statements the pastor had made in the morning meeting. A couple of quick calls resolved two of the issues right away. Lenny Granger had not recanted his letter. He said he meant every word of it and even offered to send her an e-mail to confirm his stand. That meant the pastor had lied to the elders and deacons when he had told them that a watered-down version would be sent by the Grangers to replace the one the board had presented.

Jack also verified what Mira already believed. He and Sylvester had buried any enmity between them and, although they weren't destined to be bosom buddies, at least they were getting along. He was baffled by the pastor's statements, since there were several people that had overheard the apologies exchanged between him and the old man and there had been no further problems at subsequent board and council meetings.

"I think Pastor Rafe was trying to prejudice the deacons against the board," he said.

Mira agreed. "Pastor Rafe will use anything to his advantage and if the facts aren't strong enough, he will twist and distort them to support his agenda. I'm surprised at Sylvester for going along with it and even more so at Rev. Armstrong. He should know better than to allow the pastor to manipulate and lie with his full knowledge. He knows what Sylvester said about you in that meeting and how he went on and on, until you finally couldn't take it any more."

"Well, I'm willing to meet with Sylvester and the associate pastors, if that is what it will take to straighten this out," replied Jack earnestly. "Let's get it cleared up, once and for all."

Next, Mira called Dora to ask her if she and Tom had been shocked or upset over what had occurred in the last council meeting. "Absolutely not," Dora assured her emphatically. Both Tom and I have served on prior boards and we've sustained our wounds for doing so. Believe me, you're not the first board to deal with Pastor's controlling, manipulative spirit. Just to clarify what happened, we spent about two hours with him immediately following the meeting and he was well aware that anything unconstitutional had been withdrawn."

"So there is no question that the meeting was valid and constitutional?" asked Mira.

"None," was the reply.

After concluding her call with Dora, Mira decided to call Donny to request that he write a letter, spelling out all of the finances and time that he had freely given, involving either the Rutherfords or other congregants. She knew this was necessary to show the context behind Donny's disillusionment with the pastor, which she felt stemmed from much abuse over the years.

This accomplished, Mira resolved to prepare a memo to the council. She felt sick and disillusioned over the falsehoods that had been told by her pastor. As she labored over her task, detailing each lie and countering it with the truth, a sense of futility enveloped her. *None of this will do any good,* she thought, staring bleakly at what she had typed. *They are so deceived by him.*

Her final paragraph was blunt. *"No longer should the board or council take at face value any statement made by Pastor Rutherford that has not been verified. Too many allegations have been made that were either completely false or at the very least, twisted half-truths. What a sad state of affairs when one is forced to verify every word that comes from the mouth of their pastor because his credibility is in question,"* she wrote. *"I am trying to live my life in a way that is pleasing to God and I will not be party to covering up lies or signing checks that are not above board. I refuse to endorse any other deceptions or activities that are an abomination to the Lord, including the wounding of His people. Some day we must give an account for what we have done. I want to present a pure heart and clean hands. The shepherd of the church has an even greater responsibility for the sheep he has under his care. God will require an account of every sheep that is damaged or lost."*

Mira determined that she would pass out the memo to the council members on Sunday and she was too heart-sick to care about the consequences of her action.

Pastor Rutherford was busy with his own agenda. Before flying out on the mission's trip with his wife, he prepared a letter of his own, which he gave to Pastor Marvin. It stated that, during the remainder of his sabbatical days, he was appointing Marvin as the senior pastor of the church. Grace was relegated to assisting him only. The letter also affirmed that he, as senior pastor, would be resuming his duties on April 1st.

Marvin was not pleased with his orders. The church had been growing since Pastor Rafe had been absent and he was loath to disrupt the flow of the teamwork that was currently in place.

"I want you to preach on Sunday mornings," Rafe stressed.

"I won't do that, Pastor," Marvin said firmly. "Things have been working well with Pastor Grace and preaching is part of her gifting. I won't set her aside and not use her. It wouldn't be right."

"I'm supposed to be on sabbatical, so I guess I can't insist," replied the minister coldly, "but I am making my wishes known."

Rafe spent his remaining few days in town sewing seeds of discord among his council members and parishioners, even going so far as to request that they show their support for him by staying away from service whenever Grace was scheduled to preach. "I'll be back in April to deal with this insurrection," he assured them.

On the last Sunday morning, before they were to leave on their trip, Eve Rutherford distributed a letter she had prepared to the council. In it, she intimated that she wished very much to retire and promised that she and her husband were working toward that goal. They didn't wish to leave with a cloud over their heads, she wrote.

Mira wished that it was possible to go and have a chat with her pastor's wife about what she had witnessed and experienced at the hands of her husband. She suspected that Eve didn't know much of what Rafe did or what he was capable of since, by his own admission, most church matters he kept from her knowledge. Mira's heart was torn. Although she loved and respected the woman very much, she knew that any discourse between them would certainly worsen matters between her and Pastor Rafe. Nevertheless, she waited on the Lord regarding the matter. While she delayed, waiting for His direction, the days slid by until it was too late and the Rutherfords had departed on their trip.

Mira finally put in the call to the lawyer who had helped draft the church's constitution. It turned out that Darren Amos was a distant cousin of Tom Storey's. His voice sounded amused when she told him what the matter was about. "Is that guy still the pastor at the Good Shepherd Church? I would have thought that he would have been fired long ago." He laughed easily.

"You know him? Mira asked in surprise.

"Oh yes," he replied wryly. "I know him! I dealt with an issue a few years ago that involved him and the board of directors. In fact, it was the board that retained my services at the time. I'm not at liberty to discuss any of the details with you though, since it was a confidential matter."

Quickly he gleaned all of the relevant facts regarding the current situation from Mira. "I want to contact an employment lawyer to draft the settlement package," he said when she had concluded. "I can help you with constitutional matters but you require more expertise then I can give you for the settlement. I do know an excellent lawyer that I would highly recommend. Settlement packages are his specialty. Perhaps you could arrange for me to meet with the board first, to see if they want to go ahead with this." They decided on the following Monday evening and Mira was relieved that he was willing to rearrange his schedule to accommodate them.

Toward the end of the week, Mira called Ina's cell phone number. She was on her way to spend the weekend with relatives. Keeping the conversation brief, Mira asked if she would be willing to put into writing, all of the unethical things that she had shared over the past few months involving the pastor. "It's entirely up to you, Ina. I realize that this is a difficult thing I'm asking you to do, but will you think it over and let me know?" Ina promised she would think about it.

Before Mira could hang up, Ina reported that Matt Billings had come into the office that week and had plugged a jump drive into a couple of the computers. She thought his conduct had seemed furtive and suspected that he may have downloaded sensitive information. Mira questioned her further asking if Pastor Rafe was aware of the incident. "I don't know," came her worried reply.

"I'll take care of it," Mira promised. *Oh Lord, what now! We don't need any more fires to put out!*

~

On Sunday morning after the service, Mira was approached by a tall, broad-shouldered Nigerian man who was involved occasionally in the music ministry of the church, singing solos or leading worship. Kurtis Oluwa and his family had been in regular attendance for just under two years.

His wife, Natalie, a wonderful asset to the assembly, had willingly assumed the reigns of leading the Children's Ministry. This she did with great efficiency. In the spring, Pastor Marvin had approached the board on her behalf, hoping to obtain some remuneration for her efforts. Pastor Rutherford had discouraged the idea, insisting her services should be voluntary, even though her predecessor had been a paid staff member. The board however, felt that she deserved at least a travel honorarium, since Jonas was receiving one for filling the roll of youth pastor at the time. It had seemed only fair, since her portfolio was much greater and more time consuming than his. They had voted to give it to her over the objection of Pastor Rafe.

Mira had always worked well with Kurtis, even though it was sometimes a struggle to adapt to his style of music. The pastor was using him more often lately, to the chagrin of many in the choir. Unable to adjust, one or two of the newer members had become discouraged and quit, while others had lost much of their enthusiasm and, more often than not, would skip choir when they knew he was leading.

The big man was soft-spoken with a thick accent, which demanded all of Mira's concentration to decipher. "I've heard that there are some problems between the pastor and the board," he said pleasantly, "and if you all don't mind, I would like the opportunity to address the board at the next meeting."

Mira was surprised. "Where did you hear about these problems?" she asked.

"I'd rather not say," he answered. "I usually don't like to get involved in internal strife and I'm not a member here, but I feel the Lord has laid something on my heart that I should share. I have been part of the intercessory group that meets with Pastor Rafe on Saturday mornings."

Mira's antennae went up. *It must be the pastor that has been talking to him then,* she thought. *That can't be good! Are we being set up with another false prophesy? We certainly don't need any more of those!*

"You should ask David Armstrong," she said, after a brief hesitation. "He's the president of the board. Our next meeting is tomorrow night, so you should catch him before he leaves, if you want permission to attend."

The big man indicated that he would like that very much. "My wife and I are on the verge of leaving," he confided. "That's part of the reason why I don't believe in membership. It leaves us free to move on, according to the Lord's leading."

Mira knew they weren't members. Natalie had told her as much when they met to discuss the annual budget for the Children's Ministry. She had been a little taken back by it at the time, wondering why Pastor Rafe permitted a non-member to fill a leadership role. Natalie had further surprised her by indicating that she would probably resign her position by the end of the month. She had given Mira an unsolicited letter, addressed to the council, which laid out very clearly all of the things she had been promised by Pastor Rafe which had never materialized.

Kurtis sounds as if he knows something is wrong here, she thought. Maybe he will be supportive of the board after all. I guess it can't do any harm to listen. We'll know soon enough if he's a fake."

Mira had planned to skip the Sunday night service and go to bed early, but it was not to be. David Armstrong called in the afternoon to tell her that Pastor Marvin wanted to meet with the board, immediately following the evening service. He asked her to relay the message to the remaining directors. Curious to find out what he wanted, they all readily agreed to come.

After the message ended, they followed the young pastor into the fellowship hall. "I just wanted to talk with you guys for a few minutes, about the current situation between the board and Pastor Rutherford," he said cautiously. "I feel badly that I may have inadvertently said something in the latter part of the year that stopped you from just walking away from the situation at that time. As you know, things have now escalated to a point where there could be great damage done if it isn't stopped. I think I encouraged you guys to hang in there and I now feel that I may have given you the wrong advice. I would like to ask you to consider walking away from this, quietly. Maybe that would be best for all concerned. I'm just asking you to consider it and pray about it."

They looked at one another in shocked silence, not knowing how to respond. "We're only standing for what is right," said Jack slowly. "Pastor Marvin, you of all people ought to know that what Pastor is doing is not ethical. In fact, it is immoral and wicked. I believe the Lord put us here for this purpose and I don't think you have a right to ask us to walk away now, just because things have gotten tough."

"I agree," declared Mira. "It was God that placed us in our positions. If we turn a blind eye or walk away and allow the pastor's behavior to continue, then we are partakers in his sin and the Lord will require it at our hands. I don't believe that we should turn tail and run. There is nothing in the Word of God to support that. We are required to stand for righteousness and that is what we intend to do."

"Amen to that!" replied Donny and Ian. "We're going to see this through."

"Well, I felt I had to at least make the request," replied the pastor. Mira thought he seemed relieved. Perhaps Pastor Rafe had requested that he make the attempt to diffuse the board or maybe he was just worried about whether he would still have his job when this was all over. He had four children to clothe and feed and she didn't really blame him for not wanting to get caught up in this battle with the senior pastor.

On Monday evening, just as she was getting ready to leave the house to attend the board meeting, Mira received an e-mail from Ina refusing to write the letter she had requested. Each of her personal issues with the pastor had been dealt with immediately, she wrote, and they were hopefully forgotten forever.

Funny, thought Mira, *they weren't forgotten when she related them to me. I'll simply have to reference her as my source and let it go at that. I'm certainly not going to omit them from the document of issues. They're too important!*

That evening, the directors met with Tom Storey, Dora Golding and the lawyer, Darren Amos. Both Grace and Marvin were present as well, at the request of the board. Rev. Armstrong announced that Kurtis would be speaking to the board for fifteen minutes before the business portion of the meeting. The big man appeared almost at the sound of his name. He began by divulging that Pastor Rafe had shared with him some of the problems he was having with the board.

Mira wondered just how much the pastor had told the Saturday morning group of intercessors. The thought of it made her uncomfortable. She was reasonably certain the board would be painted in the worst possible light.

Kurtis then admitted both he and his wife were very unhappy over administrative issues connected with the pastor; doubtless referring to the things Natalie had been promised which were not forthcoming. He told the directors that he had pointedly asked the pastor if he had done anything wrong and had been assured that such was not the case.

The board struggled to understand the man's accent and managed to catch the main drift of what he was trying to communicate. As he got into the meat of his speech, his key point seemed to be to protect the sheep. Then he wandered from his theme and rambled at some length telling the Old Testament story of David and King Saul. "David behaved wisely in waiting for God to judge Saul, rather than taking his life himself," he said. His address to the members was by now well past his allotted fifteen minutes and the group was beginning to shift restlessly. Still the president made no move to halt what appeared to have become a full fledged sermon.

Mira finally felt compelled to do something. When he finished his next thought, she interrupted, asking him if he was almost finished. She reminded him apologetically that the purpose of the meeting was to meet with a lawyer whose time was costly. Kurtis wound up his remarks by telling the board that they should stand their ground. The directors looked at one another, confused by the conflicted message.

After he had left the room, they got down to business quickly with the lawyer, Darren Amos, who immediately addressed the constitutional issues involving the accountability of the pastor and the mediation process. "As the employer of the pastor, the board has every right to terminate his employment with or without cause," he emphasized. "Behavior would have to be extreme, in order to terminate without compensation, however, if the termination is based on performance, complaints or allegations, then the pastor should be given notice or paid in lieu of notice."

Tom Storey added that he and Dora had agreed to be mediators at the request of the pastor if it were also agreeable to the board. The directors seemed relieved and assented readily. "Does this board believe that restoration is possible?" asked Tom. Most of the directors shook their heads doubtfully.

"I would suggest that it would depend upon whether the pastor can change in the areas of the issues and complaints being brought against him," replied Darren.

"The board needs to keep in mind that the church's reputation could be damaged if a resolution isn't found," added Tom. "What will happen if the issue goes to the congregation?"

"It could get very nasty," said Dora. "I don't think anyone wants that!"

Tom raised his concern over the brief time period allotted for the mediation and the perception of procedural fairness.

"I would suggest calling a membership meeting on Sunday, after the morning service, to extend the date of the annual business meeting or, alternatively, you could ask them for an adjournment at the annual meeting and set another date," the lawyer suggested.

"Too risky," returned Mira resolutely. "It allows too much opportunity for the pastor to mobilize a group against the board. Also, the mix of the board will change at the annual meeting and that could make all of our decisions and mediation null and void. A new board could retract everything we decide. We'd have to begin all over again with another group. Good luck with that! The pastor is already trying to pressure letters of support from church members."

"He should declare a conflict of interest to the members, if this is happening," said Darren. Everyone laughed at that. "The best solution here is a united position of both the pastor and the board," he continued. "If that can be attained and emotions kept in check, you may achieve a positive outcome for everyone."

The annual meeting, with its potential problems, appeared to be the most contentious issue in the discussion which followed. Doubts were expressed that a full slate of director nominees was even possible this year. Mira wondered what would happen if some allowed their names to stand and then withdrew at the last minute, due to the outcome of the mediation with the pastor. She questioned if the church could potentially be left without any board in place, which would create total havoc and another whole set of problems?

The issue of a retirement offer or severance package was raised with the general consensus that it should be generous. Darren apprised them that an employment lawyer would be required to work out a fair termination package if that should end up being the outcome of the mediation process. A motion was duly recorded and voted on to retain the lawyer recommended by Mr. Amos.

David Armstrong suggested that there should be guidelines included in the severance package regarding vacating the parsonage. The lawyer indicated that the usual time period would be one month, but that two might be more appropriate.

"I think we should give him longer than that," said Rev. Armstrong. Everyone agreed, wanting to be sensitive in this matter to both the pastor and his wife.

Darren cautioned them about allowing him back into the pulpit until the process was finished and the matter resolved. "This would be accepted more easily if it were a celebration of his fifteen years of ministry," he added. No one disagreed with that.

Ian reminded the directors that they would be hampered by the financial limit that they were held to by the constitution, being unable to approve any expenditure over $25,000.

Again, Tom brought up how uncomfortable he was with the compressed schedule of meetings, feeling that this would make it more difficult to obtain a solution. "If it were to become public knowledge, the members might feel that the board has an agenda it is trying to jam through and it might reflect poorly on them," he claimed. "I spoke with both Pastor Rutherford and members of the board before accepting this position and I wouldn't have agreed to become a mediator, unless I truly felt there was a willingness to be open minded."

Darren pointed out that the board had a right to make a decision, at any point along the way, if they were not happy with the outcome of the mediation process. "The letter, signed by the four board members and presented at the council meeting, must be thoroughly documented," he warned them.

"I think the pastor should be afforded the courtesy of receiving all of the documentation, prior to the first mediation meeting," offered Grace, speaking for the first time. "He must have the opportunity to see all of the evidence so that he has adequate time to prepare. To be fair, I think you should give him as much time as possible. I say this because I know he felt blind-sided by the letters he had not seen, prior to the council meeting when they were presented."

A decision was eventually reached to extend the date of the annual business meeting, pending the pastor's approval, and a potential fourth mediation date was added to the schedule of meetings. This appeared to satisfy any concerns that Tom and Grace had. The board then dismissed the lawyer, the newly appointed mediators and the pastors from the meeting, so they could deal with other pending issues.

One of these items was the termination of Matt Billings' services. Mira reported that Matt had finally returned all of the church equipment that he had been keeping at his house. She shared the information she had received from Ina about him coming into the church with a jump drive and unloading information from the computers. The board agreed that it was time to issue a letter of termination to Matt and find someone else to service the computers at the church.

20

LIFE THESE DAYS WAS so chaotic for Mira, she felt choked at times with the panic and fear that threatened to rise up within her. It became increasingly difficult to drag her weary body out of bed to face the day. She had to fight to keep from sliding back into the same pit of depression she had been so wondrously delivered out of. Her husband watched and worried over her emotional state. The two commanders shadowing her spent much of their time giving aid, comfort and strength, speaking quiet words of peace into her ear when she prayed or cried out to the Lord.

As she drove to the monthly Women's Ministry meeting on Tuesday evening with Grace, Mira allowed the worshipful strains of music from her favorite CD to wash over her soul. Although it brought stinging tears to her eyes, it also had a calming effect on her spirit.

She was thankful that her only responsibility that evening was to open the service. Following the half hour allotted to food and fellowship, she called her friend, Jeanne, to lead the praise and worship with her guitar. Her guest speaker, she knew, was a humble servant of God, so she anticipated a powerful message would be forthcoming.

Settling back in her seat, Mira tried to concentrate on the words being spoken and forget the turmoil swirling through her head, like a whirlwind out of control. Try as she might, she couldn't shake from her mind a disturbing invitation which Grace had shared with her as they were getting ready for the evening.

Apparently, Pastor Rafe had entered the weekly prayer meeting late that day and with great show, had fallen upon his knees, wailing loudly. After a few minutes had passed, he got up and making a bee-line for her sister-in-law, who was kneeling in a quiet corner, he had prayed loudly over her, more Grace had felt for the benefit of those present, than for any other reason.

The real purpose behind the encounter had revealed itself quickly, as he engaged her in quiet conversation regarding his current situation with the board. He had pressed his case vigorously, imploring her help in arranging a meeting with Mira alone; without her husband or other board members to back her up. She might agree, he suggested smoothly, if Grace were to approach her with his request. He was even willing that she come with Mira, if that would make her more comfortable.

Catching a hint of desperation in his voice, Grace had inquired what he hoped to accomplish. "I would like to kneel before Mira and invite her to pray for me," he had told her. "What do you think of my idea?"

Her sister-in-law had been repelled and nauseated by it, giving him little encouragement regarding the meeting he coveted. She had tried to enter into prayer again but the encounter had left her disquieted in her spirit. Those few, who had come for prayer, left grumbling that the pastor had disrupted their prayer time with talking, when he should have been praying.

Mira felt strangely sick when she heard what had transpired between Grace and Pastor Rafe. Their conversation was still uppermost in her mind as the service wound to a conclusion.

When most of the ladies had dispersed, Mira timidly approached the speaker who was beginning to gather up her things. "Would you please pray for me before you leave?" she asked, the tears starting to gather behind her eyes.

Looking into her face, the woman smiled brightly and taking Mira's hands in hers, she offered up a simple prayer. Caelen and Valin spread their wings over the pair protecting them from the demons that scurried forward to disrupt the flow of God's Spirit. Trembling and weeping,

Mira felt the power of God enveloped her whole being. When her tears were spent, the woman gave her a warm hug.

An intense desire to share the worrisome invitation overwhelmed her as they sat quietly chatting together afterward. She wanted to find out what this woman of God thought about it. Gathering her courage, she finally broached the subject on her heart. "I would like to ask your opinion of a situation that has been bothering me," she faltered. The woman nodded encouragingly.

"A certain minister, who has questionable ethics, wishes to arrange a meeting with a female board member." Mira hesitated. "I guess I should reveal that he's been having some problems with his board and is actively trying to divide and conquer them, as it were. His expressed wish is to kneel before the woman and ask her to pray for him."

The speaker regarded her with a horrified expression. "You're kidding! I would say – Don't do it! Don't even think of it!"

"Why?" questioned Mira. "I know the thought of it makes me ill, but I don't know why."

"The minister is an authority figure. By submitting himself to a board member, he makes them responsible for his soul, making it less likely they will oppose anything unethical he does. They will overlook and excuse his behavior because they will have a soul-tie, a connection with him." She looked at Mira intently. "Are you the woman in this situation?" she asked candidly.

"Yes," replied Mira. "You wouldn't believe what I'm going through here even if I tried to explain it." Her tears started to fall again.

"I am aware of more than you think," the woman exclaimed. "I belong to the same organization that your pastor used to be affiliated with. He was fired by his last church for his involvement with a young man in his congregation. Our organization offered to pay all expenses if he would enter serious counseling but instead he chose to try and split the church with a telephone campaign. He came here without resolving any of those issues. I have close friends at head office and I've heard many things. I know that he was asked if that was the only incident that had ever occurred and he assured them it was, but later, it was learned that many such incidents had occurred. He has left countless broken, wounded people in his wake from one end of the country to the other." Mira was stunned. "Why did you come and speak here if you knew all this?"

"I came because I felt that God wanted me to be here tonight. I thought it was only to share a message with the ladies of the church, but I think God had a bigger purpose. Mira," she emphasized her words carefully. "Please, do not go through with this meeting that he wants. It is an unholy thing that he plans to do."

Grace interrupted their conversation at this point but Mira had the answer she was seeking regarding her uneasiness over the pastor's request. She was thankful that God cared enough about her to send this woman at just the right moment to stop what might have been a disastrous encounter.

Pastor Rutherford had barely left on his mission trip when Mira received an e-mail from Phyllis Gasher, a longtime friend and follower of Rafe's. Technically, she should not have been a member of the church because, living a fair distance away, she only attended occasionally. However, Rafe had always insisted that her name be kept on the active roll because she was such a staunch supporter of him personally.

The communication was vicious in nature. Phyllis ripped the board of directors to shreds, charging them with trying to get rid of her precious pastor in secret. "*I oppose their actions vigorously*", she wrote, *"and the spirit of matriarchal witchcraft behind it. The voting members need to be made aware of what is going on."*

She followed this up with as dire a threat as she could think of. "*I have contacted several national and international ministries to pray for this situation and am seriously thinking about taking this story to the press to expose the board's evil plot to the light of truth. Mira Grant is in a conflict of interest position on the board, with her sister-in-law acting in the capacity of a pastor. In light of the present circumstances, she should resign her position immediately! Pastor Marvin must assume his role and authority of Senior Pastor (preaching Sunday morning) until Pastor Rutherford's return (as Pastor Rutherford instructed before his departure). The board must cease from all of its secret meetings and activities until Pastor returns. Have a nice day!*"

Mira was stunned as she read the malicious words which obviously came from a heart of hatred. This same woman had fawned over Grace in the past, on one occasion even insisting that the Lord had told her to bless his servant by buying her a whole new wardrobe. Obviously either she had changed her mind or the Lord had not spoken to her at all, Mira thought ruefully.

Tears stung her eyes as she absorbed the spiteful message. She knew that Pastor Rafe was behind it but that didn't make it any more palatable. "God," she cried, "You know I haven't done anything wrong here. My heart and hands have been clean before you. Please give me wisdom and help me to forgive, even as you have forgiven me." Knowing that the woman was sadly deceived didn't take away the hurt caused by the cruel words.

Phyllis sent her spiteful e-mail to Pastor Marvin as well, demanding that copies of it be sent to all of the board members and the two pastors. He responded quickly to the hurtful missive, requesting her careful discretion before making any public statement to the press or any church members. "*It may not be something Pastor Rutherford would want to have happen, especially in his absence,*" he wrote.

Phyllis wasted no time in replying. She informed Pastor Marvin that she had been the last one to see Pastor Rafe and his wife before their departure and that they were fully aware of her intentions. She threatened to name names, again ending her venomous tirade with, "*Have a nice day!*"

Grace was upset when she received her copy of the missive. Reading between the lines, she realized that she and Mira were the accused matriarchal witches, since they were the only females involved in the woman's tirade. However, this she took to her Lord in prayer as she did with everything in her life and in the end, she decided not to respond to the vicious attack. Marvin had answered the e-mail and she was content to leave it at that. She advised Mira to do the same.

"We can't get down into mud and fight with her," she said. "It would make us no better than she is. We know that what she has written is slanted and false. She has taken up a cause and there is nothing we can do about that. God knows all about it and it will be God that vindicates us in the end. It isn't easy! The natural reaction is to strike back, but it wouldn't be right or godly to do so. Be prepared, Mira, because Satan is going to bombard the board with attacks from all sides. He knows his works are being exposed and he's angry because he's afraid of losing his stronghold in this church. Like the bible says, you just need to stand for righteousness and let the Lord do the rest."

The last few days of March passed all too quickly. The last Sunday of the month Mira spent at Pastor Dave Holman's church leading worship. The special speaker that day was one with whom she was very familiar. As an evangelist, he had spoken at the Good Shepherd Church many times and was an old friend of Pastor Rutherford's.

When Mira arrived at the church, Pastor Dave asked to speak with her privately. Surprised, she followed him into his office. "You should be aware that your pastor requested a meeting with me," he explained in a straightforward manner. "He wanted to tell me his version of the problems he has had with his rebellious board. He insisted that I set you aside and not allow you to be involved in any further ministry here. He also seemed anxious that I not ask Grace to preach in my pulpit again."

Mira was stunned! She could hardly believe Pastor Rafe's audacity.

"I felt you should know what has occurred, in case your pastor should mention it," he said with a smile. "I didn't want you to find out about the meeting and worry about what was said. Pastor Marvin was present in the meeting also, at my request. I felt it wise to have a witness to any conversation between me and your pastor. I told Rafe that you and Grace have both been a great blessing here. Neither of you have ever harmed this church in any way." Her eyes filled with tears at his kind words and he patted her hand comfortingly. "I want you to know that nothing has changed. You are welcome here and I will continue to use you as worship leader and soloist and Grace as a speaker."

Mira was stupefied that Pastor Rutherford would do such an underhanded thing. Her gratefulness to Pastor Holman for his support and love was unbounded. She determined in her heart that if she was meant to leave the Good Shepherd Church, this is where she would attend. Perhaps God was preparing this place for her because He already knew she would need it.

When the evangelist took his seat on the front row, Mira smiled a warm welcome from her place on the platform. It faded quickly however under his expressionless stare. *Does he know something about what is going on with Pastor Rafe?* she thought in dismay. *You're too sensitive,* she told herself sternly. *Perhaps his mind is elsewhere.* She closed her eyes and allowed the corporate praise and worship to carry her to the throne of God.

As he started his sermon, Mira noticed a harsh spirit about the man that had never been evident to her before. "If you are having problems in your church, you shouldn't change assemblies; you will only take your problems with you," he thundered. "Go back to your church and make things right!"

Mira felt as if a knife had been thrust through her body. *He knows everything! I'm sure of it!* She was hurt that he would judge her without even talking to her, but she knew how persuasive Pastor Rutherford could be. *Surely a true man of God wouldn't use his sermon for political purposes or to threaten or bludgeon people,* she thought. She felt sorry for those whom she knew had left other assemblies out of great hurt. *What if there are those present who have come out of a cult?* She shuddered. *They might think he's advising them to return.*

As she pondered this, it occurred to her that many in her own church idolized Pastor Rafe to the point that they believed he could do no wrong. It seemed they worshipped him more than they did Jesus. *That sounds almost cultish,* she reflected soberly. Mira had never thought of it quite that way before but now she contemplated it seriously in her heart. *Have I been guilty of that?* She had to admit that she was.

Here, in front of her, was another man that she had put on a pedestal. Once, several years ago, this same evangelist had prayed for her and she remembered the wonderful visitation she had experienced from the Lord that night. She had credited the man perhaps as much as she had the Lord and now she realized how wrong that was.

Somehow Mira managed to get through the evening service. It was the first time she had ever felt uncomfortable in Pastor Holman's church. As she mulled the day over while driving home, it slowly dawned on her that people are just people, regardless of the position they hold. At one time or another, they would all make mistakes or fail a person in some way, just as she would herself. If this man misunderstood her motives and disagreed with her actions, it was beyond her control and she would have to leave that with God. It was His problem, not hers! The only thing she was called to do, was to keep herself in right relationship with Jesus, keep her eyes focused on Him, and do what she knew to be right to the best of her ability. He would take care of the rest.

The night was frosty and cold. The boots of the commanders crunched noisily in the icy snow as they traversed the narrow passageway between the two tall buildings in the center of town. Their warm breath was torn from their mouths by a strong wind that swirled the driving snow into eerie shapes around them.

Caelen looked at Jarah, the angel of the Good Shepherd Church. "What news do you bring?"

"The battle grows desperate," he replied leaning forward and speaking rapidly. "The Evil One increases his hold on the shepherd daily." His face flushed with the intensity of his feelings. "He has all but given himself completely over to the enemy. He feels that this is a contest he must win at all costs and he will brook no defeat. He is formidable in his determination to decimate this board. Behind the scenes, he moves with great cunning, like a chess master, planning each strategy carefully, totally unaware that he is being manipulated by demons. He still thinks that he is in the perfect will of God."

"Can you do anything to sway him?" asked Valin. "There must be something you haven't thought of."

Jarah shook his head in frustration. "I've tried everything I know to do. The man will not bow his knee in surrender to the Lord. He spurns any kind of prayer life giving his time to greedy endeavors and evil pursuits. The Spirit of the Lord has left him and he doesn't know it!

Caelen sighed. "I don't doubt your report, Jarah," he replied sorrowfully. "We have seen the evidence for ourselves, have we not?" He looked meaningfully at Valin and Captain Darshan.

"Yes, but I fear this will bring terrible destruction upon this unsuspecting body of believers." Darshan sounded worried. "Many of them are weak, almost useless to us in this fight. They are weary with the cares of life and have had little or no training for spiritual warfare. Others are just beginning to wake up to the battle that rages for their souls."

Valin asked the question that was uppermost in their minds. "What are we to do if the man cannot be reached or saved?"

"We must save as many as the Lord has called," he replied grimly. "But we are not defeated yet. We must find the thing that will turn his heart back to Christ."

"We will leave no stone unturned and nothing undone that may be done," exclaimed Caelen.

"Amen to that!" they replied in unison.

It was with feelings of trepidation that Mira unlocked the church for the final board meeting before they would all be plunged into the mediation process. She shrank from sharing with the others, the things she had learned about the problems faced by past boards. There was barely time to photocopy the additional five packets before they arrived, anxious to learn what she had uncovered.

After the initial greetings were over, they decided to gather downstairs in the small banquet hall next to the kitchen. Donny offered a large box of donuts he had picked up at a coffee shop on the way over and Ian distributed water to everyone. Mira busied herself stapling together the hastily copied packages and handing them around the table. She was too heartsick to eat anything. She just wanted to get it over with.

They settled into their chairs quickly without the usual friendly banter. Taking a deep breath, Mira plunged directly into the content of the prepared documents, barely glancing up until she had finished. The issues were concisely presented along with a complete pastoral evaluation.

As she turned over the last piece of paper, she looked up, her eyes meeting those of the men seated around the table. It had taken her over an hour just to read through the packet. "Gentlemen," she said, "I know this is a lot to take in. The pastoral evaluation is merely a draft, which can be changed or amended, according to your will. Darren Amos made it clear that all of the issues we listed in the last council meeting must be thoroughly backed up. He also told us that we should be evaluating the pastor's performance the same as any employer and this is in accordance to the new constitution. It states that we are supposed to do this evaluation each year before the annual business meeting. I don't believe that has ever happened, maybe because this is the first year that the new constitution has been in effect. But it is a part of our job."

Mira sighed and shook her head sadly. "I know some of the backup is pretty harsh but to tell you the truth, I didn't include in these packets some of the more explicit sexual allegations that I found. We haven't been approached as a board with any such accusations, so that is something we will have to leave in God's hands. However, the board that dealt with those issues also went through exactly what we are now experiencing - lies, manipulation, defamation of our characters, intimidation, harassment, control. This has been and continues to be, a pattern of behaviour that appears in the records of the church, ever since Pastor Rafe came here, almost fifteen years ago. Many have fallen and I think most of us are on the verge of leaving as well. The bottom line here is – what are we going to do with this information?"

David Armstrong let out an explosive gust of air. His face was devoid of color, almost greyish in appearance. "Are you absolutely sure all of this is true?" he asked in disbelief.

"I'm positive. I wish it weren't true. Here is the full binder on the moral issue. I only copied very small portions of it for the packages, but you are welcome to read the whole thing yourself."

"I wouldn't mind reading it." It was Jack who spoke.

"I'll make you a full copy before we leave tonight, if you don't mind waiting," Mira replied.

"Wow, a whole lot of things make more sense to me now," said Donny shaking his head, a bemused expression on his face.

"I'm not surprised," said Ian quietly.

"How do *you* feel about all of this?" Mira addressed Sylvester who sat in stunned silence. He dazedly shook his head and when he spoke, he sounded far-away, as if he was locked in a nightmare that he couldn't escape from.

"I don't know what to think," he finally managed gruffly, his lower lip trembling. "I just can't believe this! I don't know what to think." He repeated the last phrase several times.

"I know I can't have this man as my spiritual leader any more." Jack sounded final. "I'm done here if he stays."

"Me too!" came from both Donny and Ian.

"My wife and I moved here when I retired from ministry, so that we could attend Pastor Rafe's church," said Rev. Armstrong. "I've always had the deepest respect for him, but I've never really known him personally – just what I've seen and heard on television over the years." He paused for a moment, shaking his head in a bewildered fashion. "But this! I have to say I've never heard the like of this, in all my years of ministry! I knew he had some personality problems, but this is downright immoral...and unethical. I can't be a part of this sort of behaviour."

"Nor can I," replied Mira. "The thing is... will we do as the other boards have done...just walk away and say nothing? And, if that is the choice we make... what about the people? Don't we have an obligation to them? They have no idea who this man really is! They only know his charm and the celebrity persona that he exudes."

"Well, I can't reconcile just walking away with what Jesus would do," said Jack earnestly. "He threw the money changers out of the temple and used a whip to do it."

"What about the Apostle Paul?" added Mira. "He would have set things right in the church in short order. I don't believe for a minute that he would have run away from his responsibilities." She sighed. "I know that the hour is growing late, but I really feel that we need to make a decision tonight, on what we're going to do. For myself – I feel that God placed me in this position for a reason. I don't think it was an accident that this group of people were elected to the board at this time. God knows what He is doing. He places the powers that be, in government, and He placed us here. The question is – what are we going to do? Turn tail and run or stand for integrity and do what is right, even if we lose our friends over it. It's a hard decision and one not to be made lightly."

"It's probably the hardest thing we'll ever have to do, but maybe that's why we're here – for such a time as this." Donny shrugged. "Esther put her life on the line for what she believed was right and saved a nation. Can we do less for the precious saints here? Count me in. I'll stay and stand for what is right no matter what it costs."

"You all realize that the people may not understand," Mira warned. "I thought Pastor Rafe was a wonderful man of God for almost fourteen years. I didn't understand when the last board fell. I thought *they* were the evil ones. We will probably be misunderstood – even maligned. Are you ready for that? I say this only because I strongly believe that if we stand, we should stand together. If he is able to divide us – we're done! Either we all stand together or we all walk away from this right now!"

"I say we stand," replied Ian stoutly. "I have nothing more to lose. I can always go and worship somewhere else. Besides, there are more here than you might think who are unhappy with Pastor Rafe."

"I'm willing to see it through," said David Armstrong.

Mira went around the table, asking each one for a decision. "We'll see it through," was the reply from each one.

"And the pastor? What will we do about him?"

"Well... I guess we're going to have to fire him," said the old minister hesitantly. "I don't see what other choice we have."

"Is everyone in agreement on this?" Mira questioned. They all nodded.

"We can't allow him back in the pulpit," said Jack. "I don't think I could stomach it!"

"We would need a resolution passed by the board," returned Mira.

After much discussion, it was decided that the motion in question, should prevent the pastor from resuming his duties, until the mediation process was completed to a satisfactory resolution. It also required him to refrain from any direct or indirect contact with members of the church in an effort to influence them or to make any defamatory comments against the board of directors or council. Donny agreed to bring the motion to the floor and surprisingly, Rev. Armstrong seconded it. There was no dissenting voice.

"How could you allow this to happen?" shrieked the Jezebel Spirit. The lesser demons scattered before the fierceness of his wrath. The great downstairs hall was packed to capacity with evil spirits and devils.

A contorted, spider-like creature with numerous grotesque, hairy appendages skittered sideways across the floor with amazing speed, coming to a halt in front of the massive demon commander. Its small evil eyes gleamed wickedly in the dim light which barely illuminated the hall.

"Paugh!" spat the beast sharply. "This board will not hold together! They are full of courage now, but when our pawn returns, they will crumble and fall as before. Two of them are weak. They are as the waves of the sea and they will turn as quickly in the other direction, as they did in this meeting that has you so concerned."

The Jezebel demon-master drew its mammoth body up to its full height. Its great bulk heaved a huge shadow over scores of wraith-like creatures milling about the vast interior of the room. Its wrath was a giant weight pressing down upon the smaller, lower-ranking spirits. Those in closest proximity scattered in terror, finding a place of relative safety outside the range of its massive swing, fearing the hammering fists and undulating claws.

"They must be utterly destroyed!" he roared. "I have labored too hard to build this stronghold."

The spider-like demon rose on misshapen hind legs. Its thick, twisted, malformed tentacles reached out menacingly. "We will not lose anything here! We are too strong! No one can withstand us now! First the two will fall and then the others will turn tail and run," he predicted with a sneer. Black venom oozed like corruption from its hungry claws.

The evil commander decided it would not be to his advantage to tangle with the fiendish brute. "You had better be right," he growled, his tongue lolling between sharp yellow teeth. Saliva dribbled from the corners of his mouth as he licked his cruel black lips.

Mira spent the next couple of days preparing full packages for the mediators and council. Telephone messages and e-mails flew between them at all hours. Darren Amos called her with the news that he had consulted a colleague and they both strongly felt the annual business meeting date should be left alone and not changed, as had been discussed in his initial meeting with the board.

"All board decisions could possibly be declared illegal if they breach the by-law of the church constitution," he said. "Either the by-law must be amended or the meeting must go forward as scheduled."

When Mira called each of the directors with the news, they all agreed that it was too great a risk to contravene the constitution or to try to modify it. Tom Storey wasn't happy with the change of plan. He was still in favor of amending the by-law, but he agreed to abide by the board's decision, so Mira sent out the appropriate announcements to all the parties involved. A public announcement was made at the mid-week service that the date of the annual meeting would not be changed, but would go ahead as originally planned on April 11th.

Tom Storey set up appointments to meet with each of the board members, who promptly called Mira, wondering what his purpose was in having the private meetings. "He probably wants to know if we are all in unity, regarding what must be accomplished," she said, in an effort to reassure them. "He also would like confirmation that we are going into the process with open minds and reconciliation as our goal, rather than being focused on firing the pastor, no matter what happens."

Between phone calls, Mira dropped by Dora's apartment with copies of the package she had worked so hard to assemble. She was assured that Pastor Rutherford would receive his package on Thursday evening so that he would receive no surprises at the first mediation meeting. Tom and Dora were scheduled to meet with him that night for the purpose of preparing him for it.

After receiving his packet, Tom arranged a conference call with Mira and Dora. He had serious reservations about including the letter with the board's resolution to suspend the pastor's duties until after the mediation meetings were completed. He asked Mira if she would call the directors and request that they wait on delivering the letter, until at least the end of the first meeting, which was scheduled for Saturday morning. After some consultation, they reluctantly decided to accede to his request.

Mira delivered a copy of the mediation package to Darren Amos. After a brief consultation, he took her over to the employment lawyer's office. She liked the straightforward, professional manner of this man and was favorably impressed with his quick grasp of the case. He seemed to know exactly what the church was up against with Pastor Rutherford and did not seek to minimize any of her concerns. She felt better knowing that the board was doing it's best to provide the pastor with a more generous package than law required.

That evening around the dinner table, Grace tried to bring a little levity into the conversation which had been heavy all week.

"Donny and Rob came by the church today," she said, her eyes twinkling.

Mira perked up her ears. “What were they doing there?” she asked, her curiosity getting the better of her.

“Cleaning up… apparently.” She grinned openly now. “They were throwing out some of the clutter that has accumulating in the basement,” she explained. “I went downstairs to see what they were up to and found them having a great time getting rid of old beat-up furniture and junk that Pastor Rafe had permitted people to drop off at the church, for some unknown reason. I had a look at it and it was only fit for the garbage heap. They probably didn’t want to pay to take it to the junk yard.”

“It’s about time,” said Dan, a gleam of satisfaction in his eye. “I threw out a lot of stuff when we did the kitchen renovations, but it just keeps rolling in and piling up.”

“Dan’s right!” exclaimed Mira. “The board tried to put a stop to it, but the pastor allows his favored ones to get away with it. We don’t find out about it until it’s too late!”

Grace laughed. “You know the old couch in the youth room?”

“Yes! It’s disgusting! I think there’s cat urine on it or something. It’s all stained and gross looking! We’ve been complaining about it for ages!”

“Not any more!”

“They threw it out then?” cried Mira. “It’s about time! I’m glad! I hope no one rescues it from the garbage bin.”

“Not much chance of that.” Grace giggled. “They burned it!”

“NO!” hooted Dan.

“Yes! They doused the thing with gasoline and set it on fire!” Grace continued breathlessly. “You should have seen it! The black smoke just rolled off it and the flames shot twenty feet in the air! It was too priceless! Rob even took pictures with his cell phone. You have to see them!” That sent them all into gales of laughter.

“Did anyone else see?” gasped Mira finally when she could speak.

“Ina found out and was a little upset.” Grace dabbed at her tears. “She said they had no right because it was someone’s property. Mira,” she choked, “they wanted to get into the pastor’s office and grab his couch too! They planned to heave it over the railing, drag it outside and burn it! I think they wanted to consign it to the pit of hell… or something like that!” She was hysterical by now. “And they were serious!”

The two women laughed so hard they couldn't speak. Dan's loud guffaws just made them worse. Finally Grace caught her breath. She was holding her stomach and the tears were running down her face.

"I talked them out of it," she finally managed.

"Well..." said Mira, in a more serious tone, "I can see where it might have made them feel better, after everything they've learned recently. We've all been pretty shaken up by it."

"Too bad they didn't go through with it!" exclaimed Dan, sobering up as well. "God only knows what unholy things have happened on *that* couch!"

"I know how you must feel, Dan," said Grace. She hesitated a moment wanting to find the right words that wouldn't offend her brother-in-law. "Can you do me a favor?" she finally asked.

"Sure thing, doll," he replied cheerfully.

"It would make my job so much easier, if you would please stay away from the church during office hours when Pastor Rutherford is there," she pleaded. Dan had talked openly with her regarding his point of view on Rafe's sexuality, so she was aware of his struggle in dealing with feelings of betrayal and anger over what had occurred at his daughter's wedding. It caught her by surprise when he readily agreed to do as she asked.

When Grace had first taken the position as associate pastor, Dan had initially told her that he would not be in attendance at any of the services. "I need to focus on beating this cancer," he said, "and I can't do it, when that man is around." After the pastor left for Florida however, he would sometimes slip into the service and stand at the back of the auditorium to listen to her preach. One particular Sunday, she noticed that he had progressed to sitting with Mira; something he had not done for a very long time. As soon as Pastor Rutherford returned however, he disappeared again.

Grace had quickly learned for herself that when Rafe was in town, he was so needy and demanding of her time, she often didn't have any opportunity to work, pray or even to eat her lunch. When he learned of this, Dan would sometimes show up unannounced insisting that his sister-in-law take the time to go out for a proper meal. "You need a break from the guy," he told her. "He'll suck you dry if you let him!"

The last time Rafe was in town, Dan had come to the church on just such a mission of mercy. Unfortunately, he had run into the pastor in the lobby. Just seeing the man had infuriated him. He had called Rafe *"a Jezebel"* and *"an antichrist"* to his face.

It was Grace however, who caught the brunt of the pastor's anger, after her return from lunch that day. She noted with interest that Rafe seemed intimidated by her brother-in-law. Of course, Dan was a man that brooked no deception or nonsense and he wouldn't back away from a confrontation either, if the need arose. Grace suspected that Rafe despised him because he had no influence or control over him.

21

THE MORNING OF THE first mediation meeting found a nervous council, awaiting the arrival of the mediators with Pastor Rutherford. They had decided to use one of the Sunday School rooms in order to ensure complete privacy. The only absentee was Frank Milton who was vacationing in Florida. He would not be returning until the following week. Donny Allison and Rob Samuels brought in juice, water, muffins and donuts to fortify everyone for the task ahead of them. Even the associate pastors were present, although they were seated at a small table apart from the council members. Mira set up a recorder to tape the sessions, in order to make it easier for her to capture the minutes and still concentrate on the progress of the meeting.

A troop of twenty angelic warriors were positioned strategically behind the council members to ward them from the multitude of demons and imps who watched and waited, a savage hunger glowing in their febrile eyes.

As Tom and Dora entered the room with the pastor, the members were surprised to see Mrs. Rutherford accompanying them. They looked at one another in consternation, each one wondering how much this would curtail an open and honest approach in the meetings.

Tom wasted no time in calling the meeting to order. He defined the role of the mediators and requested that everyone respect this by addressing himself and Dora as chairpersons, rather than one another. Mira was duly appointed to take minutes and although it was agreed that the meeting would be recorded to provide accuracy, the tapes were to be destroyed after the written version was approved. Since there was no objection on any procedural point, Dora proceeded to open in prayer.

Pastor Rafe sat on the opposite side of the table from Mira. His color was high, his expression grim and foreboding, as Tom read scripture and presented an outline of the process. When he was finished, Tom requested that each person be distributed paper and pen in order to write down their own ideal solution and outcome for mediation. He assured them that no one other than the mediators would see what they had written. He felt this would give him and Dora insight to help guide the process.

When this exercise was completed, Tom read a brief statement on behalf of Pastor Rutherford. Rafe's letter announced that although it was a difficult decision, he was ready to retire. The timing and implications of leaving his role as senior pastor were not clear however. He stated his shock over being asked to resign at the fateful council meeting in early March and ended by recognizing that the situation was difficult for everyone involved and people were hurting. His desire, he said, was to discuss and work out the details of his retirement in a spirit of love, peace and reconciliation.

Watching the emotions play over his features as Tom read his statement, Mira was not convinced that Pastor Rafe was as willing to retire as he claimed. His stiff face and rigid body gave the impression of barely controlled rage, seething just below the surface.

Mrs. Rutherford rose to address the council. She was candid regarding her very strong wish to retire, but expressed shock over being told by her husband that they would no longer have a job or a place to stay.

The little group looked from one to another knowingly. *Pastor's been at it again!* - was plainly written on every face. They all loved Eve Rutherford and felt her pain acutely. Most of them were keenly aware that Rafe was accustomed to telling her only those details he wanted her to know. Her words brought a lump to Mira's throat and tears to more than one eye before she had finished.

Everyone was relieved when Tom announced that the pastor and his wife would be leaving the room, prior to any further discussion. It would be much easier to be open, honest and direct without Eve's presence in the room and indeed, without that of Rafe as well, although they were very surprised that he was not staying.

When the door closed behind them, Tom shared that he and Dora had been pleasantly surprised on Thursday evening to find that the pastor was going to retire. They had been apprehensive about giving him the board's package, feeling it might change his mind, but apparently it hadn't, since he agreed to go ahead with his prepared statement.

"There are many issues to be decided," Tom said, "and we need to consider these with open minds, including whether it is worth conceding some things, if we get the resolution we want."

"What concessions are you talking about?" queried Rob, his brow raised questioningly. "That doesn't sound right to me. Does that mean we are supposed to put aside every issue we have? I feel that we need "due process" in order for council members to be healed individually and be effective in the ministry here."

The mediator shrugged. "I only mean that we're approaching discussion from a different perspective because of the change in the pastor's attitude toward retirement. My guess is that some of you felt there could never be an agreeable solution."

"I hear it, but I'm not at the point of believing it yet," retorted Rob, his voice tight with sarcasm. "What assurance do we have that this is real?"

"Dora and I spent a few hours with the pastor. I would suggest, for the purpose of moving this process forward, we all try to accept what he's saying at face value. We can always come back to that concern later in the process."

Pastor Marvin raised his hand. "In any conversation I've had with Pastor, he's never used the word "retire". Whether it means now or later? Who knows? But I agree that this is much further along than what we've heard so far."

"If God can move him this far, God will resolve anything," added Pierre, in his broken French accent.

"What kind of time frame we are looking at?" questioned Ian. "Will the pastor be preaching in the pulpit again?"

"These are the things this council needs to identify," answered Tom gravely. "You need to talk through all of your questions and issues."

"At least it gives us a starting point." Rev. Armstrong's face had brightened considerably. He was encouraged to think there might not be any unpleasantness after all.

Mira spoke hesitantly. "I am pleased with what we heard this morning, but I too am concerned that this could be just a stalling tactic." She remembered the glowering brow of Pastor Rafe. "Can we believe it?"

"Not to minimize your concern, but we need to work from a heart of love and a good faith belief that he means it," responded Pastor Marvin.

"I'd have a better good faith belief if this were concluded before the annual meeting," was her terse rejoinder.

"She's right! We need to see something in writing," interposed Jack, a worried look on his face.

"The document must be notarized as well, so he can't change his mind," added Ian resolutely.

Tom raised his hand for order. "I agree that we need to get something in writing. But I would ask that we try and set aside any scepticism and assume that we can believe what we hear and continue the discussions on that basis. We need to come to a place where we can all agree on what needs to be done; capture it in writing, so that everyone can read it, accept it and sign the document as evidence of formal agreement.

"This all needs to be finished before the annual business meeting," insisted Mira vehemently.

Tom looked annoyed. "The time frame is a problem with the annual business meeting in less than two weeks. A more reasonable goal would be to have a resolution document signed prior to the annual business meeting, with some parts of the agreement extending beyond that time frame. We have a very short time for the mediation process and I really don't have a blueprint in mind for exactly how this will happen. We may have to set some things aside for a time, in order to proceed."

"The very fact that the pastor is resigning takes care of much of the problem we have," stated Rev. Armstrong. "I guess all of us are questioning - Is he sincere? A lot of the issues point directly at the pastor, but if he leaves, many of them are resolved."

"What has happened today is a trade-off," interjected Rob sharply. "He wants us to forget the issues because he knows that he is facing a brick wall with this board. He tried his best - right up until last night - to shake it apart. We don't have a date of resignation or any verification of it. All we have is a statement, which you got from him on Thursday night, but even after that - he didn't stop manipulating! So I have to believe that his mind wasn't set on retirement at that point."

"When we talked to him Thursday night, he was not in possession of the last package of material. We didn't want to give him the package because we felt it might derail the mediation process. He now has that package. We gave it to him later the same night, as we were instructed by the board to do, even though we were seriously concerned about the effect it would have on him after he read it."

"Well, quite a bit still went on Thursday and Friday," cut in Rob sardonically, still pressing his argument. "I had to write three letters in answer to his e-mails and I am not happy to have communications such as those on file. We need verification of his retirement! This whole process has cost us tremendously and we've invested a lot in it. We are owed something! Not just a statement that has yet to be verified! The bible says, *"Faith without works is dead"*. A statement is not works! We need to see a predictable behavior style so we can start trusting him again; so that he won't say one thing and mean another. Eve's comments were lovely and I know she was bewildered at why we couldn't have shown more patience, but we were not ever told they were working on a retirement plan."

"I don't believe he was," replied Ian.

"Exactly!" cried Rob. "We all know it! We asked for his plans at the March 10th council meeting so why didn't he share this then? Now we are running out of time! I have to judge this at face value. I judge it according to the seriousness of this meeting, the time line we have, and our responsibilities here. The heaviest load falls on the shoulders of the board of directors. They are charged, both by God and the government, with the governing of this church. They are the stewards of it. It is their responsibility to ensure that all of the pastors, employees and deacons are conducting themselves properly. I feel the weight of my position as well. I have never been told, schooled or installed properly, in the role of a deacon, so I don't come from a position of knowledge, understanding and training. Unfortunately, the problems this board is facing are inherited from past boards, but nevertheless, they are responsible to see this through to a conclusion. It is ultimately the board who carries the responsibility for everything that happens in the church, legally, spiritually and financially.

"The pastor and the elders have the spiritual responsibility for the church," retorted Tom.

"Yes, but even though the pastor may be the spiritual head of the church, the board is directly responsible for his employment and conduct. We need to get past what has happened here, but we also require verification that he means to retire; something with some teeth to it – a solid unbreakable agreement. It's a trade off. We're trading off discussing the problems that have occurred and the complaints that have been brought forward, in order to deal with the resignation; to see if we can get that moving forward. We have been fighting hell and spiritual demons trying to deal with these issues, as well as the flesh on all sides. We are still here and we know God has charged us with this and we can't escape it! I'm glad for what I've seen and heard here today, but we need to put some teeth to it – some meat on the bones. This has to happen today or you've not satisfied anyone! I think really it was just a matter of who blinked first – him or us!

"There are a lot of details that still need discussion...."

Rob interrupted the mediator impatiently. "But we have to do it today! Not a month from now! Don't do that to us!"

"The time line is under pressure," replied Tom. "This doesn't mean that we are throwing the issues out the door, but I think our focus today would be more productive if we explored this opportunity. If we talked about each separate issue now, our time would be gone and nothing resolved. We can come back to the issues. We need to be able to live with whatever is hammered out."

"The pastor will have a long list of what he would like, and council should have a list as well," added Dora. "Just having Eve here, which was a surprise to all of us, puts some validation on this. It's not just him, but also Mrs. Rutherford who is saying that they want to retire."

"I know she's sincere," replied Rob earnestly. "I think we all agree on that."

"Eve means what she says," interjected Phil, with a vexed look at Rob. "Pastor Rafe doesn't want to be forced out, under these circumstances! He had a bad kick from his last church and he doesn't want that to happen again. Let him make the choice! When he went to Florida for a month, he was confused. He wasn't sure about anything. I believe you should give him the chance to decide in his own way when or if he wants to retire. The congregation is hearing a lot of gossip about what is going on. If he tells them that he and Eve made the decision to retire on their own, they will accept that. But if the people know he's being forced out, you're going to open up a real can of worms! There will be a lot of upset people! Forget about us! You have to consider them! So let him make the decision. Eve is right there and he is not going to ignore her feelings in the matter."

"One way to handle this, is for the pastor and Eve to make a written joint public statement," suggested Tom, wanting to move the discussion forward. "To explore this further, you should all try to identify the details for agreement by making a list of what needs to be included and the time frame. What are the options or range of options that could be included? Consider his position and factor that into the discussion. Dora and I will meet with Pastor Rutherford and ask for him to do the same. We need to begin with where we are currently, to start a constructive dialogue. Try to create a collaborative environment to work together, as opposed to an adversarial position. The most important items, from what I am hearing, are the actual retirement date and the announcement of it."

"Can't we go back and change our vote on the pastor's resignation from the previous council meeting?" asked Phil.

"No," replied Tom. "Recorded votes and minutes of meetings cannot be changed. You can revisit the issue in another meeting, but you can't change what's already been done."

"It's not really important what's recorded. Most people will never see it," added Rob impatiently. "It's a fact that the pastor was asked to resign and this whole struggle is not new to him. I think it is very important that we don't deny it. Putting everything aside is denial. We can't do that! We need to transition *out* of it and move on."

"I know there are important issues here that have gone on for awhile." Dora sounded apologetic. "We are not trying to minimize them, but for now, we do need to focus on the retirement. It is the end solution for all of your concerns."

Mira looked pointedly at Phil. "We cannot put this decision back into the pastor's lap. This board has been through enough! That is not an option! If we present a united front, with the Rutherfords making it clearly known that they want to retire, then that is the best possible solution. We should start with a request that the pastor and his wife make a public statement of retirement *before* the annual business meeting, thereby diffusing any problems with the membership. Pastor Rafe should also publicly state that he has full confidence in the abilities of the associate pastors to carry on, while a search is made for another senior pastor. Any involvement by him in that search would be completely unacceptable! The constitution sets forth clear guidelines for the process and it certainly doesn't allow room for the outgoing pastor to be involved in any way. Eve has been very vocal for awhile now about her desire to retire. The pastor has been equally vocal with this council, saying that he has no intention of retiring. Either he has made a 180 degree turn or we have to assume that this could possibly be a stalling tactic, in order to get rid of this board at the annual business meeting. He would then arrange for a more agreeable board that would presumably proceed with whatever agenda he desires. We have heard so many lies that it is difficult to sort through them all and find the truth here. This is a complete turnaround from not even twenty-four hours ago."

"I think we need to adjust to today's statement that was made," reiterated Tom. "There's still work to do and we must keep in mind that there is also opportunity for things to change over the next few meetings and follow a less desirable path. I see today as a first step. In the next step, the pastor will make a list of what he would like and the council will make a list of what they would like. Council wants a letter, a public announcement and some different things. If we are willing to pursue that route and avoid a clash, then let's turn the meeting to focus that way and deal with the other issues later.

Donny Allison spoke for the first time. "I also have concerns about the validity of the pastor's word. The announcement should definitely be written out and mutually agreed upon by all parties, so that everyone knows exactly what is happening. Pastor changes his mind all the time and that cannot happen with this announcement."

"I agree," replied Tom. "Another item that could be added is the severance package or retirement send-off."

Mira asked for recognition. "I circulated copies of a preliminary severance package to the directors this evening. It was drawn up by an employment lawyer and e-mailed to me today. The documents include general recommendations set out in common law and precedents of other cases. Of course, we have to keep in mind that any amount mutually agreed upon, in excess of $25,000, must be approved by the membership at the annual business meeting."

"That would tie in with the announcement being a positive one and stated more as a send-off or pension," replied Tom approvingly.

"The board needs to move on this very quickly," she replied. "The lawyer should be instructed Monday morning to finalize a generous and acceptable package to present to the Rutherfords so they have sufficient opportunity to digest it."

"The retirement announcement should be read in the service tomorrow, if that can be worked out," stated Rob. "Then we would know that the pastor is serious. That could be followed with a big announcement in the paper for a celebration party in tribute of their fifteen years of service at Good Shepherd Church. It will bring honor to them and cover over a multitude of sins committed by the pastor. The other issues can then be moved further back so that it would take the heat off for now. It would certainly verify we are on the same page, but make no mistake, we do need it verified!"

"All of the suggestions are good," replied Tom, "but tomorrow is too soon to craft a retirement announcement, have the whole council approve the wording of it, digest it and sign it.

Mira could see that Tom was trying to slow them down. "Easter Sunday morning would be a good time for the announcement," she volunteered. "It coincides with the fourteenth anniversary of the church in this building. That will allow Pastor to keep his honor. He has spoken about transitioning into his global ministry several times in the pulpit over the past few months and people are prepared for his departure. Some have even thought that he had resigned already. They have mentioned as much to the associate pastors."

"What about the issue of him going into the pulpit tomorrow morning?" enquired Rob.

Tom suggested that it might be time for him and Dora to meet with the pastor in order to clarify some of their questions, while council continued to flesh out their list of requests. After the mediators left the room, the group gathered around the refreshment table, chatting about the unexpected turn of events due to the pastor's impending retirement. They decided to meet with the employment lawyer on Wednesday evening, if it could be arranged, in order to give them a proper retirement package to offer, in advance of the third meeting scheduled for the following day.

The members were encouraged that such quick results had been obtained, when most had been prepared for a nasty drawn-out battle. Even so, the majority agreed that some things were simply not negotiable. A firm commitment from the pastor that he would not go into the pulpit throughout the mediation meetings was at the top of their list. They also felt the retirement statement should express confidence in the associate pastors, the council and board to take the church into their future.

A generous severance package with goodwill on top was also a priority. It was suggested that two offers might be made; a lump-sum payment or a payout over the course of a year. The latter, they felt, might give them more control and hopefully minimize any damage the pastor would try to do to the church body with a telephone campaign. Left to his own devices, they all believed that he would try to divide the congregation with lies and manipulation. Adequate time to move out of the parsonage was also something that everyone was willing to be flexible on.

When Tom and Donna returned to the meeting, they announced that Pastor Rafe had agreed to make the retirement announcement prior to or no later than the annual business meeting. He was also prepared to identify details regarding what he expected in his retirement package, as well as the actual date of retirement. The mediators had asked him to involve Eve in that process as well.

"So you think they are serious about actually retiring?" Rev. Armstrong's tremulous voice asked the question. "There's no doubt about it?"

"No, there is no doubt," Tom assured him.

"I feel this is a major step that we've all accomplished this evening," added Dora.

"It's a real answer to prayer," breathed the old reverend thankfully.

"Did you address his speaking in the Sunday services?" questioned Mira.

"We chose not to discuss that issue but to put it on the back burner for a bit. We felt we needed to discuss it with council first."

"We do have very real concerns about whether he would be able to leave the issues out of the service" offered Rob. His features looked pinched and tired. "We think it wise for him not to be in the pulpit until the mediation is over."

"The pastor acknowledged some of this himself" replied Tom.

Mira raised her hand. "I have a letter here from the board to the pastor which effectively removes him from the pulpit until the mediation process is finished. We would rather not give it to him if we can get a verbal commitment from him that he will not preach during these negotiations or, at the very least, he must promise to behave himself and not say anything to inflame the current situation. We need some assurance that what has begun here will not be derailed so that we can pursue a positive resolution."

"I agree that giving him the letter would be better avoided," said Tom. "I'm aware that there is a lack of trust, but the pastor has no interest in derailing things."

"I agree with Tom," declared Dora. "The pastor is diffused at the moment. I truly believe that even if he was to take the service, he would be okay."

Pastor Marvin signalled his wish to be heard. "We had no idea who would be speaking, so Pastor Grace has been advertised in one newspaper and just a celebration service in the other."

"The congregation might wonder why he is back and not in the pulpit," offered Tom.

"We have serious concerns over whether he has enough control to keep these issues from creeping into his remarks or sermons." Rob looked around the group for verification. Several nodded their heads vigorously and expressed their own apprehension regarding the pastor's emotional state. "What if he just announces that he is back this Sunday and will be speaking on Easter Sunday?"

"He may want to share a little about his mission trip and let Pastor Grace bring the message as advertised," suggested Tom. "That would send a message to the congregation that the pastors are working together."

"I think it might be beneficial for him to share about his trip to the mission field," agreed Rob. "The congregation would probably like to hear about it. If Pastor Grace preached the main message, council wouldn't be as concerned about him taking advantage. He must be emotionally spent from the last few days anyway.

"If he should get on a soapbox on Sunday to promote his cause, it would be detrimental to him," added Tom. "People would view it as inappropriate. But I still feel that if the letter from the board is delivered to him, it might be perceived as a bullying tactic."

"We need a predictable service for our comfort level," declared Rob. "We don't want to shun him but we don't want a soapbox either."

"We will present to the pastor that this would be a wise way to handle the service," assured Tom. "I think everyone is pleased with what has occurred today and I'm sure no one wishes to disrupt the progress that has been made." He hesitated. "The pastor would be more comfortable if the packets you received tonight were collected. At the time they were prepared, things looked different. Some of the issues still may need to be addressed, but it would be seen as a positive show of good faith if we were to collect them at this time. The material is hard-hitting. Would it be acceptable to gather them and come back to the issues that need to be talked through later?"

"It shows a good spirit and an act of faith," agreed Rev. Armstrong warmly.

"It may help the pastor's frame of mind," agreed Tom.

"The secretary should hold them," countered Rob dubiously. He was worried that they would somehow disappear.

Tom suggested that Dora take them until the process was finished, with the exception of the original file which would stay with Mira. As secretary of the board, she would be required to add letters and documents to it on a daily basis. Before handing them in, the directors were requested to remove the information on severance packages. When this was accomplished, the mediators left again for a brief meeting with Pastor Rutherford.

When they returned, Tom told the group that the pastor was appreciative of the good faith shown by handing in the packages. "Pastor did raise some concerns however about not leading the service," he said apologetically. "He thought it would raise more questions by the congregation and create more issues. I think he understands the negative implications of raising any of these issues in the service and he has guaranteed us that it will not happen. We pointed out that it would be very detrimental to the process and to him. Dora and I believe him and we are asking the council for a leap of faith in allowing him to speak on Sunday."

Mira asked for recognition. "If anything should occur in the service, the board of directors has a prepared statement that will be read," she declared firmly. "I would also suggest that the entire service be taped, including the worship service." Pastor Marvin promptly agreed to take care of it.

The small group of tired council members made their way downstairs to the lobby. Although worn out from the gruelling meeting, they were also encouraged by the outcome. Things had progressed beyond their wildest hopes and now a positive resolution seemed possible.

At Mira's request, Rob Samuels sent her the letters that he had referred to in the meeting. To her fast-growing binder of issues, she added his handwritten letter of objection regarding the improper and illegal elder/deacon meeting. In it, he expressed his outrage over Pastor Rutherford's obvious lobbying effort to influence the part of council that excluded the board of directors. He felt it was illegal, ungodly and manipulative.

The reply that he received from the pastor told him plainly that he could resign if the pressure was too great to handle. Rob had promptly returned a clear statement, "I WILL NOT RESIGN!" Rafe's answering e-mail declared his shock over Rob's reply. His anger was evident as he defended his position and accused Rob of positioning himself in a posture of agreeing with those who had purposely set themselves against him.

It certainly didn't sound to Mira like the pastor had even remotely considered resigning. Since the letters had only gone back and forth between the deacon and the pastor in the past couple of days, it gave her an uneasy feeling that perhaps there was another agenda and Pastor Rafe may only be buying time after all.

22

The next morning was Palm Sunday and Rafe managed to behave himself creditably in the morning service during the time he and Eve were sharing their experiences on the mission field. As he delved into his message however, his control began to slip and he forgot his promises to the mediators or perhaps he just distained them.

Painting a picture of Jesus praying for strength in the garden of Gethsemane, Rafe veered from the scriptures, comparing himself to the Christ. "Sometimes, it is those closest to you who betray you." The cadence of his voice deepened dramatically and he allowed a tremor of emotion as he aimed a skilful barb at his leadership. "I shouldn't complain though. Jesus only had three reliable men that he could trust." Jack tried to catch Rev. Armstrong's eye but the old man stared straight ahead.

Rafe managed to get in another clever dig in his depiction of how betrayed Jesus felt over the defection of his treasurer. Since the reference was so blatant, Mira wondered if anyone outside of the board had caught it.

As he became fully caught up in his theme, he likened himself more and more to the Master. "Just like Jesus, I have prayed and fasted constantly throughout my ministry. The only thing I haven't done is sweat blood... yet." He threw out his hands dramatically. "Yes," he thundered loudly, "Just like Jesus, they tried to kill me off but it didn't work then and it won't work now!" Some of his congregants looked bewildered and confused. The directors sat in stony silence, aware that his tirade was a direct attack on them.

Sliding adeptly into prophetic mode, Rafe strode back and forth across the platform alternately moaning and shouting his Word from the Lord, which lifted him up and singled him out as special in God's eyes. "I AM the I AM; I AM the I AM," he roared at the end of his outburst. The demons exploded in hysterical glee. They rocketed through the sanctuary spewing poisonous black liquid in a deadly spray of corruption over the hapless, unsuspecting heads of the congregation.

Jack and Amy Johnson looked at one another in consternation. The proclamation that Rafe had given sent shivers down their spines. Could he actually believe that he was divine? Amy closed her eyes and sent up a desperate prayer asking God to move his mighty hand on behalf of his children.

A tall golden warrior spread his wings above her head, shutting out the clamor on the platform. A vision began to swiftly materialize. Its clarity and force startled her.

She saw the church surrounded by a large fence. Its appearance was similar to that of snow fencing with wooden slats held together by wire. As she gazed upon it, a small portion of the fence on one side suddenly broke away. Toppling from the main structure, it fell backward to the ground opening a path into the fields beyond. Although it lay flat upon the ground, it did not seem to affect the rest of the fence which remained as it was.

As abruptly as it had appeared, the vision was gone. Still she sat examining it, meditating...waiting for the interpretation. It came to her unexpectedly with great simplicity.

The fence represented the people of the church as a whole. The wire that held and bound them together was "deception". The small piece of fence that broke free and fell over was the remnant that God was preparing to escape. As they attuned their ears to His still small voice, He would enable them to break the bonds which held them fast, to follow Him and Him alone. They would know the truth and the truth would set them free. But the rest of the fence would remain as it was, still bound by deception.

In the evening service, Rafe's chosen topic was "The Judgment of God" and this time he had barely begun before he lost his grip on reality. Leaving all wisdom and prudence behind, he jabbed his vicious remarks straight at the leadership in an attempt to intimidate them by bludgeoning them with the Word of God.

"There is a lack of fear in the church," he thundered, pacing back and forth across the front. "Rebellious people, leaders even, are doing their own thing. They are motivated by madness or caught in the grip of whatever has overtaken them." His anger and outrage moved him inexorably forward until he slipped beyond the brink of good judgment. "They will be plagued with the plagues of Egypt, with death being the ultimate result, if they do not repent," he roared.

Those from council, who attended the service, wondered if they would come under a curse, as a consequence of their presumed rebellion against the pastor. Amy left the auditorium before he had concluded and paced the lobby praying. Ian's wife, Jane, joined her and they consoled and encouraged one another, reminding each other that their Savior had taken their judgment on the cross of Calvary bringing them into the perfect law of liberty, disciplined and taught unto holiness. Knowing this was not the first time that Pastor Rutherford had abused his pulpit, publicly labeling sickness and death as a consequence of rebelling against him, didn't make the bitter pill any easier to swallow.

When Jack and Ian discussed the sermon afterwards with their wives, they realized that Pastor Rafe was moving the church precariously into the cultish range. His acts of fear and intimidation had all of the earmarks of a cult leader who must use bullying tactics in order to keep his followers compliant and unresisting to his leadership.

It took Mira many hours to transcribe the minutes of the five hour mediation meeting from the tapes. Fear of being accused by Rafe of slanting the content or omitting portions, brought her to the decision to transcribe them directly. As a result very little was omitted; only when a speaker lowered his voice did she have trouble with exact wording.

When the job was finished, Mira called Dora to tell her the minutes would be ready for distribution that evening. She requested that the packages be brought in as well, in the event that any issues were raised.

When asked how the Sunday services went, Mira told her bluntly that the board was very upset over Pastor Rafe's deportment in the pulpit. In spite of his promises and assurances, he had used his authority and position to abuse his leadership publicly. Consequently, the board was now determined not to allow him any more preaching time, other than his farewell message. They were fully prepared to deliver the letter that would effectively terminate his authority until the mediation process was complete.

She shared with the mediator how frustrating it was for the board not to have something in writing by now from the pastor, given that he had indicated his willingness to resign early in the meeting on Saturday. It was particularly worrisome because they all knew how prone he was to changing his mind at a whim and no one trusted his word. Dora had not disagreed with her.

For the first time since she had arrived, Grace came home early from work. Dan and Mira knew something was wrong when she headed straight to her room with barely a word of greeting. After a few minutes, they heard the sound of muffled sobbing through the door. Dan quietly motioned his wife to find out what was wrong.

Mira soon learned the cause of her friend's distress was the result of a meeting with a self-styled prophetess. It turned out this was the same woman who, back in the fall, had counseled Pastor Rafe not to meet with the board until she had spoken with him.

Grace hadn't known what to expect when Lana Vanderwood had made the appointment. She knew that the woman was part of the pastor's intercessory group that met on Saturday mornings to prophesy and speak into his life. Grace had attended one of those meetings shortly after she came, but found to her amazement that all they did was chat. There was no intercession. Pastor Marvin told her it was pretty much the same thing every Saturday and he tried to get out of attending whenever he could. Grace didn't go again after the first time. She didn't see the point.

Mira learned from her sister-in-law that Lana claimed the Lord had shown her that Grace had allowed some childhood experiences to thrust her into ministry which she was not called to. "You have no anointing for this and you need to leave this place or God will take you out," she had scolded in a tirade that lasted an hour. She criticized Grace's sermons and recommended counseling which she said she was willing to provide.

Mira was furious! "Don't you let that woman speak anything over your life!" she commanded indignantly. "You know you are called of God and that is a foul spirit of witchcraft and divination that she is using."

"I shouldn't have allowed it to go on for so long," sobbed Grace. "She really got to me after a while. I should have stood up to her sooner."

"Did you say anything to her?" asked Mira, her curiosity getting the best of her.

"Yes, I did finally," claimed Grace, sitting up and drying her eyes. "And it felt good too!" She looked at Mira woefully. "I know that God called me to the ministry so why did I allow her to abuse me like that."

"You're too nice!" declared Mira. "You probably didn't want to offend her because she's one of the pastor's pets. Say," she added thoughtfully, "you don't suppose he set her up to it in order to force you to leave. It's rough going right now and I'll bet he'd like nothing better than for you to pack you're bags and go home."

"I didn't think of that, but I wouldn't put it past him. She probably isn't even aware that she's being used to accomplish his purpose. Well," she added crossly, "you can bet I won't ever allow that to happen to me again. Sometimes I think we Christians are too ready to allow people to use us as doormats. I don't believe that God ever intended us to be doormats."

"Amen to that!" Mira replied. "I'll bet the Apostle Paul or Peter would have put her in her place!"

She explained to Grace what little she knew of the woman. "A few months ago the board had to move quickly to stop Lana from setting up a counseling office in the church. She had already met with a couple of clients before we even learned what was happening. Pastor Rafe gave her his approval and didn't inform the board of it, as usual," she said grimly.

"Faith told me that she was putting pressure on her as well as many others to use her services," she went on. "The board felt the liability risk too great to allow it to continue, so we wrote her a letter, nicely worded, informing her that no business was permitted to operate on church property. In spite of Pastor Rafe's glowing recommendation, we all had serious reservations about what she was counseling."

"Something else happened," said Grace hesitantly, "but I honestly don't know whether I should say anything about it. You'll probably think I'm really weird or something."

Mira laughed. "My dear, you are the sanest person I know and after all we've been through together, I think you can trust me, even with the weird stuff."

"Well…it was getting pretty late by the time Lana left my office and everyone else had gone home. I had just locked the door and was headed upstairs when I heard this harsh whispering." Her eyes were huge. "Mira, I checked everywhere and there was no one there. It scared me so badly that I ran out the door without setting the alarm. There now! Do you think I'm losing it?"

Mira felt the hair on her arms stand on end. "Nooo," was her slow reply. "I don't think you're crazy at all. Dan has heard the voices too and so has Jonathan."

It was Grace's turn to look startled. "Are you serious?"

"Absolutely! I didn't know what to think when Dan told me about it. They were in the basement together last fall when Jonathan was laying the tile floor and they both heard these guttural voices whispering. Dan searched the whole building and found nothing. It scared Jonathan so badly that he locked himself in his truck! There's no way anyone was in the building. It was about five o'clock in the morning!"

They stared at one another. "Do you think it could be evil spirits?" Mira asked a chill running up her spine.

"I don't know what it was, but I know what I heard!"

"Pastor Marvin says that other members of the congregation have reported some bizarre things to him too," confided Mira. "Apparently wolf-like creatures have been seen and strange shadows have come out of the wall and gone right through people." She shivered. "Our maintenance man was changing a light and the ceiling tile started to chatter. He was so frightened he ran out of the building."

Mira remembered something else. "Pastor Rafe asked me a few months ago to have Dan check his office. He said he could hear voices talking and wondered if his office was bugged. He blamed it on the young pastor that he drove out – John Schilling. Do you suppose it was the same whisperings you heard?"

Grace nodded her head slowly. "Something is terribly wrong in that church! I've felt it off and on ever since I came. I don't know what plans God has for the place but I do know that there is a terrible battle going on in the spirit realm that we can't see. I believe the outcome will affect this body of believers forever."

As she tossed and turned in her bed that night, Grace found sleep would not come. Hearing the voices had shaken her more than she cared to admit. She pondered what Mira had told her about evil spirits being seen in the church. Finally, toward dawn, she fell into an uneasy sleep only to be awakened twice, screaming from nightmares that haunted her dreams.

The first apparition appeared as a giant snake at the foot of her bed. Its red-rimmed, lantern eyes gleamed with diabolical wickedness while its enormous leathery, scaled body undulated slowly toward her threatening to crush out her very life.

Her second nightmare seemed more like a hallucination. Black, grotesque hands grabbed her by the feet attempting to pull her down into a fathomless, black pit of horror.

Caelen issued a number of instructions to Captain Darshan and his companion, Valin as they approached the Good Shepherd Church. The Captain had chosen twenty of his best warriors to accompany them. The remainder of the large detachment under his authority encircled the building awaiting his signal. They stayed outside of the perimeter of the property, strategically placed beyond the sight of the demonic patrols.

At seven o'clock, the council again gathered for the second of the scheduled mediation meetings. The great Python spirit slithered into the room much to the chagrin of the presiding Jezebel demon-master who coveted any glory or acclaim for himself. A vast number of demons blurred through the concrete blocks in an overpowering tide. They clung to the walls, perched on the tables or skittered across the floor, gibbering mirthlessly in hoarse voices. The air reeked of attar and sulfur.

Mira noticed uneasily that several council members were absent. Rev. David Armstrong, Sylvester Zimmer and Phil Schmidt had apparently each found a plausible excuse not to attend the proceedings. Frank Milton was back from his vacation but seemed bewildered and disturbed over the whole process of events that had occurred during his absence. The associate pastors maintained their separate position at a table behind the main group. Pastor Rutherford was present, this time without Eve to hamper his style.

Mira distributed the minutes of the last meeting, but the mediators suggested that they delay approving them until a later date, so that everyone would have opportunity to read them since they were lengthy.

Tom Storey reminded the group of their responsibility to keep the best interests of the membership in the forefront. "What would Jesus do?" he quoted, "would be a good check for everyone to keep in mind during our discussions. The constitution charges us to do our best to come up with an agreeable and peaceable solution."

He recapped the retirement statements issued by the Rutherford's, which had taken everyone by surprise and turned the first meeting in a different direction. Setting aside the issues, they had begun to explore a possible resolution of the matter. Then he opened the floor for comments on the retirement option.

Frank Milton was the first to speak. "I don't understand how it got to this. I know I've been away but.....I can't see how anyone thinks that Pastor isn't doing his job. The attendance at church always drops whenever he goes away and it picks up when he returns - so he must be doing his job. I guess I'm too late though because it seems that things have already gotten past the stage of job evaluation."

"I would suggest that you read all of the documentation in the packages prepared for everyone," replied Dora.

Mira quickly handed him one with his name on it. As she was doing so, she suddenly recalled a list of phone calls that she had asked Ina to pull for her. They included all long distance calls made to and from the church over the past three months. Her purpose had been to show that the pastor was not on sabbatical but was continuing to run the church from his place in Florida. There had been seventy-three calls between the pastor and the church. In doing that exercise, she had also noticed a number of calls to another Florida location which just happened coincidentally to be the same city where Frank and his wife spent the winter.

His opinion has already been compromised by Pastor Rafe's manipulations, she thought sadly, *and I doubt if anything will change his mind now. He probably believes the worst of us.*

Rafe leaped at the lifeline thrown out by his deacon. "I think Frank poses a very good question," he said smoothly taking the lead. "First, I would like to express my deep appreciation for the mediators who have handled things so wisely and godly." He smiled benignly at Dora and Tom. Ever the politician, flattery dripped from his mouth with the ease of long practice.

"My wife is not able to attend this evening because her blood pressure has gone up and she has to be closely monitored." He tried to look appropriately distressed in keeping with such a sad turn of events. Mira doubted the veracity of his statement. Pastor Rafe had shared these same sentiments with Grace earlier in the day, but when pressed by his associate to go and be with his ailing wife, he had asked her to go instead.

The enormous head of Python shifted lower behind Rafe's head. The deadly forked tongue flicked abruptly into his ready ear. Jezebel moved closer, contempt and blood-lust alternating in spasms across his repulsive face.

"How did things get off track?" the pastor continued smoothly. "Constitutionally and scripturally, things were not followed through. That is very troubling to some of us here. I'm not trying to point a finger of blame. I just want to get things back on track." His voice was compelling, almost mesmerizing.

"I have two concerns. One is my wife; a dead wife is no good to me and I think that is my primary concern. Eve has been sensing for some time that there is to be a transition in our lives. We are not fighting to hold on to something that God wants us to let go of. That is not important whatsoever." He looked sternly around the table. "The truth is, we have been talking for almost a year now that the time has come to retire. I find it more difficult than she does to let go of that which has been more bonded to me. I get so close to the sheep, that I find it very difficult to let go."

Rafe allowed his voice to tremble slightly with emotion. "I have felt drained; some would even call it "burn-out", which is why I needed to get away. I didn't want to make decisions in a state of exhaustion and I thought I would find a place of rest to wait on God for direction. Some things got off track on that and when I returned after my first three weeks in January, I was made aware of some issues arising from the surveys. It was not clear to me what the issues were; only - be prepared - as there are some real concerns. I thought the purpose of the surveys was to be constructive."

His color heightened and his voice rose heatedly. "Never did I dream that what I created, with the help of these two fine people," he said, indicating Dora and Marvin, "would be used as a weapon against me. That wasn't the purpose. There were only about eight of the comments that would be viewed as negative. Is that enough to explode a whole congregation?" he asked, his voice a rising current of righteous indignation.

Mira wanted to scream. *Eight! What an outright lie! The survey was 85% against him. According to Dora, the only comments that weren't derogatory were submitted by his wife, grandson and the guy living with them. I doubt if he's even read the package we put together. How can he continually dismiss those surveys and letters, not to mention that package of issues, as so much trivial nonsense?*

"Those that had complaints, we could have dealt with wisely and lovingly. Even though I was warned or cautioned that there would be some reaction, I was really shocked when someone said, "What we're really saying is that you should go". I tried to follow that through with a vote to see if everyone felt the same way. My pastoral staff told me that this was going to be a reconciliation meeting," he stated angrily. "It was supposed to be a time when we would look at issues and know how to solve them, not to have it thrown at me – "It's over for you, buddy!" Eight letters are not enough to put you out!"

"One of the members...." Rafe looked around the table noticing for the first time that Phil was not there to back him up. "One of them said, "Why don't we give the pastor what he's asked for and let him finish out the three months of sabbatical. They voted to give me that time. So I went to Florida with complete rest in my spirit, thinking that the last number of weeks I would able to, without any feeling of threat or pressure, get into a state where I could really rest; only to find in my devotions, a caution by the Holy Spirit that something else was going on! I could not believe it! In meditating in the Word of God, I said, "This can't be, Lord. They wouldn't be doing this!" But it was very clear what the Holy Ghost said to me and I had it further confirmed by a phone call before I even got back from Florida. So I said, "Okay Lord, that confirms it".

Is anyone buyng this garbage? Mira felt sick that her pastor had no compunction about using the Holy Spirit to give credence to his statements. Her eyes were certainly being opened with a vengeance! Disgust was clearly written on her face as she listened to what he was saying.

"When I drove into the parking lot for that Saturday morning council meeting, the Holy Spirit spoke to me and said, "This meeting isn't what you think it is going to be". And I said, "Isn't that strange. What does that mean?" I thought that we had a week before the annual business meeting and we would be planning the agenda and going over the financial statements. I was totally blind-sided, except for the statement that the Holy Spirit brought to me as I pulled into my parking spot."

Liar! Mira ground her teeth. *Grace and Marvin prepared him for that meeting and he knows it. He's counting on their silence.*

"That meeting caused me to go into a bit of shock, which also triggered a reaction in my wife when I had to report to her what happened. My original question was, "How did this get off track?" What was it that caused this quick action on the part of the leadership here to even go beyond the motion that is still on record that nothing would be done until after March 31st. They felt I violated the sabbatical and therefore they felt it was wise that they do likewise."

Rafe looked innocently around the table. "I ask you, what was the violation of the sabbatical? They are claiming that I made frequent, numerous phone calls from Florida. So I immediately spoke to both Faith and Pastor Marvin and asked them if I made any phone calls during that second period I was away. They said, "No". I returned some messages from my office staff, but I only called Faith once."

Mira knew that was lie. Both Faith and Grace had told her about the numerous times the pastor called the church and she had direct confirmation of their assertions in the phone call list that Ina had provided her with.

Rafe carried on about the phone call issue as if it were the most important of all of the matters he had to face. He put as much sincerity as he could into his expression. "I noticed in these documents that have been compiled against me, a list of the number of calls I was supposed to have made. Faith made a number of calls when she was down there visiting for a week and my wife also called her often to chat while we were away. These calls that I have been accused of making were not my calls."

Liar, liar! seethed Mira. *This man is incapable of telling the truth about anything! I know he called every day. I certainly believe Faith and Grace over him!*

"The procedure and motion that was put into place," Rafe continued, "I feel was seriously violated and I have now been blamed for breaking that sabbatical and as that precipitated the quick action of the council, dear chairman, I am very troubled by this and it breaks my heart that this has happened. This is the only explanation that I can see how this got off track and it continues. We cannot resolve matters in anger. We resolve things in love. We are all are scriptural people. I have determined that I will only move in love but it was told to me that a number of the council are prepared to fight. I cannot believe that among God's people we would come prepared to fight."

Rafe's voice grew more eloquent as he attempted to heap guilt and shame on his listeners. He had the floor and intended to make the most of it. "I surrender to the purpose of God," he quavered, "and we are going to move in that purpose, in divine grace and in the love of God. "*He that hath begun this good work in us will perform it unto the day of Jesus Christ."* So I submit myself to God; I wave the white flag of surrender. I have nothing to prove. My record stands for itself, even though they have made derogatory comments and statements and tried to drag up things of the past that were under the blood of Jesus Christ," he exclaimed indignantly.

Mira's cheeks grew hot. She prayed with a desperation she had never felt before. "*God, please do something here. He is using You shamelessly!"* Caelen touched her shoulder and spoke inaudibly into her ear until he felt her spirit quiet down.

Rafe's seething anger boiled just beneath the surface. To restrain it took enormous effort. The demon-master squeezed his victim's shoulder and dug his claws in with implacable fury. Rafe responded instantly. His look of distress would have fooled even his own wife.

"They have put into print a package called "*Confidential"*. I felt like a knife went into me that grieved the heart of God to think that the blood of Jesus could be mocked in this when it was under the blood some twenty years ago and it be brought up – how can that be of God?

How can this be a thing to praise the Lord? My second concern is not just my wife, it is the congregation. I know that some of you were afraid that I would go before the people and expose what's been going on but I would not hurt the people. They would be absolutely devastated to think that this could happen. If you smite the shepherd, the sheep will be scattered. So I am desirous that the sheep would be protected at any cost and I would ask that that would be in the heart of every one of us. Thank you."

Relieved that he was finally finished, Jack raised his hand. "I don't want to go over all this stuff again." he said. Although normally soft-spoken, Mira could detect frustration in his voice. "We've tried to talk to the pastor for many months about all kinds of issues and it hasn't worked. He will not listen because he thinks we're wrong about everything. I feel for Eve but this is very serious to the church body. This cannot continue."

Ian asked to be recognized. "I know a few of you are confused about why we are going through this mediation exercise at all. Well, it isn't just one particular mistake made by the pastor. It's a build up of many, many things. It's the constant lying, the way he treats people and the unethical things he does. We just can't stand for it any more!"

Pierre, who had been quiet until this point, rose to his feet. "God knows everything that is going on," he said earnestly. "He knows the things that are good and the things that are bad. But He also wants us to have mercy upon one another. We are all guilty and do wrong, one time or another. We cannot dwell in the past. What is done is done. The will of God is to work together and to care about one another. We don't know how the pastor feels and we don't know how you, as a board, feel. We all go through times that are not right but we are all human. God is the answer for all things." He sat down with a troubled look on his face.

Mira could see that Pierre didn't have the remotest idea of what the board had been forced to deal with over the past few months. It was obvious to her that he believed if they forgave the pastor everything would be fine. From his comments she knew he didn't have a grasp on what they were dealing with, even though she knew he had read the package.

Her nerves were starting to fray. Their precious mediation time was rapidly disappearing and she was beginning to wonder if there was another agenda here – a hidden one! It sickened her that no resignation had been presented in writing yet. *What was going on here! Why hasn't Tom intervened by now?* Her stomach churned wildly as she slowly considered the unacceptable idea that the mediator had taken the pastor's side in the conflict. *We're supposed to be talking about retirement and not one thing has been accomplished yet. Tom seems more than willing to allow Pastor Rafe to rave as much as he wants.*

Unable to stand it any longer, Mira took the plunge and daringly suggested that they return to the retirement discussion. Tom obligingly drew their attention to a large white board where he had written the various components of the retirement package which needed to be discussed. *I guess I'm wrong about him,* she thought brightening up considerably. The butterflies in her stomach settled down a little.

"I find it kind of funny that the board has dug up all the dirt they could find on the pastor from years ago and then want to have a celebration party," grumbled Frank. "It doesn't make much sense to me."

Oh no! Here we go again! Mira's grip on her chair turned her knuckles white.

"We have to keep in mind what is in the best interests of the members and strive to minimize the impact on them," explained Tom patiently. "The worst case scenario would be a full church split."

"I understand that," replied Frank, unwilling to move on. "I'd still like to know who did it. Who went into the archives and found all of this stuff that happened twenty years ago and decided to bring it all up again? I don't see the reason for that. That was all taken care of back then. Why drag it up now?"

Mira was losing patience even though she knew that Frank was being cleverly deceived by the pastor. "You don't know what's been going here because you've been away for several months," she told him. "The package you received earlier has very little in it that dates back prior to the last year. That which does, is only included because it shows a pattern of behaviour that hasn't changed. The board has had ongoing problems, which they have been trying to address for the best part of a year. The research done in the archives was a direct result of our being told by the pastor, several times, that we are the worst board he's had in 45 years of ministry. So we delved into the past to determine if we *are* the only board who have had major issues of integrity to deal with, regarding Pastor Rutherford. That exercise proved to us that other boards have faced exactly the same lack of trust and integrity, of financial abuse, and all the rest of it."

Everything that had been pent up in Mira spilled out now. "Do you realize, it's hard to even find past board members who will allow their names to stand again? They don't want to expose themselves to him again. Most of them have left the church, wounded, hurt, and broken and we are now at that point as well. So that's where we're at, Frank. It was not meant to drag up past indiscretions. It started out as a simple exercise to find out whether we are indeed the worst board in history. What we found was the same pattern of abuse going back as far as we could trace. The problem is that the board changes somewhat every year and the new members have no clue what they are facing. I'm sure that every member of this board, when we began, thought the pastor was the best thing since sliced bread. I know I did!" Several of the directors nodded their agreement.

"As time went on," she continued, "we started to realize there were serious issues regarding the pastor's trustworthiness. We have seen lying, dishonesty, gross manipulation, dividing and conquering and maligning of our reputations with our own eyes. We looked back and what we found was the exact same pattern. That's why that document was put together. It was to educate the council as to where the board is coming from and why we are at this point today. And what's more," Mira said heatedly, "this has to be finished before the annual business meeting. If it is left to drag on, this board will leave and the next one will face the same things all over again. Also, you should be aware that there are quite a number of people in the church who will be leaving, if this is left unresolved.

Rafe broke in angrily, eyes blazing, his face distorted. "You use words such as *dishonesty* and *loss of integrity.* We have some deacons here at this table that have served as board members. Why Phil, Frank and Pierre have been here since I came."

Yes, thought Mira, *and they will approve anything you say, regardless how ungodly or profane because they believe you're a prophet. Well, I don't! Not anymore!*

"This great exodus we're hearing about," he scoffed, "I would like names and details. Anyone can throw out numbers. My integrity is at stake here."

Mira watched him, fascinated by what she was seeing. *He's being controlled by demons. My God! Help us! We can't overcome this! Is this the end result of pride, disobedience and an unrepentant attitude? God give us wisdom!*

He stared mockingly at Mira as if he knew what she was thinking causing the hairs to rise on the back of her neck. "Someone told me, "They did you a favor..." and I said, "What do you mean? This is terrible." They said, "This has now become a *legal* document and very serious." He attacked viciously now, sure that the hint of a lawsuit would strike fear into their hearts.

"Talk about manipulation! There's no truth in this packet," he sneered. "You accuse *me* of twisting things, well there's certainly a lot of twisting here. If you want to go through it, we can go through it, but it will prove nothing because it is slander and defamation of character for which you could all be legally charged. Of course, I would never do such a thing," he added hastily, while glancing reassuringly around the table. His smile was sickly sweet, like sticky syrup and it made Mira want to vomit.

"I would never take God's money to prove a point. We can go through every issue you've mentioned and build a case, but I will not do that because you'll just accuse me of always having to be right. Well, that is not the case. I've been wrong many times. I'm not running from the issues. You think you're going to be able to say, "We gave him the scare of his life and put the run to him," but I want you to know that that is not the case. I deal with issues and I will deal scripturally with each one that wrote a letter. Some of them won't answer my calls. By the way, I did not say that Lenny would recant his letter. I merely said he regrets how he did it and admits that scripturally, he should have come to Pastor first. See how they are capable of twisting a thing that is partially true?"

I wonder if he's actually read all the way through the package, thought Mira. *Doesn't he know that Lenny followed up with an e-mail that says he will not change one word of his letter? It's in the package. Are the deacons so blind to his lies or haven't they read it either?*

"We would not be here tonight if the Word of God were honored. Instead, you gathered against me and forced these ones to write letters against me which has caused them great harm. And you talk about losing trust! I would have been very pleased to meet with each person to resolve their issues."

23

TOM FINALLY DECIDED TO take back control of the meeting. In order to move things along, he suggested that Pastor Rutherford leave the room so that council could discuss how they might proceed and reach some agreement. Rafe walked to the door with an arrogant swagger.

When he was gone, Dora told Frank that he should read his package as soon as possible so that he would be up to speed with the others. In her heart, Mira was pretty sure that he wouldn't bother with it. She didn't think Phil had deigned to read his packet either. Nonetheless, she went over to Frank to talk with him while the others milled about the refreshment table.

"Frank, you need to be made aware that this is not sudden," she explained quietly. "We have been trying to address the issues in this package for a long time, but he will neither listen to us nor discuss them. He claimed tonight that he's not afraid to go through them, but you've seen for yourself what he does. He justifies, lies and skates all around the issues and treats us as if we are a bunch of school children. We cannot win a war of words and he's made it clear that he is not answerable to anyone."

Frank seemed to listen and even nodded his head and agreed that the pastor had been difficult when he had served on the board. "It's just hard to comprehend that things have gotten so bad while I've been away."

"They've been this bad for a long time. We just haven't involved the deacons in what's been going on," she answered. "They have only been added to the mix recently. That's why is seems such a shock to you. You need to read the packet and all of the other letters and minutes in your folder downstairs."

"I'll read it," he agreed, but his tone was still doubtful.

The council hammered out what they considered an acceptable agreement. They felt the ideal solution for everyone would be a mutually agreed upon written announcement that should be read by the Rutherfords in the next Sunday service which was Easter. This would eliminate any surprises. They balked at permitting the pastor to preach again. Their trust had been too damaged by his inflammatory comments on the prior Lord's Day for them to risk a repeat performance or worse. The moving date from the parsonage was a minor issue but for the sake of the agreement they thought three months would show generosity along with the proviso that they could stay beyond that time if they had not found another place.

Their primary focus was the Sunday announcement. Everyone was keenly aware that if it wasn't made, they would be looking at going into the annual business meeting which could easily become a blood bath. A retirement statement would also pave the way for the settlement package to gain approval at the members meeting. They decided the document should be finalized and signed by all parties in the final mediation meeting on Thursday.

"Has the pastor actually agreed to read a statement?" enquired Mira. "All we've heard so far is that he is retiring at some unknown date."

"I'm not sure if he has specifically agreed to that," answered Tom noncommittally.

Mira probed further. "But he did say he was willing to make an announcement prior to the annual meeting?"

"I think he might be persuaded to do that," he replied.

"We don't want a repeat of what happened on Sunday," insisted Donny stubbornly.

"The idea of this is to soften the blow to the congregation," offered Mira. "Back in February, the pastor gave the congregation the impression that he was resigning or at least preparing to resign. He's been talking about transition for some period of time now and moving into a global ministry. This is not new to the people. If he presents it in a positive light then most people will not be that shocked except for the ones he's been calling the last two or three weeks. There are going to be issues there, but that's his own fault!"

"The sharing of the announcement on Sunday would facilitate the acceptance of the financial package because the membership would know at the annual meeting that the pastor is leaving," agreed Tom.

"Since we're meeting on Thursday, it should be here for everyone to look at and sign," added Mira. "The board has scheduled a meeting for Wednesday night with the lawyer to discuss the financial end of it. We have recommended to Mr. Amos that the settlement be generous. I will meet with the employment lawyer tomorrow to go over information he feels is relevant to the preparation of the package. Everything will be fully explained to everyone on Thursday.

"The retirement date may be different from the announcement date," proffered Tom cautiously. "There may be some value to having the retirement date later to give the congregation some time to get used to the idea and convey the message that this is a decision the Rutherford's have made."

"That is unacceptable," protested Rob Samuels. "We have a problem with a retirement date that is after the annual meeting because of legal issues. There is an implied authority that extends beyond that and there is a consensus that we don't want that.

"I understand your preference for it being sooner, rather than later, but I would encourage that you consider some flexibility."

"I don't think we can be flexible on that point because of the legal implications. Why must it be such a big deal?" Rob asked, obviously frustrated. "There isn't any salary consideration. We're only talking about a date and a supposed authority that goes with that office. That is the big thing that we have to deal with. We have agreed to shelve the issues but we expect the trade-off to be getting the retirement announcement and date set for Sunday. It won't affect how we treat him or how we are going to respect him, but for us to have any satisfaction, this has to be cleaned up now. We don't trust him not to change it with the next board. There are a lot of issues here that are very foggy. A delayed date would only work if his authority was taken away. That's the problem we have. He can get a new board in and flush all of this down the toilet!"

"I agree with Rob," said Mira decidedly. "I've already spoken to Mr. Amos regarding this issue. Pastor could reverse everything we decide, if he keeps his authority. At this point, he still has say over the associates, he's still in the pulpit and we've already had problems this past Sunday because of it. The evening service was more inflammatory than the morning, so as time goes on and he gets a little more secure, it will spill out into his sermons. We know he's been calling people and trying to foment an uprising against the board. Does his authority have to be taken away as senior pastor? Absolutely, it does! The only way to accomplish that is to make the retirement date on Sunday or lift his pastoral authority. I don't even think the latter option will work. His retirement has to be finished on Sunday – period! The celebration party can be announced then for a later date. We have a lot of ladies available that can pull together a large function held here in the church. This board mix is going to change in another week and anything else allows a hook we cannot risk.

Tom seemed unwilling to take the ultimatum back to the pastor. "I would be very surprised if a lawyer cannot craft a document that addresses these issues."

"No!" insisted Mira. "If we were to delay the actual date, the damage he will do from now until then is incalculable. No! We've gone through enough hell. Enough is enough!"

"You don't seem to get that we're not dealing with someone who is rational," agreed Rob.

"We can't trust him even for the Good Friday service," put in Jack. "He was very close to doing a lot of damage on Sunday. He has anger that I don't think he's even tapped yet and he's hurt so many here. Since this began, all of us have cried our hearts out. Donny went to another pastor and cried on his shoulder. This man is vicious and he is not to be trusted and if we can't nail this thing down....It goes beyond the letters that were written and you have to understand, we all thought, like everyone else, that he was the best thing God ever stuck on two legs. But he lies so often that I don't think he recognizes truth any more. He has misused funds. I know it's hard to believe what he's capable of. I believe there's a spirit behind it, but he's got to be shut down here solid or .....He says he cares for the congregation but I don't trust him! He's lied too many times!

Tom tried again. "There may be a deal or arrangement that both parties might not be entirely happy with, but both would hopefully be able to live with. Are you prepared to potentially throw out a peaceful solution by taking a hard line on one issue?"

"I'm a peaceful person," replied Donny. "I think everyone here prefers a peaceful solution, but I have to say that what I've seen from Pastor this evening is not peaceable. He's claimed that we have told untruths and slandered his name. Not true! We need to back up here! The only reason we are in mediation at all is because we dared to confront Pastor with issues he doesn't want to deal with. He appeared to concede to retirement in the first meeting, but he has been working behind the scenes ever since in an attempt to unseat this board. He doesn't want to deal with the issues! He even lied when he said he would be very careful not to make any statements or say anything that would upset the board last Sunday. There were things said that should not have been said! We need to realize that this man cannot be trusted! He is not a rational person and the longer we allow this to go on, the more risk we take that something awful is going to happen. More people are getting hurt this way and that is why I believe we need to bring this to a quick end, particularly in lifting his authority. The work here will have to be rebuilt without him running interference. There are too many hurting people to prolong this. Mrs. Rutherford wants out. Her health is not good. He should be saying, "My wife's health is in jeopardy. I need to stop my ministry and deal with this situation and retire quickly." The truth is he only cares about himself. It is imperative that we get this done before the annual meeting so this doesn't continue with another board."

"I believe that in last few weeks your number one priority has been to achieve a separation between the pastor and the church," said Tom. "The pastor's willingness to entertain retirement has achieved your priority. Having achieved this, what is most important and what can you compromise on that is not worth being a deal breaker?"

"This board's term expires shortly so this is only relevant during their term," insisted Rob stubbornly.

"Mira can explore tomorrow the legal opportunity that may be available to you towards some flexibility," Tom insisted.

"I think we have to assume there isn't any flexibility because we have only one more meeting left of mediation and then there are going to be some serious decisions made," replied Rob. "If we're still sitting here at 10:00 pm Thursday night, that's a serious problem. This board wants a resolution. We're going through the same thing that happened six years ago because a board fell. All of the allegations and even the mediation process could expire with a new board. The only legal thing we can do is make sure that the authority he has expires and is gone because with authority comes power."

"He's already threatened to get rid of the constitution and the board," put in Jack. "He wants control of everything! As elected officials of the congregation we have to do the best we can, as Spirit-led people. The stuff that he has done is really out of line. I think it's safe to say that he does not have the mind of the Spirit. We've failed to bring him to any kind of accountability all year. He's just taken over in our meetings. Now, I believe he wants his way, just like always. We can't allow it to happen again!"

"Jack is right," affirmed Mira. "He controls all meetings, one way or another. He uses word power and spiritual abuse to shut everyone down. In that elder/deacon meeting of March 12th he tried to destroy the reputation of every board member that was not there. Unfortunately, those that have not worked in leadership positions believe every word that comes out of his mouth because he's their pastor. I went through and checked every statement he made in that meeting. I spoke directly to Lenny and he sent me an e-mail stating that he *did not recant* his letter. He denied the pastor's statement that three board members put pressure on him to write the letter in the first place. Pastor represented all of the letters that came in as trivial and stated that they had already been taken care of. He has not once talked to me about the letter that I wrote. Not once! So I have to assume that there are some other people that he hasn't talked to as well. Has he dealt with any of your letters?" she asked looking around the table. The men all shook their heads.

"He sent me one e-mail and I couldn't even understand what he was trying to say," replied Rob. "There were a lot of words in there but not one rational statement. Before he went back to Florida, I blew my stack out of frustration. He doesn't even know why I was so upset. It should have triggered something, but this guy needs help."

"He thinks that if he talks to you at all about a situation, then any issue surrounding it is resolved," cried Mira, passion and frustration mounting in her voice. "Nothing has been resolved! We've been trying for months! He doesn't hear us! He pays no attention to what we say!"

She grabbed her package and held it up. "I documented the phone calls from Florida. It's all in here. Seventy-three phone calls from January through to mid March and now he claims his wife made them. How can we fight that? We can't. Do I believe it? Absolutely not! But can I say he's a liar? No, because I haven't got absolute proof that he was on the other end of the line. That's just one instance! And why did he pick on that item as the only issue he wanted to talk about? I can tell you why! Because it breaks his sabbatical and he is desperately trying to fire this board for bringing any of this to the table during his so-called sabbatical period."

"He scheduled a trip in the middle of it himself," she snorted, "but I guess that's okay. It's all so one-sided! He set the sabbatical time period himself to expire at the end of March. Then he goes away and returns a week and half later. He's supposed to be on complete rest. He spent the first month and half overseeing work at his home in Florida. He wasn't waiting on the Lord! We've seen no evidence of a plan or purpose for the church. Seventy-one percent of the leaders surveyed have no clue what the direction of the church is? He lied when he said only eight people made negative comments in the surveys. The vast majority are disillusioned and fed up! We have people now that will not get involved in any ministry until this is settled because we are all in waiting. We've been waiting for months to see what is going to happen here! We have tried to make him address the issues and he keeps putting us off because he's determined to wait out this board. Well, we are not going to allow it! We are going to deal with this now and we are not going to fall, like every other board before us. We're not!"

"Many have tried to warn him that he needs to seek the Lord and repent before it's too late but he won't listen," added Jack. "He only hears those that uplift him and feed his pride and there are plenty of them around."

Ian added his voice to the mix for the first time. "It is the desire of this board that we have a peaceful resolution but we do want a resolution. Our first choice is a peaceful resolution but if we can't have a peaceful resolution, we *will* have a resolution."

"This date of retirement has got to be a real sticking point for Pastor," said Rob. "Why? What's the big deal?"

"I think he wants a little bit of time with the congregation to announce retirement," replied Dora.

"That doesn't make any sense," cried Rob. He has been hinting at it for months. I can get you tapes of the sermons. What is the problem? Mental? Emotional? Get some help and get over it! This is not our problem or a church problem. It's his pride! His retirement will come as no surprise to the congregation. They all swarmed him after those services, loving on him, thanking him for his time among them. Now suddenly he's wants to take baby steps to ease the congregation into it? Does he think they're children? He's had a forty-five year career and you're splitting hairs over a few days. What is it?"

"It's about control," Mira exclaimed in disgust. "It's about him having a say over who the next senior pastor is.

"Well, we're deep into this now," said Rob, frustration showing in his voice. "We're experts at what's going on and weighing this out and understanding it. There's got to be something behind this! There's no money on the line, no career on the line, there's nothing on the line but there has to be something, because that's all he's focused on. If he can drag it past this board then he can do whatever he wants. That's the motive!"

He was on his feet now. "The last council meeting, I told him that we knew him and he said, *"You don't know me at all."* Why don't we know him? He's supposed to be our spiritual father. It shouldn't take a year to address problems but with him it takes a year or two or three. I've been waiting for ten years for him to address problems. It hasn't happened with me and I've sat his dinner table almost every Sunday for seven or eight years. I'm talking out of conviction, wanting to do the right thing in righteousness. None of us are schooled on this."

The date of retirement shouldn't be a problem" he continued earnestly. "What does he want and what is his motive behind it? We haven't held anything back from him! It's all in black and white but we haven't seen anything from him! What does he want?"

"He hasn't said he wouldn't retire so he probably would, wouldn't he?" asked Frank naively.

"Sure! On his own terms! And after he's got a team in here that he can supervise," snorted Rob. "What he wants is to be daddy bishop and keep his authority but not do any of the pastoral work."

Tom finally gave up trying to persuade the group to his way of thinking and he and Dora went to break the news to the pastor. When they returned, Rafe marched into the room with them. Unseen demons hung from his hair and clothing. The Jezebel Spirit loomed behind him, satisfaction in his eye and a grotesque leer on his ugly, misshapen face. The massive coils of Python were clenched effortlessly about the trunk of Rafe's body. Faint plumes of smoke issued from its grinning maw. Red-rimmed eyes gleamed with malignant satisfaction.

The angelic beings held their ground behind the council members they warded but their power was limited to those they had legal access to; those who had prayed and waited on God before entering the meeting.

Tom instantly deferred the floor to Pastor Rafe who carried an unspoken authority that brooked no delay. There was fire in his eye and his demeanor didn't bode well for their hope of a quick resolution. His voice dripped unspoken threats.

"My concern is the importance of timing. My wife and I have been trying to adjust to this transition but now we've got to transfer this from us to the larger body of Christ because they're going to have to sort it all out. Some of the congregation have already told me how happy they are that I'm back and they don't want me to leave again soon. I've just told them that God is working it all out. I want what God wants. I have to get the people adjusted to this, so I would ask everyone to give some consideration to the congregation. Some of them are not prepared. Some of them don't sort out things quickly. Emotionally they are not ready to let me go. You'd only have to be around Sunday to see the admiration and love they shower on me. It seems unfair to now just drop a bomb saying that I am going for good. There needs to be a smooth transition. I don't want damage to happen and if it's not done properly it could be very damaging to the people. In places where I've pastored, we have given them a good measure of time to sort it out because there is an unusual bond between a shepherd and his flock. I am still the shepherd and if the shepherd is removed, you must replace that position with another very loving and caring shepherd. We must believe God for the right one. Who is the one that can bridge this whole situation? I've considered this and some time ago I talked with Brother Armstrong and he said, *"What could we do? Who do you feel that's so appreciated, that has years of maturity and strength of ministry that we could use?"* Some names surfaced, one being Hal Chatsworth."

Mira stiffened. That was the evangelist who had spoken at Pastor Holman's church and told them to return to their churches if they were having problems. *He's trying to get his own man in here so that he still has foothold!*

Rafe continued, allowing some well-nurtured excitement to creep into his voice. "This is a man who is so well loved by the people and he has the maturity of years; a man of the highest caliber; someone who has recognition. So I said, *"Well, I don't know if he's willing. He knows the people and loves them, but I don't know."* Brother Armstrong urged me to call him which I did and I was very amazed to hear him say that he was willing to come. Of course I asked him when he would be available, because if we don't have someone of his stature to bridge the transitional period, this thing's not going to fly!"

"I've noticed that the numbers in the last three months have dropped drastically with my absence," Rafe said, preening self consciously. "I'm a good shepherd and I know my sheep! I know their response and I know what some have said as recently as the last few days. I know how critical it is! My concern is not for me anymore. I want you to know that. God will take care of us. But I am concerned about the sheep. These precious people; they will not survive if things proceed as they are going here right now."

"Hear the Word of God," he thundered, sliding effortlessly into his practiced prophetic voice. "I know the heart of God and I know the sheep. This thing is that critical that it could cause a very severe, abrupt damage to this flock. And that is my appeal, I ask nothing of myself. I ask for the sheep."

Rafe was truly magnificent. His deep voice alternately crooned and wailed with deep pathos. "I will be going," he said sorrowfully. "God has plans for us but I am burdened and broken over the sheep. The decisions we make around this table will have lasting and eternal effect upon people that are fragile, that are new in the faith, that are little children. They're lambs and so we need a mature person like Brother Chatsworth.

There may be somebody else.... I don't know." He kept his face deliberately turned away from the table where his two associate pastors sat.

"Hal was the only one that surfaced," he repeated, "and it was Brother Armstrong that said, *"Call him! Call him!"* - knowing what was happening here. I asked Brother Chatsworth how quickly he could come and he thought as soon as the end of April. I believe that this would be the bridge to this whole situation. The sheep already know him and they trust him. He has established such a relationship that I would feel it an absolute gift from God that this should happen. So I lay that out before you." The cunning old fox sat down fully satisfied with his performance.

"So I believe what you're saying is that you would look to a retirement period by the end of the month with an announcement to be made this Sunday?" clarified Tom.

Rafe's answer was curt. "Yes".

"Would you address the concern of how strong your commitment is to following through the process and not being side-tracked or changing direction?"

Deep distress filled Rafe's trembling voice. "We had felt this would be a very sweet time and now we have to recover to *make* it a sweet thing." His eyes flashed dangerously. "It is not sweet right now! It is extremely difficult! We can make it a sweet thing if we all, in love, move together. And we can let the people know that Rev. Chatsworth will be coming. That takes the focus off of me and gives some hope to the situation. Why, the people will hardly be able to believe that I could pull it off – getting a man of his caliber. It would be just a God's gift. And with that in mind, I could build up the excitement and anticipation over the next three weeks.

"You're talking about Hal coming in as an overseer though, not as the next pastor, correct?" asked Tom seeking clarification for the council.

"Yes, as an overseer. I don't know of anybody else that could do this and hold things together for a period of time. My concern, as a pastor of fifteen years here, is for the flock. That may be questioned, but God knows my heart and those of you who know me and those whom I have touched over the years, will know that to be true. And that has not changed. I love the flock of God. And I want to go with a memory of pleasantness, with a contentment that we've done what we could for

God and that the Lord did do some wonderful things. I'm not fighting it. I only object to the timing of it. If we can work with the Lord on this and see it come to pass, it would help the flock to adjust. It still may be too abrupt for a lot of people. They'll say, *"The end of the month? Oh, my God!"* ....but we can steady them. I know we can build up some excitement and say, "Look what's going to happen though? Brother Chatsworth is coming!" We certainly don't have to sell them on Hal. He's already established himself in their affections here as an evangelist. For me to be negative would be the worst thing that I could do. All I can do now is to build them up and get them excited and bring an exhortation of strength to them. I know it's a short time, but God's Holy Spirit can bring that enthusiasm and the realization that God's in this."

Jezebel's yellowed fangs widened in a grotesque grin. Black venom dribbled in rivulets down his chin onto the leathery scales that covered his chest. He relished the control he had over his victim, especially with Python watching.

Rafe loved the spotlight even when he found himself in a tight spot like his one. He loved the challenge of it! The blood raced in his veins leaving him giddy, almost euphoric. "One dear sister told me on Sunday that if God was leading me out than she would release me as well. I don't know what she knows, but she told me that she had been putting me on a pedestal." He tried to look humble without any success.

"The Lord told her to let me go," he said poignantly, "and she wept over it for a long time but finally yielded it to God. That's one example of those that the Lord now is adjusting, so I have to believe that there are others too that need some preparation time. Soon with anticipation we can say, *"Praise God, look what's happening - what God is doing."* My concern is not for me. It's this bridging of a godly overseer and I don't know of anybody ... because it's going to be very traumatic for many, many people – my going."

Rafe caught several grimaces and rolling of eyes. Rage boiled in his heart. "You may find that hard to believe but I hope you understand what I'm saying. I'm not boasting. That is a very humble statement. I know the sheep and they're going to really feel the loss tremendously. But my three months being away was a good preparation. I think it was timely. I believe it can transition very sweetly, very effectively and God will be glorified. To me it's awesome to think that this has already been put in place and I didn't have to do anything about it. God had already worked it out. It was such a confirmation to my heart. It gives me great contentment that I can freely walk away knowing that things will be strongly in place."

Tom suggested that Pastor Rutherford leave the room again so that council could digest his proposal. Mira spoke heatedly as soon as the door closed behind him. "I would like something clarified before we move into discussion. The pastor made a statement that the church attendance had dropped drastically while he was away the three months. I know that the numbers have been consistent. I've been keeping track. The only exceptions have been when there were bad storms. They would have dropped then no matter who was here. I would like to hear that addressed by the associate pastors, please."

"We had roughly 160 out on the last Sunday morning before Pastor Rutherford left, replied Marvin, "and outside of those storm days you mentioned, we had actually increased the attendance, until Pastor returned this last time and then it dropped. I think that may have been because there was so much that happened then and there was a lot of talking."

"You also have to compare January with January," added Grace quickly. "Some of the numbers from the end of the year are hard to track, because there were times they were deliberately discarded. Faith told me that when Pastor Rafe doesn't like the numbers, he destroys the sheets. It's unfortunate because when the numbers are written down they don't lie. They can be considerably different than the embellished number that's remembered in the minds of people some time later. For January, the numbers were good and we had growth. We also had excellent altar call participation." She hesitated wondering how blunt she should be. "You all heard the statements made by the pastor but you were also all here, so you know the truth. As Marvin said, there was increase right up until he returned."

"One other point I would like to make," declared Mira, still disturbed over Rafe's arrogant speech. "When the pastor came back at the end of January before he went away again, he expressed extreme confidence in the team that we have here – Pastor Grace and Pastor Marvin. He said that now he could go away, with confidence, to his sabbatical because he realized that he had an excellent team in place and he didn't have to worry about the church. Tonight he virtually ignored both of his associate pastors and even tried to cast aspersions on their work here. I must confess that I am deeply disappointed in that."

"You're right," replied Donny. "They deserved some recognition from him. I believe he did it on purpose. He's angry and he's lashing out at everyone within reach. This is a very sad situation and we should never have allowed him to leave without confronting him on it."

"I think he might have had concern that any statement he might make about them would be perceived as wanting to exercise control over staff," said Tom. "That's my words though, not his."

"Oh, come on! Let's face it," cried Mira, sarcasm dripping from her voice. "He made it seem like the staff here is not doing their job because "*the numbers have dropped so drastically*". Funny how he can suddenly cast his wonderful team aside; the one he bragged about less than two short months ago. Now they're incompetent? Give me a break! He thinks he's going to make a deal with someone to come in here as his overseer. I say a resounding "NO"."

"He's anointing his man to follow him," added Ian. "Of course it's not acceptable."

"It says in the constitution that any new pastoral staff position is established by the board of directors or if there is a vacancy in a staff position then the board of elders shall establish a search committee." stated Jack.

"Yes, that's true," replied Tom. "That is the procedure for an appointment of a new senior pastor but as a bridge overseer, whatever that means, it would be a type of appointment."

Mira threw up her hands. "He is still trying to control everything! The answer is "No"!

"I see this whole scenario as just more of the same type of scheming that we have endured and it is just going to keep on happening," put in Donny angrily.

"Why can't the two associate pastors carry on as they have been in the interim?" questioned Jack. "They're excellent and well liked by the congregation. Of course Pastor has been on the phone trying to slander their reputations, so there will be some who will believe him, but anyone with any sense won't. Do you think this overseer thing could be just another stalling tactic?"

"I wouldn't put it past him," replied Mira. "The whole thing is stupid anyway. If we're required to come up with a big settlement package, there won't be any money to pay an extra pastor, unless this is his way of getting rid of the two associates. I personally believe he hates them. They're too well liked so he will make every effort to destroy them before he goes."

"I would have to agree that for the last while, under Pastors Grace and Marvin the people are doing well," volunteered Pierre. "They are gathering around the altars to pray at the end of the services like never before."

Rob spoke up. "Pastor's key words in his little speech were to excite the people and to get something new and fresh going. That's superficial at best. That's what we've been running on for a long time - excitement. It doesn't work anymore. It may have worked for awhile, but we need something that people can take to the bank spiritually and emotionally. We need something solid."

"I would like to propose that we bring things to a close in view of the time," said Tom. "Basically, in my view, the retirement process and differences of opinion have been put on the table today and have been fully explored. There is time to pray and consider what this all means to us over the next couple of days and come back on Thursday with a good place to start."

Before they closed, the board told the deacons they were welcome to join them Wednesday evening for their meeting with the lawyer to discuss the settlement package. Wearily, the group straggled from the room in silence, their faces grim and their hearts filled with foreboding.

24

SHE FINDS HERSELF OUTSIDE of the Good Shepherd Church. On the roof, a solitary figure struggles for its freedom. It has the appearance of a mummy bound with grave clothes, rocking to and fro. She watches with bated breath as the thing pitches back and forth, moving ever closer to the edge of the roof. A deadly fall seems imminent. Directly below, a small child plays with a toy, oblivious to the danger above.

The figure reaches the edge and with one final surge, it topples and falls- as if in slow motion - landing on top of the playing child. The tot is terribly wounded. Blood streams from a large gash at the temple.

Abruptly the scene changes and she finds herself in a baby nursery. An infant is lying in the crib, its wee face pressed into the pillows. The small body is very still, the skin already blue from lack of oxygen.

A man steps into room to check on the baby. Calmly he transfers the infant to the change table close by. He sees the blueness of the tiny lips and hands and notices the stillness of the limp form. Unconcerned over its condition, the man changes its diaper. Then he lays the infant back in the crib and walks indifferently from the room. The baby dies.

Mira rolled out of bed Tuesday morning feeling exhausted and depressed. Her muscles seemed stiff and aching with a weariness that would not be shaken off. The remnants of her dreams haunted her as she went about her morning ablutions. *What did they mean?* Perplexed and distraught, she sought for the answer, an interpretation that made sense.

Caelen drew a deep breath and a great blast of cleansing air filled the room. It touched her brow softly and the unrest and confusion dissipated. With sudden clarity, she heard a still small voice speak to her from the depths of her being.

The mummy represents the church, bound and shackled by the Evil One. It struggles for freedom – for its very life. The new thing that God desires for this place will suffer a terrible wound – a blow from which it may never recover.

The second dream is connected with the first. This time the baby is the church. The shepherd has an opportunity to save the fragile little life. He believes he has the answer but does not understand that the only need he sees is superficial. It is not the real dilemma. Caught up in his own wants and desires, he watches it die, unconcerned for its plight.

Mira was shaken as she contemplated the import of what the Lord was saying. Surely there must be something that could be done to save the situation. The minutes of last night's meeting were waiting to be transcribed, but the thought of going through the tapes for hours on end was more than she could stand. She laid her head her head on the kitchen table and sobbed until there were no tears left.

"God, I don't know what to do," she cried. "I know my times are in your hands and I think my journey is going to take a different path in the future. I can't see beyond the next bend, but your Word says that You will never leave me or forsake me. I trust you, Lord."

A Women's Ministry planning meeting with her executive had long been scheduled for that evening, but Mira found that she dreaded the prospect of it. Eve always attended the planning sessions and her heart sank as she grappled with the thought of facing her. "It's too hard, Lord," she cried. "I don't even know what to plan. I can't see beyond the annual business meeting. It's all a blur. I haven't even got the heart for it any more."

Her Bible was laying in front her and flipping it open she began to read from the first passage of scripture her eyes fell upon. It was chapter 34 of the book of Ezekiel and the words leaped at her from the page. "*...prophesy against the shepherds, the leaders of Israel. Give them this* *message, from the Sovereign Lord: What sorrow awaits you shepherds who feed yourselves instead of your flocks. Shouldn't shepherds feed the sheep? You drink the milk, wear the wool and butcher the best animals, but you let your flock starve. You have not taken care of the weak. You have not tended the sick or bound up the injured. You have not gone looking for those who have wandered away and are lost. Instead you rule them with harshness and cruelty. So my sheep have been scattered without a shepherd and they are easy prey for any wild animal.....*

Therefore my shepherds, hear the word of the Lord. As surely as I live, says the Sovereign Lord, you abandoned my flock and left them to be attacked by every wild animal. And though you were my shepherds, you didn't search for my sheep when they were lost. You took care of yourselves and let the sheep starve. Therefore you shepherds, hear the word of the Lord. This is what the Sovereign Lord says: I now consider these shepherds my enemies, and I will hold them responsible for what has happened to my flock. I will take away their right to feed my flock, and I will stop them from feeding themselves. I will rescue my flock from their mouths; the sheep will no longer be their prey."

In the next passage she read about the Good Shepherd and how he would search for the lost, bandage the wounded and strengthen the weak. As she meditated on what she had read, Mira felt an awesome presence of the Lord surround her, bringing with it a sense of his overwhelming love. Answers to the dilemma of the church, she still didn't have, but she knew that the Almighty Lord of Hosts would keep his sheep safe in the very hollow of His hand. A holy fear filled her heart; fear for her pastor and the road he had chosen; fear of what it must be like to fall into hands of the living God, if you were responsible for abusing his sheep.

She threw the mediation tapes into a box just as Dan came through the door. "I've decided to leave the minutes alone today," she told him. "I really don't have the time to even start them and the last ones weren't approved anyway. I have a feeling I'll be long gone from the church before I get them all done. I have a meeting with the lawyer this afternoon and a women's meeting tonight."

"Can't you cancel the night meeting?" he grumbled. "I hardly see you any more."

"I know, Hon, but if you'll just hang in there another eight days, I think it will all be over. I should have lots of time on my hands then," she said with a smile.

"Good! Maybe we can go somewhere," he said brightening.

"A nice quiet cottage on a lake would be heavenly," Mira agreed. "I could certainly use the rest and a change of scenery as well. It would be nice to get away."

The afternoon found her dashing off to her appointment with Darren Amos and the employment lawyer. They went over the details of the financial package which was promised in time for the Wednesday evening meeting. They decided that Darren would be the best one to present the documents to the rest of the board.

Her last meeting of the day was still of the utmost concern to Mira. She breathed a thankful sigh of relief when she walked into the room and saw that Eve was not there. The executive went ahead with the planning of the monthly meetings through until their summer break.

Grace had agreed to be the speaker for the April meeting, scheduled in two weeks, and a general testimony service was decided upon for the May meeting. Mira offered to approach four ladies from the church membership to share what God had done in their lives. June was easy because they always had their annual women's picnic so no speaker was required.

This was the first year, since Mira had assumed the reins of president, that the ladies' annual spring retreat was cancelled. Realizing her own future at the church was foggy and unsure, there had been a definite check in her spirit as the time approached to make plans. God must have been looking after her, she thought gratefully, knowing she lacked the strength to deal with a project of that magnitude in addition to her other duties. It would also have troubled her greatly to let her team down on the eve of such a crucial event. To her executive, she said nothing about the reasons behind the cancellation.

As she locked the doors behind the last woman, Mira wondered if this would be her last planning meeting. She had grave doubts that she would be opening the April meeting. The posters, as always, would be prominently displayed in the church lobby on Sunday announcing Grace as the speaker and the assigned ladies would distribute the flyers, but only the outcome of the mediation meetings and the annual business meeting would determine her presence or absence.

The next day Mira slept in. Her eyes felt so heavy, she allowed her tired body to drift in and out of consciousness until the morning was well spent. A phone call from Darren finally got her out of bed. The settlement package was ready and he had already e-mailed them to her, in order that copies might be prepared for the meeting that evening.

After printing the documents, Mira called David Armstrong and talked to him at length about delivering the letter to Pastor Rafe that would suspend his duties and authority until the mediation process was completed. The president agreed that it should be sent, so Mira called the rest of the directors.

When she reached Sylvester, he told her that he was resigning his position from the board due to poor health. His wife would leave his official resignation letter in Mira's folder at the church office.

The remaining directors agreed that it was time to deliver the letter, but asked her not to inform Tom of their intentions. Although they were loath to think such a thing, by the end of the second meeting, all were beginning to wonder if their trust in his position as unbiased mediator had been betrayed. When the process started, they believed he was completely unprejudiced to either party, but as the meetings progressed, he seemed more slanted in favor of Pastor Rutherford as he advocated the pastor's position over that of the board time after time. His determination to delay the retirement date until after the annual business meeting, in spite of the legal implications, worried them.

As chairman of the proceedings, Tom had permitted the pastor to ramble on with lengthy speeches, openly flouting his own request to keep statements brief and to the point. The board felt frustrated at every turn, as the mediator talked them out of presenting the pastor with letters and motions which could have prevented much grief had they been delivered immediately. They felt the delays had significantly undermined their position, causing untold anxiety, which might have been prevented if Tom had not involved himself so prominently in every decision.

Mira wanted assurance that the pastor would receive their directive this time, but she had no desire to face him alone. When she shared her dilemma with her husband, Dan offered to deliver the sealed letter directly into his hands.

While her husband was gone, Mira heard from Dora Golding, who had some startling news. Pastor Rutherford had advised her that an elder's meeting had taken place on Tuesday night for the purpose of appointing four more elders and an advisor to his elder board. He had tried to make her believe that the nominees for eldership had been considered in the fall, so she wouldn't think this was something he had cooked up to nullify the board. They were duly installed, he proclaimed, and would be attending the final mediation meeting.

In the ensuing conversation, Mira learned that, of the three existing elders who had voting rights, only Rev. Armstrong had been physically present. Sylvester had cast his vote for the new nominees by telephone, being too ill to attend. A second proxy vote was obtained from an elder who had been on a leave of absence for over two years, due to his deteriorating cancer condition. Since the constitution demanded their physical presence for voting, they did not have a legal quorum which made the whole induction vote illegal.

Dora told her that Pastor Rafe's new hand-picked team consisted of the big Nigerian, Kurtis Oluwa; Tad Booker, a hitherto unassuming, quiet little man who taught a new believer's class in the church along with his wife; Larry Chaput, the newly appointed head usher who had replaced Ian by the pastor's order and finally, Jimmy LaCross. Jimmy had served as president during Mira's first year on the board. Prior to that, he had held the office of treasurer but according to Ina, he had never darkened the door of her office to request a report.

Wilhelm Hahn, an elderly man of German origin with stern countenance and military bearing, was the new acting advisor. Oddly enough, he had been the person responsible for installing Rafe as pastor of the church in the first place. Even so, he had left in anger several years ago, after serving as president of the board, and had only been back for about a year. Mira had seen Wilhelm's name on some of the documentation surrounding the moral issue with Pastor John Schilling. From what she had read, she was reasonably sure that he left because he knew or suspected that Pastor Rafe was guilty of the charge of sexual impropriety. Why he had returned was a complete mystery!

She was completely taken aback by Dora's latest revelations. Their implications made her head spin. It had to mean that Pastor Rutherford had no intentions whatever of resigning. That was now obvious! The certainty grew in her heart that he was determined to overthrow the board.

What does he think he is winning by this move? she thought in dismay. *He will truly be the cause of a major split and there is nothing we can do about it except to follow it through to the end. If we leave quietly, we abdicate our duty as directors. If we stay...*her stomach revolted at the idea, knowing full well they would be misunderstood and possibly even reviled for their stand.

Tension crackled in the air when Caelen and Valin approached the building followed by Captain Darshan and his warriors. Instantly they were accosted by belligerent antagonists who raved and imprecated dire threats and consequences should they attempt to breach their stronghold.

The commanders drew their swords. Their bodies shimmered with white-hot power in the crisp cool air. The sentries fell back in fear and consternation. Demanding entrance on legal grounds, they led the small band of warriors past the guards into what felt like the pit of hell. A tight knot of snarling, ferocious demons, arranged in formidable wedge formation, accosted them savagely.

Caelen faced the brutal beast at the forefront without flinching. "We have a legal right to be present." His voice was stern and his manner forceful.

"You are finished here," taunted the demon scornfully. "Go back to where you came from. This territory is ours!"

""Not as long as there are praying saints," Caelen grated stiffly.

"Bah!" retorted the creature. "There are precious few of those here!"

"Nevertheless..."

The evil spirit continued to mock the heavenly beings while his underlings spread out and encircled the group, watching avidly for any sign of weakness. Caelen's fingers moved rapidly in a pre-arranged signal. At Captain Darshan's sharp command, his warriors shot straight up through the ceiling to the second floor.

~

There was a certain resignation in Mira's mood that evening, as she copied the financial package in the downstairs office of the church. When she had first arrived, the pastor had appeared in the doorway of the accounting office but when he saw Dan standing protectively beside his wife, he merely nodded coldly. Dan was determined that Rafe be given no opportunity to bully or intimidate Mira.

People were starting to straggle in for the regular midweek Bible Study. Instructions had been issued by Pastor Rutherford to show a film in place of his usual message. He wanted to be free to direct his offensive against the board with his new elders.

When Darren Amos arrived, Mira and Dan escorted him through the hallway and climbed the stairs to the second floor. A high level of excitement greeted them from the group assembled there. Mira noticed that Rev. Armstrong was conspicuously absent again.

Dan was about to leave when he was stopped by Rob Samuels. "If you don't mind staying for a few minutes," Rob said with a twinkle in his eye, "there are a bunch of new elders that are expecting to crash this meeting."

"They are not real elders," exclaimed Mira. "The meeting they had was illegal and unconstitutional. In any case, they shouldn't be here tonight! Pastor Rafe told Dora they are coming to the last mediation meeting. This meeting is for the board to decide the financial package. It isn't for mediation!"

"Well, I'm telling you, they're all down there in black suits, looking like they're going to a funeral." He chuckled. "They're certainly not a happy lot.

Mira turned to the lawyer to explain the latest development adding, "I guess they've confused this with mediation. I think they're planning to try and fire the board."

Darren threw up his hands. "This is the first time I've ever heard of the like of this in all my years of practice. And we're supposed to be Christians!"

Grace entered the room in a rush, clearly out of breath. There's a whole line of men in black suits coming up the far stairs," she said, her eyes wide.

In moments, the file of men trotted down the corridor. Much to their chagrin, they found Rob and Dan blocking the entrance of the doorway.

"This is a closed meeting," stated Rob, his manner formal and his tone even. "It is not a mediation meeting. The board of directors has an appointment with their lawyer. Council members are welcome but only those who have previously attended the mediation meetings are permitted entry."

He signaled to Frank Milton. "You can come in and so can Phil Schmidt. Both of you have been part of council." He scanned the group for Pierre but didn't see him.

The two men entered the room and finding chairs they sat stiffly with grim, foreboding expressions. Arguments ensued at the doorway, until the rest of the group finally came to the realization that they would not be gaining admittance to the meeting. Turning around, they solemnly filed back the way they had come, to report their failure to the pastor, regroup and decide what to do next.

Frank and Phil, realizing that the new elders could not bully their way in, scrambled to their feet and left the room grumbling, presumably to go and join their compatriots. Dan went out to his car in the parking lot, where he sat and waited for the meeting to end.

After things had settled down, the lawyer went through the proposal. The package was generous in the extreme and if the group hadn't been shaken by recent developments, they might have hoped for a good resolution the following evening. As things stood now however, the best they could hope for was to persevere until the member's meeting and then leave. This little group, the only ones still standing, felt the bond of their purpose drawing them together as one unit. They would see it through to the end and it was close enough now that they could almost taste their freedom!

Before the meeting ended, there was a knock on the door. Rob opened it to find Tad Booker standing there with a letter from the phony new elder board. It served notice on the directors that the elders had declared a vote of "*no confidence*" in the board of directors.

Darren took a look at the letter and dismissed it with a laugh. "They can't fire you without a full membership vote, so I wouldn't worry about it. It may become a moot point in any case, should you decide to terminate the pastor tomorrow night. It appears to be the desperate act of a man determined to keep his job at all costs. Let me remind you that you do have the right to fire him. You are his employer."

As everyone was gathering up their things to leave, Rob beckoned Mira to a quiet corner of the room. "Faith noticed something the other day that might be of interest to you," he said quietly." She raised her eyebrows questioningly.

"She saw Tom coming out of the pastor's office." His face was serious. "He was alone. Do you think it means anything?"

"It's odd that Dora wasn't with him," she replied thoughtfully. "It was my understanding that they were to attend all meetings together. It certainly doesn't look good for us, I'm afraid." The conversation left her with a sick feeling inside.

Later that evening, Mira and Grace scrutinized the elder's letter more closely over a soothing sup of tea. They discerned several issues that had previously gone unnoticed. The elder meeting had been secretly called, purposefully omitting notification of the associate pastors who, according to the constitution, were part of that board. Besides the illegal vote to install the elders, Kurtis was not even a member of the church, which exempted him from qualifying for a leadership position on any board. The *"no confidence"* vote taken by the quasi elders showed votes from Sylvester Zimmer and David Armstrong. Both of them served on the board of directors. In fact, David was the president of the board.

Mira and Grace couldn't help but laugh as they realized these two aged gentlemen had voted against themselves. "What were they thinking?" Mira asked as they broke into gales of laughter. The more they thought about it, the more they howled. "I can't help it," giggled Mira, wiping away tears which were a result of overwrought nerves taking their toll. "They just voted themselves incompetent. How nuts is that!"

There was a paragraph in the letter stating that David Armstrong had no knowledge of the board's letter that suspended the pastor from his duties. "That's just wrong!" exclaimed Mira indignantly. "He knows the board voted unanimously for it at the March 26th board meeting. We even talked about it in the first mediation meeting. Tom wanted us to hold it back and we agreed... much to our sorrow! I talked to him for a whole half hour about it yesterday and he agreed that it should be sent. You and Dan both heard my end of the conversation."

They were up half the night after that, talking things over and trying to make some sense of the situation. The pastor's ability to suddenly gain control over so many good men in the church, mystified and intrigued them. Mira thought perhaps it was because he had brought them together and submitted himself to them, thus making them responsible for his spiritual well-being and creating a soul-tie, just as he had tried to do with her.

She was grateful, beyond measure, to have her sister-in-law with her during this battle she was going through. She could see God's hand was in it and knew now that He did indeed have a purpose for bringing Grace into the midst of the mess at the Good Shepherd Church. This woman of God, whom Mira had grown to love and respect for her Christ-like walk, always seemed to know just the right things to say to encourage her and strengthen her for the battle that lay ahead.

The morning of the final mediation meeting dawned bright and clear. The first thing on Mira's agenda was to e-mail David Armstrong to ask him about the elder's meeting directly. *There's nothing like getting it straight from the horse's mouth,* she thought.

In her letter, Mira carefully documented the various violations of the constitution which made both the induction of the new elders and the *"No Confidence"* vote illegal. She showed the old minister clearly that he was in a conflict of interest position since he had voted at the board meeting of March 26th to suspend the pastor from his duties, and then subsequently had voted against the board, of which he was still president. She delicately reminded him of their telephone conversation where he had agreed to send the letter.

Rev. Armstrong called shortly after opening Mira's e-mail. In a tremulous voice, he told her that he had felt pressured to attend the elders meeting called by the pastor and forced to vote with the others in the *"No Confidence"* vote. "I will not be in attendance at any more meetings – that includes board, elder or mediation meetings," he assured her, "until after the annual business meeting. I will abstain from all further votes until then as well."

Mira called Darren to inform him that she expected trouble in the last meeting. It certainly didn't bode well for the board that these new elders would be crashing it. "I think I should have a legal termination letter handy, just in case," she said.

He agreed that it was better to be prepared for any eventuality. "I'll e-mail you something that you can use, if necessary," he replied, "but try not to do anything at the meeting unless you're forced into it."

Grace called late in the afternoon to inform Mira that Pastor Rutherford had directed her and Marvin to absence themselves from final mediation meeting. Mira promptly countered his order with a request from the board that they both attend. Too many times, the pastor had lied about things. She felt it imperative that they be present to keep him as honest as possible and the other director's agreed.

25

As CAELEN AND HIS warriors passed through the guards and sentries that evening, they sensed a great swelling of evil, even before seeing the vast army that was arrayed against them. An upsurge of malevolent power brought cold dread to the heart of the commander. It felt as if the very walls throbbed and pulsated with the malignance of thousands of hungry corrupted spirits. As the heavenly host assumed their positions, waves of demons rippled through the walls.

Captain Darshan met Caelen's gaze grimly for a moment. "We're in for it tonight, I fear."

"Hold fast, Captain. The Lord of the Host of Heaven's armies is with us."

"The Creator cannot help you now, sssniveling coward!"

Caelen stiffened. The repulsive head of the massive serpent, Python, shimmered through the wall beside him. It looked like an ethereal, disembodied member until large leathery coils suddenly appeared shoving the head further into the room.

Caelen ignored the thrust. Knowing they were vastly outnumbered, he wanted to keep the peace as long as possible, allowing his warriors to provide as much aid as they could muster under the circumstances.

The directors arrived early, going straight upstairs to the meeting room. Mira was relieved to see both associate pastors already in place at their separate table. She greeted Jack, Donny, Ian and Rob warmly and they milled about the refreshment table laughing and talking while they waited for the appearance of the mediators who were still downstairs with the pastor and his elder/deacon entourage. There was a kind of giddiness in the air that was almost intoxicating. This was it! The final mediation meeting! They could see the light at the end of the long dark tunnel.

Rob was called from the room briefly. When he returned, he shared with the group that he had been fired from his position as deacon by the new elder board. He threw the letter on the table.

Mira's eyes grew wide. "You've got to be kidding! How could they fire you?"

"For not supporting the pastor, or at least that's the excuse they gave. They have no authority anyway. They're not a legal board. Besides, if part of being a deacon is following a corrupt leader blindly, then I want no part of it."

Mira had to stifle a giggle when the pastor walked in with his little army trailing behind. The whole scene was surreal. Their severe demeanor reminded her of a movie where the mafia was converging to annihilate their foe. They sat on the opposite side of the table from the directors, a hostile force attempting, in vain, to bring fear to the heart of the enemy. Rafe glowered when he noticed the associate pastors were there in spite of his orders. He leaned over and whispered in Tom's ear. Mira heard the reply that the pastors were there at the direct request of the board.

Since they had arrived some twenty minutes late, Tom wasted no time reviewing the rules of mediation for the benefit of the newcomers. He felt a good place to start would be with the financial package which he and Dora had presented to Pastor Rutherford the night before.

Rafe took the floor with obvious relish. As the Jezebel Spirit pressed a massive claw on his shoulder and leaned into his ear, he felt raw power course through his body. It had become an addiction to his soul. His opponents, he viewed with contempt. He would smash them and grind them into the ground for having the audacity to stand against him. His smile however was bland and his voice without tremor as he flattered the mediators before beginning his prepared speech.

"These excellent mediators came by with the proposal from those gathered last night and I took it to my wife and had her review it. I am committed both constitutionally and to the wisdom of the board of elders. Without their knowledge or consent I could not make any decision, so we met with them and a couple of the deacons as well. I felt pushed, even bribed and threatened to cooperate. I did not in any way influence the others, but only shared with them what was proposed and they felt very much the same as I did. So I need to go back, if I may, to a little background on what happened as a result of the Monday night meeting."

"I must say that our plans for retirement are not changed," Rafe reiterated smoothly. "If you think I'm trying to manipulate something here.... in fact, my wife has boxes in the kitchen already packed. But my concern is for the work of God. Don't worry about me! It's not me any more. It is the congregation - the membership. This was my concern and it still is... that we consider the congregation. When I went home Monday, I have to tell you, I did not sleep hardly one minute – maybe collectively an hour that whole night, if that. I went downstairs and I had a visitation of the Lord giving me divine direction throughout the night. I wrote down the Word the Lord gave me."

Rafe put on his glasses and picking up a paper from the table, he began to read. ""*Those who have come against you; God will take care of them. Be strong and of good courage and hearken unto the voice of my Spirit.* The Lord reminded me, there are many voices, but the Lord has said, *"You are going to hear my voice, son. Tonight, I am going to speak to you. The time for you to go forth is at hand... but not now. I will gather those around you whom I have appointed to stand with you. My purpose shall be accomplished in my way"*, says the Lord. *"Stand still and see the salvation of the Lord, your God. Set the House of the Lord in order, according to the Word of God. The things that are being done to you are not of me, for it has been done in secret, and it is not holy unto the Lord. God will bring to naught the things of those who persist in doing them. It has been done by force and manipulation and I have revealed their works, which have grieved the heart of the Lord. Many have cried unto the Lord over this situation and the Lord has heard and will take swift action.""*

Rafe paused to remove his glasses. "This has not been given to take any offence, but just to share what was the experience of that night. And whether received by any or all is up to you to decide. The Lord reminded me that there were those that I had spoken to last fall, a slate of names, that we were working on to add to the elders. The whole process was delayed by the holiday season and my being away the three months."

In an attempt to justify the appointment process, Rafe stuttered and stammered over dates, seeming confused as to when he actually spoke to anyone. His lie was getting too involved and his memory of the dates he was actually in town was hazy. He realized that he shouldn't have tried to be so specific, especially with the men present and listening. But his little troupe were gazing at him attentively, totally enraptured by the charismatic personality of the man.

"Two days ago, the Lord told me that it was now the time to call them and bring them all together. I was quite amazed at this and knew that this was an awesome visitation by God. I asked them to bring their spouses so I could share what has happened. I believe God has fulfilled this and is now giving guidance as to what we should do. This last week, we have been overwhelmed with the calls that have been coming to us..."

Rafe suddenly stopped. The director's heads were not down as they usually were during his carefully prepared discourses, deliberately crafted to heap guilt and shame upon them. Instead they were held high, as if they were unashamed of what they were trying to do to him. He tried to start again, but nothing would come out of his mouth. "Uh...um," he struggled, mortified at his sudden inability to speak. His face reddened noticeably. Their eyes were still upon him, watching him intently. The lack of emotion in them pierced him with uncertainty. After a few agonizing moments, he managed to grind out, "I can speak further, but the looks I'm getting from them are hard to take."

"I would ask you to please address the Chair," replied Tom.

"Yeah... okay." Rafe still looked shaken. "It would seem that this has become a national piece of information now, and this is what I was trying to save us from," he appealed, forgetting that he had just told everyone that it was he who invited his new appointees to bring their spouses, so they could be informed on what was happening.

"I will not disclose how this information is getting out, but we around this table know," he announced with a defiant glare. "This to me is very troubling and I am trying to protect the flock from the things that are being said...so abusive and detrimental and inflammatory."

He raised his hand and looking straight across the table at Mira, he wailed dramatically. "It breaks my heart that those I thought of as family have betrayed me. Now that tie is severed...." He paused to let that sink in before he softened his voice. "But it *can* be healed; that's what I'm praying for; "Lord, heal the breach with some of you that I have loved so much." I've been proud of you! I took delight in you and rejoiced to see the work you do in ministry." His voice rose magnificently. "I believe if we can humble ourselves before God and yield ourselves before the Lord that God can and will overrule the current circumstances and situations and bring glory to His name."

Mira felt sick. She knew that he was only playing a part, like an actor on a stage. It infuriated her that he was still able to tug at her heartstrings, if only momentarily. *He would plunge me back into depression in a heart-beat without a thought or a care, as long as it suited his purpose,* she reminded herself.

"Thank you, pastor," replied Tom. "The next step to the meeting would be an opportunity for the board to respond, ask questions for clarification and then the others may have an opportunity." They presumed he was referring to the new elders.

Jack Johnson took the lead. "The documents that have been read by council, as well as our own personal letters, state clearly what we believe," he said. "The pastor has read them and he knows the truth. A shepherd should serve - not dominate."

Mira's heart was pounding as she raised her hand to address the newcomers. "The appointment of the new elders appears to this board as a last minute effort to take us down and make us of no effect. Kurtis is not a member of the church, so he does not qualify to be an elder. Beyond that, the board has had some serious issues to deal with in this past year. There have been lies and manipulation; checks have been put in front of us that I, as treasurer, had no knowledge of, until I was asked to sign them. None of you have even seen the letters and documentation that have been prepared for council to deal with. You are coming in at the last moment, in the final meeting, when we should be finishing up the details of whatever resolution this exercise is going to bring."

She took a deep breath and forged ahead. "You talk about reconciliation and your first act as an elder board is to fire one of our deacons because he dares to be honest. Not one of you can appreciate what this board has been through in this past year. If you've not read the documents then you really need to or maybe you should meet with the board separately, so we can at least tell you what agony we have suffered. We have not been able to be heard. We are still not being heard! Not one issue has been addressed! Our letters have been dismissed as trivial."

As Mira spoke, she prayed silently for help to stay steady and calm. "We are the legal governing body of this assembly. The buck stops here! We are the employer of all of the staff in this building. We are responsible for the actions of that staff. In the real world, if you had an employee that constantly lied and misused funds, you would fire him in a heartbeat. But you expect us to turn our heads and say, "Oh well, maybe he will change!" As a Christian charity, our standards should be higher than that of the world! I am at the point where I cannot sit under this shepherd any longer. He does not care for the sheep! He has hardly been in the pulpit this past year and when he is, he only tells stories of his life. I am starved for the Word of God! We had so many guest speakers last year that fifty-one second offerings were taken. A lot of our congregation are retired and live on fixed incomes. Our youth and children's ministries are struggling and there are a large number of potential workers who refuse to get involved in those ministries because they are waiting to see if this pastor can be dealt with."

"Make no mistake, gentlemen," she continued. "Regardless of what happens here we are going to have a split in the church. The board may ultimately decide to step down and walk away but let me assure you, if that occurs, there are a large number of people that will go with us. Or conversely, if the pastor leaves, those that support him will probably go with him. Either way, it doesn't look pleasant for the future of this assembly, unless we can reach a united resolution that is best for everyone, including the congregation."

Mira thought she saw some response in Tad Booker's eyes. Perhaps it wasn't too late for a resolution after all. "You must appreciate the tough position that this board is in," she pled earnestly. "We've watched the pastor sow seeds of division between the directors, defaming and maligning one to another. Sylvester has already quit and our president now refuses to attend either board or elder meetings because of the position he has been put in by the pastor." She had lost Tad. She could see him stiffen his back the moment she accused his pastor of unethical conduct.

In desperation, she turned toward the table where Grace and Marvin sat quietly watching the proceedings. "I would like to ask a question of the associate pastors," she said bravely, pleading forgiveness with her eyes. "Have you ever heard Pastor Rutherford say bad or evil things about any of the people who are present in this room tonight?"

Marvin hung his head, but answered in the affirmative, as did Grace. Mira took it a step further, trusting that both pastors would answer honestly. "What about the pastoral staff? Has he ever tried to drive a wedge of dissention or discord between the two of you by talking to one of you about the other in a disparaging manner?" Again the answer was "yes" from both pastors.

"I too have had offensive comments made to me about other board members," Mira continued, "and I'm sure they have been told derogatory things about me. In the last mediation meeting, our associate pastors heard Pastor Rutherford say that the attendance dropped while he was away. That was a lie! The only drop we had was when there were storms and they would have dropped no matter who was here to preach. My sister-in-law came here at the request of the pastor. He pursued her vigorously to get her to come and she came with no agenda. She came here because she thought there might be reconciliation between the pastor and the board. She has preached the Word consistently without political agenda and as a result, we are having altar services that we haven't seen in a long time. The offerings have been consistent as well. Both she and Pastor Marvin have done an excellent job. The pastor, himself, when he returned in February said that he was happy with job the associate staff was doing and he felt he could go back to Florida and rest, because he knew that the church was being well taken care of. And yet in the last meeting, he lied, claiming the attendance had suffered under their care. In fact, he would have us believe that should he leave, we would have to bring in a big name evangelist as an overseer because otherwise the church would fail."

Mira gestured toward Grace. "I have watched this woman and she walks the talk. She spends hours in prayer and the most important thing to her is the Word of God. I have also seen her come home in tears more than once because of the agony the pastor put her through that day. So, gentlemen, how would you have us resolve this? Do you wish to hear statements from the associate pastors about what it's like to work with Pastor Rutherford? Pastor Marvin, Pastor Grace, please speak. Marvin just shook his head. He looked frightened.

Grace rose slowly to her feet. "I will only speak about my coming and I will speak about the rumors of my agenda. I came here, on a four month contract, knowing there was difficulty but believing that reconciliation could take place. We had worked out an agreement so that, during my time here, I could expand my evangelistic base by doing a little speaking at other places. However after I got here, there was a change of plan and I was not able to do any traveling. Even on Sunday night when Marvin spoke, I was expected to be here. I submitted. I've enjoyed this church. I've enjoyed Marvin's ministry. I came believing that eventually my family would join me and I would do work in the church and evangelistic work in the area. That was my plan. If it didn't work out after four months time, I would still have had the opportunity to perhaps gain some evangelistic contacts."

She looked directly at Pastor Rutherford. "I did not come here to take the senior pastor job nor did I come to steal your church to give to Dave Holman. I've been asked three different times about that rumor. I don't know where it came from but it has never been my agenda. I wouldn't steal a church! There is no conspiracy between me and any other minister. I am heart-broken because I know that I've been misrepresented and slandered even to some of you. I have already received a vicious letter from a church member who believes all of these things to be true of me. I'm hoping that as resolution takes place, the damage can be rectified because, in all sincerity, with a clean heart before God, I came with no agenda except to work for this church. I will say that a good resolution here appears dismal at this time.

Rafe bounced to his feet. He felt his control over his entourage weakening a little with Grace's comments. "Statements have been made of money fraud! This is critical! I've been accused of abusing people! I would like to see every document of money fraud. I have never taken a cent!" he stormed. "I even pick up pennies and dimes from the floor and I will not even put them in my pocket. I have spent hour upon hour laying tile here and it is all over the tile issue." He wasn't even making sense by this point.

He ranted on jumping from the tile to the Christmas dinner claiming the board had accused him of being a shyster. Afraid that his new elders might actually take a second look at what he had told them, he justified, blamed, excused and obfuscated his actions until he felt his little entourage was back on board with his agenda. Loudly proclaiming his innocence to all of the accusations, he lied further, giving his assurance that he had always spoken highly of his pastoral staff. He did however admit that he had been disappointed in them because they hadn't stopped the board in their attempted coup, as he had trusted them to do. The inaccurate attendance figures, he craftily blamed on his secretary figuring that most of his elders wouldn't know that it was the ushers that took the attendance.

"I will not ask my staff to respond as others did," Rafe said, throwing a contemptuous look in Mira's direction. "I would not put them on the spot as they were put on the spot a few moments ago. That is not fair to them and I can see by the look on their faces that it was very embarrassing for them. They know that I was always loving and gentle with them. It was only the Lord that prepared me that day, that the council meeting I was going into wasn't what I thought it would be. I admit I felt somewhat betrayed by my associates personally, that I was not forewarned that this was going on behind my back, as they attended all the meetings. I went away to my sabbatical in confidence, until the Holy Ghost revealed to me the Spirit of Absalom was running loose in the place."

Absalom, King David's Son had tried to usurp his father's throne so the implication was clear to all. *On one hand, he claims love for Pastor Marvin and Grace and on the other he is blatantly accusing them of trying to take his pulpit from him,* thought Mira.

Rafe moved on in an attempt to further justify his position. "Some here..." He looked accusingly at Mira over his glasses. "Some here are trying to discredit my sabbatical by accusing me of making phone calls to the church while I was away. That shouldn't even matter. *They* are in violation of the terms of the sabbatical. I did not make the calls. I returned a few calls and I called Faith only once for some phone numbers that I needed. The premise that I broke the sabbatical is false and we're here now because of an action of the board. So let's not be pointing fingers!" he said sternly. "There has been a serious derailing of this process and activity that has been not pleasing to God. And I could go on but that's the answer to some of these situations and accusations."

Mira raised her hand. "One serious issue that we have had to deal with is the fact that the pastor never asks the board for permission to spend money. We get the bills after the fact and must then be forced to pay because otherwise the church's good name will be jeopardized. We cannot allow the bills to be put into the hands of a collections agency."

"Faith and Ina were the ones that wanted to go ahead with the Christmas party for the volunteers," Rafe replied heatedly. "I told them it might create a problem."

That's the first time he's said that, thought Mira disgustedly. *What a liar!*

"I didn't know if they were going to call the treasurer on this and it was all coming together so fast because we usually plan a party at the parsonage but that got changed. It was just a simple thing that got off track. I put about $200.00 of my own money in to help cover the expense," Rafe added triumphantly. "So I don't think there was any problem."

Why would he pick this issue when there are so many that are far more serious? Nevertheless, Mira called him on it, trying to expose his lying behaviour before the elders. "Actually that's not true! The pastor told me after a Wednesday night service about the party. It was a last minute thing, thrown together, as most things are! I told him clearly that there was no time to call a board meeting to discuss the issue and approve the expense. He wanted me to call the directors for permission and I refused. I was too worn out to deal with it. Pastor assured me that he would make the calls himself. That never happened! No one received a call from either him or the office staff." *There! I hope that is the last time we have to go over it!* she thought.

"The amount was so insignificant that Ina, Faith and I were going to cover it between us," Rafe argued, "but somehow it fell between the cracks. Is that a major sin?" he sneered. "It was a simple misunderstanding of procedure that the treasurer refused to take care of? If it is such a great sin, then we ask your forgiveness." Mira didn't trust herself to speak.

Kurtis Oluwa got to his feet. "I would like to address the issue Sister Mira has raised over my church membership," he said. "I believe I've been here a little over two years now. I'm an ordained minister. When my wife and I asked about having our baby dedicated, I received a membership form from Sister Faith along with the dedication form which we filled out and turned in. Sister Faith did mention later on that she probably must have misplaced our membership. After that, I was considered for the board of elders. Pastor had talked about this to me two months ago but I was hesitating. I have ministered here under the anointing of God. Why, at a time like this, would you bring up membership? If it's about the constitution or books, there is the Word of God that weighs more than that. My membership is somewhere in Sister Faith's office, if that is important to you." His voice was tinged with sarcasm.

Puffing out his chest, he fixed a commanding eye on Mira. "The integrity of this board of directors is in question by the pastor and the elders. Issues and disagreements occur between parties from time to time. It happens! But it is wrong to take a stand on personal issues without considering the church as a whole. The board of elders, which I'm part of, will be making a statement here soon."

Mira couldn't believe Kurtis' denial regarding his membership status. She looked him straight in the eye. "Not long ago, we had a conversation in the sanctuary of this church. You told me that you did not believe in membership and that you were not going to take out membership here because you were thinking of leaving. I also had conversation with your wife, Natalie, when we were talking about the budget for the Children's Ministry. She also said that you had no intention of taking out membership. She had her resignation prepared for the end of January and was willing to hold off submitting it until the end of February to see whether any of the promises she had received from the pastor would ever come to pass."

"Can I respond to that?" replied Kurtis. His tone had sharpened. "If membership takes you to heaven, I'd better get one right away," he sneered. "What you understand by membership is different from my idea of membership. We're all one body of Christ. I filled a form out – it's there. It's in the records. Now if that is a thing that bothers you or if you feel threatened with that then I doubt the integrity of the question."

"Let me repeat - you told me that you did not want to take out membership because you didn't believe in it and you were thinking of leaving the church," said Mira hotly. "This was verified by your own wife so either you were lying then or you're lying now."

Kurtis repeated his story about the old membership form, claiming his wife for a witness and blaming Faith for losing it. He ignored Mira's account of her conversations with him and his wife, figuring that it was her word against his. In a further embellishment, he alleged that he had joined alone, not submitting membership for his wife or children. He admitted his wife's frustration with the pastor over administrative issues connected with the Children's Ministry. The group looked at one another in confusion when he sat down.

"I have just one last response to this issue," replied an exasperated Mira. "When you do get around to filling the membership form out - until that membership form is approved by the board of directors and until you are inducted into the church membership - you will not be voting at the annual business meeting and you should not be an elder."

Rafe jumped to his feet. "Why don't you deal with that right now? We are here in a council meeting and this can be submitted. He already filled out the form and has been approved constitutionally by the elder board. It is the elders who approve, set and accept the memberships, which are then given completed to the board of directors for record purposes because they are in charge of records. They do not decide whether or not they accept or refuse a member. Only the elders do that. So read that in the constitution!" he ended defiantly.

Ian spoke out, a look of disgust on his face. "Mr. Chairman, would you ask the pastor if it is his intention to gather up people wherever he can and anoint them as his posse. Never mind, I withdraw the question. You don't have to ask him. This is a farce! A joke! It's disgusting! It makes me sick to my stomach! I'm ashamed to tell people what church I attend. If people ask me, I do not mention the name of this church. There was a time when I looked up to the pastor as a father figure - a loving father. It wasn't until I got on the board that I experienced the abuse of a father to a child. And now my heart cries out for those people who have been abused."

"I agree with that," put in Jack feelingly. "He has hurt us all. He may have a charismatic personality and even be a gifted speaker and he can certainly talk his way out of pretty well anything, but we know what we've been through and it's just too much. We can't step back and let this go. Not this time! If we have to go further, we are prepared to do that."

Rafe indignantly came to the defence of his hand-picked crew. "I have been given the support of these fine Christian men who have been in leadership." He pointed out each in turn, announcing their titles as if he were a king bestowing knighthood. "Larry Chaput is head of the ushering, Jimmy LaCross is head of the building department, Tad Booker is head of the New Life class and the chairman of the missions department and Kurtis is a minister who has been very active in worship and music ministry here. I think it very distasteful that you have labelled him an impostor and I apologize if that has offended you folk."

"I'll tell you what is distasteful!" Mira had fire in her eye. "This letter that Rob received tonight from these elders is distasteful!"

Donny cut in. "They don't get it! They haven't seen Pastor as he really is. I've had a difficult time myself trying to understand how this man, whom I trusted like a father, could be so abusive toward me. I'm still struggling to grasp it. You don't understand," he said, gesturing to the new elders. "You haven't walked in our shoes this past year. Not only has he been abusive to me, but to all of us. I wish to God that I had never met this man! I've helped him in every way that I could - with my money and my time. Whatever he asked for, I did. I didn't deserve to be hurt by him. I didn't deserve it!"

Rafe quickly signalled Tom that he wished to respond.

"Save it!" replied Donny bitterly. "I really don't want to hear anything more from him. I'm sick of his lies and fed up with his garbage. He manipulates good people, twisting everything around until he eventually destroys them. He has to control everything and everyone around him. I think he actually believes that he is above everyone. He's special!" His grim chuckle was humourless.

"Oh, you'll get along fine and dandy with him as long as you're in agreement and doing everything he says," he continued. "But watch out if you ever take a stand or try to bring up any issues. Suddenly you'll become his sworn enemy! He'll cut you off and throw you to the wolves without a thought or care. You'll no longer be his friend. This man deals in deception! I was very deceived myself until I became a director. I sure got my eyes opened up then and I started to see it all. I'm so sick of it! Everything within me has been turned upside down and inside out! This should not happen in a church! It's wrong! There has been no repentance from this man whatsoever, so any comment he could possible make is not going to cut it. I'm sorry gentlemen, but you are deceived and time will prove me right. I'm done listening to his lies."

"I am not going to seek to justify," rejoined Rafe jumping in to begin his defence.

Donny pushed his chair back. "I'll be back when he's finished." He strode from the room.

"He left because he knew the truth was going to come out," Rafe cried, incensed over Donny's remarks. He launched into a tirade against the man blaming him for overstepping the bounds of his authority the day he committed the unfortunate faux pas of blurting out the board's decision to suspend Jonas' travel allowance. By the time Rafe was through, he looked like a suffering saint under vicious attack by his board. Donny, in particular, had been painted in an extremely unfavourable light. Not satisfied that he had said enough to discredit the man, he went on to shred his reputation further by relating how a couple in the church had come to him repeating some alleged comments Donny had made against him.

"We've had letters that have come," claimed Rafe, "very critical letters, but I wanted to protect him from an accusation that I thought was severe. I said, "Let's work it out". I wanted recovery, redemption for the man. I wanted to protect him. I could have been mean and nasty and brought it all out but I did not do it. I must apologize to this church for being neglectful and not dealing with one who went about belittling and undermining me because he was going to show me that I am not going to run them. I can't even share with you what Donny told me. I cannot share this! It's that bad! So now a little sore has become a festering wound that I should have dealt with sooner."

Marvin and Grace shifted uneasily in their chairs. They knew very well that it had been the Rafe's intention to use any means at his disposal to oust Donny from the board and they had protected him. They were also aware of the identity of the couple who had written the letter at the pastor's request. The man was sitting in the room; part of the pastor's new elder board. It upset them that they were unable to speak out to bring clarity to the circumstances that had precipitated the letter, but they had been cautioned before the meeting to keep silent, unless asked a direct question.

Tad Booker also sat on his own personal knowledge of the letter, for it was he who had written the offending epistle, at Pastor Rutherford's bidding. It had been a relatively bland letter stating that Donny had spoken words against the pastor. Yet the new elder held his peace, allowing Rafe to embellish the truth as much as he pleased, casting grave suspicion on Donny by referring to his words and deeds as so vile that they could not be repeated.

Rafe pushed it to the extreme. "Even today another party called me and said that it was being told around that I meet with witches and fortune tellers." He laughed as if he was embarrassed to even mention it. Grace and Marvin looked at one another in bewilderment. They hadn't heard anything of the kind. More lies?

"He is in contradiction to the constitution," Rafe continued ruthlessly. His little group hung on every word. "As a matter of fact, as soon as anybody works out of harmony with the constitution, their position should be immediately vacated. We haven't pushed this. I did not want to do this. I'm not a confrontational person. I wanted reconciliation but Donny won't talk to me."

26

THE DOOR OPENED AND Donny re-entered the room, stalking to his seat in silence. Rafe's tone immediately changed to one of pleading. "I miss Donny's friendly calls and I'd like to work things out," he said plaintively, looking mournfully at the director. "I've walked with him through some painful times in his life and we had such a sweet friendship. I stood by him. I still believe God can restore things between us..."

Donny shook his head in disgust. "Well, if you don't want it," Rafe whined, "if your spirit isn't right, then I'm sorry, because the heart of the Father is for restoration."

Jack interrupted. "Pastor has said different times that he's never had a board like us and that is upsetting. We've been praying and crying about this thing and we've searched our hearts as to whether what we're doing is wrong. I asked Mira to check in the archives to see if any other board has had these problems that we've experienced. She has found the same problems and issues repeated over and over again with past boards. We found more than we bargained for! There were even greater moral issues that have been swept under the carpet in just the past few years. There's talk of homosexuality and different things have come up that really put a big question mark in my mind about who this man really is and what's going on here! We know from experience that he is impossible to deal with and whatever he gets involved with creates a terrible mess which we are expected to clean up or ignore. Oh, he has word power and he is able to twist things around and cover things up in a way I've never seen before. The end result is always hurt people and he'll hurt more if we don't stop him."

Tad Booker raised his hand. "I hear a lot of emotion here and some generalities but there doesn't seem to be any substance. I just want to publicly state that my wife and I have supported Pastor Rutherford's ministry for some twenty-five years which pre-dates his history at this church and we were blessed under his ministry. We found his character to be stellar. In fact, I have used him as my number one role model. I can't tell you the indebtedness we have to him and his beautiful wife, of ministry to us. I just wanted to set the record straight from my view point. Pastor Rafe is not perfect. We all sin, but its unfortunate when we take an antagonistic or opposing view point. I believe that we can work things out for the glory of God."

"I think the biggest problem here is a lack of knowledge of the truth and of what has really gone on here," replied Donny. "Knowledge brings with it choice. We all have a choice on how to use what knowledge we have been given. If we use it wisely, then people will be benefited; otherwise they can be hurt. You don't possess the knowledge that we do in this case. You have been brought into a situation that you know nothing about. You have not been properly briefed on documents, letters and issues that we have to deal with. You have not been a part of this process and it would take hours to bring you up to speed. It is unfair to expect us to now begin all over again, in the final mediation meeting, because you do not comprehend the complexity if the issues that are at stake. If you didn't care to do your homework before stepping into this situation then you shouldn't have agreed to come in the first place. Furthermore, I will state for the record that there have probably been scores of people that have ended up like me and others here; abused and very seriously damaged spiritually because this man used his power and position in an ungodly way."

"I ask you," Rafe replied hotly, "how can I be reconciled to Donny? He doesn't want it! I have apologized very sincerely to each one. But it has not worked! I don't know what to do! I'm at wit's end! These comments are derogatory and everyone here has now heard them. I did not become spiteful. I did not even become offended. I continued to reach out for reconciliation. Sure, I was hurt", he whined. "Now I feel strengthened by a spiritual board of elders that maybe can help negotiate." He settled back in his chair feeling satisfied that he had accomplished his purpose.

Fascinated, Mira watched her pastor change like quick-silver between rage and compassionate love. *I have never really known him at all! He already has them completely hooked! By submitting himself to them, he has effectively created a soul-tie with each one and they are blind to it! He controls them and they don't even know it!*

Jimmy LaCross raised his hand nervously. "I served on the board for two years and I have to say that I did not experience any of these allegations I am hearing about during my term. It's true that we had projects sometimes that the pastor would get involved in that he probably shouldn't have. There were also cases when he overlooked decisions that the board made. But these allegations are much stronger than what I experienced and I've only been off the Board for one year." He looked bewildered.

Kurtis quickly stepped into the gap. "The board of elders here speaks with a unanimous voice," he stated firmly. "The spiritual health of this church is more important than any dispute between the board and the pastor. If that understanding is not clear to the board members tonight, then they are in trouble. The Lord told me that this church is going to be shaken, but God is not going to give in to man. It's still His church. The man of God should be treated with honor. We are all here tonight because the board has had a misunderstanding with the pastor. When I came here, about two and a half years ago, I walked through that door and the Holy Spirit showed me that there are a lot of hurting people in this church. But the enemy also comes in through the same door and he plants his own seeds which germinate and grow. It has taken effect like a worm and a virus upon everybody. I'm sure you're feeling stressed and would like a way out of this. Well, I believe in miracles and I believe that God doesn't want us to go home without a peaceful resolution to all of this."

"I want to comment on what Jimmy said," volunteered Jack. "We served together on the board for his last year along with Mira and Ian. Things weren't too bad that year. There weren't any major projects so it was pretty quiet but this last year, things have changed drastically.

This package of letters and documents is not a trivial whim or something trumped up to get rid of the pastor because we disagree with his methods or don't like his personality. There have been pyramid schemes fostered by the pastor, mismanagement of funds, unethical practices and moral issues. The man can't speak the truth! There are those in the church with evil spirits attached to them that have been allowed to run amok causing great spiritual damage to many. Some are laying hands on people, hurting and upsetting them. This type of thing will not be dealt with as long as we have this pastor as our spiritual head. He is a partaker in it. Our trust in him is gone."

"There is great deception in this place," added Donny earnestly. "It's a spirit and it's been allowed to operate for years. As soon as people get their spiritual eyes opened up to see it and they try to confront it, a war is waged against them. They all leave because they can't deal with the strength of it. We've had to stand against what we believe is not right according to how God has led us. If you would take the time to read all of this documentation, you will see for yourselves the pattern that has been recurring for years. I have no problem stating that I considered myself a friend of the pastor's for many years, but as soon my eyes were opened and I realized the wickedness in his heart, everything changed. You are still deceived."

The comments were starting to unnerve Rafe. Afraid that they might reveal something to his new elders that he hadn't told them, he interrupted. "They didn't have any grip on anything until a document or a survey was constructed by one of our dear mediators and Pastor Marvin Gates. It was never intended to be a weapon turned against me! We want to be up front. We're not hiding anything. The Holy Spirit had revealed to me an uprising was underway. I'm glad that these elders can now help and I am grateful for those who have helped mediate as well. The problem is that when you lose love, bitterness operates. Then you see a person in another way and I've been wounded by this."

Rafe's voice trembled with emotion. "They have told me I'm incompetent. You know, let's just get rid of the old horse. We had a good ride, he was a high sprinter and he had some good races but he's slowing down now so put him out in the field and let the glue factory pick him up." He paused to allow the emotion of the moment to saturate and infuse his elders. Mira's stomach wanted to heave.

"It was very painful to have that sort of feeling and then to follow it up later with violation after violation of the constitution!" Rafe's voice rose dramatically. "It left me feeling like I was all alone in this because I had now lost the confidence of a few good leaders. I did make the statement and I regret it - that they've been the worst board I've had in forty-five years, but it was only because I got so frustrated. It wasn't right. Mira has been one of the most efficient secretary-treasurer's we've had. I've told her that and she knows it."

He looked expressively at Mira. "I'm sorry that I made that comment, Mira, because you have carried a tremendous load in this. I've told you many times how much we appreciate it. But one negative statement has perhaps washed away all the other positive statements that I've made. I feel sorry that I've done that and I ask you to forgive me for that statement which has hurt you and I can only say out of frustration that I should never have said it."

"We all make mistakes," replied Ian. "I've made mistakes. I'm the first to admit it. My wife will probably be the second. But what I'm saying is - if I make the same mistake time and time and time and time again or do the same thing over and over, it is no longer an incident or an issue, it is a life style. That's why we went into the archives to see if this was one time thing, because we all make mistakes. But when you go back and the same things are recurring over and over again, it's not just an incident or an unfortunate thing that happened. It's a life style."

Tom halted the discussion. "I think we really need to get back to the pastor's response to the board's proposal and some specific discussion on that. I'm not exactly sure where we are, other than it's after 10 o'clock. A couple of options, I guess – one is that we pick up the meeting the way we left off. Another is that we break up into sub-groups for a brief time and then come back; for example, the board could meet, the deacons could meet and the elders could meet. The mediators might like to meet with one group at a time. Comments or questions?"

Mira raised her hand. "I just have a couple of comments first that I would like to make. It isn't our personal wounds we're addressing here. It is issues of integrity and trust. There have been innumerable lies and so much manipulation. Do you know that in this crisis, not once has the pastor called his board or council to pray together? Not once has he called his own staff to pray for this crisis."

She struggled to keep from breaking down. "We, as a board, have been before the altar weeping over this situation. We have seen the pastor use illegal meetings and manipulations and whatever it takes to get rid of us! This latest letter firing Rob is inexcusable! What!" she retorted. "He is not permitted to come to a meeting and speak his mind without suffering a consequence? We are supposed to be able to be honest here but instead his concerns have been twisted and turned against him in an effort to discredit him. Are we then supposed to just keep our mouths shut and take whatever the pastor hands out because he's always right?"

"That letter wasn't drafted by Pastor Rutherford," retorted Kurtis. "It was drafted by the board of elders and it is because of Rob's reaction to the meeting yesterday. Now if you disagree with that for any reason, I think that's where it ends. A new season will start and we want to put the old behind us and begin to move forward."

"We started this final meeting to discuss the retirement package," cried Mira, "and at this moment I am totally confused! Is the package accepted or rejected because I believe the board is now ready to vote?" Her face was white and defiant. "We are ready to take comments from the council and then we will go and vote."

"If you decide to go ahead with your vote," responded Kurtis insolently, "then it's the understanding of the board of elders that the board of directors is not in unity. The president of the board calls the shots and the meetings."

"No he doesn't!" she fired back. "Any two members can call a board meeting."

Kurtis pushed back his chair and jumped to his feet. "It is the understanding of the board of elders that the board of directors are not in unity and cannot function as a board recognized by the church," he stated boldly. "Based on that fact only, if you do take your vote, you have to consult first the board of elders and we have the right to place disciplinary actions on individuals within the church for misconduct regarding spiritual matters. This night, we will be serving disciplinary letters to all of you."

Mira stood, her hands shaking. Her whole body started to tremble uncontrollably. "Way to go, Pastor!" she cried, catching the triumphant smirk on his face. "Way to go!" Several chairs scraped the floor loudly. The whole board was now on their feet.

Jack's anger flared. "This is a set up! You've done a good job with them, Pastor! They don't know how they're being used!"

"They're deceived!" observed Donny, a look of utter disgust on his face.

The Jezebel spirit snickered while the great serpent's maw opened in a crooked, evil grin. Its red-rimmed eyes glittered in satisfaction. Victory was assured!

Grace hastily stepped from behind her table and moved to a position where everyone could see her. She couldn't keep silent any longer. "There are some very unhappy people in the church that have already threatened to go to the press. I have spent much of my week keeping people calm, so they don't do something stupid - like go to a newspaper and let us read about ourselves on Sunday morning."

"Let's all settle down!" she cried. "This is still the church and I have seen more ungodliness, lack of integrity, lies and manipulation since coming here than I have ever seen in the Kingdom of God or in the secular workplace, for that matter. Excuse me for saying so, but the fault here doesn't lie solely with the board, as some of you have been led to believe. We need to really back up and say, are we truly caring about the sheep or are we playing a game that we are insisting we must win? And what will we win when our fight is done here?" she queried, her voice trembling with passion. "What will be the trophy that you will walk out of this room with? You tell me! What will you hold up and say, *"We won!"* Another fragmented and split church? Another three or four dozen people going to hell, losing their faith in God because they couldn't handle the abuse they have gone through! What will you hold up and say, *"Applaud me for my victory!""* She clapped her hands mockingly.

"We've got to really back up! You had an opportunity here." She pointed at the new elders. "You came in under a cloud. And you!" She singled out Kurtis. "You are not a member! I'm sorry, the list is out there and your name is not on it! None of you reached out to Rob Samuels. You know this man, he's served this church well for over ten years but you slapped him with a disciplinary procedure. You said, *"Let's put a wall up."* You had an opportunity! I'm so sorry, but I'm passionate about this. I've watched so many churches split." Beads of perspiration stood thickly on her forehead. "You had an opportunity to extend your hand and instead you kicked their butts! And so we'll all go down at the end of the day and nobody will win. And don't you dare think that you will shake the bible and stand in the face of God and He will applaud you! We will all grieve the heart of the Father together! If you guys want to start looking at some things rationally, then stop badgering the people with this spirit stuff and bible stuff and all that! If you really want to get down and look at the heart of the matter, they have trust and integrity issues with this man and they can't listen to him preach. Somebody is going to have to go and maybe it *should* be them! But go ahead, put the gloves on and fight it out and you will *never* stand before God and hear Him say, *"Well done."* If they have to go or he has to go, you make it in such a way that this church is not destroyed in the process or you will never, never stand before God and hear Him say, *"Well done"*, about this issue. Forgive me!" she threw up her hands. "I was out of order but somebody had to say something. BACK UP!"

Grace's impassioned speech had brought tears to the eyes of many in the group. Several were starting to waver. Jezebel barked swift orders and a score of demons quickly moved into wedge formation and began their dark incantations of power. The serpent struck with deadly force driving Caelen to his knees under the unexpected viciousness of his attack. In a flash, the commander was overtaken and buried under a seething mass of evil spirits.

"To arms," howled Captain Darshan to his warriors. Bright blades cut a swath through the black bodies, splitting the air with their conflagration. Valin plunged after his companion wielding his weaponry with deadly accuracy as he hacked his way through the enemy. Caelen regained his feet.

Rafe quickly moved to control the situation. He was determined not to let Grace's speech deter his plan to have the board removed from their positions before the night was over. "I appreciated your passion and desire," he said, feeling his way with caution. "I can't speak because they don't trust me and so somebody had to. But when my elders are told that I lie! I want documentation of any lie that I told..."

"Come on!" retorted Ian in disgust. "You've heard it before. There's fifteen years of documents!"

Rafe threw his hands into the air. "How can I address this? I've never had a meeting yet about the issues. I've had letters that I didn't even know I was getting until the moment they were opened up. I asked them, "Can I not take a moment to look at them?" How can I address something that was thrown in my face? They wanted an answer for it right then! Talk about trust! I went from the meeting in February, told that nothing would be done 'til I got back. I trusted and my trust was seriously violated. So I'm struggling too. I shared it with my two associates and we did have prayer together," he added defensively. "I wept with this lady." He indicated Grace with a wave of his hand. "We had a very special time of prayer together."

"Pastor," interrupted Grace in disgust. "That was a five minute prayer that disrupted an intercessory prayer meeting. We have never knelt before the Lord and wept, as I've wept with these people, as messed up as you might think they are. I'm sorry," she said addressing the elders, "but there are integrity issues! There really, really are!"

Rafe's eyes flashed dangerously. He had to rescue this situation immediately from further disaster. His elders might start to believe the allegations if one of the associates backed them up. It took a herculean effort, but he put as much tenderness into his voice as he could manage.

"I don't think they're messed up. I still love them. I wasn't invited to their two prayer meetings. Well, the first one, I could say I was invited, but they knew I could not be there on a Thursday night. And another one, I was told there would be a prayer meeting before the board meeting. The way it was said," he whined, "I didn't know if they wanted me to come or not. So I didn't go. Anything I say is not believed now anyway. I'm at my wit's end! I'm trying to be scriptural. I'm trying to follow it through. It doesn't work! Hopefully the elders can mediate." The old fox sat down, satisfied that his victory was assured.

"They are not trying to mediate," stated Ian coldly. "They are trying to use a hammer to threaten us."

"We've had skilled people study the constitution," replied Rafe defiantly, "and as they looked at it they said..."

'My God, help us!" Mira's mind spun as she saw his evil plot fall into place. She knew that the fatal blow had already been struck and nothing could turn things back now. It was too late! "This isn't about the constitution!" she wailed. Misery, anger and disappointment choked her so she could scarcely speak. "It's about the trust and integrity of our pastor!"

She turned on him heatedly. The words, when they came, burst from her as if torn out of her chest. "I can't even sit under your ministry any more! My husband won't come to church because he's been told by friends of ours that you hit on a gay waiter at our daughter's wedding and that with your wife present! He's angry and upset! And I don't blame him! I don't blame him!" she repeated in a shaking voice. "I have to get out of here," she gasped, looking appealingly to the directors. "Let's go to another room. Pastor Marvin and Pastor Grace, can you please come with us? We need some counsel."

Mira turned and fled from the room. Tears spilled down her cheeks unchecked and her knees shook so that she had to grasp the railing for support. Her breath came in ragged gulps. Behind her, the other board members clattered down the stairs, followed by Rob and the associate pastors.

Kurtis appeared at the top of the stairs. He tried to stop Rob to speak with him but the deacon would have none of it. "Why won't you speak to me?" the big man challenged. "Is what she said true? I demand to know if it's true!" He advanced down the stairwell to the landing, his voice loud and insistent. "Sister Grace, I just want to talk to the board."

Grace stopped short and turned on him. Indignantly, she pointed her finger back up the stairs. "Go to your room!" Mira laughed hysterically between sobbing breaths.

The Nigerian still descended the steps. He looked huge and menacing as he repeated his request to talk with the directors. "We are willing to look into any allegations," he insisted loudly.

Grace pointed inexorably to the upper floor. "Kurtis, we both know you lied about your membership. You have no right here. Go!"

Caelen and the angelic host were still locked in vicious battle with the demonic forces. A trumpet sounded. Instantly scores of warriors melted through the walls, pouring into the room with swords drawn and shields ready. The stone walls shimmered as if they would melt with the brightness of their coming.

Weapons brandished like lightning opening a path for Caelen and Valin to escape. In a blinding flash of light, they disappeared only to reappear a split second later in the sanctuary below. Captain Darshan assigned what warriors he could spare to follow them.

~

Grace followed the little group into the main auditorium where they collapsed on the first chairs within reach. Mira was still shaking uncontrollably. "She told him to go to his room!" she shrieked, laughing and crying at the same time. It was a few minutes before everyone was composed enough to consider their next step.

"They mean to serve us with the letters of discipline tonight," Mira said finally when she had regained her composure. "I don't think we have any choice here. Either we walk away or we terminate his employment. If we go back in there and they serve us first...." Her voice trailed off.

"I don't believe they have a legal board of elders," said Jack stoutly. "Anything they do wouldn't hold up in a court of law. It's ridiculous! I say let's just fire him and get it over with."

"You have to know that if you choose to do that, in the end, it will be you guys who will be leaving, not him," Grace told them. "He has too much of a stranglehold on this place. I just want you to count the cost before you do anything irrevocable."

"It's the right thing to do," replied Donny. "The man is evil. We have the authority to fire him and I think we should do it."

"I don't care if we get thrown out of here or not," added Ian. "I won't be coming here anyway, if he stays."

"I move that we terminate his employment, effective immediately," said Mira.

Donny raised his hand. "I second the motion." In a moment, the vote was taken and it was done!

Mira took out the termination letter with trembling fingers. She was thankful that she had remembered to grab the folder that contained it before she left the meeting. Filling in the date, she quickly signed the document. The other directors all signed it as well.

"What you said up there..." Marvin looked pleadingly at Mira. "Is it true?"

Mira looked him straight in the eye. She knew what he wanted to know. "Yes, it's true. That is part of the reason that Dan has been so angry at Pastor. He feels betrayed and refuses to sit under him any more. I have been in denial over it for months. I just couldn't bring myself to accept it until I went through the archives. There is far worse in those binders and documents. That's when I realized the truth of it and it made me sick! My husband has also caught Rafe in a number of lies which the pastor claimed were only little white lies, so Dan has no use for him on that count either. I'll be lucky to ever get him inside a church again," she finished despairingly.

Pastor Marvin looked crushed. He sat shaking his head in disbelief.

"I have to go back in there to get my tape recorder and documents," said Mira tremulously. "I absolutely dread facing them again! One of us will have to serve him with the letter?"

"Jack should because he is vice-president and acting president in the absence of David Armstrong," volunteered Donny. "I'll back him as a witness."

"We'll all go," said Ian.

They entered the meeting room together. Pastor Rafe stood laughing and chatting with his elders. Mira made a beeline for her chair and swiftly threw her documents and recorder into the box while Jack and Donny approached the pastor with the letter.

"We have voted to terminate your employment. This is your official notice," announced Jack.

Rafe laughed as if they had done him a great favor. "Oh, look at this," he chortled. "They're firing me!"

Darshan's warriors fought bravely and desperately for survival in the enclosed space. Fire blazed from their weapons as they battled their deadly foe. Glee illuminated the black misshapen faces of their opponents as they sensed their enemy weakening under the sheer force of their vast number.

Rob picked up Mira's box while the directors surrounded her protectively to escort her from the room. Her heart thumped mercilessly in her chest and her knees were as weak as water. Surely everyone would see. Someone took her arm to steady her as she started down the steps.

As they reached the lobby, Tom leaned over the rail and asked them to wait a few minutes. It wasn't long before he joined them. Shaking each of their hands, he thanked them for their participation in the mediation meetings.

Grace wasn't far behind Tom. "I'll see you at home" she whispered patting Mira's shoulder comfortingly.

~

The angelic host was failing. One by one, they fell beneath the terrible onslaught of the enemy. The captain waded back and forth, reigning heavy blows on every demon within his reach. His fiery hair was plastered against his head, corrosive black fluid sticking to him like sin. *Where are the commanders?* he thought wildly. *We are going to fall.*

Suddenly, a high shout and a thrilling blast from a shofar cut through the mayhem around him. Looking up, Darshan saw Michael. The powerful archangel bore down on the seething mass of angels and demons like a blazing star of destruction. Behind him streaked Caelen and Valin. Scattering the foe before them, like firebrands in the wind, they hurtled toward the evil commanders. The force of their momentum slammed the creatures to the ground in a shattering concussion. Locked together, in a deadly struggle with limbs flailing, they rolled through the pulsating company of demons and angels.

Captain Darshan felt God-given strength pour into his being. With a roar he leaped upon the enemy, defying arrows and ruinous weapons. The fallen warriors stumbled to their feet and fought with renewed vigor.

The high angel, Michael, flanked by the two commanders, continued his relentless attack bearing grimly and deliberately down upon the two dark leaders, Python and Jezebel. He ignored the fiery darts of the enemy, brushing them aside as if they were inconsequential gnats. Jezebel's face was livid with surprise and rage. Unclean spirits, like putrid frogs, spewed from his great jaws. His massive claws, bent in clenched frenzy, scrabbled for a stranglehold on his elusive prey. With a loud cry, the archangel plunged his sword into the thick, leathery hide of the beast burying it to the hilt.

The shofar blew two long blasts. Captain Darshan signalled his troops to withdraw. Michael withdrew his weapon and slammed it again with powerful force, this time, into the coiled body of the mammoth serpent. Then he raised the sword with a glorious cry to the heavens. In a split second, the whole host of angelic warriors had extricated themselves from the boiling horde of demons. With a great shout they disappeared in a brilliant flash of pure white light. The demon horde howled and shrieked in impotent fury at their disappearing foe.

~

Mira walked into her house as if in a dream. The reality of what had happened still hadn't caught up to her. Dan looked up as she entered the kitchen. "What happened?" he asked.

"We fired him!" she announced dazedly.

"Praise the Lord! God will bless you for it!" was his answer.

Grace came through the door a few minutes later. "What a night!" she said plopping herself down in a chair. "Can you believe that Rafe suggested prayer to close the meeting after you guys left? It's true," she said, seeing Mira's look of disbelief. "I told him that it was a little late for that now."

They sat and shared the night's events over steaming hot cups of tea. Dan whistled about the kitchen as he whipped them up something to eat. It was almost midnight when the phone rang. Startled, Mira picked it up to hear Dora's voice on the other end. "I just had to call you to congratulate you and the board for what you did this evening. I am so proud of you," she said. Quick tears came to Mira's eyes and a lump rose in her throat.

"I think you broke something in the spirit world over the church tonight," Dora continued. "This is something that should have been done years ago but we didn't have the guts. I just want to say – thank you. I don't know if anyone else will understand what you've been through, but I do and anytime you want to talk, I'm here."

Although the mediator's heartfelt comments stunned Mira, they were exactly what she needed to hear. She took it as a confirmation from the Lord that the board had done the right thing and that meant the world to her. Exhausted as she was, her adrenalin was pumping too high to allow much sleep that night. Before she sought her bed, she sent an e-mail to Darren Amos telling him about the action the board had taken.

27

Mira woke on Good Friday with scarcely the strength to crawl out of bed. Before she was able to drink her second cup of tea, she heard the warning buzzer on her computer signal an incoming e-mail. It was from Darren, assuring her that he would prepare a *"no trespass"* letter to warn Rafe that if he disrupted a service, appropriate action could be taken to enforce his removal from the church premises.

Mira decided against attending the Good Friday service. She had no heart for it after what had happened the previous evening. Grace was obliged to go but returned to the Grant home disgusted and shocked over the spectacle that took place on what should have been the most holy weekend of the year for Christians. In her hands she carried a tape of the service which Rob given her as she left the building. Mira and Dan settled down to watch it with her.

Pastor Rutherford had opened the service in direct defiance of his termination. Wasting little time on preliminaries, he had moved forward with his planned agenda immediately following the singing. He had chosen one of his newly appointed elders to implement his carefully staged propaganda. Sporting his best black suit, Jimmy LaCross had ponderously made his way to the platform, his sombre appearance and grave countenance giving him an almost funereal air. This was exacerbated by the dirge-like tune that Eve played on the organ throughout his entire speech.

Jimmy conveyed to his audience that he was there to address the various rumors that were circulating in the church. "Pastor Rutherford has come under personal attack by some members of the board of directors," he said solemnly. "This all happened while he was absent which is regretful. This situation has been handled by the board of elders, the details of which will be disclosed at the annual business meeting on Wednesday."

"Yesterday," he continued, "the pastor was asked to resign and to have no further contact with the members of this church. The letter he was given dictated that he must have all of his belongings removed from the house in just a few days. We would appreciate it if everyone would be involved in the annual meeting."

Mira watched the tape in disbelief. "He lied! We never asked them to be out of the house in a few days. They have three months or longer if they want! How could he lie like that?"

"I know," replied Grace indignantly. "Everyone is angry and upset and you can't blame them after what he said!"

"We'll just have to make a statement of our own," Mira flashed, "and expose the lie! What else can we do?"

She called the other board members but, not surprisingly, none of them had attended the service. After she hung up the phone, she noticed an e-mail on her computer from a woman who was a faithful church member. Although Nina Perry was a close friend of Faith and Rob Samuels, Mira knew her only slightly. She had always struck her as straightforward and honest; someone who spoke her mind freely and would brook no nonsense or subterfuge. The note was brief, asking Mira to read an attached letter which she had written and sent to Pastor Rutherford. "May God have mercy on us all," she ended.

Mira opened the attachment curious as to the letter's content. In it, Nina highlighted how heart broken she was over the "God forbidden" statement that Jimmy had seen fit to read in the morning service. She did not believe a word of it, she stated, and it was hard for her to see that her beloved pastor made no move to prevent it.

"The platform is not a temporal battleground," she wrote. *"I fear that all the elders have done is to cause a big split in my church. Pastor, your*

lack of action has wounded my spirit deeper than anything I have ever experienced." Nina went on to say that due to her losing faith in the leadership, she could not let her name stand for the board nominations on Wednesday. She reaffirmed her love for the pastor and his wife but shared that the Holy Spirit had spoken to her, letting her know that she had put them on a pedestal and been guilty of worshipping them. *"Last night,"* she said, *"I experienced a horrible feeling in my spirit and knew that something was terribly wrong. I haven't been able to shake it and now I know why. I heard the lies this morning! Those involved will be required to give an account for what they have done,"* she wrote, *"and the church will never prosper with this kind of thing going on."*

Nina ended the letter saying that she still loved her pastor but hoped that he would find his way back to being the man of integrity that she had known and loved these many years. Telling him not to contact her, she asked that her letter be read to the church council so they could see first-hand how a poor decision could cause much pain and damage to the faithful.

When Rafe received Nina's letter, he e-mailed her immediately pleading that she meet with him in order to learn from his own lips the gravity of the situation he had been placed in. He admitted that Jimmy had misquoted the board's letter and assured her it would be rectified.

Nina decided that perhaps it would benefit her to talk to her pastor directly so she agreed to the meeting. She had found it painful to listen to him defend his actions and those of his elder board, while maligning the reputations of the directors.

Rafe, for his part, was very concerned that Nina and her family might possibly leave the church. That could translate into quite a drop in finances since they were all generous givers. Knowing that she held a strong bond of friendship with Rob and Faith Samuels, Rafe devised a plan to drive a wedge between them. This he did without any qualm of conscience, feeling that Rob deserved what he got since he was one of the ringleaders in the revolt against him.

Toward the end of the meeting, Rafe found an opportunity to cunningly plant a seed of doubt in Nina's mind against his former deacon. "The Lord revealed to me that Rob has problems with the internet," he insinuated craftily, stopping just short of accusing him of dabbling in pornography. He left the implication to do its dirty work, well aware that Rob and Faith were surrogate grandparents to Nina's granddaughter.

Nina now knew beyond a shadow of a doubt that Pastor Rafe had indeed lost his way. Catching him twisting the truth more than once, she realized that he was not the man she had thought him to be all of these years. Before she left, she implored him to abstain from saying or doing anything that would desecrate the sanctity of the Easter Sunday services and managed to wring the required promise from him.

Later, as she mulled the interview over in her head, she decided it would be best to lay any doubts to rest. Even if what he had said about Rob were true, her pastor's purpose in revealing such a thing struck her as unscrupulous. She suspected there was a corrupt motive behind it. Going straight to Faith, Nina told her squarely about the accusation against Rob. Faith was both incensed and bewildered that her pastor and friend would say such a thing about her husband. After stewing over it awhile, Faith told Rob what Rafe had said.

"Faith," her husband replied, looking her straight in the eye, "I have never used the internet for anything other than my business. I have no interest in pornography! To the best of my ability, I have always tried to do what is right in the sight of the Lord, ever since I accepted Him into my heart and made Him my Savior. We have sat at that man's table almost every Sunday for ten years. We have helped them entertain and we've cleaned up after them. From what I've seen and felt in my spirit, Rafe is the one with the *"internet"* problem, not me! Do you realize I could have his license for this! His only purpose was to estrange us from Nina and her family because he knows that we are considered second grandparents to her grandchild. That's just about as low as anyone can get! I really fear for his soul if he doesn't repent and get himself right with the Lord! What he has done is just more proof to me how truly dishonourable he is!"

~

On Saturday afternoon, Grace received a phone call from Pastor Rafe asking her to come to the church immediately. Shortly after her departure, Jack, Donny and Ian arrived at Mira's home for an emergency board meeting. Together, they worked on the preparation of a memo which would inform the four newly-appointed elders that their induction meeting had been illegal, according to both the constitution and legal counsel. They sited the lack of a proper quorum and the non-membership of one of them as valid grounds for not recognizing the appointments. In the last paragraph, they included a reminder that Pastor Rutherford had been legally terminated from his position and had no authority to make decisions on behalf of the church.

When the memo had been completed to everyone's satisfaction, they discussed the damage that had been done on Good Friday and the rising anger of the congregation against the board. Realizing this would only escalate leading up to the annual business meeting, they decided to draft a statement to rebut Jimmy's lie that the board was throwing the pastor and his wife out of the house in three days. They struggled with the dilemma of how to present the statement. Eventually, they resolved not to stoop to the pastor's level and try to read it in the sanctuary, but rather to hand it out quietly to the congregation at the door as they entered the lobby on Sunday morning.

In the middle of their discussion, Grace burst through the door. "He's fired me," she exclaimed breathlessly. Her voice trembled and tears were close to the surface. She threw a letter onto the table. It carried the signatures of each of the new board of elders with the exception of David Armstrong, who abstained. Pastor Rafe's name was at the bottom.

"I haven't done one thing to deserve this," she cried. "I preached the Word of God and tried to help the people." The tears she had been trying to restrain tumbled down her cheeks. "Look at this! I gave hours of my time to Sylvester and still he signed this unholy document against me."

"Grace, you're not fired!" exclaimed Mira. "All of those elders are illegal except David and Sylvester and the pastor is terminated so he has no authority. Your contract isn't finished until May 5th. Pastor Rafe will be delivered a legal *"no trespass"* order today so you will likely have to preach the Easter service."

The phone rang. It was Rob asking that the board put a package in place for his wife. "She can't go back to work if Rafe remains," he said. "She's a mess right now. I can't get her to stop crying."

"We'll take care of it right now," Mira promised.

The directors hammered out an acceptable agreement, allowing Faith two months stress leave and a settlement package at the end of that time, in the event that the pastor was still there. Mira prepared the appropriate memos for the Samuels and the church accounting office after which she drafted the statement that was to be distributed the next morning. The four directors affixed their signatures and adjourned the meeting with prayer. Jack and Ian offered to deliver the *"no trespass"* order together that very evening.

The sun shone brightly on Easter Sunday morning but Mira didn't enjoy the drive to the church. She was nearly sick with nervousness when she entered the main lobby but Pastor Rutherford was nowhere to be seen. Quickly, she ran the copies of the statements for Jack and Donny to pass out. Thankfully they had also arrived early, along with Ian.

Each of the directors found a letter in their folders from the elders attempting to relieve them of their positions. These were obviously the infamous disciplinary letters they had expected to serve on them at the mediation meeting for they were dated the 5th.

There was also a short list of new members approved by the elders in Mira's folder. They consulted briefly over the names agreeing to allow the memberships with the exception of Kurtis Oluwa. They felt his membership was suspect after his recent untruths regarding his application, coupled with the fact that he did not support the church with tithes and offerings, which was one of the requirements of membership. A letter would be given to inform him of his rejection by the board of directors and welcome him to re-apply in six months time.

The Samuels arrived together and Mira followed Faith into her office to give her the memo regarding the package the board had set up for her, if required. "Why did you even come in?" she asked her.

"I had to finish up a couple of things that I left hanging and I'm supposed to run the overheads today," she replied unhappily.

Captain Darshan had filtered a small number of warriors into the sanctuary but many of his angels had been excluded. The magnitude of the evil force they encountered upon entering was monstrous. It exuded a palpable power that told the commanders that Python was undoubtedly in the house along with the formidable demon-master, Jezebel. Imps of darkness and wicked spirits hissed and clawed at the heavenly beings as they passed by.

The angels knew they were vastly outnumbered. Their orders from the captain had been clear. Do not engage the enemy! Protect the board at all costs! Do whatever you can to provide some protection for the praying saints.

Caelen felt impotent and helpless in the face of this enormous tide of demonic power. His sword glowed faintly at his side but he knew better than to draw it without a powerful reason in this formidable stronghold of Satan. He adjusted his shield cautiously sending a warning signal to Valin who was nervously fingering his weapon. The dark-skinned commander dropped his hand to his side.

Mira was about to leave the office when Phyllis Gasher hurtled through the door, with fire in her eye; a virtual tempest of fury. The angry woman raged and screamed calling Mira a matriarchal witch and accusing her of attempting a coup to overthrow dear Pastor. "You and that sister-in-law of yours are after the property here," she screamed pointing her finger at Mira.

"Phyllis," said Faith firmly, interrupting her tirade, "this is not the time or the place for this. I'll have to ask you to leave."

The woman leaned over desk while Mira retreated in shock before her vitriolic frenzy. She was practically incoherent with rage. The secretary rose and walked toward the door, stepping protectively in front of Mira. Again she asked the woman to leave. Half crazed, Phyllis tried to step around Faith in order to get her angry claws into Mira.

Faith's voice rose in indignation. "This is not appropriate behavior in church on the Lord's Day! Please leave my office immediately!" But the woman was so far gone that she had to be physically pushed through the doorway. Faith locked the door with a snap and then slid shaking into her chair.

Mira felt sick inside. The only words she had been able to speak were, "You just don't understand." She felt dirty and violated, almost as if she had been raped. Through the glass door she saw Phyllis spitefully rip the Women's Ministry poster off the wall. Seething over Grace's picture prominently displayed as the next speaker, she tore it in half and stomped it under her feet in the lobby in full view of everyone.

Grace had come to church at Mira and Dan's urging. "You're going to have to preach this morning," Dan had said confidently. Mira wasn't so sure but as it turned out her husband was correct. Pastor Rafe had decided not to flaunt the "*no trespass*" order by preaching so he slipped unobtrusively into the building and surreptitiously hauled Grace into the fellowship hall to ask her to take the service.

"I thought you fired me," she said, looking him squarely in the eye.

"I didn't have anything to do with that," he whined. "That was the elder board, not me."

"Let Pastor Marvin take the service," she replied stubbornly.

"He really isn't capable...I mean.... he doesn't do so well at the last minute." Rafe looked at her appealingly.

"Alright, I'll preach," she promised shortly.

That morning, in honor of Easter, there was a special presentation with banners and dancing during the praise and worship portion of the service. Mira knew the woman who organized it fairly well, having worked with her previously on a large convention. As the banners paraded by her aisle, the woman slipped out of line and throwing her arms around Mira, she hugged her close.

"Hang in there, honey," she whispered softly. "What you're doing is pleasing to the Lord. The outcome, you just have to leave with Him."

After what she had experienced with Phyllis earlier, the unexpected kindness moved her as nothing else could have, in the harsh atmosphere that pervaded the room. Tears spilled from her eyes and sobs tore at her throat. The woman allowed the parade she had organized to pass her by, while she drew an overwrought Mira out of the sanctuary and into the fellowship room. Here she spent time praying with her and speaking words of encouragement until Mira felt calmer. When they finally returned to the sanctuary, Mira slipped into an empty seat beside her daughter and son-in-law.

Powerful wedges of demons traversed the aisles of the big auditorium, chanting their mighty incantations. They howled and yammered incessantly building in savage frenzy to a deafening roar. Great black vultures swooped over the crowd spewing fire and venom, relentlessly coercing the will of the hapless people, inspiring hatred in their midst.

When Grace took her place on the platform to minister, she almost wished she hadn't been so quick to agree to speak that morning. Rafe had been on the phone rallying the troops and stirring them into near frenzy with his lies. The auditorium was three quarters full of hard, angry, upset people; a difficult crowd to preach to. They glowered fiercely at Grace as she brought a brief Resurrection message. Mira was proud of her sister-in-law. She preached well, in spite of great opposition, allowing no trace of a political agenda to seep into her sermon.

When Grace was finished, Eve Rutherford immediately stepped to the podium and called for the elders and deacons to join her. Deliberately, she named each one, purposefully omitting Rob Samuels. When he saw what was about to take place, Rob, who was taping the morning service, popped out the sermon tape and replaced it with a fresh one.

Solemnly, the men lined up across the stage in their dark suits. David Armstrong fidgeted nervously, hopping from one foot to the other, while Sylvester looked uncomfortably at the carpet. Pierre stared blindly toward one side of the room. One of the parishioners, an old man who liked the spotlight, but unfortunately not part of the favored group, grabbed a microphone and droned on confusedly while the rest suffered in silence.

After he was finished, a letter of censure against the board of directors was read by the wife of the elder who had sent his proxy to the illegal elder induction meeting. Mira felt sad that none of the elders or their wives had cared to talk with her or any other member of the board. They had known her for many years and to be publicly humiliated and misjudged was a hard thing to suffer through.

Tad Booker was next and he informed the audience that they should all be present at the annual business meeting on Wednesday to take care of the two rebellious board members, Jack and Mira, who still had another year to serve, by a free vote. He then invited two men from the congregation to join them on the platform, proclaiming them to be advisors to the elders, Wilhelm Hahn and Rev. Ben Vicente. The latter sang on a semi-regular basis in the choir on Sunday evenings with his wife. It was unusual for him to be there on a Sunday morning as he held an associate position in another church.

While the two elderly men were making their way to the platform, Tad told the congregation that the propaganda distributed by the board that morning was ungodly and untruthful. He urged them again to come out on Wednesday to hear the details that would bring godliness back to the church.

Ben Vicente was next on the agenda. "This church is governed by a constitution," he explained, "and there has arisen a situation involving Pastor Rutherford and his board of directors. The church council is the highest governing body in the church structure. These people are all elected by you, the members," he stated impressively.

"No they're not, are they?" whispered Krysta to Mira.

"No, only the directors are elected. The rest are appointed by the pastor," Mira replied.

Phyllis Gasher leaned forward. Mira hadn't noticed that she was sitting right behind them. "Shhhhhh. Keep quiet!" She shook her finger at them angrily.

Krysta turned around and gave her a look. "I will not keep quiet!" she retorted.

Ben continued, trying to choose his words carefully. "After a series of meetings on how to resolve the issues between the pastor and the board, there was a serious disagreement between council at a meeting on Thursday evening. Now the constitution says there must be agreement but four members of the board decided, on their own, that other remedies had to be taken."

He stopped and looked out at the congregation. "By the way, I'm not judging anyone. I'm just reporting the facts. Pastor Rutherford has not been dismissed by the church council." His voice dripped with sarcasm. "The directors went to a lawyer and found out that, as directors of the corporation, *under the law....*" he stressed the phrase, giving it bold emphasis. "*Under the law,* they have the right to fire the pastor. This is not church law or council law. This is a governmental law. By the way, I spoke with my son-in-law about it. He was a former president of the board here. As a matter of fact he wrote our constitution."

"That's not true," whispered Mira gripping her purse until her knuckles turned white. Krysta reached over to hold her hand. "His son-in-law had another document prepared. He didn't want this one that was drawn up by Darren Amos. He said it took too much power away from the pastor and he warned Rafe last year not to allow it to go forward."

Ben's tone was cynical. "*Under the law,*" he drawled again, "an employer has a right to fire an employee without any cause." He raised his hand dramatically. "A corporation is sovereign in this respect. So Pastor Rafe was fired. Now who fired him?" He pointed theatrically at the people. "*You* did!" he bellowed. "The board is elected by you! What they did is perfectly legal..." His disdain could be felt to the back of the room.

"It's perfectly *legal* under corporate law," he continued, emphasizing the word "*legal*" as if it were something dirty. They did nothing illegal and in their wisdom, we must not judge their motives. That would be propaganda. I will not engage in propaganda. I'll give you the truth and the facts and let them speak for themselves. Examine them in your heart and before the Lord and then make your decision. Yesterday evening, two of the directors knocked at the door..."

Eve interrupted. "They didn't knock, they just walked in."

"Oh...well, they have that right," he chuckled sardonically. "They *are* the directors, after all." Mira caught a disgusted shake of the head and a murmur from the row where Jack and Amy Johnson sat. She knew it wasn't true that they had just walked into the parsonage without knocking.

"The letter delivered came from a lawyer hired by the directors. They have every right, as your elected officials, to take this action. It says that his termination is lawful. That's correct, according to the law," he stated ponderously, "however, the elders here say that the constitution has been violated. The board of directors will continue in office until replaced by the member's vote at the next general meeting."

He laid the letter down. "What remedy can you take to bring about your wishes? Well," he paused for effect, "the directors were voted in by you - the members - and the only remedy you have is to vote them out. You must look at the facts, the legal requirements, but the only say you have, is to get out and vote." He handed the microphone to Jimmy LaCross.

Jimmy looked somberly out over the congregation. "I would like to extend Pastor Rafe's greetings to you on this Resurrection morning. On behalf of the board of elders, I would move that all who wish to express their support for Pastor Rutherford will, by a show of hands and voice, demonstrate that support. Do I have a seconder?" The confused old man who had spoken first raised his hand. Eve pointed him out and Jimmy nodded in recognition. "Those who wish to support the pastor will now rise and show their support," proclaimed Jimmy solemnly.

People stood all over the sanctuary, clapping and shouting for the pastor. A pang went through Mira's heart as she saw many that she considered good friends stand and applaud. Even one of her closest friends, Sunni, stood. When the noise died down, she was startled by a voice behind her raised in righteous wrath.

Nina Perry stood a few steps away in the main aisle. From that position she was addressing the group on the platform. "Excuse me," she said, raising her voice to almost a shout in order to be heard. "I don't think that was right. This is not the time or place for this! It is the most holy day of the year for Christians and this is wrong!"

"You're out of order," said Wilhelm who was now standing at the podium. Rob, in the sound booth, reached over and turned off his microphone.

"No, you're out of order," shouted Jack. "She's right! This is wrong!"

Phyllis Gasher's harsh scream cut through the murmuring voices of the people. "Sit down. *You're* out of order." She pointed her bony finger at Nina.

Krysta turned around and told Phyllis to be quiet. Mira clutched at her daughter's skirt. "Never mind, Hon. Just let it go." Jason got to his feet. He'd seen enough. "So long," he said raising his hand in a stiff salute to the platform. Mira watched him go with sinking heart.

Nina threw up her hands and turned on her heel. Several of her family members followed. As they passed through the lobby they were heard to say that they would never be back. Their Easter worship had been destroyed.

Wilhelm was tapping his mike in frustration. Finally Pastor Marvin went back to the sound booth and turned it back on. Rob sat innocently by the tape recorder.

"Can you hear me now?" came the thick German accent. "I have been a member of this church for many years ever since it began," he said, ignoring his six year absence completely. "I feel very saddened after all of the victories we have had under Pastor Rafe's ministry that there is such a vindictive witch hunt going on against him. They are supposed to make every effort to restore, reconcile and forgive, according to the constitution. The agenda of this board has been to get rid of the pastor and force him to agree to all of their conditions. This is very, very sick and it has nothing to do with legality. It might be legally correct but it is not morally right."

Eve Rutherford stepped forward next to take her place behind the pulpit. "Needless to say, I am heartsick that we have come to this place today. I have been talking for a year about retiring. I told the board this on Saturday. I'm not going to get into the things that were said but I want you to know that they were aware that we are going to leave. If you come over to the house, I've got boxes packed. It was all in place – all in order. We did not have to come to this, dear ones. God is not pleased."

Her voice trembled. "God is not pleased," she repeated pointing her finger at the audience. "Now, whether we are allowed to stay and say goodbye to you as we had planned, is up to you. We love you with all of our heart. It's time, dear ones, but there is a proper way to do things. I realize that there have been complaints about the pastor. I could complain about him every day."

"Let me be clear," she continued, "there have been no accusations – only complaints. If the people with the complaints had just come to mama, I would have talked to them. I would have done my best to look after their complaints. My heart goes out to you if you feel that you have been neglected and that no one has cared for you. My heart breaks for you and I would have done my very best for you because I have a mother's heart. So the complaints piled up and this has all happened as a result of that. I'm in line too. I've got complaints, but I know how to take care of them and I would have helped you to take care of yours too." The people clapped wildly, stomping their feet and shouting their support.

"Thank you," she replied placidly. "You will say who you want to run this church. You will say if you want Pastor out. We have to go by the letter, so tomorrow he has to empty everything out of his office." She pointed at the organ. "That organ is mine, so that's got to go. The organ in the fellowship hall is ours so that has to go. I hope that doesn't have to happen. I hope that we can take the time to say goodbye. After fifteen years, I think we should expect some privilege." Again the people clapped and roared.

"Thank you." She looked out over the crowd. "You, who are the board – I have loved you dearly. I trust that you will allow us to have this time to look after our affairs and that things will be done decently and in order."

A man went to the platform. Mira didn't recognize him. "I can't be here on Wednesday night but my vote is with the pastor," he said. "I think we should remove those that have caused this insurrection in the church. You've had the privilege of an elected office and you are not willing to serve God." He glared self righteously at the people searching the audience for the unhappy board members. "Leave then and take the devil with you," he bellowed.

A great wave of exuberant shouting followed as the people were swept up in the roar of the tide. Another stranger, an Egyptian man, rushed to the stage. "Satan is gaining ground in the land. We are privileged to have a pastor such as this here. What is happening should not be allowed."

Who is this? thought Mira, *I've never seen him before.*

Krysta leaned over and whispered," Let's get out of here. I can't take any more of this. I need to find out where Jason went." They gathered up their things just as the man launched into a full blown harangue, shaking his finger at the crowd, which was now thinning considerably.

As they slipped out into the aisle, a friend of Mira's leaned over and said in a nasty tone, "How could you do this to Pastor? How could you, after all he's done for you!"

Mira hesitated a moment by her side but she could tell from the anger in her face that the woman was in no mood to listen. "You don't understand!" was all she could choke out. Then she turned and fled from the auditorium. Her last view was of Eve leaning on the pulpit drumming her fingers restlessly while Tad tried to pry the mike away from the Egyptian man who determinedly held on.

"Have you lost the Spirit of the Lord, here?" he shouted. He likened the directors to those that would crucify Jesus. "I'm warning you, don't do this mistake," he said, jabbing his finger after every word. "If this pastor leaves the church, we are the loser but if he stays, we are the winner. We hired the board and we have the right to dismiss the board, not our great pastor. God bless you."

The clapping was less enthusiastic this time. Tad stepped up again to inform the crowd that if they couldn't attend the annual meeting, they should pick up a proxy vote and signify their intent clearly on it. He encouraged as many members as possible to be there and asked that they keep their emotions in check. "We want to conduct the meeting as

Christ would," he ended, handing the mike back to Eve to conduct the closing prayer.

The elders hung about the lobby after the service to urge those who were not members to sign forms so they could vote at the meeting in a couple of days. There was no pretense of trying to adhere to the constitutional requirements for membership. They were beyond that now.

28

THE NEXT TWO DAYS were a blur of e-mails and phone calls in preparation for the annual business meeting. Mira worked on drafting an acceptable statement for the board to read. She talked to Pastor Marvin about whether he also wished a package put in place for him by the outgoing board but he declined.

She called Darren and urged him and the employment lawyer to present their final bills so that the current board could sign the checks before entering the meeting on Wednesday night. If he waited, there might not be a legal board in place and signing authority at the bank would likely be changed immediately. He agreed, given the circumstances, it was probably a good idea and promptly e-mailed her the bill which she forwarded to Ina.

More time was spent preparing the church's annual financial statements and budget. For accuracy on historical data, Mira decided to check the charity's annual returns posted on the government website. A thought occurred to her as she was scribbling down the information she required. Pastor Rafe had his own personal charity. She didn't know much about it, other than the regular monthly checks she signed, payable to his ministry for some missionary endeavor he was involved in.

Out of curiosity, she typed in the name that he used. Sure enough, she found it!

"I wonder who is on his board of director's," she murmured as she clicked through the documents. "Johanna Hanes!" She cried the name aloud and Dan came running. "Can you believe it? Pastor Rafe has someone with Alzheimer's on his board!" She shook her head incredulously. "Unbelievable!"

When Mira had completed the financial statements, she e-mailed them to Ina and requested copies for the members. This was one budget they wouldn't be happy with, she thought grimly.

On Tuesday evening, the night before the annual meeting, the board reconvened to tidy up the last minute details. They discussed the board statement at some length, adding and deleting passages, until each one was satisfied that it addressed all of the issues and clearly and concisely stated the unethical and immoral practices of the pastor. When it was completed to their satisfaction they each signed the final copy and Mira sent it off to the lawyer.

At Grace's request, they voted to terminate her contract offering a full buyout through to May 5th. Mira prepared the memos and e-mailed them to Ina, requesting that all of the required checks be prepared for the board's signature the next evening.

Pastor Rafe was busy Tuesday evening as well. Another elders meeting was called to ratify the appointment of the new elders a second time. He made sure that Sylvester was present. Pastor Marvin was asked to e-mail Mira with the results of the meeting. Tad Booker, Larry Chaput, and Jimmy LaCross were appointed a second time and Kurtis Oluwa was also chosen upon completion of his membership. Wilhelm Hahn would serve as advisor until July when he would be received into office. Apparently he didn't qualify for office at this time due to a recent personal bankruptcy which wouldn't be discharged until then.

On Wednesday morning, Mira boxed up everything that belonged to the church including her ring of church keys, office supplies, the official board book containing the minutes for the year along with several other related binders. The mediation letters, documents and tapes, she put away in a safe place along with copies she had made of certain sensitive files from the church archives. Pastor Rafe had threatened a law suit and she wanted to be sure that she had adequate back-up in case of court action in the future. Dora had warned her that Rafe was asking how to go about getting rid of the John Schilling file and any other archived documents that put him in a bad light.

Both mediators had been in touch since the final meeting to request that she finish the minutes of the mediation meetings as soon as possible. They wanted the tapes and any remaining packets still in her possession to be turned over to them to be destroyed.

"Rafe is behind it," said her husband. "Don't give them anything! He wants the stuff destroyed because it is damning evidence against him. If he should ever decide to sue, you'll need it."

"Well..." Mira debated thoughtfully. "I can see your point. The truth is, I'm too exhausted right now to spend the huge number of hours it will take to go through those tapes and transcribe them. I need a break! I'll get to them when I feel like it and not a minute before. You know what?" she added. "I don't have to turn over the tapes and documents until the minutes are approved anyway. That was the agreement. To have them approved, they first have to be typed and then all of us who were involved in the mediation have to meet to approve them. Good luck on that!" She laughed bitterly. "We're going to be done after tonight so I don't know how anyone is going to pull that one off!"

Late in the afternoon Mira received a phone call from Darren. He was concerned that the board's statement was much too provocative to be read. He had consulted with a lawyer friend and was warned that it could provide fodder for a slander suit against the directors personally. He urged Mira to allow him to prepare a blander statement in order to protect them.

"But the people need to know details," she implored. "They need to understand the gravity of the situation if they choose to keep this unethical man as their leader. We have been slandered by him and his group. We should stand up and tell the truth!"

"I know how you feel," he replied, "and my heart goes out to each of you. When I was sitting in church on Good Friday, all I could think about was the terrible situation your church is faced with. If it didn't break confidentiality, I would have felt impelled to seek counseling myself, from my own pastor. I have never been involved in anything like this in a church. However, my primary concern is for the directors. Two have successful businesses and you all have homes and much to lose if you should be sued," he pleaded. "Some of the comments in your statement could be construed as slanderous."

"Even if they are true?" queried Mira indignantly

"One never knows the outcome of litigation of this kind. My friend and I both feel that the risk to all of you personally is too great. I know you want to have your say but ultimately remember that God will have His way no matter which statement is read. The timing may not be ours, but truth has a way coming out eventually. We don't have much time. Will you let me do this?"

Reluctantly, Mira agreed to allow him to prepare the statement. She shed some bitter tears over it but felt that she couldn't knowingly risk Donny and Jack's businesses and all of their homes and savings for a few moments satisfaction. She closeted herself in her bedroom and prayed it through until she had peace in her heart again. She had fasted the whole day to ready her herself for the trial she knew she must face that evening.

With a heavy heart she prepared her formal resignations for the various positions she held in the church - director and secretary-treasurer of the board, president of Women's Ministries, and lastly, her and Dan's resignation from the church membership. Finally she was finished! Everything was in order. Nothing had been overlooked or forgotten.

Dan drove Mira to the church early. Together, they carried the boxes of supplies and binders into the building and dumped them on a desk in Ina's office. Mira dug out her keys and handed them to Pastor Marvin who came in to give her a hug and some encouraging words. Ina sat quietly at her desk, her eyes red and swollen. The checks were ready in a folder for signatures.

People were already starting to arrive although the hour was early. Excitement permeated the atmosphere. Mira scurried to put away the contents of the box safely in the archive room. By the time she returned to Ina's office, Jack, Donny and Ian had all arrived. Donny walked over to Ina and gave her a hug.

"At least someone still cares about me," she murmured. Mira felt stricken. She had always worked well with the bookkeeper and held no animosity toward her whatsoever. She went to give her a hug as well.

"It's been nice working with you," she said striving to keep her composure. "You've always been quick to provide me with everything I needed and I appreciate it." She turned away abruptly, tears close to the surface, and busied herself with the signing of the checks that Ina had prepared.

Darren had asked to meet with the board privately before the meeting to go over his prepared statement. As soon as he arrived, Mira handed him his check and they all trouped downstairs. "What is that awful smell?" asked Darren as they walked through the lower hallway. Mira explained that sometimes the sewers backed up when too much water drained into the septic system. "How appropriate," he exclaimed with a chuckle.

The board decided that Mira should be the one to read the statement before the church. They weren't happy with the last minute change to a different document but all finally agreed that it was probably for the best. Tom interrupted them to ask Darren some procedural questions. Both the board and the pastor had agreed to let Tom chair the meeting. It seemed the best way to maintain order. Darren would sit close by in the event of any legal issue being raised.

When they reached the lobby, there was a line-up of people crowding the doorway of the main sanctuary. Mira waited until the line thinned before checking in at the member's registry desk. Complaints were already mounting from those malcontents who didn't have their name on the list. Mira heard someone say that they had signed a membership form that very day. She apprised Darren and Tom of the problem and told them that the voting would have to be strictly controlled as the room was full of strangers and infrequent attendees.

Grace pulled Mira aside to tell her that she had seen Phyllis Gasher and had told her she forgave her for the nasty e-mail and for ripping her poster off the wall. Phyllis had gone up like a flame. "I never asked her to forgive me!" she exclaimed to her friend. "I don't want her forgiveness."

Grace laughed over it. "I'm glad I did it. What she said and did has no power to hurt me anymore." The two of them walked together into the main auditorium. Spotting her husband sitting among a few friendly faces over in the far left section of the room, Mira made her way in that direction. Grace disappeared into the sound booth which gave her a better vantage point to view the proceedings.

A little lady whom Mira knew quite well waved her over. "I just need to know if you really feel that what you did was the right thing and you had no other choice," she whispered. Mira quietly assured her that such was the case. She gave her a hug and moved away, finally slipping into the seat beside her husband with a sigh of relief, grateful that she hadn't suffered a verbal assault such as happened on Sunday.

Pastor Marvin took his place at the piano and prepared to open the service with some praise and worship. "My goodness," he said as he looked out over the audience, "wouldn't it be nice to have you all in church on Sunday."

The rebuke passed unnoticed. The air was filled with excitement and, for the most part, the people's rebellious attitude was almost tangible. They would not be denied! Some came for the show, their curiosity whetted by the phone calls from Pastor Rutherford, hoping for dirt and scandal. Others came for blood - the board's blood. They were defiant, bitter and angry, wanting a spectacle made of those who dared to question the motives and integrity of their beloved prophet.

Demons filled the sanctuary. Their number had increased exponentially feeding off the insolent, unruly crowd that came thirsting for scandal. They frolicked in the aisles and across the platform. Swooping back and forth over the heads of the throng, they sprayed a thick coating of black corrosion wherever they went.

Backbiting, Criticism and Gossip were having a heyday. Their cruel poisonous darts flew in every direction, finding ready marks among the people. Demons of unforgiveness vomited their toxic malevolent bile with abandon. Resentment, Hatred and Strife shot arrows tipped with cruel, venomous barbs. Most of their weapons reached their target. Superiority and Pride fastened their deadly suction cups onto their victims with savage glee.

Caelen and Valin brought a small band of warriors with them under the command of Captain Darshan but there was little they could accomplish among the people. Their mandate was to provide protection for the four board members and strengthen them for the ordeal ahead.

Worship was frenzied but flat – a lot of hoopla with no substance. The usual few danced and screeched but it was as hollow as an empty drum. Grace caught Mira's eye from the sound booth. She smiled and waved encouragement.

Kurtis took a seat at the very back of the room and prepared to tape the show with a camera. *Darren was right,* Mira thought when she saw what he was doing. *He thinks he will capture something damaging to use against us in court.* She smiled grimly to herself. *Thank the Lord for sending us a godly lawyer!*

When the singing ended, Tom Storey took his position at a small podium which been placed on the auditorium floor just below the big pulpit. He explained his presence as chairman and moderator for the evening. He clarified that the voting would occur only after statements were made by the board of directors and the pastor. He started by inviting the president of the board, David Armstrong to give the usual president's report.

Mira knew her turn was coming next. She gripped her binder with white knuckles trying to still the beating of her heart in her chest. It was difficult to concentrate on what he was saying, but she noticed there seemed to be a lot of *"Praise the Lord's"* and not too much that could be considered substantial. Something was said about unity and forgiveness and then he shouted *"Glory to God"* a few times which stirred up the frenzied few and brought a storm of stomping and clapping.

When it was over, Tom called Mira's name to present a statement on behalf of the standing board. Silently she breathed a prayer for help as she slowly made her way to the front. Her mouth was dry and her stomach was doing flip-flops like a fish on dry land. Placing her papers on the podium, she looked out over the audience taking time to scan each section. A sea of unfamiliar faces stared callously back at her. If there were any friends there, she couldn't see them. *Where did all of these strangers come from?* was the thought that flitted through her conscious mind. She didn't see the shining angels that accompanied her.

Gripping the edges of the podium, Mira began to read, slowly and distinctly, the statement that Darren had prepared for the board. When she finished the final paragraph, she laid the papers down. "I guess this would be good time to tender my resignation as President of Women's Ministries," she said with dignity, her voice only wavered slightly. "I'm sure I will have more resignations to follow before the night is over." She didn't trust her voice to say any more.

Picking up her papers, she made her way back to her seat. Tom quickly turned the mike over to Pastor Rutherford. Rafe was riding high, his mood triumphant. He could taste victory! It was within his grasp! *This poor, puny excuse for a board thought they could overthrow me? Not in this lifetime!*

He took his place behind the podium and raised his hand to stop the mighty wave of cheering, stomping and clapping. He had used the telephone to great advantage and this wasn't the first time. A master of deceit, he had planted enough malicious lies and gossip to destroy the board. Tonight was to be his finest hour. He had fully intended to lambaste the directors with every piece of dirt he could drag up. His precious reputation meant more to him than life itself. However, the much anticipated and dreaded statement from the board had been so bland that now he knew he didn't have to defend anything. He had won!

He was magnificent in his humbleness. He radiated forgiveness, mentioning Mira by name, as one who was like family to him. Knowing that he would as soon slit her throat as look at her and nauseated over his insincerity, Mira slipped out of her seat and disappeared into the sound booth. Pastor Marvin, Grace and Rob greeted her with smiles and encouragement. They told her how proud they were of how she had handled herself in such a difficult circumstance.

When Rafe was finally finished working over the people, Tom told the members that he was throwing the floor open for them to ask questions of the pastor, the directors or the elders. Member after member came forward to throw their loving support behind the pastor, many with passionate heart-felt statements of unquestioning loyalty.

Mira found it strange that not one of them seemed to question why the board had felt it necessary to take action against him. No one wanted to know what the issues actually were. Only the church maintenance man defended the board and said that he had faith in them to perform their duties well and keep the best interests of the church foremost.

The biggest betrayal for Mira personally, came when Ina went to the microphone. She threw her full support behind her dear pastor saying that any problems they ever had were resolved with love and forgiveness. Ignoring the ethical and moral issues of which she had first-hand knowledge, she painted a rosy picture of unity and made everyone believe that all was well with the office staff.

Mira saw Rob shake his head sadly in the sound booth. She thought of all of times she had listened to the woman rant about the pastor's unethical conduct and was forced to conclude that Ina was only interested in saving her job at any cost. It hurt her to know that the woman could have remained quiet, saying nothing, but instead she chose to publicly align herself with her immoral pastor.

Tom Storey cut off the comments after Jimmy rather lamely admitted that he had misquoted the letter he had spoken about on Good Friday. The correction came too late. The lie had accomplished its purpose. It was time to vote on whether the members supported the board of directors in their decision or not.

Pastor Rutherford retired to the office while the ballots were distributed. Tempers flared as those who were not on the membership list were denied a ballot. Grace heard one couple venting in the lobby because they were listed as associate members and therefore excluded from the vote.

"Were you going to vote in favor of the pastor?" she asked them. When they replied in the affirmative she patted the woman's hand comfortingly. "Don't worry," she said trying to keep the sarcasm out of her voice, "he has plenty of votes in there. He'll win."

In order to conduct a fair vote, Tom had to have the list read, name by name, so they could receive their slip of paper from an usher. While the votes were being tallied, Tom slipped over and asked Mira if she was up to presenting the financial statements. When she nodded, he quickly returned to the podium and invited her to come forward.

Mira presented a clear, understandable financial statement. She highlighted the large drop in income in the final quarter of the year as a real concern expressed by the auditors. Moving quickly on to the budget, she presented a comprehensive picture of what the members could expect for the coming year.

"I have based this budget on the premise that the church will experience a thirty member loss." Her voice rang out clear and steady. "I feel this is a conservative number so the loss could be far greater but my information is limited to only those people that I am reasonably sure will leave the church. Proceeding on this premise then, the church can expect their total yearly income to decrease by almost $100,000."

She glanced up casually to let that tidbit of information sink in. The crowd had thinned out considerably. They had not come to hear about the church's finances and so, as fickle friends do, they left as soon as the shouting was over. She noticed Mrs. Rutherford, who sat directly in front of her, thumbing frantically through her package trying to find the budget page. No one had given that a thought until now. Wilhelm scrambled through his own set of documents, frowning darkly, while Tad and Jimmy whispered agitatedly into his ear.

"I have used very conservative numbers for all the necessary expenditures," Mira continued. "All non-essential items have been cut and nothing has been allowed for special projects. Even with these obvious cuts, as you can clearly see, the projected loss is almost $100,000. Again, let me remind you that I have used very conservative numbers. If fifty people should leave, the budget would change dramatically. Any questions?"

Dead silence greeted her. "Can I have to motion to accept the budget then?" she asked innocently. Someone raised their hand. "Seconder?" Another hand was raised. "All in favor?" Hands were raised throughout the sparse audience. "Opposed?' Not one hand!

"I guess I'm done then." Mira gathered up her papers while Tom rushed to the front. Taking a seat momentarily beside Darren, she waited for the results of the vote to be announced.

Wild cheering and clapping ensued as the results were given. Eighty percent had chosen to support Pastor Rutherford. The remainder of the meeting was a blur for Mira. Because there were insufficient nominees for a new board, Phil Schmidt, Tad Booker and Ian Parker were acclaimed. No one cared! Ian had already left the building with his wife and didn't even know. Mira knew he would resign as soon as he found out. She was surprised that Rafe had allowed his name to stand. She figured he probably hadn't had time to deal with it because he was too busy making phone calls to rally support.

Darren asked Jack and Mira to step into the fellowship hall with the newly acclaimed board so he could advise them on how to proceed. David Armstrong tagged along obviously wanting to keep his place on the board now that things were settled in the pastor's favor. Someone ran after Frank and asked if he would accept a board position until a legal election could be held.

From the front office, Rafe motioned to Grace, who was standing in the lobby just outside his door. He wanted to speak with her. She looked at Dan who was waiting for Mira to surface from the board meeting.

"You might as well go home," she told him. "It's hard to say how long Mira will be. I'll bring her home with me."

"Do you think she'll be alright?" he asked worried.

"She'll be fine. I'll watch out for her. I won't let him near her," she ended grimly. Rafe was waiving at her again.

"Well?" the pastor crowed in triumph as she entered the office, "What did you think of that?"

"It was quite a show," she admitted, giving him a measured look. "You were able to drum up quite a bit of support but will they still be here on Sunday or the week after? What about all of the people that have been wounded? Who will care for them? Pastor Rafe, this is probably as good a time as any to tell you that I feel it necessary to sever all ties with you and your ministry."

"You're a wise woman," he responded. "How do I reconcile with Mira?"

Grace looked bewildered. *Is he out of his mind? I think he's really lost it!* She spoke to him as one would a small child. "Pastor, the time for that is long past. That ship sailed already. Look!" she gestured toward the throng of people milling about the lobby. "Your people are waiting for you. Go be with your fans. They want to talk to you and love on you. Go be with them." Baffled, she shook her head and walked out of the room.

In the fellowship hall, the lawyer walked the new board through the legal procedures as they accepted Jack and Mira's resignations. They seemed surprised to see that she had formal letters with her. When it was done, Darren had one further word of caution.

"The problems in this church are not over because the last board is dissolved," he said earnestly. "You have an obligation before God to address the problems and issues that have brought you to this point tonight. There are serious allegations to be dealt with and there needs to be a serious investigation into them."

Tad offered his hand to Jack and Mira. "I hold nothing against either of you," he said. The others shook their hands as well. Mira felt as if she was in the middle of a nightmare but she gritted her teeth and somehow got through it. As they walked down the hallway together, Jeanne rushed over to give her a hug. "My husband and I will be resigning our membership tomorrow," she told her. Grace was in the lobby waiting with Jack's wife, Amy.

As they walked through the big front doors, Mira drew her first full breath of freedom. "It is finished!" she cried. "I'm free at last!"

She shook each foot as she started down the steps. "Shake the dust! Just like Jesus told the disciples in the bible. If they are unwilling to accept your message, then shake the dust off your feet and move on."

Grace laughed and shook each foot vigorously. Together they walked arm in arm to the car.

"What will become of the Good Shepherd Church?" asked Valin of his companion as they walked across the parking lot behind the women.

Caelen stopped for a moment and looked back at the building. "I see "*Ichabod*" written over the threshold," he said gravely.

Valin nodded. "You mean - the glory has departed."

"Yes," he replied. "Sadly, many will not even realize it. They will go on with their services as if nothing has happened. They will still sing and dance and even pray and plan, but it will all be for naught unless true repentance comes. They have a form of godliness but they have no true conception of who God really is. They have not sought after His heart. If they had, they would not be able to wink at unholy practices and allow them to flourish in their places of worship. The Lord of Hosts is a holy and righteous God and He will not be mocked."

"Surely many are unaware of the wickedness of their shepherd though?" enquired Valin anxiously. "Many have been drawn to the man because of his charisma and personality but know nothing of his true character."

"That is true and God will not abandon them. If they will seek His face, He will surely lead them out of bondage also. Many changes are coming to this place. Dark times are ahead and they will transpire swiftly."

"What will happen to those who left tonight?"

"Their bondage has been broken. The way has already been prepared before them and they will move ahead in their new-found freedom with joy and gladness."

"Will this be true for all of them?"

"Some will struggle for a period of time. They have much to work through. Disillusionment in a revered leader is not an easy thing to overcome, but God will not see His sheep abandoned. We did not lose this battle, Valin. Even though we have been unable to break Satan's stronghold here, we saved those that were marked; the called-out ones. Others will escape also - many others. They will follow these when their eyes are opened and they realize the glory has departed and the place is but a hollow shell. Those who seek to know God in spirit and in truth and hunger after Him will grow restless under this immoral leadership. With guidance, they will leave this stronghold of wickedness and find another place to worship. A safe place!"

"And if the shepherd resigns as he has promised?"

"There must be repentance!" Caelen replied firmly.

"True," agreed Valin. "But as immoral and ungodly as he has shown himself to be, he could still find forgiveness and grace if he repents. I fear for his soul however. He is far from God and so far has been unreachable."

"There has been no spark there to ignite." Caelen looked somber. "The people are accountable for their decision this night as well," he continued earnestly, "especially the spiritual leaders who are aware of the wickedness of their minister but have turned a blind eye, thereby condoning his immorality. They have chosen an ungodly man to follow. Nay, they have said, *"We will have him regardless of what he has done!"*

"A man without accountability!"

"Exactly! Therefore, they are not innocent in this matter. These people have had many years to test the mettle and observe the characters of these board members who have stood for righteousness. In spite of this, they have rejected them by their own choice. They did not even care to ask the question, *"What has he done that caused you to take the actions you have taken?"* Do you think that mob in there prayed for God's will tonight?"

"No."

"Exactly! They cannot plead ignorance! Some of them know too well the immoral, unethical practices of the shepherd. They have covered it up in the past and now refuse to make him accountable for anything. They are therefore partakers in his evil. They want their king! They have set him up as their little god. So the Lord of Hosts will step aside now and give them what they desire."

"Even so, He is ever gracious and merciful," countered Valin eagerly, "if they will humble themselves and repent and ask for forgiveness, He will still hear their prayers and forgive them and cleanse their sanctuary."

"Yes, He will do that gladly," replied Caelen. "However, if they refuse to humble themselves and repent, then the place will be as hollow as it is tonight. It will never prosper in anything it sets its hand to."

"God forbid!" exclaimed Valin. "May they find a place of forgiveness with all speed!"

"Amen to that!"

ISBN 142518582-7

9 781425 185824